Gates of Fire

Gates of Fire

ELWYN M. CHAMBERLAIN

GROVE PRESS, INC./NEW YORK

First Edition 1978
First Printing 1978
ISBN: 0-394-50162-4
Grove Press ISBN: 0-8021-0153-4
Library of Congress Catalog Card Number: 77-18319

Library of Congress Cataloging in Publication Data

Chamberlain, Elwyn M
Gates of fire.

I. Title.
PZ4.C4424Gat   [PS3553.H249]   813'.5'4   77-18319
ISBN 0-394-50162-4

Manufactured in the United States of America

Distributed by Random House, Inc., New York

GROVE PRESS, INC., 196 West Houston Street, New York, N.Y. 10014

For *SQUAW and CHICKSUR*

It is not good for the Christian soul
To hustle the Aryan brown,
For the Christian riles and the heathen smiles
And it weareth the Christian down.
And the end of the fight is a tombstone white
With the name of the dear deceased
And the epitaph drear: "A fool lies here
Who tried to hustle the East."

—RUDYARD KIPLING

NEW DELHI (*Int. News*) A dejected Mr. and Mrs. James Weatherall today announced that they were leaving India apparently abandoning as hopeless their highly publicized and generously financed search for their daughter Laura. Addressing the modestly attended press conference at the New Delhi airport where the investment banker and his socialite wife were awaiting a flight back to New York, Mr. Weatherall conceded that the three-month quest to locate his only child had produced no information.

Joining the Weatheralls here was Richard Murray, famed American song writer and father of Jeffrey Murray, a long-time friend of Miss Weatherall. According to the parents the young Murray had traveled with Miss Weatherall to India some twenty months ago. Mr. Murray stated that he had not been in contact with his son for some time prior to the departure for India and has no idea as to his son's present whereabouts.

According to sources that have assisted in the search for the young American couple, a third member of their party was Robert Stanley. Mr. Weatherall acknowledged that Mr. Stanley may have broken off from the trip at some point and returned to England or the United States. This report has not, however, been verified.

Mr. Stanley is a well-known American entrepreneur. Often cited as a contemporary example of rags to riches success, Mr. Stanley acted as a presidential emissary during both the Kennedy and Johnson administrations. Mr. Stanley returned to private life and moved to London some four years ago. He had the reputation of being an intensely private man. His activities in recent years were the subject of widespread speculation with a number of press reports leading to actions for libel. The suits were all settled out of court.

Before her departure for India Miss Weatherall had been a social presence in her own right. She was usually referred to by the social columns as the flaming red-haired beauty from Hobe Sound and Park Avenue who acted as if she preferred Greenwich Village. The young Mr. Murray was the subject of some public attention for his activities surrounding the now famous Woodstock Music Festival.

[9]

I

§

THE AFTERNOON SUN filtered through the drawn curtains of the London townhouse on Tregunter Road. Laura felt sleepy and childlike, not in the mood for şex. "In love with the idea of his own cock," she thought, and would have turned over except he was so expert, like a magnet inside her generating waves.

"Dial Jeff for waves," she thought.

The phone rang for a long time and then stopped. There was a knock at the door. It was the manservant.

"Yes?" Jeff said hoarsely.

"A call for you, sir. The gentleman calls himself Stan. Shall I say you're asleep?"

"Say I'm just . . ." Jeff paused. Something hung in the balance, he wished he knew what it was. "Say I'm just waking up, I'll call as soon as we . . ."

"What sir?"

"As soon as we do wake up."

"Shall I take the number, sir?"

Jeff smiled at Laura.

"No, uh . . . we have his number."

§

Life, for Robert Stanley or Stan as he was known, had become a dangerous affair. By his own account he had been born cynical and doubting, a result of early poverty in the slums of New York. But at the age of five when it was found that he could read *The New York Times* from cover to cover his future was assured. In his twenties he climbed to the top of the academic heap, discovered antibiotic formulae that netted him millions, and in his thirties became a U.S. presidential appointee, trusted with unprecedented decision-making power. Now at forty, having discovered the joys of LSD, he'd become the kingpin in a far-flung underground enterprise to manufacture and distribute it. Robert Stanley was handsome, bi-sexual, Napoleonically built, and uncouth.

As Jeff and Laura arrived at Stan's townhouse in Chelsea, an old Irish hag named Jenny emerged from the front door. She had the vigilance of a policewoman and never forgot a face. She liked Jeff.

"Come on in," she yelled cheerily. "Haven't seen the likes of you two since New York, now have I?" She gestured with an upright finger. "He's either on the phone or asleep. Go upstairs and find out for yourselves. Are ye hungry? I'll bring ye some breakfast after a spell. Here, come, let me take yer bags."

They climbed a circular stairway into the three-story drawing room where an extraordinary Aubusson carpet, vanloads of vintage furniture, and priceless paintings were thrown together as if in a junk shop. Over the fireplace one of Van Gogh's last paintings gave out insane vibrations. Stan himself was in bed on a balcony, phoning Washington. An inveterate caller, he would phone anywhere from anyplace at anytime. At the moment, it was obvious from his voice that he wanted something.

"Make yourselves comfortable if you can find room," he yelled down. "I'll be right with you . . . just doing my morning round-the-world tour."

"Somehow he always manages to make you feel uncomfortable," Laura thought, "a very eccentric bird indeed." In spite of her suspicion that he might be dangerously crazy, she was attracted by a certain chicken-soup warmth, his strange perceptiveness, high powers of concentration. And his acting ability was tops: he could appear perfectly normal, in the most uncanny low key way. She had seen him do it. Pull himself together just as the scene seemed about to fall in.

"So what?" he yelled contemptuously into the phone. "So what?" slamming down the receiver.

He came downstairs wearing a pair of yellow silk pajamas, moving with the ferocious locked-up energy of a prizefighter.

"Too much speed," Laura thought to herself.

"So you've come to see me. Don't tell me why, let me guess." His icy grin warmed to a smile. "I mean it's really good to see you both . . . Mademoiselle Weatherall, and friend Jeff Murray."

"You said on the phone there was some business to discuss. That's why Laura and I came right over."

"Did I?" said Stan. "So many phone calls. What business? Oh yes."

"Another Woodstock, I suppose," said Jeff somewhat contemp-tuously.

[12]

Stan giggled. "Was it that bad? Didn't you make lots of money, lots and lots of money?

"It's pretty heavy in the States just now," Laura put in, "that's why we left, acid as cheap as a subway ride, everyone's freaking out."

"Freaking out?" Stan responded. "Not at all ... everything's happening as it should ... increasing the speed of human evolution, making some people smarter, causing others to jump out windows ... whatever. But the human adaptation rate must speed up! Otherwise we'll be finished! Not much time left." He slapped his knee. "Some people are much smarter now than before. Many people in government, highest positions, are much smarter since acid."

He looked up, smiling benignly. "Of course, as I am a natural genius it is of no concern to me whether people are smarter, but it is nice to have a few more people around one can talk to, as equals ... like you two. Of course, if people are really stupid by nature then that all comes out too."

Narrowing his eyes, he stared at them. "I want to turn on India next," he said matter-of-factly.

"India?" They both looked incredulous.

"What on earth for?" Laura said.

"Biggest market yet," Jeff muttered knowingly.

"Not at all, my dear Jeff!" Stan said irritably. "India is the soul of the world. Of course you wouldn't know that! And it's falling apart. Too many fools at the top spouting too many textbook principles! They need new solutions! They need acid there to wake up. They think they got a democracy, socialism. It's just a mess. The same colonial farce. Nobody likes it and they gotta come up with something new."

They all looked at each other. Jeff thought about the money the British made introducing opium into China and tea into India, and he doubted Stan's good intentions.

Stan droned on, pompously lifting one finger and gazing off into space. Jeff was the instrument he needed to carry out his plans. He'd be reliable because he was greedy. After Woodstock he was in deep! He was just the one. If anyone could, Jeff Murray would find a way to make money off the Indians. After all, it was a very big market.

"Do we understand each other?" Stan said to Jeff after breakfast was finished.

Jeff's eyes flashed.

"I see we do." Stan paused. "Of course it might be dangerous! India is India. You don't know of course, but they will think we're making money and they'll be after us for it."

[13]

"We won't make money? I suppose you're turning into a philanthropist then," Jeff said condescendingly.

"It won't be a giveaway but at their exchange rate we'll be lucky to break even after our own expenses."

"How many trips do we take in?"

"One million for starters."

Jeff whistled under his breath.

Laura was sure Stan had flipped.

"Now you know," sighed Stan.

§

Jenny could be heard letting someone in downstairs.

"Who's that?" Stan yelled.

Up the stairs bounded a young man wearing white buckskin leggings and numerous silver and turquoise rings, with straight black hair halfway to his waist. He padded into the room.

"Like a panther," thought Laura.

"Ah, Carlos." Stan was obviously pleased with the interruption. "Have you met Jeff?"

Jeff nodded before Carlos could answer.

"And this is his, er . . ."

"Lover," said Laura wisely.

"Lover," Stan said to Carlos.

Carlos nodded at Laura. He was Stan's number one boy, his pimp, bodyguard and social secretary. Handsome, part Indian, part Spanish, it was rumored in London that he was an Inca of ancient lineage. With men he acted seductive, to women he seemed strong, an androgynous quality about him made him desirable to both. Although he always seemed relaxed he had the reflexes of a cobra and a mind that worked like a snare. More than anything, money turned him on. It was well known that you could make Carlos dance with banknotes of the proper denomination.

"Could you pour us all a drink," Stan asked.

Carlos poured liberal doses of gin with plenty of ice and not much tonic. The afternoon wore on, thick with cross purposes and preparations. Stan was so maddeningly disorganized, Laura thought.

Finally, however, he was shouting orders to the driver, bags were being loaded, and soon the long black Mercedes slipped noiselessly out of London through the evening traffic.

Hours later the highway gave way to a bumpy country road which ended in an avenue of ancient oaks. Moonlight streamed through the branches, casting intricate designs on the snow. Suddenly a large fortress-like structure loomed up.

"My country place," Stan said, rousing the others.

Jeff peered through the car window. "What do we do now, drive through the front door?"

Moments later a young man appeared with a flashlight and they entered a vast hall where their voices echoed. A roaring fire burned in one of two fireplaces. The walls were covered with swords, daggers, and other paraphernalia of wars long past. Ancient suits of armor stood guard like iron ghosts.

"Alex, this is Laura Weatherall and Jeff Murray. They've agreed to help us out. Carlos you know of course."

"Welcome," Alex said, peering at them from behind his horn-rimmed spectacles.

Laura liked him immediately.

"Are you hungry?" Alex asked. "We have . . ."

"We are hungry, my dear boy," interrupted Stan. "But Jenny has brought along a roast duck dinner for us. Alex is a vegetarian," Stan explained.

"I think I'd like to try the vegetables," Laura said, smiling at Alex. "If you don't mind, Stan."

"Of course, my dear, have vegetables, it will mean more duck for us. Ducks aren't very big you know. You'll have duck won't you, Jeff?"

"Sure, I love it." Jeff and Laura exchanged glances.

"Then come along."

They parted. Stan followed by Carlos and Jeff went through large double doors into a drawing room beyond, while Laura followed Alex to the servants' quarters where he was living.

"Welcome again," he said setting out plates on a pantry table. Steady blue eyes smiled from an intelligent face. He had a long pedigree in the acid world, extending back to his Harvard undergraduate days.

"I'm hooked on trying to find out what really happened when I first took acid," he said between mouthfuls of bean sprouts. "Research is very expensive, you know. I couldn't afford all the equipment myself. Stan's been very generous."

"Are you the Alex who came up with different variations like . . ." Laura rattled off a few of the familiar names. Alex nodded.

"Then I've heard about you."

"Really," he said, wondering how much she'd heard.

It was Laura's first vegetarian meal. She found she didn't mind it but thought she wouldn't exactly want to make it a habit. After dinner Alex got out a strange-looking stringed instrument. She

[15]

remembered that friends had told her he had been to India a number of times and that he was on a very weird trip because of what he'd learned there.

"You have a teacher somewhere in India?" she asked, as he tuned the instrument.

"Yes, somewhere," he replied, gazing beyond her. "How did you come to know that?"

"Can't remember. Heard it somewhere. Is your teacher one of those orange-robed swamis?" Laura had had enough of swamis.

"Not a swami," he said, "no orange robe, nothing. Naked. He lives mostly in jungles, likes tigers."

Tigers interested her. "Stan has asked Jeff and me to go to India. Could you put me in touch with your teacher if I go?"

"I can give you a number where you might get news of his whereabouts. I never know exactly where he is. That's his picture over there," he said, pointing to a small photo on the mantelpiece.

Laura got up to look. Something about the face she saw shocked her deeply. The face of a saint, or a swindler. She felt the image was almost alive as it stared out at her. Or was it some sort of ghost? She felt unnerved.

"Don't worry, he won't bite," Alex said, as if he read her thoughts.

"Looks like a heavy," Laura said, returning to the table. "Thanks for the dinner. I'm dead just now, perhaps I should go and find out where I'm to sleep before they all get too high out there."

Alex lit the way with his flashlight. There were few electric lights and in the dark, the rooms full of covered-over furniture looked ominous. The whole place had an unpleasant air about it. When they finally reached the entrance to the other wing she could hear music behind the great double doors. Above it Stan was talking and laughing.

"Never stops, does he?" she said to Alex, nodding toward the door. "Does he still take speed?"

"Doesn't need it," Alex smiled. "Money's the strongest drug of all. I'll leave you here then. Stan knows where you're to sleep. Good night."

"Good night and thanks."

Through the doors Laura saw that three girls had materialized, sprawled out on fur rugs smoking joints which Carlos was busy preparing. Across the room Jeff slouched in a brocaded wing chair. Stan was running true to form, she thought.

"Have some coke?" he asked, producing a piece of paper with a line of white crystals.

Laura took some to show she wasn't ruffled by the situation.

[16]

She wondered if the girls were kept in a special tower of the mansion, and whether any more were hidden in its ninety-odd rooms.

"Where do I sleep," she asked Stan.

"You're not going to leave us?" He grinned. "We're just beginning . . . How were your vegetables?"

"Delicious. And how are your ducks?"

"Ready to eat," he whispered in her ear, "like to try some?"

Laura felt like smacking him. Instead she made herself yawn.

"Carlos will show you to your room. . . . Carlos!" he yelled. "Show Miss Weatherall to her room, eh? And take some candles with you, I don't believe we got around to connecting the lights up there."

§

Laura and Carlos mounted the main staircase off the great hall, a three-story affair branching off in every direction into corridors filled with more covered furniture. After losing their way several times they came to a door that Carlos unlocked and went in. The room smelled of tuberoses. It reminded Laura of her mother's old place at Hobe Sound.

"Where did the tuberoses come from?" She smiled at Carlos.

"There's a greenhouse here," he said, "filled with them. I thought you might enjoy."

He began lighting the candles and an apartment of several rooms materialized. The walls were covered with tapestries and needlepoint.

"Very grand," Laura observed.

"Not a bad place to spend time." Carlos shrugged.

Laura forgot the bad vibes downstairs; she felt like locking the door and sleeping for a week in the huge medieval bed with its scarlet damask curtains. Carlos lit a fire, then stood looking into her eyes until she had to look away.

"Is there anything you think you need?" he asked as though she had forgotten something. "Or want?" he added softly.

"What?" She turned to survey the room.

"This," he said, spinning her around, drawing her close.

"I'm sorry." She pulled away. "I think I'd better get some sleep."

§

She woke the next afternoon feeling rested, went to the wide bay window and sat gazing out at the winter landscape. From rows of oaks along the drive the last golden leaves blew away over the snow like confetti. Beyond lay cut fields and stands of chestnut and sycamore. In a pond at the far end of a promenade the last ducks and wild geese were calling.

A soft knock sounded at the door. It was Carlos carrying a tray with some soup, toast, and a pot of tea.

"I was thinking you might be hungry," he said smiling. "Sit here and eat." He arranged the dishes on the table.

Laura observed him while she ate. There was something about him. He seemed dangerous to her, yet attractive. The sun was gone now and the hot soup tasted delicious. Laura watched his broad back as he leaned over to fan the coals in the fireplace until the new wood caught.

"Where are you going now?" she asked as he stood up facing her.

"To lock up. Stan and Jeff, they had to go back to London, something Stan is forgetting. They will return tomorrow. What will you do now?" He stared at her.

"Oh read I suppose, something like that." She returned his stare until he looked away.

"You will need more firewood. I'll come again around nine." He picked up the tray and went to the door. "See you later," he said evenly.

§

Had she fallen asleep reading? She'd been in the middle of a strangely vivid dream in which a tiny white-haired old man was dancing naked. Now something had jarred her out of it. Carlos dropping an armful of logs by the fireplace. He sat down on the edge of the sofa and smiled at her.

"You were dreaming."

"Was I? I don't usually dream." She shut her eyes. It was so real. She opened her eyes and looked at him. "It was more real than you are right now."

"Want some Afghani smoke?" he asked.

She nodded.

"Hard to get these days." He lit a small pipe and handed it to her. "A friend laid a kilo on me."

[18]

"He must like you very much."

"He wanted something."

"Were you able to help him?"

"Yes." Carlos looked at her. "I am always pleased to satisfy the desires. But often people don't know what they want, or they are afraid to tell. Too much of repression in this world . . . better to be happy, no?" He smiled his prostitute smile. "You tell me what you want," he said softly, "or don't you know."

Gazing thoughtfully at him, she knew she had only to make a move and they would spend a long night, high, inside the warm dark curtained bed.

"Shall I go now?" he asked.

She was unable to answer.

He stood up, leaning over her. "I dig you. Go to sleep now. I'll come back later when you're asleep."

§

Laura felt too high even to bathe. Time seemed to stand still as she looked into the fire, her mind a blank. On the edge of sleep, falling off, she was suddenly jolted back into reality. Something was moving in the fire. She stared in frightened disbelief and pinched herself hard. Something was certainly moving in the fire. Some apparition, a tiny man, the little man from her dream. Now he was there before her. She bit her lip. He was not naked now, she could see that, but wore something like a towel around his stomach. "It's this hash," she thought. But the room was there, solid and real before her, and she was awake. She got up and went near the fire until she could see that the hands of the little old man were cupped in front of his mouth. He appeared to be yelling but she couldn't hear him. With a poker she stirred the hot coals hoping that he would disappear, that she was only hallucinating, but he merely jumped from one place to another. She wanted to run out the door, to yell for Carlos. Then the tiny figure beckoned her closer. Trembling, she knelt by the fire. "I can't hear you, please talk louder," she whispered.

Then, as if a broken speaker system had suddenly come booming on, she heard him, loud and clear.

"Lock the door," he said. "Do you hear me? Lock the door."

Stunned, she didn't move.

"Listen to me, Laura Weatherall! Lock that door!"

Being called by name terrified her. She got up and locked the door but returning, found him gone. She knelt and poked the coals again. She'd thought he was going to tell her something important.

[19]

Why else lock the door? Then she caught herself. Lock the door. What about Carlos?

For a long time she stared into the fire, unnerved. After a while she got up, showered, and then fell into bed exhausted, leaving the door locked. In her dreams he came again dancing and shouting words she couldn't understand. All she remembered when she woke the next morning was that he had said she needn't worry, that he would see her again at the end. At the end of what, she thought.

The dreams disturbed her so much that she got up and without dressing went to the kitchen where Alex was having breakfast.

"I think I might be going crazy," she laughed nervously over coffee. "Or perhaps it's your acid. Does it spread?"

Alex listened to her story, methodically munching his toast.

"It's the burning bush," he explained. "What seems inside is outside and what seems outside is inside. Sometimes you reach a peaceful state of mind where the two come together. Then they disappear into each other and you get in touch with things you don't understand. Space is just a function of time, and time is a function of space. Both are illusions. Don't disbelieve what you saw."

"You mean it was real?"

"What is real?"

"Wasn't I . . . projecting?"

"What is that?" said Alex. "I mean what do you think it is?"

"Isn't projecting when you go mad and start seeing things?"

He smiled. "Just believe in what you saw, keep your visions to yourself, and see where they lead you." He paused and looked at her intently. "And if you do go to India call Indra in New Delhi at 67896."

§

Four days later at Heathrow outside of London it was freezing. Even the brandy they'd drunk as the limousine sped toward the airport hadn't helped. Laura hoped the flight would be on time. She hated these departures where everyone stood around making up things to say.

"And so a new adventure begins," said Stan pompously when the flight was finally announced. "Call me from Delhi as soon as you get to the hotel. I'll be nervous about getting all that stuff through customs. Remember, if they say anything, give them money right away. Right?" He looked hard at Jeff. "Don't be shy about it, just shell it out. After all, they worship it there."

[20]

On the plane, half the people were asleep. The through passengers from New York looked gray and exhausted. A fresh platoon of doe-eyed hostesses in saris gently tucked in the new arrivals. The soft Indian music sounded out of place in the plastic interior of the "747," poetically referred to over the loudspeaker as the Emperor Shah Jehan. Finally they were airborne. "Escape," Laura thought, doubting that it was really possible, as Britain and Europe disappeared in a gray-and-white swirl outside the window.

§

But as they emerged from the plane twenty hours later in New Delhi, down the open ramp and onto the soil of India, Laura sensed that something was different. It was in the air. She had escaped, she could smell it. The metallic odor of Europe was gone, there was an earthy smell which excited her.Wood smoke hung in the air. Lights burned dimly through the humid mist. It was warm!

As planned they went through customs separately so that the crystal and tablets of LSD, all in bottles marked with the labels of known firms, would be overlooked more easily.

"You are bringing in so many tablets?" The customs clerk looked at her with implacable dark eyes, as he unzipped the first of her bags. "Do you plan to sell them?"

"They are vitamins. I am bringing them in for friends."

He stared at her thoughtfully.

"You are coming here as a tourist?" He held her passport in front of his face so that he could look over it. He'd seen many like her: skinny white witches who dropped from the sky, profaning the holy Earth of India with their flimsy see-through dresses, their bare legs, and their suitcases full of medicines and cosmetics. To him they represented a new kind of being, one that fed on magic pills and made love in public places. How thin she was! He thought of his plump wife and his eight plump children. He wanted to keep them plump. Leafing through her passport, he noted that she traveled a lot. Travel was expensive. Then he saw the fur slung over her arm.

"I'm afraid we will have to charge you for these, Madam. The customs' duty is 90% of value. What is the value?"

Laura put on her blandest smile. "Will this cover it?" she asked, palming a hundred-dollar bill over the edge of the counter.

He took the bill from her hand with a glance over his shoulder to be sure he hadn't been seen, then pocketed it. After all, it represented almost a quarter of his annual wage—who would not

[21]

forgive him? Without further word he stamped her entry papers and unsmiling passed her through.

Outside the terminal in the dawn, turbaned coolies were everywhere. A gang of them descended like sparrows on the exotic Western couple stuffing their bags into a broken-down taxi.

They crowded around Jeff. "Change money, Sahib, change money?" they shouted. "Good rate. I geev you good rate, you change money with me?"

"Did you get through without paying?" asked Jeff, helping Laura into the taxi.

"I had to pay a hundred dollars."

"It was your fur," he said. "But so what? We're here and we're in. At least it's warm."

The cab, which seemed to be held together with coat hangers, started with a lurch. Soon it was careening wildly through the early morning traffic of suburban Delhi, maneuvering between potholes and people and other vehicles that crossed the way. The driver blew his horn at everything from the oxcarts and herds of goats to the long black cars of the politicians. The eyes of India stared in through the car windows. Laura stared back, seeing everywhere disorder bordering on chaos. The dinginess, the tattered and frayed look of everything came as a shock after the bright plastic facade of the West. "You could go crazy here and no one would ever know it," she thought. "You could die and no one would care."

The hotel, however, was like a luxury hotel anywhere in the world: concrete, steel, glass, doormen, thick carpets, giftshops, palms, and fat guests. Yet there was a difference too. The soft obliging manner of the staff. A hint that clock time meant very little here where orders when given might be carried out or entirely forgotten.

The sun was just rising and the ruined tombs, the forts and battlements of the Moguls floated in the mist against the pink sky.

"Good set for a mystery movie," Jeff thought out loud.

"I feel like I'm in an elevator going down," Laura whispered. "It's so quiet."

Jeff doled out tips to barefoot boys who were bringing the luggage into the room. "It's supposed to be Lotus Land," he said, "the land of forgetfulness. Let's get some sleep."

But sleep did not come easily for Laura that morning. She closed her eyes wondering to herself about the chance events which had brought her to this unlikely spot halfway around the world. Her thoughts went back to Woodstock where this trip had all begun.

§

The rain had come down in buckets all night long drenching the festival crowd. Rip Van Winkle, his white beard flying, a twinkle in his eyes, sported over the hills roaring with laughter at the goings on. But no one looked for him that night or cared. The heavens collided while the fabled *rishi* danced, his footsteps resounding merrily from hill to kyll.

Below it was a different matter. Inside the structures and bubbles, the buses and the tents, the air was heavy with incense; the scent of group lust drifted out into the New York monsoon. Laura knelt, naked, open to receive him, her body flushed, her dark red hair loose to her waist. Jeff entered her, his green eyes intent, lips distended, muscles taut. Once they had locked together there was no movement, only .tension mounting between them, inner contractions. Did they know of the Kama Sutra or the pleasure palaces of the Moguls, their fabled pastimes at Fatephur Sikri? Not quite. But the spirit of the East had come alive here on Rip's old stomping ground. Atavistic, out of control, bent on transforming the future as it worked its way out through these sons and daughters of a New Age.

In the morning Laura and Jeff rode out on his Arabian mare to survey the scene. He was elated by the success of the strategy. Largest acid drop and distribution ever undertaken finished twenty-four hours before the advertised event was to start. The scam was a success: that it had turned into something not quite expected was hardly of concern to him. Let the gates be thrown open. All come in free.

She held his waist lightly as they trotted through the melee of people and mud. It was unreal: Laura Weatherall, 610 Park Avenue and Hobe Sound, had not exactly been prepared for this scene.

At the staging area Jeff had a fight with one of his partners over the tangled cables and equipment, touchy performers and road managers, the vibrations of greed—age-old money thing. She watched him as he gave orders and was obeyed, shucked out bread and was salaamed. It was all a game to him she'd thought, like the Monopoly they used to play as children after school, left alone in apartments while their mothers, who were friends, had their hair done at Bendel's, and their fathers got drunk at "21."

They rode beyond to the lakes. Sun pierced the clouds to glitter on choppy waves, split the veils of mist rising from oaks and willows, bathing hundreds of naked bodies with magic light.

She thought she might be in love with him. He had opened

her—with the drug, with his sex. But who was he really, this Jeff from the West Side with the rich songwriter father, the boy she had known in her childhood. They had never gone further than games or going to the movies on Saturday night and when Laura went to Bronxville to school she lost track of him. Then they remet by accident: they both had the same hash connection. She sensed a new Jeff. When he was near her a switch turned inside her, they seemed to touch essences. Even so, she wondered whether she was confusing soul with meat? She didn't even know why she had come to Woodstock, a spur of the moment thing. She wanted to forget about thinking. She wanted to let herself feel free, whatever that meant. Above all she wanted freedom from Laura Weatherall and all she was supposed to be.

Helicopters landed in the late afternoon delivering superstars, newsreel photographers, others of the hip elite. The mud dried. Portable radios announced that an entire nation was focused on the five hundred thousand people who were getting it on in the Catskills. Some said it was the beginning, others thought it might be the end. Red Rudy and some of the older hippies gathered on the hill with binoculars like Civil War generals. Whatever it was, it was an event not soon to be forgotten.

After the sun set the dwarfs peddled their wares: "Hashish, cocaine, LSD," "mescaline, mescaline," "smoke, smoke, smoke." Peeping behind bushes and lounging in trees, selling or giving to the hundreds of Snow Whites and Princes. Entranced, some lay down in the leaves for hours, even days. Some inched over the ground, seeing the microcosm. Some were on bad trips. Everyone was helpful and above all cool.

Next day there was a giant hangover. Laura and Jeff threw blankets over their bubble, hung up a DO NOT DISTURB sign, and crawled under their furs. A day later came the famous garbage mess: The press and the U.S. government began looking for Jeff. But he and Laura escaped to 610 Park Avenue; it was late summer and her mother was in Newport, her father drunk on a boat in the Mediterranean. They were safe at 610 Park under the very noses of their pursuers.

When they appeared at a party after Labor Day they found themselves superstars in an underground besieged. Having pulled off the Woodstock scam, Jeff was an overnight celebrity. People wanted interviews and photographs. Fat sons of gangsters called with new and bigger festivals dancing like sugar plums in their pea brains. Everyone's hair was getting longer and it became impossible to filter out friends from foes. They moved to a Fifth Avenue penthouse where security was tight.

[24]

Months passed and the Chicago trials began. Superstars of riot and rock commenced to watch each other nervously, wondering what was going to happen next. They had landed on top of media-fame mountain but the Mitchell and Nixon dogs, barking and out for blood, were coming up fast. Charlie Manson manifested as a pop witch, Weathermen and women united. Altamont exploded. The manic energy of the sixties was a collapsing helter skelter. The mountain had become a volcano.

One night as they lay reading in bed Jeff turned to her.

"The scene is going bad," he said.

"We could split to London, it can't be worse."

"Forget America?" he asked.

"I doubt we can ever forget it, maybe it'll forget us."

"I wonder how long we'll be gone?"

Jeff shrugged. "A day, a year. . . . Maybe we'll never come back."

II

§

"Mr. A. K. Sundaram downstairs in the lobby to see you, sir," a voice crackled through the phone.

Laura was half asleep. "Would you repeat that," she said, trying to remember where she was.

"Mr. A. K. Sundaram here to see you, sir."

"Jeff," she whispered. "Jeff! Wake up!" She kicked at him with her foot. "Someone called Sunderyumyum or something is coming up. Wake up!"

Minutes later an Indian counterpart of Stan appeared at the door: handsome and athletic, dressed casually but expensively. "I am Sundaram," he said. "Welcome to India."

"Jeff Murray and this is my wife, Laura."

The two men shook hands. Laura wondered whether Mr. Sundaram was hip. His face was an expressionless mask behind an Adolf Hitler moustache. Coffee came in behind him with a waiter.

"We've just arrived," Laura said in her best Farmington teatime manner. "You'll have to forgive us if we seem not quite awake—jet lag and all that. Will you have some coffee with us, Mr. Sundaram?"

"Please call me Sundar," he said, easing himself into a chair. "I received a cable from Stan to call on you. How is he?"

"He's fine. We just left him in London."

Sundaram's round, passive face examined them. "I haven't seen him since our Harvard days. We were close friends then but India is so far away, so many things have changed. Do you suppose he'll ever come here?"

"He's thinking of it," Laura said. "How do you like your coffee, Mr. Sundaram?"

"With cream and sugar," he replied. "And please—call me Sundar." He ventured a smile.

After the first few sips, Sundaram brightened and became almost effusive. "I am very glad my old friend Stan sent you to

[26]

me," he said. "It is good to see attractive foreigners here in Delhi. We see so many Germans and English, even Russians nowadays. They are so big and fat. They give us inferiority complexes."

"I'm afraid most Americans are even bigger and fatter," Laura said.

"But you—" Sundaram gestured grandly, "—you are not only thin but beautiful too. Ah, both are beautiful," he added laughing.

"Beauty is only skin deep," Laura said.

"Ah, but skin is what we are," replied Sundaram, "is it not so, Mr. Murray?" He slurped his coffee noisily, then put down his cup and rose. "I will not disturb you any longer, you must rest now. But you will come to me this evening, yes? I have a house near here. There's a party and I will take you. It will be a good chance for you to meet some of the 'in crowd.' And from tomorrow, please feel free to make my place your home. I am a bachelor." His eyes twinkled. "You can even move in if you like, if you get bored with this." He pointed around the room. "Friends of mine own it, very boring hotel." He laughed explosively.

"How will we find you?" Jeff asked.

"I will come and fetch you. Or if I am unable, my driver will come. You must relax and let things happen, you are in India now. Don't think, just enjoy." Sundaram's eyes glittered. "Now I must go, I'm late. May I take my leave, Madam?" He bowed formally to Laura.

"Tonight at seven-thirty," he said, extending a limp hand to Jeff and holding onto Jeff's hand as they walked to the door. "It is a great pleasure for me to have you both here. Get some rest, we'll meet again this evening."

§

"I bet you didn't dream you'd be holding hands with gentlemen the first day in India," Laura giggled.

"And with eye makeup!"

"Oh, they all wear that," Laura said. "But what do you think the 'in crowd' is?"

§

They spent the late morning unpacking. Nothing looked right.

"We have to have some new clothes, don't you think? Otherwise we'll look like hippies and scare people."

Jeff agreed. "It's still the fifties here."

[27]

"Of which century?"

"We should be able to find some things in the hotel shops," he said, not wanting to move.

Laura nodded. "First we'll have lunch downstairs and see what people are wearing. When smuggling it's best to be invisible."

After they were dressed that evening they stood together in front of a large mirror. Laura began to giggle. "You look like a cricket star," she said. Jeff had bought a pale double-breasted mouse colored suit which fit snugly over his athletic body. Underneath he wore a white turtleneck pullover and on his head a dark red turban which the shopkeeper had insisted he buy.

"You will look very handsome in thees," the shopkeeper had said. "It will make your green eyes look like zee emeralds. Then you will have more success with thee vimen, heh? You don't like? Yes, it is right?"

Laura found it impossible to get used to a sari so she had bought pale blue chiffon pants and a matching blouse embroidered heavily in all the necessary places with sequins and small glittering stones.

"How do I look?" she asked.

"You'll probably be raped before the evening is over," Jeff said. "In fact, it might happen right now." He pulled her toward him, watching in the mirror. "But seriously, these Indian men will go crazy you know. Shouldn't you wear something more than that?"

"I have my silk shawl," Laura said. She twirled a flowered fabric in the air and then wound it about her. "In public I can look just as wrapped up as they do." She opened her jewelry case and began to put on some of the most impressive items. "But they won't see me, they'll only see this," she laughed, holding up a bracelet of matched rubies and diamonds. "Isn't it dreadful? Belonged to old Aunt Ethel in Palm Beach. They're supposed to be impressed with glitter here, I've heard, even pray to it. It may open some door—eez not right, Meester Jeff?'

The phone jangled. "Good evening," Sundaram's voice screeched. "Are you ready?"

"Be right down," Jeff said.

There was sputtering on the other end. "You are not ready?"

"No, no. We'll be right down," Jeff yelled into the phone.

When they reached the lobby they spotted him pacing nervously in a tight-fitting mod evening costume. He failed to recognize them at first, but then noticed Laura.

"How very clever you are, Madam," he exclaimed, eyeing the rubies. "Extraordinary, most extraordinary." He turned to Jeff. "And you, sir, you look just like a Pathan."

[28]

"Is that all right?" asked Jeff good-naturedly. "It was the shopkeeper's idea." He pointed to the turban.

"The Pathans are our most accomplished enemies. But we love them nevertheless because they are so beautiful. They are an ancient race of thieves who like to think of themselves as Moslem—really they are just thieves. They all come large like you, six feet or more, sometimes seven. And many are green-eyed, like you, and very dangerous." He tittered, rolling his eyes.

There was a pause during which they all looked at each other like strangers in an elevator.

"So," Sundaram finally said. "Shall we go? It's not far away."

A series of costumed doormen guided them out of the never-never land of the hotel to where Sundar's sleek grey limousine was waiting. The driver saluted and opened the door. Jeff was impressed. Obviously Stan's friend was important.

A few minutes later they were driving past guarded gates into a luxurious compound somewhere near the center of Delhi. Hidden by lush gardens was a sprawling stucco and cement villa. It had round windows and rounded corners and made Laura think of Santa Monica. The scents of jasmine and gardenia mingled in the soft night air. From somewhere inside came a loud imitation of the Rolling Stones.

Sundar introduced them to their host, Dorje, a Tibetan aristocrat's son who escaped from Lhasa with a fortune in gold six months before the Chinese invasion. He was very fat. Laura thought he looked like a gangster. It was impossible to guess his age. His huge face sat on his body like a moon on the horizon. He led them through several rooms full of people engaged in animated conversation.

"It's a cocktail party," Jeff whispered.

They both laughed. "Then we'll have to play cocktail party," Laura murmured.

There were numerous well-dressed young people chattering in a mixture of Hindi and English. "It's the fifties all right," Laura thought.

"It's like Rock Hudson and Doris Day with sincerity," Jeff whispered.

A number of young couples were talking about their "kids." Laura wondered where they picked up this sort of thing and what all the mod clothes from London had to do with talking about the kids. She spoke to Sundar of it.

"My dear, in India all foreign imports are just fashion," he explained. "They are shuffled, re-shuffled, jumbled in the most preposterous combinations, because in the end we know that they are just passing fads."

[29]

Laura wondered about the India outside the compound. She had already seen enough to understand that India was a great sea in which one could easily be drowned. And these people, with their fake sincerity and their talk about the "kids," were they not also nervous about drowning?

Groups of voluptuous girls from the Bombay film scene twittered like finches around handsome young army officers, who strutted about catching glimpses of themselves in mirrors. A number of Westerners were scattered through the crowd.

"I give this party once a year," said the moonfaced Dorje in a high voice with an Oxford accent. "It absolves me of most of my social debts—really it's nothing. In fact," he turned aside to them, eyeing Laura's rubies, "in fact, it's a drag." He winked at Jeff.

Jeff wondered how turned-on Dorje might be. Laura noticed a familiar tired face nodding to her from across the room. It was Charles Hooker, her brother's old friend.

"Laura Weatherall, of all people," he said, ambling up gimlet in hand and sounding like the Yale Club. "You're the lahst person I expected to see in India, absolutely the lahst. Are you alone?"

"I'm the lahst person who ever expected to be here," she replied. "I'm with Jeff, remember Jeff? He thinks he might want to make films here."

"Yes, the film scene here is very exciting. It seems that absolutely everyone is coming to film in India. I may build a studio in Delhi. I wanted to return to the West for a little while but they—" He snickered, gesturing toward the room full of people. "They won't let me leave."

Laura, thinking of the Hooker steel fortune, could guess why.

"Where's Jeff?" said Hooker.

"Over there, talking to that . . . er . . . girl."

"You mean the great Sharma." He nodded. "Of course, but where is Jeff? I don't see him."

"In the turban," Laura said.

"But you can't mean it? It isn't—?" He gaped. "But it is. The suit and that turban." Hooker burst out laughing. "You know, I'd been trying to decide whether he was an Army man or a cricket star. I might even be able to use him in my next film."

"He's very good at acting," Laura said wryly.

"Woodstock wasn't too bad for starters," said Hooker. "But how on earth did you get to this party?"

"A friend of a friend from London," Laura said. "Calls himself Sundar—you know him?"

"But, of course, my dear, doesn't everyone? He brought you here? You're very lucky. He's a Cabinet Minister, practically in her arms." Hooker looked impressed. "He's very powerful."

Laura couldn't imagine the neurotic-looking A. K. Sundaram a powerful Cabinet Minister.

"Would you like to meet a few people?" Hooker asked. "I'm sure you'll find them most amusing."

Laura's sleek body moved freely beneath the chiffon and sequins, sending out tantalizing waves of freedom and sensuality. Many of the women present would have destroyed her instantly had they the power. The men on the other hand would have eaten her alive if they'd dared. She found she rather liked causing a sensation. It made her feel womanly after wearing blue jeans for so long.

Hooker introduced her to three young Sikhs who were standing together near the bar sipping drinks and watching her with large serious eyes. Their swarthy faces were set off by pale pastel turbans, and Laura wondered what they would look like with their long black hair hanging free. She was also aware of the difference between their probably lascivious thoughts and the formality of their outward behavior: the stiff gestures, the handsome masks.

As they stood playing this wordless game, Laura's attention was caught by a movement at the periphery of her vision. She turned and saw a man whose body seemed to be shining through the clothes he wore. Later it was hard for her to describe that first impression even to herself. As she looked he too turned, and their eyes met across the crowded room. She thought he might be Alex's teacher, the man in the photograph. She excused herself from her admirers and trying to look casual made her way hurriedly among the guests. She wanted to get a better look if even to be sure she really had seen him. She entered the room where he had gone and there he was again standing in a dark corner talking with an old woman. Sundaram was not in sight but the fat Tibetan host was. She took Dorje aside.

"Who is that man talking to the older lady?"

"Ah, you mean Indra," replied Dorje. "He is talking to my aunt. She has known him for years. She is so fascinated by him that I am afraid she may someday give him all her gold. Then she would have to come and live with me." He tittered.

"But who is he?"

"Ah, he is Indraji. He was a great athlete and major in the paratroopers under the British years ago—Rajput, I believe. He is very mysterious even to those who know him well—disappears for long periods of time."

"I'd like to meet him if you would introduce me," Laura said.

"But of course."

After they had been introduced, Dorje left and Indra continued talking to the old lady in Tibetan. Laura waited patiently, trying to connect this tall man in the Saville Row suit with the photo Alex had shown her.

After some moments he turned aside from his conversation. "Don't be put off by these clothes," he said to her. "It is I, the same one as in the photograph." He smiled. "Just now I must talk to this old woman who does not understand English. Please go out onto the terrace and wait. I will come presently."

On the terrace the air was filled with the scent of roses. There were roses in urns, roses in the garden, and climbing roses on the house. He came out finally.

"How could you know I've seen your picture?" Laura asked immediately. "Has Alex written you, or—" She thought somehow she'd made a mistake.

"How do I know—" He cut her off with a wave of his hand. "Do not go into it too deeply ... not too deeply. But how did *you* know—that is the question which is interesting." He laughed and turned to face her. "Are you all right?" he asked, matter-of-factly like a physician.

The question made Laura uncomfortable. Why should this perfect stranger ask her if she were all right? It made her wonder if she were really "all right," something she had not stopped to think about for quite a while.

"I'm still a bit weary from travel, I suppose," she said. "I've only been here twenty-four hours, not long enough to really see India yet."

"You are seeing it now," he said, staring at her.

"Now?"

"Yes." He was still gazing at her intently.

"What brings you to a party like this?" she asked to change the subject. "I was told you stayed naked in the jungle. I didn't recognize you in these clothes with a turban."

"But of course you did," he said. "How else did we meet?" He waved one large hand in a graceful arc toward the house. "Roses," he muttered under his breath.

"What?" asked Laura, bewildered.

"Nothing, nothing but ... roses. I like them, I grew up with them once, I like sitting in rooms heaped with rose blossoms." He sighed. "But nowadays I try to remain invisible as much as possible. Life has become dangerous and cheap here in India. I risked coming to this party thinking you might show up."

"But how could you have known I would be here? Are you a friend of Sundar's? We didn't know we would be coming until this morning—"

"I came three days ago to Delhi," he said. "To be at this party.

[32]

The old lady invited me and said there would be someone I should meet at a party being given by her nephew."

"Me?"

"Yes, she described you in detail three days ago, how you would look and what you'd be wearing."

Laura's heart jumped.

"Then when Dorje brought you over she said to me in Tibetan 'that's the one' meaning you."

"I don't believe it," Laura said without thinking.

"I know you don't. Nevertheless, it is true. And if our meeting had not taken place in this manner by chance as you call it, you can be sure I would not be talking to you at this moment."

"If I had phoned the number Alex gave me . . ."

"It's an inoperative number." He looked at her and burst out laughing at her perplexity.

"How old are you," she said, deliberately breaking into his laughter.

He laughed even more. "Don't be frightened, don't try to break my waves," he said calmly. "I'm sixty."

Laura was amazed, he looked thirty.

"Look," he said, taking hold of her shoulders. "We must not be seen here by too many of these people. Delhi is full of gossips, I prefer remaining invisible. Can you remember numbers?"

She nodded.

"Can you remember—" He gave her a number. "Can you remember it until tomorrow?"

She nodded again.

"Then tomorrow morning at exactly 11 A.M. please call that number and we will arrange to meet somewhere quietly. What is the number again?"

She repeated the number. He dropped his hands. "I must go now," he said perfunctorily.

Before she could say goodbye he had disappeared from the terrace into the thick shrubbery of the garden. Laura turned to see Sundaram standing in the double doors leading to the terrace.

"I see you have been talking with Indraji," he said.

"Yes, do you know him?"

"He was a classmate of my father's at Simla. They were on the wrestling team together." Noting her surprised look, Sundaram chuckled. "You will find, my dear, that nothing in India is what it seems—this is not a standardized place like the West. He's a most unusual fellow. Did you like him?"

"I don't know," Laura replied. "Something about him seems unreal, as though he's not quite alive."

"Or more than alive."

"Is he really sixty?"

"Yes, he's really sixty, perhaps more." Sundaram smiled. "Will you see him again?"

"Yes, I think so. He's the teacher of a friend of mine."

She told him about Alex and the picture he'd shown her and about the old Tibetan lady, Dorje's aunt, and the "coincidence" of their meeting.

"You must not tell these things to anyone else," he said earnestly. "People might think you are crazy. It might be dangerous for him as well as you."

"Should I not see him again?"

"By all means, by all means, see him again if you like—but be careful and be quiet about it." He shook his head. "He's rather extraordinary—disappeared completely from '47 on, reappearing only three years ago. He has my father completely 'freaked' as you would say."

"Why?"

"Because twenty-five years later my father is an old man, but Indraji looks exactly the same as he did when they last saw each other, at a dinner for Mountbatten just before Independence!" Sundaram laughed. "There are many stories about him, he's a tough character," he added. "I should be extremely careful if I were you—most women go nuts over him." He glanced inside. "Would you like to meet the Prime Minister's yoga master? He is talking with your husband."

Sundaram introduced her as Mrs. Murray to a black-bearded man in white robes. He nodded and continued to talk to Jeff, who was arranging to take Yoga instruction from him. Laura knew Jeff meant to use the contacts from this party to get his acid distribution started. She stood aside, bored yet still shaken by her meeting with Indraji. She felt almost as if she were tripping. She had tingling sensations and for a brief moment everything turned red. She noticed that the three young Sikhs to whom Hooker had introduced her were still at the bar. She decided a drink would steady her.

"Gin and tonic, please," she said to the bartender, who was busy and did not respond.

The youngest of the trio came to her rescue with an imperious shout and the drink immediately appeared. "Won't you join us?" he said, displaying a dazzling set of white teeth. "Right over here, come!"

His machismo annoyed her somewhat. "Sure, why not?" she replied, trying to mirror his toughness. After a second gin and tonic she felt better. Still why had this Indra disturbed her so? Something familiar but unrecognizable had peered through a crack inside her. She resented it, yet was unable to mend the crack. She felt immobilized psychically, like a chicken with a circle drawn about it, unable to move.

"I am Harpal," her new acquaintance was saying. "And these are my brothers, Harjith and Kuljit."

Six obsidian eyes projected wanton waves toward her. "Want my body," Laura thought, but she didn't mind. Sex put her on more solid ground. Harpal talked while his eyes undressed her. She decided to play the same game and could see that it excited him. She kept talking about nothing, laughing at him with her eyes. He asked her for a drink at his flat, wanted to take her home, cracked his knuckles in anticipation.

"Really," she said, catching sight of Sundaram, "I've just arrived from Europe and I'm still dreadfully tired. I think I have to go to the hotel just now. Rest. We will meet again, no doubt."

"No doubt," Harpal said seriously, holding her hand. "No doubt."

She left the bar then and found Sundaram.

"I have to go to sleep," she said, "jet lag, I guess."

He looked surprised. "So early? Wait until the crowd has thinned. The scene will become more interesting."

"I'm exhausted. Sorry to be such a bore, Sundar." She took his hand. "Do you think you could send me to the hotel in your car?"

"But of course."

"Jeff must stay if he likes," she said. "He recovers from flying faster than I do."

"Of course."

"Please tell him I'm leaving, yes? And thanks for a very interesting first evening in India."

Sundar led her to his car. "Your friend Hooker is having a few people for dinner tomorrow. I will probably see you there."

"I hope so." She smiled her best ladylike smile. "Good night."

"Good night."

§

A. K. Sundaram watched his car disappear down the drive and then returned to the party. The remaining guests were gathered in the library listening to the latest Mick Jagger tapes. His contemporaries in the diplomatic corps had left and there were no foreigners except Jeff and the longhaired son of a high ranking American

[35]

diplomat. The boy, who was the bane of his father's existence, offered Sundaram a smoke.

"Ganja?" he asked.

The boy nodded. Sundaram refused politely. Two young Army officers were smoking with their girlfriends and several sons and daughters of Delhi's rich merchants were dancing frantically. Dorje was standing with his back to Sundar.

"Now that we're alone," he announced in conspiratorial tones, "would any of you be interested in dropping some acid? LSD," he said, holding out a handful of orange colored tablets.

Sundar flinched. He knew that Dorje had the reputation for being outrageous and could afford it, but he wished the Tibetan had waited until he, A. K. Sundaram, Cabinet Minister, had left. It seemed like a plot. To his horror Dorje turned toward him.

"Well, who will try first?" Just to prove it was like eating candy, Dorje popped three tablets into his own mouth. Sundar took one which he pretended to swallow but didn't. He would send it for analysis the next day.

"So acid has arrived in Delhi," said the longhaired American boy languidly, taking two and pocketing them for later.

"Here—open your mouth," Dorje said, making a show of popping one onto Jeff's tongue.

"That's a surprise," said Jeff coolly so that everyone would hear.

Skepticism filled Sundar's alert mind. He wondered just what was going on. Jeff, unaware of the suspicious Indian nature and what it could lead to, was elated that Dorje had been so cooperative. "Here we go turning on India," he thought to himself, and settled back in his chair.

§

Laura awoke to find herself alone in the big double bed, unable to recall where she was and where she'd been. When she remembered she sat up for a moment to look out at the sunrise, and then plunged under the sheets for more sleep.

The next thing she knew the phone was jangling. She hated the idea that one couldn't hear on it and hesitated to answer but the ringing persisted. Finally she picked up the receiver and slid it into bed with her.

"I say Laura, it's Charles—yes Charles Hooker. Hi!" he yelled. "Are you there—are you awake?"

"What time is it?" she answered as loudly as she could.

"It's ten-thirty."

She came awake suddenly. Her call to Indra was to be made at eleven. She tried desperately to remember the number he had given her.

"I wanted to ask you and Jeff for dinner. I'm having just a small—"

What was the number he had given her?

"Small dinner party this evening." The phone crackled. "Are you there?"

"Yes, yes. I can't say for Jeff . . . No, he isn't here just now. No, exploring Delhi I suppose. Yes, yes, I'll come with Sundaram then, he's already . . . yes, okay dahling . . . lovely, byeeeee."

She fumbled blindly to get the receiver back on the hook. What was the number. The number! She jumped out of bed and rummaged in a suitcase for her traveling clock. She called for the time, and put the clock beside the phone. "Don't write it down," he had said, so she had kept it in her mind, repeating it until—until the gin and tonic. She flopped back on the pillow, closed her eyes to concentrate and finally recalled it.

The room boy came in with coffee and pretended to clean while casting furtive glances at her. He was young and handsome and spoke good English. He seemed to be waiting for something to happen. "Like Carlos," Laura thought. She could feel waves of frustration coming from him. Were all the men here uptight? Was Indra uptight?

At exactly eleven she lifted the receiver and asked the operator for the number. The phone rang and rang. Her heart fell, she was certain she'd remembered it wrong. Then his deep voice was on the other end.

"Can you remember an address?" he said. "And come as soon as you are ready?"

She had her pencil. The phone was crackling again. She cursed it under her breath.

"Don't worry, you'll remember it." He repeated the address. "Don't write it down," he added.

"But I already have."

"Then look at it for a few seconds and tear it up. I'll be waiting here for you."

There was a click at the other end.

Would she go immediately, was her first thought. And what was this about tearing up the address he had given her? Some sort of test she supposed. "Might as well play the game," she said aloud, tearing up the slip of paper. Should she hurry? No. She decided to take a long bubble bath.

Afterwards she took great care dressing and putting on make-up.

[37]

She would go down to the coffee shop, have a Bloody Mary, scrambled eggs, and coffee and it would be mid-afternoon when she went to see him. She was thinking of Sundar's warning. She must be careful to avoid giving this Indra the idea that her interest in him was anything more than casual.

§

It was exactly three P.M. when she arrived by taxi at the address he had given her. A half-open rusted gate was the only break in a high crumbling wall that stretched for a full block. Several "shops" made of tin and wood scraps grew on it like barnacles, beggars and a a few lepers lounging against them. A skinny old man wearing only a turban and a pair of ragged shorts darted out of the gate to open the taxi door. He ventured a kind but toothless smile from his stubble of white beard, and after a verbal battle in Hindi with the driver, beckoned Laura to follow him. Inside the gate was a jungle of vines, ancient mango trees, and palms whose untrimmed brown fronds rustled in the dry January wind. Hidden in this tangle of vegetation were the remains of a vast mansion dating from early colonial times. Decaying pillars and fallen beams marked the long veranda where once, Laura supposed, handsome regimental officers and their ladies had sipped tea. The old man led her down a long hall past silent dusty rooms smelling of mold and rotted wood, full of Victorian furniture and large engravings, photographs of swarthy faces, faded color reproductions of gods and goddesses. At last they came to a small terrace that opened onto a patch of well-kept garden, planted with flowers and vegetables and bordered with roses. There was a well and a small fountain splashing into a white marble pool.

Indra was laying naked on a charpoy, a long low wooden platform. A cherubic young boy was rubbing his legs. In one corner an ancient fan rattled. Laura sat, not daring to speak, as he turned on his stomach so that the boy could rub and knead his back with oil. He appeared not even to notice that she had arrived.

After what seemed like an eternity he propped his head up on his arms and smiled. There followed another long silence during which he continued to smile, studying her with his dark eyes while the boy massaged his feet and hands.

"Is this your house?" she asked, unable to bear his look.

"They say it belongs to me." He sighed and turned over to sit up. His body glowed like that of a young athlete. "They say it is an inheritance after a long family feud during which the man who

[38]

called me his son was poisoned by another who called me brother." He shook his head as if to shake the memory out of his mind. "A long story, filled with episodes of infidelity and deceit."

"Now what will you do with it?" she asked sympathetically, familiar herself with property and family feuds.

"Not sure," he said. "Thinking of setting fire to it, thinking of climbing on top—on the roof—and having this boy set fire to the whole thing."

He placed his hand affectionately on the boy's head and spoke to him softly in Hindi. The boy, who was squatting at Indra's feet, grinned. "You see, he would do it, he would really do it. A very grand fire it would make too, would it not? Light up all Delhi, ha! These houses are prisons. Always remember: it is better to live in a shack, a shack won't dictate your life. . . . Better yet, live naked out of doors and be free."

His nakedness and wild talk were so bizarre—was he putting her on, she wondered. At the same time there was an element of dead seriousness about him.

"But it must be very valuable," she said, trying to keep some thread of conversation going, "here in the center of Delhi."

"Delhi!" he laughed. "You can't imagine what Delhi was really like. But it is no more, it is Leningrad or Detroit, not Delhi. Money is not a problem for me. I can do very well without it. The problem is that if I sell it some greedy beggar on horseback will make a bigger prison here, a skyscraping hotel where he and his fat friends and their fat spoiled quarrelsome children and even fatter wives will live with pants, shoes, and miniskirts. Let them." He gestured gracefully. "They are all going to the dogs. The best people are all gone, killed in '47, dispossessed, gone crazy; only the garbage is left. They have no teaching because they hate teachers—they are without proper gurus. They think they know everything and that life is—" He paused, arching an eyebrow at her, "just a bowl of cherries. But what will happen? All they want is money for jam." He grinned, showing his teeth. "It will probably be given away," he said, matter-of-factly.

"By you?"

"If that's the way it happens." He gazed at her a long time, scratching one leg and trying to see into her.

She found it hard to look at him directly. She was nervous and not accustomed to having philosophical conversations with naked men. His body glistened smooth and sleek in the failing light. Far away a faint roar signaled the mounting confusion of Delhi's rush hour—the "cowdust hour" with its pungent odor of thousands of fires kindled in preparation for the evening meal.

[39]

After some time the old man brought out an oil lamp and the boy fetched tea and a concoction of what appeared to be dumplings floating in cream.

"Do you always flavor your sweets with bhang?" asked Laura, recognizing the dish cooked with cannabis, cardamom, cinnamon, and nutmeg.

"You have a dangerously perceptive taste, Laura Weatherall," Indra said.

"I've had some experience."

"In this weather, in Delhi, a small amount of bhang is sometimes taken in the food," he said, ignoring her challenge but interested in her show of strength. "It is good for the health at this season. We grind the spices together into the batter of the dumplings which we call pakoras. Bhang and opium and many other poisons are used in small amounts by us to regulate the system. If you are neurotic or have too many attachments to body or property, and if therefore you are filled with frustrations, then you should not use drugs, even as medicine."

"Do you mean me, or one?"

"You," he said, staring up at her. "You have had too many drugs."

She looked skeptical.

"Yes, yes. I know you do not believe me—you do not understand too well. These drugs are all poisonous, very toxic. All poisons are initiators into different states of being with the world. Each has its special path, its ritual and rite. The power that comes can kill you if you do not understand the procedure that must be followed. It is too complex. You have to have a teacher with you. There are many things we don't tell—"

"Unless?"

"Unless the student passes certain tests."

"And I am not kindly or pure, am I," Laura said.

"No one has given you the opportunity," he answered listlessly, closing his eyes.

"How come you came to Delhi anyway," he said, after a pause. His accent had changed to imitation American slang. He sounded like a police sergeant.

"My husband is a . . ."

"Be careful what you say, don't incriminate yourself."

"Quite right," Laura said. "He is *not* my husband."

Indra grinned.

"We're here together to make a film."

It was no use. He just grinned at her. She felt extremely

[40]

uncomfortable but she couldn't tell him the truth—at least not now.

"Why are you grinning?" she asked finally.

"That's a riddle for you to unravel. You can though," he said. "You *can* unravel it—all of it. That's why you are here at this moment."

For the first time the seriousness of this meeting confronted her.

"You spoke about some power coming," she said. "What power?"

"Ah, you Americans, you are always so interested in power. Don't you have some story in the West called the Sorcerer's Apprentice?"

"Yes."

"Well then," he said, laughing, "there is only one power, *the* Power." He made a careless gesture with both hands, accidental yet beautiful. "It comes automatically as a result of practicing the ancient teachings—if you know the methods. If you use the power in this world, however, it will finish you. It is meant to be used only in getting people out."

"Are you a sorcerer then?"

"Sorcery is the application of power in this world. Your Western scientists are sorcerers. Mathematics is their secret language. They have stolen it from the gods. But they are neither kindly nor pure and so the power they have is about to destroy them and their system. The only reason for using power is to bring people to their senses so they will want to go across."

"Go across—what does that mean?"

"That's a Buddhist expression." He sighed and leaned back on one arm, smiling at her as though she were a new toy. "Hogwash, all this talk is useless, it only drives one crazy. Ask me no questions and I'll tell you no lies."

The old fan rattled on in the early evening silence. As Laura watched him she had the peculiar impression that he was not really there at all, that if she rose to touch him there would be nothing.

"The world is a bridge," he whispered, almost to himself. "Pass over it but do not build on it. He who hopes for an hour may hope for eternity. The world is but an hour. Spend it in devotion. The rest is unseen."

"What is that?"

"Oh, just an inscription on a gate." His voice drifted off. Then he asked, suddenly, "Will you come with me to the Himalayas tomorrow?"

"Tomorrow? With you?"

[41]

He nodded. "Tomorrow or the day after."

Laura panicked. "Actually I'm late now, for an appointment."
She seemed to hear her own voice echoing outside herself and it
frightened her.

He smiled.

She felt immobilized, disconnected, and when finally she was
able to get up she lurched toward him as if propelled by some other
force.

But his hand came up in a gesture that signaled both a blessing
and a halt. "You will call me tomorrow," he said.

She stood still, fiddling with the fringe of her shawl. For an
instant she felt like a child standing in front of her mother. The
sensation was so strong she could even smell her mother's perfume
in the air.

"Yes, I'll call tomorrow. By then I'll know about going with
you."

"Of course," he said.

The boy had a taxi waiting. "What a strange being," she
thought as the driver wheeled off into the night through the dimly
lit streets. "So young yet so ancient.

"And I'm not pure, I'm filled with attachments, like sex and
comfort."

Outside the car window a gray and uncomfortable India slipped
past. She knew instinctively that he wanted to throw her out into it
to test her mettle. "How can I go anywhere with him, out there,"
she sighed, "I'd never make it."

Would she phone him in the morning? She didn't feel up to it.
"He knows all my weaknesses," a voice stammered inside her, "he
wants to test me and I want to be tested . . . but not yet."

They were passing through the wide boulevards of a suburban
development—expensive but absurd whims rendered into concrete
and tile at the command of the petulant nouveau riche. The car
slowed, then stopped outside the gate of a house set deep within an
oasis-like compound. She paid the driver and walked in. "Poor
Charles," she thought, looking around her, "he can't seem to get
out of Beverly Hills."

She was greeted by Sharma of the night before, who as it turned
out was Hooker's girlfriend.

"Sorry I'm late," Laura said, "I got lost shopping."

She felt relaxed with Sharma, a woman of great strength as well
as beauty. Laura admired her magnificent breasts, naked beneath a
wisp of sari.

"Never late," said Sharma, laughing melodiously. "Come, your

Jeff is here. He's waiting over there for you." She gestured and then disappeared into another room.

§

"Sorry I didn't make it back last night," Jeff said. "Business."

"I can imagine."

"But really, Laura—it was good for us," he protested. "About ten people got turned on after the rest had gone. No freakouts, all good trips. Everyone wants more."

"Did *you* give the acid out?"

"No, Dorje did, he's a beautiful cat. He was the host after all, very hip underneath the mask."

"I thought you might have been fucking all night."

Jeff grinned sheepishly. "The important thing is the contacts I managed to make. The sooner we get rid of the acid the sooner we'll be *out* of here!"

"You don't like India?"

"Not much, there's too much frustration—people are too uptight here."

"How about the girls?"

"They're funny, like rabbits. They want you to be like a rabbit too, quick time." He noted the angry look that crossed Laura's face. "Don't be a jealous wife," he snapped. "You're free too, you know."

"Free to do what? This is a man's world. Look around you. All these male chauvinists think of me as a whore, I can tell."

"That's because at home they're all ruled by their wives," said Jeff. "Wives still mean something here because they still make homes men want to come back to. They know how to take care of men."

"Don't be romantic," Laura said. She gestured around the room. "These chicks aren't exactly what I'd call homemakers."

She was angry. First Indra had called her impure, now Jeff was down-tripping her. Men were all the same the world over. "Where they have the power," she thought, "they want to squash us like bugs."

Jeff turned away and wandered off into another part of the house. Watching him go, Laura felt depressed and somewhat frightened. Indra had touched something very deep within her; the cellars and sub-basements of her mind, long shut up, had been pried open a little. She looked through the crowd and saw Harpal, the

[43]

Sikh from the night before, at the bar. They locked eyes across the room.

This was more certain ground, an inner voice told her. But was it? She sighed, a new voice also told her that it was not. The certain ground of sex and parties . . . "Money for jam," Indra had said. She felt on the verge of some new insight, but what was it? Her old habits were familiar, easy, and reassuring. Change was an unknown quantity. She hated the idea of the unknown. If she forced herself in a new direction, there was no telling what might come of it. She might even go crazy. She decided not to interfere with the course of events, but only to respond positively to whatever was happening around her. If that meant being a whore, then she would be a good one. She moved toward the bar.

Harpal watched her, his face impassive as a Greek athlete, handsome under a magenta turban pinned with a large blue stone.

"Good evening," he said. "Do you want a drink?"

Something inside her wanted to act fearlessly, aggressively, whatever the consequences. "I want *you*," she said with a calm smile, making her eyes travel down his body and up again.

That threw him off guard and he looked away momentarily before taking up her challenge.

"You come and have a drink," he said huskily, as though she were a naughty child.

"We were introduced last night, were we not?" he said formally.

"Oh, yes," she said. "Your name is Harpal, isn't it?"

He nodded. "And yours?"

"Laura."

"You are from?"

"The moon."

He didn't smile. She knew he considered her behavior insubordinate, but she enjoyed upsetting him. Seduction scenes must be heavy here, she thought. He stood very still, his legs apart, at ease in the military fashion. Only his left leg moved slightly, rhythmically from the knee.

"You have missed eating," he said.

"I'm not hungry."

"Then will you have a dance before we leave?"

They danced in a dark corner. To her surprise he moved well.

"Where did you learn to dance?" she whispered in his ear.

"On South Randolph Street in Chicago," he answered. "I was supposed to be going to the University of Chicago but I spent most of my time on South Randolph learning to boogie. They liked my turban, you know." He paused.

[44]

"And now?"

"Now I'm a landowner. Our father called me back. We all have to live on our land now, otherwise under the new laws we might lose it."

Her body relaxed him, she felt so warm and soft. He never went to the Indian prostitutes, getting it free in America had killed all that for him. He wondered whether she could sense the extent of his sexual frustration. How long it had been since he had a Western girl! But the ethics of his tribe still governed him: his Rajput ancestry wanted mindless submission. Though fascinated by her open sensuality, something in him disliked a woman who talked back.

"Now we can go," he said. He caught her hand and pulled her outside onto a terrace. The evening had turned cool, almost cold. As they walked down the drive he motioned to a jeep parked just beyond the gate.

"Sorry about this car," he said, helping her up. "But we have many roads where only jeeps work. We are a poor country you know. We have to use the same vehicles for everything."

A few minutes later they pulled up at the side entrance of an imposing skyscraper hotel somewhere in downtown Delhi.

"One of Indra's prisons," Laura thought.

"We keep an apartment here," Harpal said. Everyone at the door saluted him.

The elevator opened onto a small mirrored alcove of white marble. Beyond lay a large room with polished wood floors and at one end a wall of windows overlooking the city. The room was crowded with expensive furniture and old treasures: campaign chests with brass fittings, carved screens, trophies, and animal skins. There were hallways on either side leading to other rooms. Outside rose a waning saffron moon.

Harpal excused himself to make sure no one else was in. Neither of his brothers had lived abroad. They would never understand that she was not a prostitute.

How could he explain to her the customs and demands of his crazy older brothers? Could she imagine how the total lack of privacy had infected all of them? His brothers were primitives, echoes of another time, another life. Himself, he was split in two: half Western, half Indian.

"Take the science but keep the ancient customs," his father had often said to them. How naive, how idealistic. It had proved an impossible combination that was going to kill them all. Now they wore uncomfortable pants and owned hotels they disliked living in. Day by day their lives seemed more confused and useless. They

[45]

were going toward destruction, to be lost forever in a sea of uniformity called "modern."

"We are alone," he said when he returned and faced her in the darkened room, silhouetted against the long glass wall. He embraced her and then with a sudden violent movement ripped off her blouse, buttons and all, leaving her large white breasts glowing softly in the half light. She reached up and began unbuttoning his shirt.

He felt her cool hand and then his muscles rippled involuntarily as she moved close to him, letting her breasts rub lightly against the skin of his chest. South Chicago flashed across his mind. She fumbled with his belt. He thought he would explode. Before she could go further he picked her up and carried her to a smaller room that opened onto a roof garden, locked the door and lowered her gently onto a low sofa. Standing over her he removed his clothes until only his loin cloth, the last remnant of the old ways, remained. Then he took hold of her long red hair and lifted her head up against his erection. She could feel it against her cheek, solid and throbbing. She gazed into his dark eyes as her hands removed the cloth.

He felt like a burning fuse at the end of a bomb. Pushing her back on the sofa he arched over her and tore away her other clothes blindly to ease himself down between the softness of her thighs, his hands forward on her breasts.

Free of the turban, his hair swung over her, a mass of silky jet black curls. He came up in a crouch beside her, brushing his hair back with a defiant sweep of his hand.

"Now you see the Harpal of Hindustan," he whispered.

He stood up, bringing her with him, lifting her into the air by her buttocks. She straddled his waist. Slowly then he let her slide down onto his large uncircumcised penis. She could feel the column of hot blood throbbing inside her. She thrust her tongue into his mouth and locked her arms around his strong neck as he lowered himself to the floor, still inside her, until he was sitting cross-legged.

In this way he had her, slowly, deeply, on the floor of the room, holding back the orgasm, letting it come on and shutting it off. The muscles of her vagina opened and closed on him.

"I'm going to fill you with a flood of sperm," he whispered.

"And I'll digest you," she said coolly.

That enraged him. "You digest *me?*" he hissed. He pulled back and slapped her hard across the cheek, then held her head on the floor by her hair, his teeth showing between taut lips.

"You digest me, a Sikh, the son of sons of sons of warriors?" He

[46]

laughed crazily and lowered his mouth onto hers, fastening his eyes unblinking on hers as he thrust himself further inside her, then withdrew and thrust himself in again. The pain on her face pleased him.

"You wanted to know how it is to be fucked by one of us, didn't you?" he whispered into her mouth. "To take a little taste? Ah, but now can you take it?" He thrust himself in again brutally. She winced. "Digest?" he said, panting. "You may eat, you crazy bitch, but you will never digest. Understand? Never digest." He slapped her again.

She went limp as he forced her to open further, probing deeper and deeper inside her.

Then suddenly she felt him tense, listening, like an animal in danger. He looked up, brushing his hair back. Laura turned her head. The glass door to the roof garden was open. Two figures stood in the dark. They came closer, loosening their belts. Fear gripped her. Harpal felt it but held her still, continuing to fuck her.

She had expected him to rise up against the intruders but her fear turned to rage as she recognized his older brothers, Harjith and Kuljit, and realized that to them she was a prostitute. According to custom, she was to be shared.

Harjith undressed, and squatting near her head took her hand in his, drawing it up under his loincloth. At that moment Harpal exploded inside her and she cried out, started to struggle. But reason and a will to live took possession of her; to fight might mean suicide. She knew she must forget guilt, enjoy and give pleasure.

Harpal withdrew and stood up trembling. Harjith pulled Laura between his legs, guiding himself into her mouth. She turned on her stomach and lay sucking him, her head held firmly between his strong hands. Then she felt two other hands massaging her buttocks and inner thighs. Kuljit drove himself into her brutally, like an animal. She felt herself tense and wished she had some cocaine to ease the pain. It was rape but she had to go through with it. Just then Harjith came in her mouth, discharging with violence down her throat. As he came he yelled out something in Punjabi, a primitive yell which sent needles through her. She gagged but was unable to move her head from his viselike grip.

For a while after that Laura lost sense of where she was and what was happening to her. When she came to she was alone with Kuljit, who was the eldest. He smelled of sandalwood. He had turned her on her back and covered her with a fur. He squatted beside her, a naked giant stroking her forehead and speaking in broken English, his handsome face serious if not kindly behind a flowing black beard flecked with gray.

[47]

"I am oldest brother," he whispered, taking her in his arms as though she were a small toy. "Harpal my babou, I teach him everything. Now you meet the teacher."

He manipulated her body skillfully into different positions like a sculptor playing with clay, each time entering her slowly, pressing her thighs and buttocks into new shapes.

The pressure of him inside her increased, filling her to the bursting point. Her nails dug into his back. She started to scream but he filled her mouth with his tongue. She opened her eyes to see his inches away, wide open too, watching, as he fucked her like she'd never before been fucked. Laura exploded. Waves rocked her body, wave after wave of pleasure and pain engulfed her until finally she lay senseless.

She floated off then, a child in a rowboat, floating on a lake where beautiful white water lilies nodded heavily in the sun. She could hear the slap slap slap of the water on the sides of the boat as she lay snuggled between her father's legs.

When she finally opened her eyes again, Harpal was standing over her, staring down at her gravely, a blue silk lunghi around his waist. She couldn't speak but extended her arm, catching his leg just above the calf, drawing him closer. He sat down beside her on the floor.

"Now you know how bad we are," he said sadly. He looked away. "But you must forgive them, it is our custom and you must forgive me as I must observe custom."

"Always?" Laura asked.

"Usually only with prostitutes," he said, with a sidelong glance.

Fury gave Laura back her strength. She was seething but kept it hidden. Drawing his face down to hers, she kissed his eyes and mouth. He stretched out beside her as she moved down, kissing his neck, sucking and biting his nipples. He became excited again, her freedom aroused him. He knew she wasn't a prostitute but maybe she was worse. A witch maybe. Her head went down kissing his thighs, caressing his penis, pulling back the foreskin like a sacred object unveiled. Then abruptly she raked her long nails across the small of his back, drawing blood.

"Bitch!" he yelled and struggled to pin her down. But she got free, and jumping on top of him, sank her nails into the tender flesh just under his armpits. He cried out, twisted away. Blood trickled down his sides. Before Laura could get up he had his knee on her back and had pinned her, face down. But she was too wide open to please him; he could feel the sperm of his brother in her vagina. He decided to bugger her. He had never before buggered a woman, only young boys—kept as prostitutes and trained especially for the

[48]

purpose. He liked it. His grandfather's boys were famous, a few even dressed as girls and were kept in the harem. The boys were tight and he, Harpal, was big. The victim usually squirmed and cried out at first, but then groaning with delight, succumbed.

With the tip of his penis he touched Laura now, watching her sphincter muscle expand and contract as it swallowed him up like a mouth. She struggled but he was strong and skillful. For some time he stayed motionless just inside her. Then he withdrew, relubricated himself with sperm from her vagina and thrust himself into her deeply. Her scream was lost in the mass of her hair. He lay on top of her and massaged her clitoris until she began to arch up involuntarily, panting with rage and lust. She cried out but he slammed her face down again, pumping himself into her until he could feel her orgasm. Then trembling he exploded, over and over again, emptying himself.

For a while they lay silent and motionless together. Then mechanically Laura got up and brought a hot damp towel to bathe him but he was asleep. She felt tired but triumphant. She'd outlasted all of them. She showered, and when she came back wrapped in a towel he had awakened but was still lying there on the floor, his eyes like slits.

"I'm sorry about all this." He gestured weakly.

"Turn over and I'll do your back." She pushed at him gently. The nail marks had stopped bleeding, but the muscles of his back were tense. She kneaded and stroked his back, applying pressure to a special place that Jeff had shown her low on the spine. Soon he was asleep.

Quickly she examined her clothes. The snaps were gone on her pants. She put them on and tied a turban cloth around her waist to hold them up. Her blouse was ripped to shreds, but she decided it wouldn't be noticed beneath her shawl, which was still intact.

The door key was lying on a table in the marble alcove. She glanced at herself in the mirrors. "Good enough to get to the hotel," she thought. With her hand on the elevator door she paused. What else, what else? She wanted to teach them a lesson. But what was the lesson? She'd been treated like a prostitute: prostitutes are always paid.

She bent over his sleeping form and carefully removed a large diamond ring from his index finger, another with rubies and diamonds and from a third finger an enormous plum colored ruby set in gold.

"Gentlemen never wear jewelry," she could hear her mother saying. But then Mother had never been to India.

She put the rings into a gold snuff box she found on a shelf.

[49]

It was past three in the morning when Laura arrived at the entrance of the hotel, deserted except for Jeff who happened to be waiting for a taxi with two girls.

"I'm taking them home," he said quietly. "Be back in a few minutes. Don't go to sleep, we have to make plans."

In the room she threw off her clothes and ran for the tub. When Jeff returned she was still in it. He noticed the bruises where Harpal had hit her.

"I went off with a Sikh," she answered coolly. "I wanted to taste, like you've been doing. Turned out he had two brothers and it's their custom to share."

"You took on all three?" He stared at her in disbelief.

"And you were right, they did treat me like a prostitute," Laura went on. She hoped her confession was upsetting him.

"So I tried to think of myself as one and didn't put up a fight. Anyhow, I'm alive and that's something. They were all over six feet, very rough, very expert. You don't know a country really until you've fucked with the people, do you? It was very enlightening . . . but corny too."

"Corny?" Jeff's eyebrows went up.

"I can't explain . . . There was no contact—I was just an object. I'm sure *you* understand that."

"But don't prostitutes get paid?" he said coolly.

She splashed him. "Hand me my bag."

He held it out to her.

"My hands are all wet, open it and see what you find."

He brought out the gold box.

"Open it."

"They *gave* you these?" he asked, withdrawing the rings.

"They treated me like a prostitute so I behaved like one. No?"

"But you can't do this, Laura," he said, as if she were a naughty child. "Do you have any idea how much this thing alone is worth?" He held up the gold box.

"That's not the point, it's the idea that's important."

He sighed. "This box, it's solid gold. Must be worth a hundred thousand. They'll be coming around here mad when they wake up."

"No they won't." Laura smiled and began to brush her hair. "They're afraid I might tell the wrong people. That," she pointed to the gold box, "will keep them from telling anyone. It would cause too much embarrassment."

"But they'll be after it on the sly," Jeff worried.

"Maybe, but I'll be gone by then. I've decided to go to the Himalayas tomorrow with Alex's teacher."

[50]

Jeff gaped at her.

"You certainly don't need me here. We've more or less established our identity, now it's just a waste of time for me."

"How long will you be gone?" he asked uncertainly.

"No idea. Can't you do without me?" Her sarcasm was evident. "You seem to be doing very well on your own."

But Jeff feared his own weaknesses if left alone. How could he ever explain that? Although he hadn't been treating her well he was deeply attached to her.

"I have a certain amount of work here," he said. "I want to get rid of as many trips as I can. It's starting out well. But I'd like to leave as soon as possible. Bombay by the middle of April."

"That's three months," she said. "I won't be gone *that* long."

"But this is India, Laura."

"What is that supposed to mean?"

"I mean you can't say just like that how long you'll be or how long I'll be. Nothing works, there's no communication system. Once you leave you can't really say you'll ever be back."

"Nonsense," she retorted.

"Don't you feel it in the air?"

"No, I don't. Just because you have to yell on the telephones doesn't mean they don't work. And there are trains and the mails. Don't worry. I don't plan to disappear. I'll be back long before you think."

"It's important for you to come to Bombay."

"Then I can meet you there." She found it ironic that he should treat her so casually when she was with him but resisted her going on a trip by herself.

"I think we should leave this place in a few hours," he said, "I don't want those three guys storming in here. Too much at stake."

"I'll stay up and pack then," Laura agreed. "Where will we go?"

"To Sundar's. He's invited us and it's what Stan said to do in case of any emergency. Have you made arrangements to leave with this *gooroo?*"

"You don't have to say it like that," she said irritated. "You'd better phone Sundaram."

§

"He wasn't even pissed at being dragged out of bed," Jeff reported after he'd called. "Said he more or less expected it."

"What did you tell him?"

[51]

"Nothing. Just that we were fed up with this place. That we'd be round before breakfast."

"Does he suspect you're dealing the acid?"

"No. He took some himself the other night at Dorje's, though. Probably thinks Dorje has it."

"Anyway you'd better keep the suitcases locked at his house." She paused. "I think I'll call him now."

"Who?"

"Indra. Alex's teacher."

"Can't you do that at Sundaram's? We should get packed and . . ."

"It's almost 4:30, he'll be up. Maybe if I call this early we'll be able to leave today."

She picked up the phone and asked for the number before Jeff could protest further. There was an immediate answer on the other end.

"Hello, yes. No, I'm not asleep. Yes, we can leave anytime . . . what is this Sundaram's address?"

She gave him the number which he repeated.

"Then I'll be there for you at eleven. If you have warm clothes bring them. Otherwise you can get what you need where we are going."

He hung up abruptly, leaving her holding the receiver. "Certainly don't waste talk in this country, do they?" she said.

"No," Jeff said, "Things happen fast and without discussion. A guy bought 200,000 trips from me this evening. The whole transaction took ten minutes."

"You've got that much money on you?" she gasped.

"Not quite. He gave me a check on a Swiss account. It has to go to Stan first, when it clears he'll get the stuff."

Laura was relieved. "Really, you know, these people are all heavies. You must promise to be careful."

§

A. K. Sundaram's face remained expressionless as Laura described her evening. That she took some loot amused him immensely.

"My South Indian soul revels in such mischief with Sikhs," he chuckled. "It will drive him absolutely crazy when he finds the jewels gone. You'd best return them though or his brothers will make things rough for him."

"Poor Harpal," she said. "But couldn't he have sent them away?"

[52]

"Certain clans from Punjab are very incestuous, especially theirs. They enjoy doing things together you might say—communal life, you know." He laughed. "Shall I return the trinkets for you?" he added after a pause, looking straight at her. "You certainly don't want them?"

"Firing from the hip," she thought.

"No, I don't want them, of course," she said aloud. "Just wanted to stop them from gloating or gossiping. I may look it but I'm not a Methodist missionary."

"My dear," Sundar retorted, "all you foreigners are. Everyone who comes here from abroad thinks they are on a mission of one sort or other. After all, India is supposed to be underdeveloped." He guffawed, staring directly at Jeff. "But I think I will let Harpal spend the day trying to locate you and at five this afternoon I will send word that his trinkets are in my possession. When he comes here and receives the good verbal lashing he deserves he'll have been sufficiently reprimanded. These people have their private mafias, you know. India has always been ruled by family gangs. . . ." Sundar thought a minute. "I will demand a commission, and I'll donate one ring to a good cause—in your name. To leprosy, maybe. At least you'll know your efforts weren't entirely in vain."

He paused and took Laura's hand.

"My dear girl," he said, "India is an odd place. You might be in a dangerous situation four months from now, who knows? Maybe hanging from some Himalayan cliff. And there, out of nowhere, would be Harpal to save you."

She gave him the box with the rings in it. He held it, clicking his tongue.

"So they are putting their money in gold nowadays? Very interesting. I doubt they have paid any tax on it. If they leave things like this lying about what do they have locked up? They'll be most upset that I have seen it."

"That's what I thought," Jeff said. "Why I didn't want to stick around the hotel."

"I'll call them later this morning," Sundar said. "No point in prolonging the agony. They might all push each other off the terrace of their hotel."

III

§

AT EXACTLY 11:00 A.M. Indra was waiting in a car outside.

"Will you come and say hello to him?"

"This is not America, dear Laura," Sundar replied. "We in India are not really one nation but a collection of fiercely independent clans, and although we respect each other's rights we aren't gregarious. He's a very shy man. Useless conversation between us would embarrass him."

"Be careful," Jeff said, taking her in his arms. "Got your backpack?"

"Yes, everything. See you in Bombay. Do you know where you'll be staying?"

"Ambassador, I guess." He glanced at Sundaram who was smiling broadly.

"Yes," said Sundaram, laughing. "By all means, the Ambassador. It belongs to your friend Harpal. You see, Laura? One Himalayan cliff, coming up in Bombay!"

§

"Are you all right?" said Indra quietly from the deep padding of the limousine.

"There it-is again," Laura thought, "that frustrating question . . ."

"Hello," she said aloud. "Yes, of course." She slipped into the opposite corner of the seat as the car moved out into traffic.

"This is for your sake." He gestured at the car. "I usually travel by bus or train, but I thought you might be tired after last night. In the car you'll be able to rest. Here, lie down on the seat and I'll sit here." He pulled down one of the jump seats.

She lay down thinking what a weird scene it was to be riding in a limousine with a half-naked yogi whose matted hair hung to his waist. "What makes you think I'm tired?"

"Didn't you have a rather strenuous evening?" he asked.

"I did stay up quite late." Nervously Laura brushed a strand of hair out of her face. "I suppose I look tired."

"The loot you took," he said pointedly. "What has happened to that?"

"How do you know about that?"

"I was watching."

"Watching?" she gasped. "From where?"

"From here." Indra pointed to his brow.

"You were watching me from here." She repeated the gesture.

"I watched some of it. I hope you were persuaded to return the loot. These boys can be extra tough. It would be dangerous for your friend Jeff."

"You mean you watched all of it," she said, staring wide-eyed at the limousine's padded ceiling. "And you—you still let me come with you?" She wanted to scream.

"But why not," he answered calmly. "What is all that to me? I am out of this world already. Not interested in this humdrum morality, that is all custom ... all relative. Balance is always restored one way or another." He laughed softly. "One man may like to eat roast pig, another drinks all night, another prays all day, another has intercourse all night. But every act bounces back. It goes on forever: action, reaction, action, reaction." He turned his palm up, then down. "Each action is echoed back and balanced out by opposites. It is the law of *this* world." He gestured outside the car. "When you get partly out of it, you'll know. That's why I can go and see whom I like whenever I like."

"Do you know Harpal?" Laura asked.

"You mean the Harpal you were with last night?" he countered. "Yes, many times over, he is one of our mass-produced nouveau riche. But my dear Laura Weatherall, you are testing me," Indra said sternly.

"Yes, I was," she admitted, sitting up. She was truly shaken. Like so many others she had found the idea of clairvoyance groovy or far out. But now confronted with its real implications all her systems signaled *Danger*. She curled up on the seat feeling very cold. "Should I feel guilty?" she asked.

"Do you feel guilty?"

"That's the problem. The Laura Weatherall part of me feels guilty, but there's another part that feels free and unblemished, that feels no guilt, only joy ... pleasure. Is that wrong?"

"Are these joys and pleasure feelings beyond fear?" he asked.

[55]

He leaned forward, athletic-looking, intense. "For if they aren't, isn't it true they're not free?"

Laura couldn't answer.

"Is it unafraid, this deeper part of you that feels only joy and pleasure? Does it embrace the fearful? When pleasure is over does this deeper part still feel a joy that is able to resist the outer one, the Laura Weatherall one?

"Wheels within wheels," Indra whispered, gesturing with his long forefinger. "Onion skins within onion skins. But it isn't inside or outside, only more and more. You are getting at this knowledge through sex, which is one way, but not the best way. Liberation through the world of desire can catch you in the skin trap. Yes? Trapped to this." He pinched his smooth flesh. "As I said, nothing is forever. But it is important to go through it if there is no other way."

He sighed, and leaning back, gazed out the window at the poverty of outer Delhi. "A hole is a hole," he said with a sidelong glance at her, "and what fills it, fills it. And the pleasure liberates you for a little while. But there are other ways, even more pleasurable," he said emphatically, "once you learn them."

§

He sat, watching the landscape slide by, a landscape so altered by the cutting of the great forests, by man's machines and the grids he had imposed, that it bore little resemblance to anything Indra had once known. He let her sleep and finally as dusk overtook them, unpacked some food from a compartment under the jump seat. He felt fed up. "Why go on with this?" he thought, looking at her. But it had happened that way. It was not his action.

The smell of coffee woke her.

"I've been asleep a long time," Laura whispered, lifting herself on one elbow.

"Sleep is good," he said gently. He handed her the coffee.

It tasted of spices and pepper and real cream.

She glanced out the window but saw only her own reflection in the dark glass. "How long have we been driving?" she asked.

"It's almost midnight now. Just before dawn we'll arrive at the outskirts of a village. I'm known there under a different form, and have a place to stay. You'll change into clothes I've brought for you. Then we'll walk about three miles into the village, which lies just at the beginning of the Himalayan foothills, in the jungle land called the Terai. From there we'll walk to another place."

[56]

She finished the coffee and then drifted off again. She saw her father—whom she'd never been permitted to disturb from his endless financial negotiations. He was alone in a vast hall, waving an American flag and shouting orders to people outside who did nothing but look at him through the windows. Then she saw her spoiled unbalanced mother, her face a disaster at fifty from years of martinis and sweet desserts. She was trying to drive her Rolls while eating a chocolate ice cream cone that dripped into her lap. Laura woke giggling. In her infrequent dreams she had never seen her parents looking so real. She felt relaxed.

Soon the car stopped. The first pink glow was showing behind the stark outlines of the foothills as she slipped into the plain rust skirt and blouse which were to be her only clothes. There were also a pair of rubber sandals—chappals—and a faded red wool shawl. When she finished dressing Indra braided her hair and placed a few roadside flowers at the top of the braid. Then he handed her a small cloth bag, also dark red, into which her essentials had been put, and said a few words to the driver. The car made a fast U-turn and disappeared.

They were alone. The real India rushed in from all sides.

§

It was the first time in years Laura had walked anywhere in the country. The rising sun shot up rays of light and the smell of wood smoke drifted in layers through the early morning. Then roosters crowed and peacocks screamed, breaking the silence. Crystal water from the great rivers of the Himalayas rushed through streams and irrigation canals to the plains beyond. Flowers of every description—hibiscus, lantana, morning glory—bloomed in the hedgerows and the fields were high with wheat and mustard. There were also acres of marijuana.

"Ganja." Indra gestured. "See. Isn't it beautiful?"

They came to several roadside "shops," patched together haphazardly of discarded boards and covered with tin roofs. Inside, open fires were already glowing; young boys prepared food while old men in white dhotis and turbans, some with scarves wrapped around their ears to ward off the morning chill, sat stoically sucking on hookas and sipping tea from brass cups.

At the outer limits of the village, numerous people were squatting at the edges of neat green fields performing their morning ablutions, each seemingly oblivious of the others.

[57]

"Them that shits together stays together," Indra said in a Texas drawl.

"Where did you learn to talk like *that?*" asked Laura, startled.

"American soldiers. I knew some long ago in Burma."

Past the fields they came to mango groves surrounded by old crumbling walls. There were houses too, most of them mud, with thatched roofs. Several early morning passersby clasped their hands in prayer upon seeing Indra. "Salaam, Babaji," said an old man in a long black frock coat, bowing his shaved head. A boy ran up to them and after touching Indra's bare feet, turned shyly and ran back toward the center of the village. There were no motors. The only conveyances were slow creaking ox carts, pony-drawn tongas carrying children to school, and bicycles that shared the road with donkeys, pigs, water buffaloes, cows, and stray horses.

Soon there were many villagers coming out to meet them. "Nameste, Maharaji," and "Salaam, Baba" mixed as both Hindu and Moslem paid their respects. Some were smiling, others deeply serious, some touched Indra's feet and some fell flat on the ground in front of him. A number of children trailed behind them. "Vat iss your name? Vat is your native place?" they yipped at Laura.

Indra said something in Hindi and they stopped.

"I told them you are French," he said under his breath. "They are taught those two ridiculous sentences in their classrooms nowadays and want to practice their 'English' on you. They don't study French."

A leper caught sight of them and came shuffling, his stubby oozing hands outstretched. "Maharaj," he wailed, "Maharaj."

Indra threw him a coin which landed in the dust. Smiling, the man picked it up between his toes.

"His too is the smile of the Divine One," Indra said, "note it well. The smile of destruction."

The village was a jumble of decaying British provincial administrative buildings, a few large mud and brick houses, and other haphazardly erected dwellings in various states of disrepair.

"What happened here?" Laura sensed some disaster.

"Many things," Indra said, "from time out of mind. Much blood has been spilled. The last calamity was an epidemic of cholera about fifty years ago, brought about by the magic of some fakir who had been mistreated by the inhabitants. After a year most of them were dead." He winked.

They came to a small hut of mud and stone in a grove of old mangoes, surrounded by a low stone wall. Behind it a grassy pasture, clipped like a lawn by grazing cows, sloped gently down to a small river where some villagers were beating wet clothes on rocks.

[58]

Herons and kites wheeled in the air, glittering against the sun.

Indra stooped into the low opening of the hut, and beckoned her to follow. Inside a fire smoldered in a pit filled with white ash.

"Sit here to my left and slightly behind. Cover your head with the shawl. The more motionless you can sit, the higher you'll score in their estimation." He smiled, indicating the villagers who were gathering outside.

"Women will come to wash my feet. There will be singing and worship and one of them will feed me. They will also set out a plate for you. You *must* eat all of it even if you don't like it. After some time, we'll be left alone. Then in the evening there will be a repeat performance. There's a small room behind this where later you may sleep."

He grinned, his dark eyes twinkling. "Eat, rest, and be merry," he whispered, "for tomorrow I begin to kill you."

Although he had startled her there wasn't time for Laura to consider the meaning of what he'd said because just then a woman entered. Her steel gray hair was pulled back tightly above refined features, and she carried a large brass bowl filled with pungent water which she placed in front of Indra. She knelt and gently lifting his leg, put his right foot into the water.

"How would you like to go," he said, glancing at Laura out of the corner of his eye while the woman bathed him. "By fire or water?"

"What?"

"You must answer," he said. "How would you prefer to go?"

"To go where?" she said flatly.

"Out of your body, to go out of your body."

"You mean when you kill me?"

The woman was now washing his left foot.

"Yes."

"But I don't want to go anywhere," she whispered, "I'm very happy right here where I am."

There was a pause as the woman wiped Indra's feet gently with a fresh towel. Then she lifted up the bowl of dirty water and gazing directly into Indra's eyes began to drink from it.

Laura winced.

"Are you all right?" he said aside to her, placing his hand on the woman's head which was now on his knee. "Are you still happy where you are?"

The woman began to back out. Laura felt slightly ill.

"You will see many strange things you may not understand. I am going to kill you, my dear, before we have parted but do not, as you say, 'freak out.' Nothing can harm her." He gestured out the

[59]

door through which the woman had vanished. "If you drank that water now," he went on, "you would probably get typhoid." He leaned toward her with the kindest expression she had ever seen.

"If you believe me, nothing can harm you either. Remember, *nothing.*"

Laura thought that she would never have enough faith to drink bath water.

"That woman has faith by birth," she said.

He nodded.

"I would have to learn mine," she thought, and doubted it was possible.

A young man wearing only pants and a turban came in with a small hand organ as well as some tobacco and hashish which he presented to Indra. Then he prostrated himself. Indra warmed his hands over the fire, seemingly indifferent to the supine boy.

"You can't 'learn' faith," he said to Laura, staring into the fire. "It comes either by circumstance of birth, or through certain experiences, usually at times of great danger to you. According to the ancient teaching, you must be born on this soil, Aryavatha." He thumped his fingers on the mud floor. "Otherwise, you must die here and be reborn. I know it sounds parochial, but I can't help that," he said smiling gently. "Shall I kill you?" He laughed and placed his left hand on the head of the prostrate boy.

The boy rose and backed away meekly, his hands pressed together.

"He's been extremely unfaithful and mischievous. That's why he had to wait. Infidel," Indra hissed.

Laura found he was already unnerving her. This man who moved in so many worlds so easily—Delhi . . . here—who was he really? Or was that a valid question. Was he joking or serious?

A group of women of assorted ages had come crawling into the small space. They held the ends of their saris firmly between their teeth, forming a half-veil to indicate modesty. Their leader presented a large brass pot filled with tea which Indra placed on the glowing coals. He had prepared a small chillum, a kind of Indian pipe held in the hands, of the tobacco and hashish, and was drawing deeply from it.

After finishing the chillum and cleaning it, he poured tea into brass cups which he passed to each woman and to Laura. The women held their cups and began singing softly. To Laura the cup seemed so hot she thought she must drop it. How did *they* manage, she wondered? One woman beat a drum. Another led the singing and the others followed in a haunting and plaintive chorus. Finally Indra coughed, sipped more tea, and took up the hand organ. He began tuning it while the women were singing. They droned on as if his action were not in the least discourteous. Then he began to accompany them, lifting their off-key voices to the proper level before he took up their song and drowned them out. They sat silent, entranced, swaying from side to side.

His voice was incomparable; Laura had never imagined he could sound like this. There was more in the voice than the song, some powerful force, an echo of supreme courage. It seemed to come from far inside—a bridge across life manifesting itself through Indra, the medium. It made her want to faint, to wail, to dance. He turned and gazed at her. His eyes were like slits and as the music faded, only his eyes were there, floating in the smoke.

The women swayed mechanically, one or two continued to sing off key until he stopped.

Then they left one by one after prostrating themselves and receiving an ash mark from his thumb between their eyebrows. Indra began tuning the instrument again, and taking a pair of pliers from his bag, started to dismantle it.

"That stupid clout of a boy has ruined this instrument," he said irritably.

It was already midday. Only a few people remained outside in the shade of the mangoes. Waves of heat and light filtered through the leafy cover, but inside the hut it was dark and cool despite the smoldering fire.

After some time a woman entered with food. She spooned quantities of a gruel-like substance onto two large brass plates heaped with rice. From another pot she added big round pieces of unleavened bread. After pouring water over Laura's hands and giving her a towel with which to dry them, the woman presented her with one of the plates. This procedure was repeated with Indra. Then seating herself in front of him, the woman began stuffing food into his mouth.

"This is the standard fare of India," he said. "Poor people's food."

With a singleminded relentlessness, the woman continued to stuff food into his mouth with the fingers of her right hand.

"Healthiest food you'll ever eat. Remember," he said, swallowing hard, "you *must* clean your plate. But not too soon or she will give you more." He raised an eyebrow. "See my plight. I must eat until she thinks I'm full—it's part of the ritual."

The flies had found the food and hovered in swarms. There were so many it was difficult for Laura to get the bread from the plate to her mouth without swallowing a few accidentally.

"Don't think about it," Indra said. "Eat the plate if necessary.

[61]

Remember, they're *giving* it." He opened his dark eyes wide. "For them it is a great sacrifice."

She looked weakly at her plate, still half full, crawling with flies.

"You must learn how to stock up like a camel. Some days we may not get food."

Finally Laura forced the last morsel down her throat and water was quickly brought for her to wash a second time. She found a certain irony in washing when it was obvious the flies didn't wash.

"Rest now," Indra said, motioning to the small room in the rear. "It's the hot time of day. I'll lie down out here."

She was thankful to be able to stretch out on the straw mat she found in the room. She felt bloated by the meal, which seemed to have formed an insoluble lump in her stomach. There was a low window about a foot square through which she could see the river through a haze of shimmering heat. Here and there groups of people dozed beneath the ancient trees.

"Out of time," Laura thought. "How fortunate they are. . . . Paradise never seems to choose those who inhabit it."

The sharp cries of birds roused her.

"Peacocks," his voice said softly as she opened her eyes. A long arm handed in a cup of steaming tea. His face hovered in the doorway.

"It's cooler now," he said. "Time to go for a bath. Bring your towel and that large cloth."

When she emerged from the door of the hut he was there waiting. A crowd of about fifty people had gathered, all sitting silently. Laura noticed a number of naked men who appeared to be yogis.

"They came to test me," Indra said. "Most of them are sorcerers. I will deal with them later. First the bath."

At the river's edge boys bathed hedonistic blue-black water buffaloes, who lounged in the water chewing their cuds. Young farmers, both male and female, bathed their sinuous bodies in the crystal clear water. Nearby the grinding stones of a mill clattered cheerfully. The air was filled with the scent of cannabis and jasmine. Golden fields of mustard and emerald cane sloped away into the late afternoon haze toward the great basin of the Ganges.

Indra took Laura by the hand and led her far out into the shallow river. Jumping from rock to rock and wading through small pools, they reached an area surrounded by bullrushes and papayrus. There he showed her how to gargle, to blow water out through her nose yogi fashion and how to bathe under a cloth.

"It is extremely important that one never be seen while bathing," he said. "Don't ask why."

[62]

Then he hurried away through the rushes to have his own bath. When he returned she was floating on her back, listening to the water bubble about her. He showed her how to put a cloth around herself and to dress inside it.

They returned in the failing light. Smoke from the evening fires hung in the still cool air like veils. At the hut the waiting crowd of devotees and curious villagers had doubled. Their faces glowed the color of burnished copper in the light of a large fire, which had been built in a pit outside the door. Laura ducked into the hut to dry her hair over the inside fire. She watched hidden as outside Indra, naked, dried his hair in front of them all. He squeezed out the four-foot long strands and snapped them—whiplike—until they dried. Then he twisted the separate jutas into one skein, curling that into a neat circle on the top of his head.

A young woman darted out of the crowd and timidly tucked a large scarlet hibiscus blossom into the crown of hair.

Indra sat down cross-legged facing the fire and the crowd, smoke undulating about him. Without turning he flung back his left arm, and snapped his thumb and forefinger as a sign for her to come out.

Laura covered her head with the red shawl and emerged from the door, seating herself behind him to the left. All around Indra were piled fruits, sweets, and other food offerings. A very dignified old man wearing a Gandhi cap sat to his immediate right, waving incense around.

Indra picked up a heavy iron fire tool called a chimtah, a three-foot long silver pincer resembling a sword. One large and three small iron rings were attached to the grasping end. When he brought it crashing down onto the burning logs the clang of metal on metal and flying sparks caused a ripple of ecstatic fervor through the crowd.

He withdrew a quantity of white ash with the chimtah and applied it to his entire body. After patting and dusting for almost five minutes, he again plunged the chimtah into the fire. This time he withdrew a small black coal which he ground into powder and applied with his thumb to his forehead, holding the residue over the fire in both fists and blowing it away muttering as he did. He applied the same mark to Laura and the old gentleman on his right. Then with a substance from a small round box he applied three red spots in a triangular pattern around the black.

A strange man who appeared to be in his late thirties kept looking at Laura, muttering what seemed like nonsense syllables at her over the silent crowd. His athletic body was partly covered with rags. Hundreds of buttons, bangles, and trinkets were sewn, tied, or pinned to them. He could have been a freak, a court jester, or the village idiot. His head bobbed up and down quickly, like a water bird, and his weird predatory eyes glittered. Even at a distance she could feel his attempt to unnerve her.

"A Moslem sorcerer," Indra said in an aside to her. "A veritable rascal, he needs punishment." He paused. "Would you like to see him dance like a woman?"

Sitting very erect, arms held stiff, he stared at the fire, muttering under his breath. Then, after some time, he slumped, relaxed his arms, and untied his hair. It was then Laura saw that he was becoming invisible. She could actually see through him, and what remained took the form of an old disheveled being—a sphinx. Many of the women covered their faces in fright.

The strange man toward whom he now focused sat perfectly still, although he made faces and obscene gestures and shouted in a mixture of Urdu, Hindi, and Bengali.

Laura heard Indra's voice out of the almost invisible form beside her.

"Within five minutes he will begin to dance. Watch."

The next moment the man began gesticulating wildly and yelling at the other yogis and sadhus, or disciples, who sat silently watching. Then rising slowly, he screamed and pointed to the place where the transformed Indra sat. When he had got up altogether he began to dance as if his legs, arms, head, and body were being manipulated like a marionette. As he danced he removed his clothes until he was naked, all the while humming nervously. Then he burst into a high-pitched song. "Like a prostitute from the brothels of Lahore or Dacca," Indra told Laura later. Someone in the crowd began to accompany the singing with weird sounds from a hand organ. The sorcerer whirled and wriggled in the flickering firelight. At last in a frenzy he fell and rolled in the dust, clutching his stomach with both hands as though he'd been shot. The dust stuck to his sweaty body and turned to mud as he jerked spasmodically like a dying animal. Resuming his ordinary shape, Indra stood up, and with his foot gently nudged the body until it loosened and sprawled full length on its belly.

Laura found she was holding her breath. The scene was strange beyond anything she had ever imagined. Less than a month before she had been sitting in the bay window of an English bedroom. Now she was in front of an open fire, under mango trees in India, with a strange being who seemed ageless and could change his form.

"I have just managed to—as you would say—exorcise this animal," Indra said softly to her. "Are you all right?" He smiled. "I have removed a demon from him and have frightened it away.

Really, the demon business is all wrong. The Christians are always looking for devils and demons because they believe only in what they call 'normal.' Christ got it all from India, but then they mixed it up with Aristotle, Augustine, and *sin*. All trash! What they call demons are just disembodied souls that manage to squeeze into a body at certain times. Sometimes these are better than the one already there. This one will be a different person when he wakes up, but not for long. He's a very bad case—quite mad from having two people inside him. Of course he will want to follow us now, but I am too lazy." For a moment Indra wavered. "And I will not allow it," he said finally, "he's just another fourth class sadhu. He would never be able to get the real thing so there is no point."

Many of the yogis who had been waiting to test him now prostrated themselves before Indra, touching his feet, leaving presents and offerings. One young Moslem fakir poured out a number of sparkling gems from a chamois bag.

"Now I have frightened them," he murmured, blessing each with a smudge of ash on the forehead. "Please observe. If I had used words to describe the problem of this man—that is, given a lecture on insanity or schizophrenia—they would've wanted to argue with me or wouldn't have understood. Instead, I have used some of my shakti, my spiritual energy. A yogi gets more of this shakti than others through his practices. They are scared stiff and have now come to pay their respects. Ridiculous, yes?" He patted the head of a very old woman who nuzzled his right foot, waiting for his blessing. "You can't cure insanity by words. What you have seen is the only way."

Indra put a smudge of ash on the woman's forehead and then fell silent. A stream of devotees, many of whom had walked long distances, now came forward respectfully, whispering a word or two as they prostrated themselves before him. Whole families approached. Children were pushed to the ground by nervous parents. On each Indra would place his hand, muttering softly but not looking. He remained aloof: serene and implacable.

After the people had gone there was a long silence, broken only by the crackling of the fire and the cries of night herons hunting in the river. Indra smiled and said something in Hindi to the old man in the Gandhi hat, who was preparing a chillum. With his chimtah Indra withdrew from the fire small glowing coals which he placed on top of the pipe. After inhaling deeply, he let the old man smoke while he played his stringed instrument and sang.

His voice floated gently over the strings which kept the rhythm, an otherworldly sound, running past stops, syncopating, crying out

[65]

at men and gods alike. The music affected Laura strangely: it wasn't just notes but a catalyst dredging up memories, opening doors, bouncing off her inner self. She felt like weeping.

A quarter moon hung in the sky over the mangoes and a warm wind had come up from the plain. The fire was low. The old man with the Gandhi hat loped off into the night.

"Are you all right, Laura Weatherall?" Indra said smiling. He looked as fresh as when the evening began.

She nodded.

"Then you'd better get some sleep. There will be horses here for us at three-thirty in the morning so we can escape this place before the sun rises and people follow us."

IV

§

MISTS WERE RISING. The night sounds of the jungle gave way to the chattering of monkeys, the whistling of mynah birds. Laura could just make out that they had come to a river wash strewn with twisted driftwood, thorn trees, and massive boulders. Beyond, the foothills of the Himalayas rose like a wall against the first light of morning. It was cold. The horses' breath steamed white in the darkness.

Indra dismounted. "I will make some bread and tea and then we will rest," he said, helping her down off the horse. "Come gather some wood with me, it will get your circulation going."

He lit the first small pile of twigs while Laura gathered more. Soon the pungent smell of spicy tea filled the air and he was kneading wheat flour in a round brass bowl.

Then he took the ball of dough and rolled it gently between his palms, pressing it and slapping it until it became a pie-shaped disk about nine inches in diameter.

"I'm a roti wallah, ha ha," he growled, grinning as he held out the disk of dough. "You have seen them, no? The men who sell these rotis on the streets?" Into the fire went the dough, which puffed up into a little balloon that he turned until it was golden brown. "Catch," he said, tossing the bread into her hands.

She caught the balloon but it was too hot to hold.

"Put it in your lap to cool," he directed, handing her a brass cup filled with tea. "Watch out, that's very hot too."

She waited while he prepared his bread and then after it was finished, tore some off and returned it to the flames as a sacrifice along with a few drops of tea.

They ate in silence. He wolfed his food like a hungry truck driver.

"Don't you ever have indigestion?" she asked.

"Too full of poisons," he said, chewing. "Best not to think too much about food. As I told you before, eat the plate if necessary."

"Could you eat that?" She pointed to the brass plate.

"If you ground it up with a file I would happily eat it," he replied laughing. "But it's copper underneath. I'd be out of my senses for a week or so and you'd have to take care of me."

§

He stretched out on his shawl. "Alone at last," he sighed, then rolled over on his stomach to look at her. "Laura Weatherall." He smiled. "It's not right. I must think of another name for you." He rested his head on his hands. "Don't let me sleep too long. We have twelve hours to go before we reach the tops of those hills. At the temple there we'll rest for a day or so before going on."

Soon he was fast asleep. Something about his smile and the way he had pronounced her name gave Laura the impression that she had at last taken on some sort of reality for him, had passed some sort of test. "What a strange being," she thought, observing him asleep. She knew that she was deeply attracted to him. He looked like a hero resting after battle, a young Ulysses. The thought that he was sixty only increased her feeling. He said that he was out of this world. But why then was he so sensual, so full of energy and vitality? She wished he would touch her, hold her. She would have made love to him in a moment, and wondered whether it was entirely out of the question. Yet she was also afraid he might know her feelings for him, for she feared his power, and the deep mystery that surrounded him. She spread out her blanket near him and lay down. Her sleep was fitful and filled with frustrating unfinished dreams.

§

She was awakened by a sharp blow on her leg, and opened her eyes to see an enormous monkey the size of a small man. He was standing only a few feet away, about to throw another rock at her. She tugged at Indra's hand. He woke up and was instantly on his feet, chimtah in hand and running after the animal, who seemed to be the leader of a large band that had surrounded them. "Ahoo, Ahoo," Indra yelled. "Ahoo, Ahoo." He chased them for a some distance, jumping from rock to rock, like one of them. After a while he returned, covered with sweat.

"Ah," he said, "it's getting warm. I slept too long. It's just as well that they woke us. Can you see that white spot there?" He pointed to the hills. "That's where we're going. Our first stop. We must reach it by sundown. It's a safe place, out of the jungle. Now let's bathe in the river, it's only about a hundred yards from here. The horses can bathe too, and we'll be on our way.

"From now on I'll call you Uma," he said, as he helped her pack up the utensils. "That's your new name. I saw it in my sleep. I can't stand that Laura business."

"Uma?" she asked. "What does it mean?"

"It's the name of a most high and fearful goddess." He laughed. "That will give you something to live up to."

§

After a week of walking and sleeping in small temples, they arrived at a sizeable town on a ridge overlooking the Himalayas. Beyond, the mountains loomed: icy, remote, unreal. It was bitter cold and the streets were crowded with dirty shivering coolies, some almost naked, huddled around open fires. In the bazaar old men sat smoking hookahs of opium and eating majoun, while they spun out raw wool or knitted it into sweaters.

A handsome young man dressed in Western-style tight pants and a cable-stitched sweater appeared suddenly. Smiling at Indra with deep affection, he took the reins of the horses and led them through a maze of alleys that stank of open sewers and the rancid mustard oil used in street shops for frying food. Finally they went through an archway into a compound where they dismounted at the foot of some steps. Half-naked servants scurried out shivering, and disappeared with their saddle bags.

"It's like the keep of a medieval castle," Laura thought as the young man beckoned them to follow him up the stone stairway.

"Where are we, and what's happening?" Laura whispered.

"Don't ask questions," he chided. "It spoils the drama."

"I will go now and tell my father you have come. He will be so happy to see you," said the young man in English, touching Indra's feet again.

"Will he indeed?" Indra muttered to himself.

A servant conducted them to a small room high in a third-story tower of the enormous fortress-like house. A charcoal fire burned in an elaborate brass box with ornate legs in the shape of lions. Carpets and tapestries hung on the stone walls to keep out the dampness. They sat down, warming their hands. Soon the wife of the household arrived and prostrated herself before Indra. Taking no notice of Laura she proceeded to wash Indra's bare feet with steaming water and afterward to anoint them with oil. Laura wondered whether she would drink the foot bath as the other woman had done, and when she didn't, Indra winked at Laura across the fire.

After this, the room began to fill up. First the old men of the family hobbled in one by one, grunting as they flopped onto the floor to prostrate before Indra. Then the younger men arrived, and last came a stream of women and girls who crowded into the back. Tea and a tray of sweets were brought in. One of the old men began to sing softly, facing Indra and gesturing dramatically.

"He's the elder brother of the head man of this house," Indra said to Laura. "He's spent his whole life running away to the jungles and mountains to sit with sadhus and yogis, but he never had the guts to stay, to give up the high life and the jam."

When the singing was over and after Indra passed the sweets to everyone, they were taken downstairs and through passageways into a large three-story room magnificently paneled with slabs of carved oak. Ladders went up to tiny sleeping rooms at the top. On one side, the paneling had been opened to reveal a large curtained section. They sat in front of it. Another ornate brazier filled with hot coals was brought in and placed before Indra.

After a short time a jaundiced hand appeared from inside the curtains and a gaunt man of about sixty struggled out, groaning. He fell on his knees where he remained for some time until Indra blessed him.

"After so long a time, now you have come to me," the sick man wailed. "I have been waiting a long time for you, Maharaji." He fixed his watery eyes on Indra. "Look at me! Nothing is left—even my eyes are losing sight. I am becoming a skeleton."

"This is Miss Weatherall—'Uma,' " said Indra.

But the man took no notice. "Why have you taken so long to come?" he continued, declaiming so the entire household might hear. "Why?" He thrust his bony hands toward Indra in supplication.

"Because you are an infidel," Indra roared. The man fell back as if Indra had hit him.

"A faithless hypocrite you are, piling up money, drinking on the sly. You have cancer of the liver—I warned you not to drink but you continue. You don't believe me," Indra said. He narrowed his eyes and showed a demonic toothy grin.

"But I watch you. I can watch you from anywhere, anytime I want—and I have seen all the mean things you do."

[70]

The man shielded his face with his arm.

"Boozing slyly, there in your bed, bossing all the poor women of your household, emasculating your sons with your sarcasm . . . They are all tired of you, you miser. Even your old mother over there in the corner has begun to despise you. Why should I do anything for you . . . devil! You are lucky to see me at all."

The man prostrated himself again and clutched at Indra's toes with trembling hands. "Please," he whispered hoarsely, "you must. You are a great saint—you must show kindness."

"Sometimes kindness means dispatching," Indra said, loosening the man's fingers. "You know dispatching, Mohan Singh? Now that you have reached the end you are frightened, eh? Get back into your bed, it is not good for you to get so excited. Your liver will get worse and I will be blamed."

Clutching at the side of the bed, the man lifted himself slowly and painfully through the curtains.

"It is easier for a camel to pass through the eye of a needle than for a rich man to enter into the Kingdom of Heaven," Indra said quietly. "I smell death in this house."

He stirred up the coals in the brass fire box while the youngest daughter placed a number of elaborate dishes of food before him.

"Don't eat too much," he cautioned Laura. "Don't ask why."

"I am fasting," he told the daughter in Hindi, "but this lady will have a little."

The girl looked disappointed but obediently took all the dishes away after Laura had taken as little as she could without seeming ungrateful.

The old mother, who had been watching from a corner, lurched across the room like a spider and knelt reverently before Indra. He kept her prostrate for some time before placing his hand on her head and bestowing the smudge of ash with his thumb.

"This animal is trying to outlive her son," he said to Laura under his breath. "They are all hypocrites. See all these photos?" He pointed to large framed portraits of chubby-looking men with shaved heads in orange robes and turbans. "They read all these false prophets and yet they call on me to come and heal them. All infidels, utterly lacking in faith. Let them sink, I say."

Laura was too tired to reply. She longed for sleep but she knew she was on exhibition and would probably have to sit as long as he sat with her knees flat on the floor and her back erect. She wondered whether a hot bath were a possibility.

Some time later the sick man's wife came in and after a few words with Indra in the local Pahari language, she motioned Laura to follow her.

"She'll show you to a room where you can bathe and rest until evening," Indra said. He smiled. "I will have to sit here. I'm not supposed to need any sleep, I'm considered immortal." He chuckled.

§

There was a knock on the door and a small boy appeared with a tray of tea and sweets. Her body ached all over. For a few moments she had no idea where she was. She had been with Jeff in a dream, they had become separated and she was vainly looking for him. Then she caught the musty smell of the room and the present rushed in on her. The boy leaned against the bed, staring at her as though she were an apparition from space.

"Vat iss your name?" he asked.

"Laura," she answered.

He held the teacup out to her. "Maharaji is waiting for you," he said in stilted English. "Drink!" He handed her the cup and ran out of the room.

By the time she had bathed, dressed, and rejoined Indra, the large room was full of people. The bed curtains were open and the sick man lay dazed, propped up by pillows, his head wrapped in a white silk scarf. Indra sat on the floor gazing into the fire. On his left were the women of the household and some curious friends, on his right the men filled up the remaining floor space. A large group of students, friends of the sons of Mohan Singh, had found places at the rear.

Indra motioned Laura to take her place beside him. A group of musicians hired for the occasion were tuning their instruments. The wife of the dying man lit incense sticks, waved them in front of Indra and stuck them in one side of the brazier. Then she lit bits of camphor on the end of a large brass salver, and waved the lights in front of him, clockwise, while her daughters rang bells. She passed the lights to her husband who struggled from his bed, muttering sacred syllables while he waved the lights spastically at Indra, almost burning him. After that followed sons, daughters, and grandparents until the entire family had worshipped him. "To them he is a living god," thought Laura.

One of the musicians began an invocation that was half song and half declamation, accompanying himself on a miniature hand organ called a shruti box. He was joined by a violin and then a harmonium and after a while the room was rocking with music and song. Women and girls clanked chimes together in fast time. Some

[72]

of the students began impiously to clap their hands. Indra held his
silver chimtah horizontally, bouncing it in his open palms to make
a metallic clanking that sounded like chain mail. Some of the
students shouted in rhythm with the music: "Jai Govinda, Jai Jai
Jai Ram. Hari Krishna, Jai Govinda." All the gods were invoked.

When the song-story was finished, Indra picked up his three-
stringed instrument and began to tune it. He tuned and tuned,
waiting for the people to stop fidgeting. They dared not leave, yet
they were rich and not accustomed to waiting for anything. Laura
had noted before how he used the tuning of his instrument as a
psychological weapon. When the impatience of the trapped
audience had reached its peak he began his song, a salute to Kali,
the goddess of destruction. The fidgeting stopped at once. Kali was
dangerous; her name was rarely mentioned in the houses of the rich
though she lurked everywhere beneath the surface of their lives: Ma
Kali, the destroyer-defender, the Goddess of death, of battlefields,
cemeteries, and burning places. Ma Kali with her bowl of blood
and her necklace of human heads.

No one sang with him. A hush fell over the room and servants
peeked from corners. The students in their modern pants and
expensive imported sweaters folded their hands and stared into
their laps. The middle-aged sons of the dying man looked nervously
here and there while the older folk stared intently at Indra as if
entranced, hearing a voice out of a long gone past. They knew the
song well, and the power of the dark voice that flowed from his lips
and from his eternally young body. He had turned a salute to
himself into a celebration of death.

Then the old mother of the dying man, overcome with
emotion, began to sing in a high, faltering voice, off key:

"Jai Kali, Jai Kali, Kalabve Nasane, Jai Kali."

The others looked at her disapprovingly but she went on and
was joined by her brother, the old man who had sat with many
sadhus and yogis.

Then Indra did something that jolted them all. With one hand
strumming his instrument and without stopping his song, he
reached out and tossed his chimtah to Mohan Singh.

Laura could feel a wave of energy go through the room.

The dying man caught the chimtah with his feeble yellow hands
and began bouncing it up and down in time with Indra's music. A
boy grabbed the tabla from one of the musicians and started
beating it wildly. The other boys all straightened up and began
swaying. The middle-aged sons left the room.

"Ah," thought Laura, "these are the dangerous ones. They want
to see their father dead and are afraid Indra will revive him." She

had a sudden feeling, here in this medieval house tucked in the foothills of the Himalayas, that everything she had been trained to think of as reliable and bright might be a giant mistake.

The excitement was mounting. Indra had closed his eyes and was projecting all his power into each phrase. She noticed that he had begun to make himself transparent again and wondered if they could see it.

Before them all the dying man appeared to have come alive: his weak body now sat erect, held up by some force awakening within him. He bounced and rattled Indra's chimtah in time with the music. Color seemed to be returning to his haggard yellow face.

One of the sons reappeared with servants bearing hot drinks and sweets. It was obvious he wanted to put a stop to a scene which to his mind was getting out of hand. But seeing Indra the servants squatted down with their trays, afraid to pass out the food in spite of the nervous prodding of their master's sons.

Suddenly Mohan Singh jumped out of bed and began to dance. To the horror of his family his white dhoti unwound and fell to the floor. He went on, his emaciated body clothed only in a pair of undershorts, bouncing on his skinny yellow legs, and flailing his hands and arms in poses of the Goddess Kali.

The old women began to groan and the old men to clap their hands. The dancer threw his glasses into the crowded room.

The old mother crept into her alcove off the main room and began to worship her private idols, waving a tiny oil lamp in front of them.

The students thought it a big joke: the great banker Mohan Singh, the bad tempered Scrooge, scrounge, and secret drinker, was freaking out in front of their faces.

They clapped together in unison, egging him on, shouting:
"Hoy, Hoy, Hoy, Hoy!"
It sounded to Laura like a Cossack drinking bout.

Indra sat seemingly withdrawn except for the tips of his fingers and his lips as he guided the pace of the music, coming in just before the end of each round, and speeding up the rhythm imperceptibly so the momentum increased.

Neighbors began to wander in, having heard the sounds they knew meant something more than the usual evening of music at Mohan Singh's.

His sons stood in the corners near the doorways, their arms folded on their chests and their dark moustached faces flushed with embarrassment at seeing their father in such a state. They welcomed the new arrivals loudly, trying to disrupt the scene. But it was useless. Indra was too powerful for them. The room was spellbound, Mohan Singh was bewitched. Sons and neighbors squatted finally with the servants, their eyes fixed on Indra, waiting.

The music reached a frenzied peak. Mohan Singh stood immobilized in front of Indra, shuddering, his tongue locked outside his open mouth. Everyone knew that the malignant spirit which had inhabited his body was ready to come out. Indra had enchanted the beast that lurked within. Now he would kill it.

Just then the old man collapsed in front of Indra. He seemed to shrink up like a deflated balloon and then lay motionless on the floor.

There was an audible gasp.

At the same moment Indra was crouched on his haunches, beating the body of Mohan Singh with his chimtah.

One of the sons lunged toward Indra but his uncle who had sat with sadhus caught his pants leg and brought him crashing into the laps of two astonished young women.

The wife of the sick man counted furiously on her rosary of rudraksha beads, her eyes fixed on Indra and on the body of her husband.

Then the body moved. The hands went out, reached for Indra's feet, held them.

For a long time the room was silent; no one moved, only the smoke from the fire box curled into the air above the crowd. Then the servants left, carrying their trays to the kitchen. The students backed out through the doors. Everyone else vanished into the recesses of the house. Only the brother of Mohan Singh and his old mother remained. Both prostrated to Indra, received his blessing, exchanged whispered conversation with him, and disappeared.

Alone now except for Laura, Indra remained crouched over Mohan Singh, gazing into space. After a long while, he lifted the man into bed and shut the curtains.

"Are you all right, Uma?"

She stretched her cramped legs and was about to speak when he put his finger to his mouth.

"We must go at once," he whispered. "Tomorrow that animal will find he has been healed. I will have his disease. I must be at a certain place by that time. If I am here I'll be trapped for weeks by all sorts of sick people wanting to be cured. If I can be alone where I won't be bothered, I can heal myself in three days." He helped her up. "Go to your room and collect your belongings. I will arrange for the horses to be brought round and to have two boys accompany us part of the way. We must make haste. I will meet you at the rear of the house in a few minutes. Lose no time!"

[75]

V

§

IT WAS PITCH DARK in the deserted streets as the horses, bridle bells tinkling, made their way through the ancient maze of the town toward its eastern gate. Two boys holding burning tapers ran beside them. At the old gate Indra dismissed them after tossing a few coins into their open hands.

As the cobblestones gave way to sand and clay and the road broadened, Indra urged his horse into a canter, then into a full gallop. He was a superb horseman. Sitting erect with his hair piled high on his head, naked except for a loin cloth and billowing cape, he sped through the night with Laura riding hard at his heels. Again a feeling of dreamlike unreality possessed her. She felt involved in an otherworldly drama in which the gods were embodied in the particular events. Was she still a witness or had she become one of the players? She wondered.

They were riding up a steep walled canyon. In the east the sky had lightened. Reaching the summit they turned a corner and there were the peaks of the Himalayas glowing pink in the darkness like gigantic lamps, reflecting the first rays of the sun. The sight was so awesome that Laura reined in her horse without thinking and almost fell off.

Indra slowed to a walk and turned around.

"Are you all right?" he called. "There's a tea shop just ahead, we'll stop there and rest."

Unbelievably as they rounded the bend there was a small stone building which seemed to be growing out of the cliff. A young man in ragged clothes ran out, greeted Indra, and helped them to dismount.

Laura was shocked when she saw Indra in the light. He had aged perceptibly during the night and looked like an old woman. He could see that she was disturbed and wrapped a shawl about his face, which only added to the transformation.

"This is the ancient road to Mount Kailas, the holiest pilgrimage place in all of Asia." he said. "These tea shops are spaced along it for hundreds of miles. Once the road was thronged with travelers—but now that is all finished. Our destination is only about five miles from here. I will take a bath down there in that stream and perform my morning prayers. Then we will go on. You can take a bath if you like, but the water is very cold."

He disappeared toward the sound of rushing water. Laura stumbled down a rocky hill toward a water course in the opposite direction. There seemed to be water everywhere, bubbling out of the mountain. She could feel the cold as she approached and wondered if she could bear it, but without letting herself stop to think she took off all her clothes and jumped in. The water was so cold it took her breath away. She climbed out feeling burned rather than chilled. Shaking, she wrapped herself in a cloth, gathered up her clothes, and stumbled blindly up the path to the tea shop.

The proprietor, modestly excusing himself, bade her dress in front of his kitchen fire. Tea was bubbling in a brass pot. Laura removed the cloth and squatted naked before the fire until she stopped shaking. All the aches and pains from the long night's ride had vanished with the shock of the cold water. Feeling revitalized, she dressed and went out.

The great mountains were shimmering now with blinding white light. She sat on a stone wall that edged the terrace in front of the shop, watching clouds form at the bases of the peaks, and patches of sun begin to light the forest below the snow line.

Indra came up the hill covered with his shawl and went directly to the kitchen. After some time he came out, bringing tea and freshly made bread. He looked refreshed, but she could see that the whites of his eyes had yellowed.

"Yes," he said. "Old man Singh's disease is on me. But don't worry," he shrugged. "I only require three days alone and it will be gone."

An old man and two boys were sitting nearby slurping their tea stoically, their pinched faces framed by ragged woolen scarves wound tightly against the morning cold.

"Maybe they'd feel better if they took a bath," Laura commented.

"Don't judge," said Indra sternly. "You never could survive what they've survived, the solitude and poverty, the bad food—always getting the last and worst of everything shipped up from the plains." With a shrug he got up and paid the proprietor.

Mounted again they left the main road to follow the stream. They rode all morning. A path wound precipitously down the

[77]

mountain. Barren hills gave way to thickets of scrub oak, then forests of towering pines and deodars, and ancient rhododendron trees with scarlet blossoms.

The stream, meeting others, had become a river. Delicate green fern and white orchids thrived on its misty banks. "This is the way everything was forty years ago," he whispered. "From the first hills to here it was paradise—before the human greed got let loose."

Far down in a lower valley rose the gray stone towers of a temple complex. Gigantic fir trees hovered over it, their ancient gnarled branches like protective arms above the walled compound. A small village perched on a knoll opposite the temple. The houses and roofs were of unmortared fitted stone. There were stone steps and terraces with covered balconies of intricately carved wood.

No life seemed to stir as they entered.

"Is the place enchanted?" asked Laura. "Where have all the people gone?"

"To the cities to make money. This is a most secret place of pilgrimage. The stones of these temples were dismantled hundreds of miles away across the plains and brought into the hills by oxcart over a thousand years ago."

"But why?"

"To escape the Moslems. Long before the Moguls, the Moslems invaded India. They were fanatics."

Indra reined in his horse, looking from window to shuttered window. "This place is run by a gang of Brahmins now," he said quietly. "Keep close and do as I say. Long ago they were extremely rich, but then the treasures of the temple—rare diamonds and so on—got stolen. Many of the people left, and the real treasures of the place—its great secrets—were forgotten and are unknown to most of the degenerate animals who now run it. You will see them soon. Their principal wealth now is hashish. The finest in the world is grown and made here and given to the temple by the devotees. But the priests are thieves who sell the hashish to smugglers and then report to the police. The police pick up the smugglers, extract a handsome price for their release, and return the hashish to the priests to be resold to new victims. They also smuggle gems from China and Nepal.

"Nevertheless the place has thousands of years of holy vibrations. The temple you see now goes back only a thousand years. Before that there was one of copper and wood, sheltering only a single stone worshipped since the beginning of time. It's now in one of the temples buried under a statue of the goddess. I'll show you.

"What the place needs is a good epidemic to clear away all the human trash. Anyhow we'll do what we've come for, and they

[78]

won't disturb us. They're afraid of me. I killed one of them once."

"You *what?*"

"It was an accident," he said grinning.

Laura had the strange sensation that she was being drawn toward the center of something. They dismounted and walked through the empty streets. No one was in sight, even the shops and tea stalls were shut. Then as they neared the temple they heard music and singing.

"Kali puja," Indra said, "a three day celebration."

They stopped at a small door built into the high granite wall of the temple. "This is the only way in," he said. "Come, I see the proprietor of the tea shop across the way is on duty. He'll tend to our horses."

The man bowed deeply to Indra and they exchanged a few words before entering through the small door.

Inside under the ancient firs a solemn dance was in progress. Concentric circles of devotees and villagers were dancing around the principal shrine, moving clockwise and counter clockwise, alternately. There were seven circles in all: children in the first, old ladies in the second, and old men in the third. In the fourth and fifth were married householders, in the sixth priests and their families, and in the seventh sadhus.

Large torches burned at the four corners of the temple and at the entrance a gold statue of the many-limbed goddess glittered in the flickering light.

"Look," Indra said. "Do you see something green on the statue?"

Laura noticed a flashing object about the size of a turkey egg. "Yes, what is it?"

"It is a four hundred eighty carat emerald, mate to the Kohinoor diamond."

"But I thought they were broke?"

"Confiscated by the government. It was all they had left and they would have sold it if they could."

The stone flashed like a traffic signal. The dancers circled, singing in rounds to the slow, methodical beat of a drum. The priests were everywhere, young and nearly naked, wearing only scarlet loincloths, scarlet cloths over their shoulders, and peaked hats of scarlet silk.

"They do look like a gang of pirates," Laura commented.

"Come, we'll find our spot," said Indra, moving on.

Some distance away, through a maze of other temples and shrines, they came to a place where alcoves had been constructed as resting places for pilgrims and mendicants. They found a large-sized one with a fire pit cut into the stone floor, worn smooth with use. The arches facing the courtyard provided a degree of privacy. In minutes Indra had a blazing fire going in the pit and the man from the tea shop arrived with their bags.

"It's the last night but the dance is only beginning. It will go on until sundown. Then they'll take the goddess inside and do sacrifice and worship her," he said. "Come, let's go down to the river now and bathe." He led her to a place where two rushing rivers came together to form natural pools among the rocks. The late afternoon sun had dropped behind the hills and under the ancient trees it was dark and cold.

Laura dipped her hand into the water. It was icy but warmer than her morning bath. Indra disappeared downstream. She replaced her clothes with a cloth and jumped in.

Although she was an expert swimmer, she wasn't prepared for the force of the current and had to struggle immediately to prevent herself from being sucked under. She clutched desperately at the rocks, thinking she might drown and cursing Indra for not warning her about the whirlpool. It seemed almost by accident that she was able to drag herself out at all. To her surprise she noticed that she wasn't cold but no sooner had she thought about it than she was overcome by a fit of shaking and hurried to put on her clothes.

Scrambling up the path she collided with Indra. "Did you enjoy your bath?" He smiled. "Are you all right, Uma? Come, the fire waits for us."

The drum beats had quickened. Inside the inner circle of dancers the goddess was being carried clockwise on a palanquin by four priests with shaven heads. Naked sadhus and mendicants rolled over and over on the stones in front of the procession.

"The dance will end soon," Indra said as they warmed themselves in front of their fire. "Then I would like you to go into the temple with me. I want to show you something."

He appeared pale and transparent, almost golden in the flickering light, and he gazed at her a long time with narrowed eyes, as though looking through her for someone else. Then he spoke again. "The statue is now in a small structure at the center of the temple. The holy stone is under the statue. Each day it is uncovered, anointed with water, oil and flowers, and worshipped."

He was whispering to her now even though they were alone.

"At my signal you will begin to say the following words over and over, either to yourself or aloud. You will say: 'Oh Mother, forgive me. At the heels of your precious feet I come. Oh Mother, forgive me.' And you are to meditate on just what you want to be forgiven."

He looked at her, opening his eyes wide. "Got it?" he said in flat imitation American.

She nodded.

"Do you agree to try?" A faint smile curled his mouth.

A flicker of hesitation passed across Laura's consciousness and she knew that he had seen it. "Oh Mother, forgive me"—it sounded so absurd. Could she really trust this strange being, this ancient youth? She felt profoundly alone for the first time in her life, wondering what the result of this "initiation" would be and at the same time repelled by her own deep skepticism.

"Yes, I'll do as you ask," she answered, seriously. "But will you stand by and not abandon me?" She stared into his eyes, hoping to make some sort of compact with him.

"I am a madman, Uma," he said, staring back. "Some day you will know everything—how and why I left this world, how I come and go. You will come to know of my other lives, as I have learned to know about them." He looked away from her, poked at the fire to ease the tension between them.

"If at this moment I asked you to come with me, to leave this world forever—would you do it? It *is* possible."

She got his point.

"See, hah—you turn pale. You lack faith. You want me to stand by you but will you follow me?" He poked at the fire again. "But you will," he said confidently. "You will. That's why we're here together. Come, we'll go inside now. It's time."

Mammoth twin statues of naked gods, their penises erect, guarded the passageway to the inner sanctum. They were carved from huge blocks of jet black stone smoothed and polished from centuries of touching. Flowers were tucked here and there in the crevices under the arms and at the genitals. Inside the sanctum it was warm and damp. Torches and lamps glowed. Priests who looked like long-haired toughs performed rituals for groups of bare-chested devotees who crowded the small covered courtyard.

A number of people were walking around the stone structure at the center, where inside shut doors the goddess and the stone were being prepared for worship. An atavistic energy seemed to resonate from the structure its lf.

A way cleared for them at once as Indra walked in, tall and gaunt, holding his chimtah like a riding crop so that its rings rattled loudly.

"Like a prisoner in chains," Laura thought. "Am I that prisoner?"

As they walked around she began to have the sensation that a rope was tied to her navel, an invisible umbilical cord fastened on a

[81]

winch inside the sanctum sanctorum. It was so strong that she could let herself lean back and be pulled along.

Many of the devotees gaped at the sight of Indra walking with a Western woman. On the third time around, they were directly behind the statue when she heard his voice.

"Now," he said turning to her abruptly. "Here. Prostrate yourself full length on these stones, let your hands touch the stones at the base of the shrine and repeat what I told you."

He placed a firm hand on her back and pushed her to the floor.

Then she heard herself saying: "Oh Mother, forgive me. At the heels of your precious feet I come. Oh Mother, forgive me . . ."

At first it was as if some other Laura were repeating the words. She became aware of a warm dampness oozing from the stones through her shawl. She heard the shuffling footsteps of devotees as they passed by or stopped to watch her. Then she remembered that she was to meditate. She began to enumerate the things she hated in herself: pride, faithlessness, skepticism, the sensuality that haunted her. Everything else faded. She was alone in the warm dampness. "Oh Mother, forgive me. At the heels of your precious feet I come. Oh Mother . . ."

Suddenly, as though a curtain had opened in the darkness behind her closed eyes, she saw a young and beautiful woman. The woman, about her own age, was lying in some grass smiling at her.

"Mother," she gasped, realizing it was her own mother. "Crazy mother before she was crazy." The picture was so real she felt filled with joy.

She began to repeat the words directly to the vision before her inner eye, telling the image of her young mother about her hangups, and asking for forgiveness. Each time she repeated the plea she felt a ripple from the base of her spine up through her entire body. Then she would relax and let the ripple turn into a wave, then begin again to repeat the words. A sound like a chorus of bell-like voices began inside her. She had the sensation that she was lying on a giant tuning fork resonating at a low vibration and awakening some ancient connection with the stones.

Nevertheless one part of her resisted, kept repeating in a masculine voice: "You are Laura Weatherall of 610 Park Avenue, New York City." This had been with her in whatever circumstances, even with drugs it had always been there. "You are Laura Weatherall of 610 Park Avenue," like a tape loop.

The voice was becoming stronger, even though she was asking that it be taken from her: "You lunatic, Laura Weatherall, prostrating my body on this filthy floor to a statue . . . to a stone . . . you are Laura Weatherall of New York City, you don't do things like this, nasty things like—"

[82]

Yet the image of her smiling young mother was still there and the waves were getting stronger. If Laura Weatherall was not in control who was? Were things out of control? Over and over she repeated "Oh Mother, forgive me . . ." and after each repetition, somewhere near her rectum the rippling spread out. Her body was a pond, a very still pond into which someone was throwing stones.

Then there was a hand, Indra's hand. She got up, dazed. He led her around the sanctum to an intricately carved spout that jutted out from the stones.

The ripples inside her had become waves.

A small pool carved in the shape of a lotus held the liquid from the spout. It looked like slop water. Indra filled his cupped hands. Lifting them he let the whitish water spill down over her hair and forehead. Then quickly another handful was thrown in her face, and a third.

"Now, drink it!" he ordered, holding a cupped hand to her lips. "The milk ocean of eternity," he said softly. "Drink!"

Something inside her screamed. The body she imagined she inhabited was becoming a sea, a sea rocked by mountainous waves.

She felt his hand then leading her before the golden statue. The space was packed with devotees, pilgrims, and priests. Hundreds of lamps waved crimson and gold, flashing gem stones, the matchless emerald flashing Go. Suddenly bells of every pitch and timbre began ringing together.

"Now again," whispered Indra, pushing her to the floor.

Something inside her frayed and snapped as she fell down. From an infinitely distant point she felt Laura Weatherall and all her burdens leaving—through her eyes, through her mouth and ears. Sucked out by a powerful force inside the sanctum that was absorbing Laura Weatherall into itself.

The great waves were all around now but some newly awakened part of her remained centered, an irreducible nucleus. Everything went blue, streams of golden light radiated out.

Then the air filled with the sound of a woman's voice she had never before heard. It was very cultivated, very old, and very hard, and spoke broken English with an Asian lilt.

"What do you want? What do you want?" the voice repeated. "Ask and it shall be granted . . . What is it you want?"

"I am tired of Laura Weatherall, can you take her back?" she answered. She could see nothing but waves going out into infinity, blue and gold in every direction.

"Is that what you ask, eh?" The voice echoed over the waves.

"Yes."

"If I take her, the price is very high." The voice hesitated. "If I take her then I take everything. Do you understand . . . the price is very high, eh?"

There was a long pause.

"Why don't you ask for something else? Ask for something else," the voice said.

"I feel you are already taking her. Please can't you finish the job?"

"If I take that burden, then finally I will have to take everything. Do you understand?"

Suddenly the last of Laura's resistance seemed finished. She felt open, she was emptying. It was physical, like an orgasm, yet not of her physical body. It seemed to go on and on and on.

After a long time she opened her eyes. All the people had gone, only the priests remained and were staring at her. As she got to her feet something about that look enraged her, brought her down. It was like coming down from acid.

Indra leaned over to help her. Something possessed her and she struck him across the face with the back of her hand. He struck back instantly with a force that propelled her out of the sanctum. She found herself in the temple courtyard running. She wanted to escape. It was dark and cold. Fear swept through her body.

Then one of the priests was running after her, a crimson figure, torch in hand. She kept running but she wasn't fast enough, and turned to see a long thin willow stick just before it landed on her back. He caught her with the tip of it repeatedly as they ran. Rounding a corner she stopped short; three more priests were waiting for her, all with willow sticks.

"It's too unreal, none of this is really happening." But she had no time to think further. She was in a trap.

Rushing at the three priests ahead of her she grabbed for the sticks, caught one and broke it and then pushed past them into the darkness of the courtyard. She remembered where the gate was and ran toward it but it was locked shut. She could hear them shouting to each other like bloodhounds. She slipped between two small shrines hoping to hide but they were too clever. They came toward her now, all four of them on the run, and surrounding her, beat her sharply with the willow sticks.

Inside her the waves began again.

Somehow she wrenched loose and blinded by tears, ran around a corner of the main temple, stumbled, and fell headlong into a deep pool of water. Again the waves inside her exploded, again she felt everything going out of her, and the voice came: "Stop. I will fulfill your request," it said. "I will take Laura Weatherall from you. Do not bother to think about it anymore."

Then Indra's hand appeared near her in the water. She took

hold of it and he lifted her out onto the stone. Then he carried her to their fire where she lay sobbing. Laura Weatherall was gone.

Indra bent over her in front of the fire, his hair loosened. "Please repeat after me," he whispered, his lips almost touching her cheek. He uttered a set of syllables over and over. She repeated them after him until they were firmly in her mind.

Then without speaking he turned her over to examine the places where the priests had beaten her and applied some yellow liquid from a bottle. After that he covered her with his shawl and she at once fell into a deep sleep.

When she awoke the following morning she saw him lying stiffly in a blanket opposite her. The fire had almost gone out. His face looked thin and bright yellow. She examined her body and discovered that the cuts and bruises from the night before had vanished.

"Are you all right?" he said, opening one eye like a parrot.

"Yes," she answered. "But *you* are not."

His eye blinked at her from under the blanket. "That is something I can handle." He smiled. "I will go just outside the wall near the river. There is a small hut there, across the river on a hill, where I will finish off this jaundice.

"That's what comes of healing these animals," he said after a pause. "I should stop it. Do you feel I abandoned you?"

"No, of course I don't."

"Do you feel I might abandon you?"

"No, I think I understand more now."

"Then that is good, we can proceed. You have surrendered to something very deep, very big. It is a first step. We'll remain here a week. I'll give orders for you not to be disturbed. There's a cell next to this one with a door. You'll move in there and someone will bring you lemon water twice a day. I'll see you at the bathing place at four in the morning and four in the evening."

"And then?"

"The remainder of the time close your eyes and repeat the syllables I have given you."

"All day long?"

"About fourteen hours each day if you can do it. You get the benefit—not I. It's up to you."

He got to his feet. "Come," he said, "we can't begin another day without battling the whirlpools, can we? Come on!"

VI

§

A. K. SUNDARAM TAPPED delicately at a soft-boiled egg.

"You must have some breakfast, my dear fellow. You look tired. Here, at least try some of these South Indian rice cakes, they're called idlis."

"Seeing you all dressed up and headed for the office so early in the morning makes me sleepy," Jeff said, stifling a yawn.

It was over a month since Laura left. He tried to spend as much time in bed as possible. He disliked Delhi. He disliked India altogether. The later he got up, the less chance there was of his having to carry on a conversation with this enigmatic man in whose house he was a guest. Sundar's round passive body was expertly covered by Saville Row suits, his handsome face a mask. Everything about him was passive and suppressed. Jeff thought of him as a neurotic turtle.

"I know it must be a shock to you, old man. But we do get up and go to offices—even in India. At least some of us do. We have a most alarming amount of paperwork to do. So many people, you know."

"You should let me teach you some American slang, Sundar," Jeff said. "You're so hip but you talk so square."

Sundar tittered. "It goes along with the early morning hours, I guess. But you don't realize, dear fellow, what a perfect disguise it is for me. And we must disguise ourselves here. We have so many castes, scheduled castes and tribals, not to mention religions. None of them get along. In order for me to be effective, I must sound neutral. The British were quite neutral so my way of speaking always suggests that."

He marveled at the American opposite him, so relaxed, so urbane, so sloppy!

"In America you all feel so free—you let it, as you say, 'all hang out.' This is impossible for us. We are governed by the idea of karma which predetermines our lives. And there are threats everywhere—no privacy, someone is always looking. Freedom is impossible unless you are very rich and also in the government. Even then," he glanced around quickly, "at any time one's most trusted servant may become a spy if he's offered enough money."

Sundar munched his toast. Did this foreigner take him for a fool? He—a South Indian Brahmin? Had he not known only three days after the party at Dorje's exactly what Jeff and Laura were up to? Although at first he had suspected Dorje. But Dorje's safety, and that of his entire family—as well as the gold they had been allowed to bring in from Lhasa—was subject to pressure that he, A. K. Sundaram, had easily been able to exert in the right places. This Jeff had no idea how easily information was obtained in India. Yet what was happening in the West remained a mystery to him. He wondered about his old friend Stan.

"But you haven't really seen anything yet, have you?" he said to Jeff, wiping egg from his moustache. "I fear you have only met film folk and embassy couples—most boring."

His lips were set in a superior smile that irritated Jeff.

"You want me to visit the Taj Mahal, I suppose?"

"No, no, that's not necessary." Sundar giggled.

Jeff laughed too.

"There is a place I would like to take you, though. A woman I think you might be interested in meeting."

Jeff shrugged.

"You don't like it here, I can see," said Sundar. "But you will. You will come with me and I will show you. You'll see how sensual we can be. We're so oppressed by our idea of 'duty' that when we let go it is something terrible! Don't forget, we worship pleasure. You vant to buy—hey, comm'on, buy, eat, vat you vant? I geef you." He stared at Jeff. "You will come then tomorrow?"

Jeff nodded. "Who's the woman?"

"That is a surprise for you. She's an old friend of mine. And do you think you could bring some of your lysergic acid diethyl-amide?"

That caught Jeff off-guard. "Sure, of course. How many?" he replied coolly.

"Oh, say a hundred. Yes, a hundred will do very well for a start," Sundar answered, feeling triumphant.

"Only a hundred?" Jeff smiled. "Are you sure that will be enough?"

Sundar fiddled with his napkin. Jeff had called his bluff. "For the moment," he murmured.

Jeff would have liked to know how Sundar found out he had the acid, and how much else he knew.

Sundar was waiting for him to ask.

[87]

"What time?" Jeff said matter-of-factly.

"What?"

"What time is this . . . meeting?"

"Ah, yes, tomorrow evening," said Sundar, thinking that Jeff was very slippery indeed. "Tomorrow evening about eight—will that be suitable? We can have a drink here and then go."

"Anything you say, Boss." Jeff slouched in his chair. "I'll look forward to it."

The next evening he found himself on the third-floor terrace of a severely modern house which would have been impressive in any country but in India was outrageous. So this was A. K. Sundaram's vanishing point!

He noticed that it was isolated in a very large compound of its own and that there seemed to be no servants. The polished marble floors of the roof garden gave way to teak inside, with thick white carpets covered with tiger and leopard skins. On the walls hung Bokhara rugs, Persian miniatures, and other expensive bric-a-brac.

"All the jazz of a Hollywood pad," Jeff thought, slumping into a pile of cushions on a low sofa. "Soft, so very soft." For the tough folks that used them he supposed.

Two tall young men with long hair appeared arm in arm with Sundar. "Jeff, I'd like you to meet Abhrim and Ismail."

Jeff nodded. Cruelty lurked around their artificially darkened eyes and their movements were the grown-up gestures of pampered children, self-indulgent and sensual. On the long fingers of their bony hands they wore numerous rings.

"Abhrim's grandfather was from Hyderabad," said Sundar. "He kept a diamond the size of a golf ball in his desk drawer wrapped in an old newspaper. And Ismail's great-uncle had his own railway train given to him by Queen Victoria. And a fourteen inch . . . uh, as you say, cock—famous throughout India. He was awarded the title Son of the Empire by Victoria."

"Did she ride on it?"

"Who?"

"Queen Victoria."

"On what?"

"On the train."

"But Queen Victoria never came to India, my dear fellow," said Sundar, pretending not to get the joke. "You don't know much about our history."

Ismail took a pipe from a leather bag and held it out to Jeff. "You like some smoke?"

He lit it as Jeff puffed. "Very interesting mixture."

"You know it then?" Abhrim sounded surprised.

"No," Jeff said, coughing, "but I know it has jimson in it."

"What?"

"Jimson weed. Large white flower."

"Jimson we don't know," Ismail said. "It contains datura ... a special variety."

"That's jimson."

"Yes, and other ingredients."

It was obvious to Jeff that drugs were nothing new here, they were all connoisseurs. He wondered if they had tried acid and whether Sundar would give some out.

Two young girls wandered onto the terrace and came toward them. Their thighs and curving buttocks were balanced by wasp waists and high protruding breasts. They wore filmy saris glittering with sequined beadwork and tinkling ankle bracelets. Jeff realized this was something he'd never tasted. His flesh told him he would enjoy himself even more than usual and that after he'd had one, he could have them all.

Sundaram introduced them. Jeff stood up. One of the girls sat down with Ismail while Jeff and the one called Ija remained standing.

"You have just come to India?" she said in a voice too mellow for her age.

"Yes."

"You must find it difficult, adjusting?" Her large eyes assessed him.

"Not too difficult."

"But the pace is so much slower than in America, don't you find that ..."

It was the same conversation he'd had everywhere in Delhi. He let his eyes travel between her lips and breasts.

"Let's sit down." He guided her to a place on the thick rug and heaped pillows behind her back.

"Are you in films?"

"Oh no, we don't go in for films," she laughed. "My sister and I come from a family of courtesans—all dedicated to the god."

"You mean part of the worship?" Jeff's mouth dropped open.

She nodded. "Don't think about it too much; it is hard for you to understand, I know."

"Why?"

"Here, sometimes, religion and sex are combined. But tell me ..." She reached up and brushed a strand of hair from his forehead. "Why are you Western men all wearing your hair so long?"

"Don't think about it too much ... you know the story of Samson?"

[89]

She nodded. "Should I cut your hair tonight and make you my slave?"

Jeff's green eyes glittered. "You wouldn't want me to lose my strength, would you?" He focused again on her full lips.

Abhrim came over to them and tugging at Ija's arm, spoke sharply to her in Urdu.

She loosened his grip on her arm casually while continuing to talk to Jeff. "Abrhim is too old-fashioned," she said lightly. "His grandfather had over one hundred wives, so you can see it is somewhat hard for him to adjust to the . . . new equality."

"In those days if we wanted something, we took it," Abrhim declared.

"Now you must ask," Ija said sighing, "and I must show you the manners of our new society."

"I don't want them," Abhrim retorted.

"You are too much a man." She cast a furtive glance at Jeff. "You should have been born less handsome, Abhrim—your good looks are going to ruin you."

He melted under her words, forgot about wanting to interrupt the conversation, and began lighting up a pipe.

"Opium, you join us?" Ija asked Jeff, motioning to Abhrim to sit beside them.

"Not just now." Jeff excused himself and wandered off to join Sundaram. He had caught sight of a new arrival, an American girl followed by two men wearing turbans. She was frail but very sensual, with a freaky look that interested him. "You've been in India for a while?" he asked after they were introduced.

"Five years," she said flatly.

"That's a long time."

"Depends on how you look at it. Long for a Texas girl like me, but India's got plenty of time." She rolled her eyes.

"Do you like it?"

"Like it?" she echoed, as if that were beyond anything she had ever thought of. "It's not liking, it's love/hate, you know . . ." She looked at him hard, then her expression changed. "No, you don't know at all. I *have* tried to leave. Once I got as far as Geneva. I checked into a hotel and said to myself, 'you're going to stay here and do something constructive.' The next day I went outside and saw the faces of all the Swiss, the Americans, the French, and English, the fat ugly bodies all doing constructive things—even the men I once thought handsome weren't handsome anymore. It was all dead there. I went to the airport and caught the first plane back. But say, where's your wife? I saw you both at the party Charles Hooker gave."

"She's not my wife," Jeff replied. "She's with a yogi somewhere."

She sighed. "I had enough of all that preaching stuff in Texas. My father was one, he used to sell Bibles, a strict religious man, you know? I couldn't even wear makeup—I mean in 1965! Now you tell me what that has to do with anything?" She laughed. "I rocked Bombay for a few years but it's getting to be a drag now—everybody's getting so uptight."

"How'd you 'rock' it?"

"Well, I came here to study yoga—and well, there's all sorts of yoga, you know?"

"And those are your . . . gooroos?" Jeff indicated the two men.

She giggled. "Them? Oh no, they're my dates sort of, they're smugglers."

"Your dates!"

"Ha, funny isn't it? But smugglers are like Texas ranchers, I understand them. And they give me diamonds, bags full of them." Her eyes sparkled. "They're old friends from Bombay. I brought them here to meet Kamala. You've met her?"

"Not yet. She's the . . . she runs this place?"

"Yes, she helped me get started. Just as I ran out of bread I happened to meet her and I studied with her. Not sex—everyone knows that—but all the other things, especially how to get the loot." Her eyes were mocking him.

"Takes guts," he said, shaking his head.

"Not guts, just an empty stomach, and then you have to learn to be somewhat detached."

"I'll bet."

"Sometimes these guys are very freaky—hot climate you know. They're ready to pop all the time." She looked around the room. "See how they keep twitching their toes or their knees." She paused, looked at Jeff. "You're ready too?"

"Always," he murmured.

Sundar came over to them. "Did you get some of the punch?" he asked.

"What?" said the girl curiously.

"Sundaram, she hasn't had punch," said Jeff. "Come, Miss Texas—my friend Sundaram will get you some. He's promised me a most unusual evening."

She rested her hand lightly on his arm. "Be careful," she said, "India's a rough country. They're not simple here like us. They know things we've never even dreamed of. You'll see—fifty-seven varieties and more."

They went to a room off the terrace that was dimly lit; long, low divans with cushions hugged the floor around three sides of it. On one wall was painted a Mogul palace with the walls cut away. In each painted room princes and concubines were depicted in erotic scenes and postures from the Kama Sutra.

There were half a dozen couples sitting around: young men with girls provided by Kamala, one more beautiful than the next. In a corner a small orchestra was playing.

The sensuous melody of a large flute filled the room. Hashish joints were passed. Sundar dimmed the lights so that the candles in the bronze wall brackets seemed to burn more brightly.

"Is the punch strong enough?" Jeff asked him.

"Quite," Sundar answered. "These are supposed to be some of the more advanced people in Delhi. I'm interested to see just how, as you say, 'cool' they'll be."

Jeff noticed one or two of the males doing double takes as their perception of the girls they were with began to change. Suddenly he realized that Sundar was a voyeur. Like Stan, he preferred to look on rather than get involved.

Just then a tall woman arrived and seeing Sundar came toward him.

"Ah," said Sundar to Jeff, "here is your guru." He stood up to greet her but his diplomatic mask crumbled. "Kamala, this is my friend Jeff," was all he got out before collapsing.

She was not a girl. Her dark kohl-rimmed eyes were veiled as though meditating. Her jet black hair was piled high and entwined with garlands of jasmine, revealing velvet soft skin at the nape of her neck. For the first time in his life Jeff felt humble. Here was real woman, a dangerous challenge, primeval and infinitely devious. She dwarfed the other women in the room.

Kamala refused the hashish he offered and instead drew his attention to a nearly naked girl who had come running to the center of the floor. There was a hush, only the drone of the tampura could be heard. The girl had large darting eyes, like a frightened bird.

A small jeweled triangle hung from a silver chain around her waist. The tinkle of bells at her ankles blended with the tampura. As she gestured with her hands her large breasts stood out as if they might give milk at any moment.

"Ah—ah," groaned one of the men.

Then a young man appeared, high hipped and wasp waisted, with broad shoulders like a figure from an Assyrian bas relief. His oiled body was naked except for a silver codpiece in the shape of a stylized erection, fastened to a silver belt around his waist and between his buttocks. From the tip of it, like a flood of sperm, a

[92]

shower of gems sparkled on silver and gold threads. He walked solemnly to the center of the room, balancing a large flat basket on his head.

An uneasy murmur flowed through the room as the girl lifted the basket from her partner's head and placed it on the floor. The youth began a ritualistic dance around her, crouching and side-stepping round and round her quivering body. Then he squatted in front of her and moved his hands slowly up her thighs as his torso began to pump, involuntarily like a male dog. He parted the jeweled covering between her legs, fingering it and letting it fall. Then, positioning himself so that all could see, he parted the jeweled strands and began sucking and licking her hairless vagina, pumping his body so that the jewels on the tip of his silver phallus rattled.

The tampura was joined by the tabla and violin, the pace quickened. Suddenly Abhrim stood up. His pants were bulging. He cheered wildly in Urdu, crawled on his knees to the girl, and pushing her partner aside, thrust his tongue into her. The girl swayed trancelike, waves of pleasure moving her body while Abhrim slobbered over her, emptying his pockets of hundred- and thousand-rupee notes.

After Abhrim had resumed his seat, the young man unfastened a catch on the lid of the basket and fell still at the girl's feet. At her command the top of the basket bobbed up slightly, and with a sudden loud hiss an enormous jet black cobra reared its head.

Jeff noticed the skin tighten at the corners of Kamala's eyes and around her forehead. Without averting her gaze she muttered to him, "It is a very dangerous animal, this one. This one is the king of cobras, rarely it ever gets tame."

A few of the girls well into their punch trips cried out or went under the pillows, moaning. One of the smugglers threw wads of hundred-rupee notes onto the floor while the other pushed the girl from Texas down between his legs.

Sundaram smoked serenely on an opium pipe, but his legs were twitching against each other at the knees.

The cobra hooded out, a hand's breadth, hissing. The girl began to dance in front of it, moving slowly, contrapuntally against the fast rhythms of the musicians, swaying like a reptile herself until she and the serpent were locked in a simultaneous undulating wave of recognition.

Slowly the serpent calmed and reclining itself in a graceful sweeping S, began to wind itself about one of her legs, then curled around her thigh, across her waist, over her breasts.

Someone else was throwing out thousand-rupee notes. "There's

[93]

enough money on that floor to feed twenty families for twenty years," Sundar whispered. His eyes bulged like Mickey Mouse. Jeff couldn't tell whether he felt this was good or bad and wondered what Kamala's cut was as the "producer."

The music trembled and shrieked. The cobra wound its body several times about the girl's neck and then began a slow descent between her breasts. She trembled, her legs were apart and her body pumping as the serpent swung down and arched out in front of her, hissing and swaying like a pendulum. Then it turned, its forked tongue lashing out nervously, and stiffening itself, slowly poked its head into the folds of her vagina.

Jeff felt Kamala's hand, rigid with excitement, close tightly on his. The girl whimpered, then moaning with ecstacy grasped the body of the snake as she collapsed on the floor in an orgasm of pleasure.

Only a few candles remained burning. The orchestra shifted to a slow raga. In the dim light, Jeff made out one of the smugglers with the girl from Texas. Her clothes were off and he had covered her with them, and was fucking her covertly on one corner of a divan. "Corny," thought Jeff, "the whole thing." He had a hard on and wanted to fuck, he decided, not watch some goddamn snake do it.

The cobra's head glistened as it withdrew and slipped back into the large basket. Jeff felt Kamala's hand relax. She turned an expressionless gaze toward Sundar.

"You didn't think it was possible," she said. "Well, what do you say now?"

"Extraordinary," Sundar mumbled, rolling his eyes. He made a move to rise but couldn't. "I think I need some air ... it seems stuffy in here. Ah, shall we—can we make a move? Come ..." he motioned to Jeff.

To Sundar's horror, however, Jeff had begun removing his clothes.

Kamala leaned back. A faint smile passed over her lips, as he removed his shirt and then standing, let his trousers fall and stepped coolly out of them.

He was expert in playing the acid game. Sundar deserved to be bum-tripped, he thought.

He made his way across the floor acutely aware of the effect he was creating. Even without a full erection, his penis was larger than most of them had ever seen. One girl reached out and grabbed his leg, trying to get to it with her mouth. But he shook her off and went to the snake girl. In one movement he squatted, took her in his arms and stood up. Then holding her against his body he began to fuck her slowly.

With a muted yell Ismail threw a wad of notes onto the floor. Jeff moved toward him, continuing to fuck as he moved, then let the girl down on the divan without withdrawing from her and with his free hand guided Ismail's erection into the girl's mouth. The musicians played on like machines, gaping open-mouthed as Jeff stood up and began forcing one after another of the stoned girls to suck him. Stretching up his arms luxuriously, legs apart, he observed with satisfaction the crouched form of Sundar nearby, afraid to look but too fascinated not to.

Then he noticed that Kamala had disappeared. Save the first one for her, he thought, turning away, the first big orgasm for her. He put on his clothes and went outside.

The terrace seemed to be floating in the tops of the palms. Someone asked if he wanted a drink and he turned to see Kamala, her face a disinterested mask. She handed him a frosted glass. Though their eyes met, she seemed to be gazing through him.

"You didn't enjoy," she said.

"Don't like snakes much." Jeff shrugged. The sperm inside him was ready to pour out for her. Some old and deep vibration that seemed to flow from her, resonated in him: love, death, love, death. All his nerves were on edge.

"You have beautiful body," she said. "I am sorry you did not enjoy our little show. Perhaps you want more serious medicine, eh?"

She made him feel like a victim but he found himself digging it.

"In India we worship Goddess," she went on, gazing steadily at him. "Each spring, the most beautiful youths were chosen to mate with her and after to be killed, like the drone bee who leaves its organ imbedded in the Queen. In late summer they were set free to wander naked, flowers in the hair, worshipped—free to have any woman, anything until the hour when their beautiful bodies were cut up and scattered over the fields." She smiled, sipping her drink.

"Desire is irresistible, it manifests the world." She gestured. "It is a great secret. If you know how to arouse and satisfy the Goddess of Desire, she will give you anything."

§

It was very still. He was lying somewhere soft and it was absolutely still except for the sound of his breathing. He opened his eyes trying to remember. Remember what. A face hung in the air over him. With great effort he tried to focus on it. It was Kamala's face. Or was it? Was he hallucinating? He closed his eyes. He didn't

[95]

want to look, he wanted to remember, but he couldn't get past standing with Kamala. It seemed days had passed.

Then he felt warmth beside him and opened his eyes again. She was lying there, reclining on one arm gazing down at him. He tried to move but couldn't. He tried to think. She had given him a drink. Then nothing. Fifty-seven varieties he thought, remembering the girl from Texas. Be careful.

Now there seemed to be spaces between his perceptions, empty gaps when his mind would slide away from him. He could feel her warmth, but otherwise, nothing. His body felt as though it had turned to stone.

He made out the form of breasts just beside him, like the plump buttocks of an adolescent girl. "You need awakening," a voice was saying from far away. Was it Kamala's voice? He couldn't remember. It seemed to come from a great distance. "You need awakening," it said again, "you are asleep. You could do so many things, but you waste it all . . . you need fright."

Then he saw the face, her lips moving, then the dark, ageless eyes he had found so hard to meet.

"You got no shakti, no power; you don't know how to love because you never had the real thing. You are too vain, too tight, you are half-woman yourself but you can't see it. And your Western women, they have no knowledge."

She put her hand inside his shirt, stroking his pectoral muscles, pinching his nipples between her long nails. He saw his nipples stand up straight, saw small drops of blood.

He hit out at her arm forcefully. He thought he did it, but nothing happened; he could feel nothing.

She saw though, and he knew that she had seen him wanting to strike her.

"You see, you can't do nothing." Her mouth seemed to open and close lazily above her breasts, her eyebrows arched slightly, the lips curled. "Can't do nothing . . . Don't do anything, don't even think of doing . . . anything. I will teach you everything, I will teach you how to do nothing. Then you will have anything you want."

Her voice was like thunder in his ear! Was he going crazy?

Then he noticed a young man: big, heavyset, ghoulish, his dark skin set off by a white cloth around his waist.

"That is my servant," she said, seeing a look of terror in Jeff's eyes.

He forced his lips to move. "Why is he watching us?" he whispered.

"He guards this body." She pointed to her breasts. "He is eunuch, sexless. He serves me."

[96]

Jeff looked again. The servant looked unreal to him. He noticed long black hair and long fingernails painted bright red.

"His testicles were removed when he was a child." Her voice sounded flat. "He was given to a friend of mine, an Arab, who gave him to me as a servant when he had grown tired of him. He is most reliable. Hassan," she said. "Come. Take Sahib into the other room, remove his clothes and bathe him.

"You must have bath before coming to me, do you understand?"

Jeff didn't like the idea. Again he thought of moving his body, and again nothing happened. He felt nausea and wanted to piss badly. With what was left of his thinking apparatus he reasoned that he was strung out on something . . . not the punch, not the majoun . . . unless he was ill. It was almost impossible to think clearly. Paranoia shot through him. Can't trust any of these bastards he was yelling deep inside himself, his mind moving like a film that made no sense. And he had to piss.

Then he was aware that he was being carried in the bare arms of the eunuch. But where? He was sure that Kamala was going to castrate him, that this fiend, Hassan, was going to cut his balls off.

Now he was in a large tiled bathroom. Why was he in a bathroom? He saw a tub sunken in the floor, saw himself being lowered into it by Hassan; flinched with the heat of the water but couldn't feel the wetness. Couldn't move or get out. At least he could piss. He watched himself and tried but nothing came. Did he really have to piss after all? His mind wandered again and came back. Hassan was kneeling by the edge of the tub, scrubbing his body roughly with a wad of coconut husks, grunting as he worked.

Jeff went out of his body completely, watching himself from somewhere near the ceiling. Hassan dragged his body out of the bathroom into a dressing room where he managed to get it onto a low cot covered with a sheet. The face of the eunuch looked tense and excited as he shook a bottle of liquid and let it dribble onto the body. Jeff could feel the oil come onto his skin, though the sensation had no location.

The servant rubbed the body with oil, his large hands flying over the white flesh, slapping the thighs, burrowing into the muscles with his fists, harder and harder. Jeff wanted to hit him. The pain was sharp now, but he was not in his body, had no control over it, only the feeling of it. He watched as Hassan flipped his body over and began the same procedure on his back: the neck and shoulders, astride the body working the muscles of the back with his thumbs, down to the buttocks, the eunuch's hands working adroitly the muscles close to the anus.

[97]

He noticed that Hassan was loosening the cloth around his waist. "My ass," he heard himself yelling hoarsely, "the bastard's going to fuck my ass." He could see him getting ready to do it, hard black cock, no balls. He felt it ripping into him, tried to tighten but could not, had no control over his own muscles.

There was sharp terrible pain. He was killing mad. He would kill this bastard, if only he could get back into his body. If only.

Then suddenly he *was* back. Like a fast cut in a movie, he could see now the dark hands with the long red fingernails pinning his wrists down, felt the sullen heaviness of the eunuch riding his back. Waves of nausea overtook him, he thought he might vomit or shit his guts out. Instead he pissed. Whatever it was, the drug was going out of him. As the warm piss flowed out under his stomach he knew that he had crossed a threshold. He had come back into his body and pissed and some of the poison had gone out.

Then it was over and Hassan withdrew. Jeff found he could move his hand but dared not risk a fight, he was too weak. He must pretend to be drugged until he could take full revenge. Goddammit, he could hear his voice echoing inside him somewhere, goddam bastard! He let himself be dragged again to the tub, doused with warm water, and dried. Then the eunuch picked him up and took him back to the bed where Kamala was lying.

"So now, Hassan has given you good bath and massage, I think? Yes, no, yes?" She bent down gazing into his eyes, her voice was heavy and mocking.

He wanted to spit in her face but the time wasn't right. He pretended to be weaker than he was. "Bastard," he whispered hoarsely, "where is that ball-less bastard?"

"No, no, no," she said, reprimanding him as though he were a child. "It was necessary for you." Her eyes narrowed. "It was my command. You Western men are too tight, got too much pride, like to show off too much—like tonight." She slid her arms around his waist. "Come here now, you beauty." She pressed herself against him. "Comm'on."

For a moment he had the funny notion that she was a lady psychiatrist seducing him.

"What the hell," he heard himself yelling, "but get that son of a bitch out of here." He gestured to where Hassan was standing in a corner of the room. "Out of here or I'll kill him."

She took his head in her hands and the strength he had managed to recover seemed to go out through them.

"Now, now, now," she said, "do not try to shout. It is too frightening. It is not necessary for you to be so angry, you will exhaust yourself. It was me who did it through him." She glanced

[98]

at Hassan. "We do not think of him as human. He is a loyal animal, something to be used, that is all. He is out of this sex business anyhow. Only my power controls him, he can do nothing by himself. Come!" She spoke to the eunuch in Urdu. "Kneel before this man here. Put your head at his feet and show him you aren't bad."

The servant did as he was told. Jeff winced, and closed his eyes, not wanting to see it.

"Ah, I forgot," she sighed, "you do not have slaves in America. Or you do not admit it. Here we are on good terms with them. Sometimes they are our best friends. You can buy anyone here for a few rupees," she said bitterly. "For a few rupees, in India. Do you understand that, Mr. USA?"

"What is the drug . . ." Jeff managed to whisper.

"Ah ha!" she laughed softly. "He is asking Kamala what drug he has been given . . . It is I! I am the drug. You know? No, you don't know. This is a tropical country. There are many plants to cure or kill you, even plants that can kill you six months or a year from now as though you'd had a disease. Ah, I could even take you to a village of women in the Himalayas, where when a man comes he is given food and wine with certain herbs that make his organ hard for weeks. The women enjoy, he dances to their tunes, then . . . phtt, he dies. It is said they eat him then, I dunno."

He was able to turn himself now so that he could see her. She lay beside him naked to the waist with a shawl of purple silk about her thighs and legs. He thought of a painting he'd seen in the Louvre, an exotic harem nude. She was nude, not naked. Her body was so free from imperfections of any kind it seemed unreal. Her breasts were large and full, the outcurve of her stomach matched the incurve of her hips, the high waist curved back to her perfectly rounded buttocks. And the skin that shone as though lit from within, the black silky hair, the eyes like moonstones set with black diamonds.

She motioned to Hassan. He came forward and began to massage her neck and shoulders.

"You are a most beautiful specimen," she sighed to Jeff, bending back under Hassan's touch. "Very beautiful male animal." She stroked his thigh, let her hand slide to his penis. Her voice was soft and lilting. "But you have the great defect, my darling . . . do you know it?"

Jeff stared at her without expression.

"You are too proud. Your pride is killing everything for you and it will kill you too, in the end." She stroked his chest."Don't be so proud," she said softly, "it is most dangerous. You look in the mirror, you see the beautiful body. I know, I look, I see mine." She held her hands above her head, stretching. "Is it not so? Yes? But always remember," she whispered, "it is not your body, it is a gift. What luck, eh? Think of this eunuch here." She rolled her eyes toward Hassan who was still massaging her. "Without balls—or worse, the body of a leper." Her eyes narrowed. "You have seen them, yes? So it is a great gift. Don't be proud because also it is illusion. Shall I tell you a secret?"

Jeff nodded.

"Nothing is beautiful," she whispered. "Nothing. You think I am crazy, but think. To the tiger or the monkey or the cockroach we look loathsome and hairless. The mountain is beautiful until you have to climb it, thunderstorm is beautiful until the lightning strikes you." She arched up on her knees beside him, letting the shawl fall from around her. "So where's the beauty? It is only our pride echoing back at us from the other side. Ha, it is so."

Jeff wanted to bury his head between her legs but he dared not move, not yet. He could see the folds of her vagina glistening through the silky hair around them and felt himself getting hard.

"My name is Kamala, Kama-la. Kama, it is Desire, it is indestructible . . . Creating worlds, makes the world move . . . As long as you're in this world you must go with it. Worship it. If you do not . . . if you misuse, then it will kill . . ."

Jeff was obsessed now with her body and understood little of what she was saying. She was an other-worldly being manifested before him. It frightened him. He wanted to take her by force. He trembled, waiting for the right moment.

The moon came from behind a bank of clouds, shining in on the bed through large windows that overlooked a garden. Motioning Hassan to a far corner of the room, she lay down beside Jeff again, her distended nipples rubbing against him. He noticed that he had broken out in a cold sweat.

Slowly she took his face in her hands and kissed his mouth, deep long kisses, sucking and biting his lips. He felt like he was experiencing a woman for the first time.

"You want something," she whispered, "yes? Then you should take it."

She pushed his head gently across the smooth curves of her body until it rested alongside her sloping thighs, then opening her legs in a wide arc, she guided his mouth toward the wet lips of her vagina. It seemed to him like the moist opening of a great cave. His tongue shot out automatically, licking and plunging into it. He looked up and could see her face above like a second moon watching him.

[100]

She had bade Hassan return. He was combing her hair out now, her long black hair, red at the edges where the moonlight caught it. For a long time she watched him as he sucked at her.

Then sitting up, she caught his hair and pulled his head up. "You are a fool," she whispered. "I cannot buy you, but you are a most beautiful fool and I will have you all the same, one way or another."

She fell back, pushing his head again between her legs. "At least you are lucky," she said softly almost to herself, wrapping her legs around him. "I am very clever woman. I know everything. Clever enough to take care of you well." She tugged at a shock of his hair forcing him to look at her again. "I will teach you . . . then you will do my work."

She lay back, stretching her arms above her, pushing herself out toward him, opening her legs wide.

He could feel his strength coming back now, his senses of touch and smell returning. For sure, the drug was wearing off but he was in no hurry for his revenge, especially as he was now more able to enjoy her.

He lay for a long time on his stomach between her legs, watching the expressions of pleasure cross her face. Then slowly he moved up her thighs, licking and sucking, sliding, up to her breasts where he sucked at her nipples, biting them gently.

This aroused her. "Yes, yes, so you can move now," she murmured, "yes."

He knew the drug's effect was passing. He could feel his erection steel hard and the pressure of sperm in his swollen testicles. He let the tip of his penis go into her slowly, almost imperceptibly. He waited as she contracted, sucking the full length of it into herself, groaning with satisfaction. Then he withdrew quickly and thrust himself in again hard and fast. He felt her flinch and withdrew again, and again plunged in with force.

"You are too large," she whispered hoarsely, "you must be more gentle."

Again he withdrew and without pausing drove himself into her, biting her breasts savagely. She cried out in pain. Hassan was there at once with a long bamboo stick. At a signal from her he laid it sharply onto Jeff's back.

Jeff sprang up. Two well-timed karate blows had Hassan on the floor. He kicked the limp body to make sure and then turned. But Kamala had got the stick and as he moved toward her he felt a sharp pain across his cheek. Another blow fell on his shoulder, bringing him down.

"You must not be so violent with us, darling fellow, or

[101]

something not nice will happen to you," she hissed, standing above him on the bed waving the stick. "Get down on your knees."

He knelt before her, panting, out of breath from the effort of the struggle and waiting for more strength, his penis still hard.

Then quickly he grabbed her at the knees, throwing her off balance and onto the floor. He got the stick away from her, and fixed both her arms behind her back. She was shrieking obscenities in Hindi, her dark eyes bulging with rage. He tore a strip of her shawl, stuffed part of it into her mouth and with another part tied her hands together.

Then he staggered into the bathroom, where he washed the blood from his cheek and shoulder, and returned with the stick.

"We'll see who is master," he whispered, bringing it down sharply on her buttocks until large welts began to appear. "Now," he said breathlessly, crouching above her, "let's see how tight your ass is."

He straddled her, boring his knees into the backs of her legs, parting her buttocks with both hands and spitting on the anus which lay exposed like some dark flower.

"Baby, you sure got a tight ass," he said as he slowly but firmly buried the full head of his organ inside her. He rested a moment watching her sphincter muscle twitch on it, listening to her whimper. Then, holding her down he jammed into her with one motion of his pelvis. She screamed, a deep cursing scream through the gag.

"Listen to me, bitch." His lips were at her neck now, his voice hoarse with the excitement of riding her body as it writhed with pain. "You and your Hassan and your India . . . bitch . . . you feel that?" He withdrew completely and jammed in again. "Do you feel it?" He pulled her up by the hair until their eyes met. "Fucking bitch. You're going to get your ass fucked all night long, baby, and if that eunuch wakes up . . . ugh, I'll kill him. You're not going to sit for days." He slapped her buttocks hard, over and over again, and bent her arms further up on her back.

It was like riding a beautiful mare. His memory spun out. He was a boy in Hawaii riding a horse he'd received for his fourteenth birthday, riding it naked on the beach. He had his first orgasm riding it, never forgot the feeling of the warm animal beneath him and the hot sperm as it rose and shot out onto the animal's neck.

He let go, pumping into her, thought it was over and then again came in spasms that left him trembling, his whole body convulsed in a long orgasm that seemed to be going on and on.

Finally he lay quiet, bathed in sweat. But he must act fast before she turned things to her advantage. Before withdrawing he tightened her bonds. Then he went to Hassan, who was moving

[102]

slightly, bound and gagged him and dragged him into the bath where he pissed on him in one corner of the room.

As Jeff showered and dressed he could hear vague noises below. End of the evening he guessed, the sudden cry of a girl, the crash of a glass, music still droning on. He decided not to leave through the house.

The drug effect was still strong enough to keep him moving slower than he wished. What sort of madness was all this he wondered, looking out over the terrace at a silent Delhi. He felt overcome with loathing. Too much blood, too much violence here. He found a stairway outside the house and slipped unseen to the gate. First he would go to Sundar's place to get his one bag there. The others with the acid, he had been careful to check in an airport locker.

Sundar's car was still in the compound, the driver asleep. Good, he thought, he would be able to get away without any scenes or explanations. He hailed a passing taxi and gave Sundar's address.

"You will stop there for only a moment," he said, "and then you can take me to Palam airport, please."

"Double the rate after midnight, the double double rate, sahib," said the driver lazily.

"Sure," said Jeff, "but hurry. I want to get the three-thirty plane for Bombay."

§

A. K. Sundaram was having his bed tea late because it was Sunday and because the evening at Kamala's had proved more interesting than usual.

"Is Mr. Jeff sahib awake?" he asked his servant.

"Oh, no sir, he is not here."

"He has gone out early?" asked Sundar, sipping his tea. "Did he say where he was going?"

"Sir, he has gone. Last night, sir. About two in the morning, sir, came by taxi. I had to let him in the gate. Picked up his bag and left in the same taxi."

"He's probably moving to Kamala's," thought Sundar wistfully. "It will be more to his taste there. Perhaps they'll exhaust each other. Get Miss Kamala on the phone at once," he said, "tell her I wish to speak with her."

The servant withdrew. Sundar stretched out. The evening had been most amusing. Ismail and Abrhim had really put the girls through their paces after Jeff was out of the way. It had been amusing to watch them as the acid took effect. "This LSD is very unusual," he thought, "something one must look into seriously. It might prove useful in certain areas of investigation and ... persuasion." He wondered how much of the stuff Jeff had brought in and whether Stan was involved in it or was just a friend.

The servant returned looking embarrassed.

"What the devil is the matter, James? Did you get her?"

"Yes sir, but ..."

"But what?"

James was a devout Seventh Day Adventist. "Sir," he said, blushing, "she cursed me very bad."

"But why? What the devil for? Is she still on the phone?"

"No sir, she rang off, said you had ..."

"Had what? Confound it, James, what is it?"

"Said you had better get the hell over there at once if you know what is good for you, sir."

Sundar smelled trouble. He was afraid of Kamala and she knew it.

"So she did, did she?" he said, acting as though he would avenge both himself and James. "Have the driver bring the car at once," he said in his most official manner. "I shall go round and find out just what is bothering her. Perhaps she's drunk."

Sundar arrived to find a bruised and bandaged Kamala lying in state on her bed. Hassan was applying balms and ointments to her injured parts. When she saw Sundar she rose from the pillow.

"It is very dangerous for him, this thing that he has done," she screamed, hoarse with rage. "Why you give me that drug to give him in the drink, what was it anyhow?" She hissed like a wounded serpent. "It is you who have given it, Sundar—you, not I. It made a problem." She displayed the bruises on her buttocks. "Kamala does not need these drugs, she uses her shakti."

"I gave you the drug, my dear, because you asked for something, don't you remember? If you got so much shakti, why did you ask? Didn't you say you wanted to teach Mr. USA a lesson?"

"I had Hassan bugger him," she whispered.

"Well, that was certainly a mistake," Sundar shouted. "No wonder he ..."

"No wonder nothing!" she yelled. "And no mistake! The mistake was that your drug wasn't strong enough—he came out of it."

"Yes, Guruji," Sundar said mockingly.

"Listen to me, pig, you—neurotic! Don't tell Kamala what to do and what not to do, understand?

"Director of Planning—ha! What planning can you do, you little know-nothing, you—Peeping Tom! Because you went overseas to school you think you can play with me, bring scum to my house.

Be careful, Sundaram. Remember it was I, Kamala, who got you this planning job."

"Yes, Guruji."

"Don't yes 'ji me," she yelled, throwing a banana at him.

"I mean it, I mean it," Sundar stammered, lunging toward the bed to touch her feet. She must be appeased at any cost he was thinking, it could be too dangerous.

"You don't mean it, I know, but you will before this life is over for you, you will!" She smiled down at him. "That scum American ... he is going to be finished, do you understand my meaning?"

Sundar nodded.

"No one slaps Kamala around."

The telephone sounded somewhere beyond the thickly carpeted room. A boy appeared with an extension. "There is a call for Mr. Sundaram," he said. "Someone has come to the airport."

"Yes," said Sundar flatly, "who is it?"

"Sundaram, it's Stan—Stanley from Harvard."

"Ah, Stanley—so you have come to India!" Sundar put the phone to Kamala's ear.

"Yes. I'd like to see you for a few hours. I'm on my way to South India tomorrow."

"But of course, dear Stanley, a car will be there at once," Sundar shouted. "Stand by—yes, at the Air India counter. My man will fetch you." The boy was called and Sundar scribbled a note for him to give to the driver.

"Who is this Stanley," said Kamala suspiciously.

"An old school friend," Sundar said cheerfully, hoping Stan's arrival might give her something else to think about besides Jeff. "He's an American."

"I don't trust these Americans," she grunted. "They're all blown up. They think they know everything."

"My friend isn't like that, really. He has held many secret positions in the American government—he may still. We must find out what he's up to." He decided against telling her that Jeff was a friend of Stan's.

"I can't see anyone until I'm healed."

"But none of your bruises need show, they aren't where ..."

"How do you know whether they will show or not? It depends on who might be looking."

Even bruised and tired, she was so overwhelmingly beautiful that it became painful for Sundar to be with her alone for very long. It depressed him that he could never satisfy her. You had to overpower her to satisfy her. "Jeff overpowered her," he thought, "but I am her slave." He hated Jeff thinking of it and was secretly glad that Hassan had been able to bugger him. "I will take my leave then," he said, getting up off the bed. "I must receive my old friend Stan."

"You will bring him to me?"

"He says he is going south tomorrow."

"Then delay him," she said, "delay him for two days and I will see him. And meanwhile—" She fastened her eyes on Sundar. "Find out where that Jeff has gone. I want to know."

§

Sundar was waiting behind the shutters of the veranda when the car pulled in. He wanted to watch his old friend unseen; first impressions he had learned were always the most accurate, especially if one did not have to react. Stan bounded out of the back seat somewhat like a cricket player coming onto the field. Sundar had forgotten how much he resembled an Indian with his olive complexion, brown eyes, and thick black hair. He had gained weight, otherwise he was the same.

As planned, it was James who greeted the guest at the edge of the terrace, took his luggage, and asked him inside. Sundar noted that Stan didn't sit but began pacing. "He's in a hurry," Sundar thought. "Maybe he's in trouble."

"Welcome to India, Stan," he said.

"Land of mystery and intrigue." Stan hugged him.

"Well, you'll see that for yourself. Your friends were in Delhi for a few weeks," Sundar said. "I took them around to some parties and so on. In fact, Jeff was living here until he vanished yesterday."

"Perhaps he'll come back."

"And Laura met a yogi. Last seen heading in the direction of the Himalayas."

"Yes, I knew Laura had gone because a friend of mine is also a disciple of that yogi. We flew in together. He's just gone looking for them."

"But what brings you here?"

"Oh, the usual thing, I guess," replied Stan. "Sightseeing, elephants, a Maharaja, an outcaste or two." He shrugged, wondering how much Sundar knew about the acid, whether Jeff had turned him on. "How about girls? I hear India's famous for them."

"How many do you want?"

"I can have as many as I want?"

"As many as you can afford," Sundar said blandly. "It's good karma to have money. Eat. Live. Take. Enjoy. We know all the human weaknesses, we have to. We have *all* of them."

"But you also know how to play them," said Stan.

[106]

"Yes."

"You mean I should be careful?"

"Yes!" Sundar repeated.

"But what have I got to lose—only money?"

"Your soul," said Sundar.

"Oh that. You really think I have one?"

"Perhaps not. But you can lose your mind here and sink into a sort of soullessness. The Moguls did, so did the British. It's our Indian rope trick, a specialty for invaders."

"Is it possible?"

"You don't think so? Ha! You don't know the full spectrum of human behavior. In the West you only have a segment—here we have the full range, from animal to saint. And nobody will stop you from going in either direction."

"We've liquidated all the dangerous extremes in the West."

"Quite right," said Sundar. "But as long as there is danger all around as there is here, man stays strong."

"I felt the people pushing to get off that plane."

"Yes, it's physical. Hunger brings sanity."

Stan slouched back in his chair. "Shall I tell you why I've really come to India?"

"The truth at last," replied Sundar. "I probably won't believe it."

"You may or may not. I have cancer."

"I don't believe it. Your Western doctors have invented that disease. What you mean is that doctors have said you have cancer."

"No, x-rays did," Stan said seriously.

"You've had all that?"

"Yes, and biopsies too."

"Oh, I see," said Sundar. "What type?"

"Lung."

"But you don't smoke?"

"I know." Stan laughed. "Ironic, isn't it?"

"But why come here of all places? You want to die in India? Of course, they say it is auspicious."

"I came to see your saint, Ananda Baba—the one who heals people. I'm supposed to fly south tomorrow, he's someplace outside Bangalore. Do you know him?"

"Quite well," Sundar replied thoughtfully. "I shall give you a letter of introduction, otherwise you might have to wait for some time."

"Will he be able to heal me?"

"That, my dear fellow, is between you and the Baba. He's a very holy man." Sundar wondered whether Stan was telling the truth.

"Fine," said Stan, "Now tell me more about the girls."

Sundar looked surprised.

"Well, I might as well get it as long as I can," Stan said. "How much did you say they were?"

"Oh, five thousand—perhaps higher."

"I'd like three of the five-thousand variety for starters. Can they be delivered this evening?"

"I think it's better you rest first," said Sundar, determined now that Kamala accompany Stan to Bangalore as an agent for him. "You've had a long trip, you need sleep."

"Now, Sundar . . ."

"Tut, tut," Sundar replied. "You *must* rest, this is a tropical country. You are sick. I insist! At least for three days. Then you can go to Bangalore. In the meantime I'll make all the arrangements and I'll have three of the five-thousand variety waiting when you arrive in Bangalore." He was determined to delay Stan's departure.

"Land of mystery and intrigue," joked Stan. "It's a deal."

"Meanwhile, there is someone here in Delhi I would like you to meet."

Stan looked hopeful.

"But only after three days rest in my house. Her name is Kamala. You might say she's the fifty-thousand rupee variety."

"Sundar, you're deeper than I had imagined. Do you by chance have any sleeping pills?"

§

"America will abandon us, you'll see. They can't cope with the Hindu mind. Negativism, that's what they call it. A Mohammedan may marry a Catholic or a Jew, it's all the same God, but he may not marry a Hindu because they say we're idol worshippers. That's true. What they don't understand is that it's just a technique like so many others. Anything is an idol. Try ripping up your American flag and see what happens!"

Sundar's usual wit had turned pedantic, the result of too much wine, too much chicken tandoori, and the nervousness he always felt in Kamala's presence.

Stan was only vaguely listening. Across from him lay Kamala, reclining on scarlet and pink silk cushions. She wore heavy gold bracelets, earrings of an ancient design, and a large diamond in her nose. Her body seemed to vibrate under her transparent sari. Stan sensed at once that she was dangerous: a priceless object in a display case. To become involved with her would mean slavery of the worst sort. He knew that he could never satisfy such a woman physically, on the other hand he was sure that like anything rare and precious she could be bought.

"But it's the soul that's at stake in the world today," Sundar continued.

"You mean it's the soul that's for sale," corrected Kamala. With a feline smile she stretched out on the cushions, displaying her breasts under the sheer silk.

Stan felt as though the nipples were aimed at him like eyes, projecting hypnotic waves to snarl him. He imagined jumping on her, riding her like a stallion. Although he wasn't a stallion and he knew it.

"Is your soul for sale?" he said to her, shifting his gaze up to her eyes.

"Before you can get to the soul you must conquer the body, is it not so?" She nodded slightly. "This body has never been conquered. It is waiting to be conquered. But I hear you are going south almost immediately," she added. "What a pity. I would have enjoyed getting to know you better."

"Why not come with me, then?" Stan heard himself asking her, somewhat to his own surprise. "You can have your own suite of rooms in the hotel. I understand there's racing this time of year. You can go to the races while I go off to visit my saint." He wanted to let her know at once that he had no intention of entering the lists as a potential conqueror of her body. But he thought he might enjoy having her around. She was bound to attract interesting people.

"Your saint?" she asked.

"I am sick. I need a saint to cure me."

"You don't look sick."

"Cancer. Lung cancer."

"Oh, I see," she said with a glance at Sundar. "Which saint?"

"Ananda Baba," Sundar offered.

"Oh, him. Perhaps I should go. Do you think you could get me on the same plane, Sundar?" She was really asking whether Sundar wanted her to go.

"I think it would prove a most interesting experience for you, my dear," confirmed Sundar. "You will see India through expert eyes," he said to Stan.

A phone was brought in.

"Sundaram here. Yes, I need an extra seat on tomorrow's afternoon flight to Bangalore. From the government allotment. Good, yes, in my name. Yes, but make the first name Kamala. Yes." He hung up smiling. "So you see, that's done," he said, silently congratulating himself, delighted that he would be able to spy on his friend and protect him at the same time. "You'll be under my care wherever you are in India," he said to Stan. "If anything happens, or if there's anything you need, don't hesitate to call."

§

"You are Mister Stanley?"

Stan was waiting for his luggage at the Bangalore airport. He turned to see a tall, good-looking young man smiling down at him.

"Yes, I'm Stanley."

"I am Saladin," the young man said. "Mr. A. K. Sundaram has asked me to look after you and Miss Kamala. This way please, do you have your baggage checks? Thank you, I will take care of everything. The car is just over there."

The air of the south was sweet and moist after the cold dry air of Delhi. The red earth seemed to breathe and the scent of blossoming trees was everywhere. They drove from the airport to the well-kept gardens and clipped lawns surrounding the East End Hotel, an old Victorian structure that reminded Stan of a spa in Weisbaden or Saranac in New York.

"I have arranged an audience for you tomorrow with His Holiness. Is that too soon?" asked Saladin. "We will have to leave very early in the morning as the ashram is near Raichur, almost a day's drive from here.

"And you are wanting three beautiful girls for tonight?" He looked toward Kamala, who was inspecting a boutique window.

"And the lady? She will also come?"

"No, no, no. We are only traveling together."

"Of course."

Saladin waited until Stan had gone. Then he slipped up a side stairway to Kamala's suite and knocked softly at the door. "Ah, Kamala, what good luck for me to see you again after so long." His eyes sparkled. "It's been nearly two years."

"Has it now?" she said, appraising him. "And look at you. You've developed . . . no longer a boy, eh?" She chuckled. She had seduced him one day out of boredom and he had proved more interesting than she'd expected.

"Then you remember?"

"Of course. And how is the pimping business these days?"

"Oh, it is excellent," he said enthusiastically. "The Russians are especially good customers."

"Russians?"

"Yes, there are many here selling tractors and they are very generous." He smiled. "The girls are getting fatter and healthier from all the vitamins and medicines I can give them now."

[110]

"And you have a date with the American for this evening?" she asked.

"Yes."

"To bring him three five-thousand rupee girls?"

"Sundar has told you then," he said, realizing at once that Kamala would be collecting a commission for Sundaram.

"Of course. Listen to me. This man is very rich. Just now, he is carrying over thirty thousand dollars in travelers checks and thousands of rupees in cash and he's not much interested in having the girls himself."

"You mean I must perform?"

"Most likely," Kamala said.

"Then . . ."

"Tell the girls the pay is a thousand rupees each, not a paisa more, understand? And make sure they don't understand English. When you deliver them, tell Stan that you'll wait in the lobby until he's finished, that if he needs you, he can call you. But he will ask you to wait instead in the sitting room of his suite. When the girls are undressed, he'll ask you to come in and will tell the girls to do something with you. He enjoys watching, that is his pleasure." Her eyes narrowed. "Then you must say at once that the girls charge an extra thousand rupees each for being watched, and that it is up to him what he feels your performance is worth; but that usually you do not do these things with your own girls and you would want the same pay as commission. He cannot give you less than the girls and so when it is over you will have twenty-one thousand rupees in your pocket."

"Ah, correct. I understand." Saladin followed her calculations, his gaze turned inward.

" But don't be in a hurry," Kamala said. "He'll want it to go on for some time, after all twenty-one thousand rupees is almost three thousand dollars. Have you understood now?"

"Oh, yes," he said, "it is a very good idea, you are too intelligent."

"And when it gets late enough, make him have the big orgasm. Then just after he has come and is lying in a weakened condition, whisper to him that he should rest up for the trip to His Holiness. That will send him to bed. And another thing—"

"What is that?"

"Bring the girls to me here one hour before you are to see him. I will make sure they obey you. I have a potion . . ."

"Ah," he said, teasing her, "will you give me some?" He put his hand on her thigh.

"You don't need potions," she said, laughing and pushing his hand away.

[111]

"But how can I repay you for your good advice?"

"We'll see about that later," she said stretching. "Now let me sleep. Oh, you might get a fat one just for the variety."

§

From speakers on the minarets of mosques, the amplified voices of Mohammedan sheiks floated out over the city. *"Allah is God, there is but one God, Allah . . ."*

Kamala couldn't sleep. She sat in one of the Victorian bay windows gazing out at the purple and orange blossoms of jaccaranda and mimosa. "In Bangalore," she said to herself with a sigh, "there is still something of the old days left."

There was a soft knocking. She opened the door. Saladin was dressed in expensive white flannel pants, a pale pink cashmere sweater, and imported Gucci slippers.

The girls trailed in after him, one suitably fat as she had suggested. She had thought that a dying man might be distracted by the sight and feel of so much healthy tissue. The others were Goan Christians of extraordinary beauty.

"Come here," she said cheerfully in Hindi. She began to rearrange the fat girl's hair, pretending to push and tuck it up in a more flattering way, while actually looking for lice.

"You don't imagine I would bring girls with bugs, do you?" Saladin said in English.

"I know you wouldn't do it intentionally, but one never knows. We don't want Mr. Stanley to get lice, do we?" She stepped back appraising them. "Are you sure they're clean? No VD? These Christian girls are so permissive, you know."

"Yes, of course," said Saladin, "but what does it matter? I'm the one who has to fuck them, right?" He pretended to look sorry for himself.

"You can't be sure, that's what I imagine may happen. But after watching you he may get excited enough to do it himself. He might even want to fuck you." She laughed.

"No, no, there is no price for *that*," he protested, slapping his buttocks.

"There's a price for everything, Saladin," said Kamala dryly. "You just haven't thought of it yet, or you've never been hungry enough!"

Then she spoke to the girls in Hindi.

"You must do anything and everything Saladin says, understand? Whether you like it or not. It's a job just like any other and must be well done. Especially as you will be paid one thousand rupees each."

She took out her purse. "Now I'm going to give you each two hundred and when you've finished you'll get the balance."

One of the girls protested, demanding half-payment. "But my dear," said Kamala, glaring, "if you get half now, you won't work half so well, will you? Shall we replace you?"

The girl shook her head.

"Then do your work well and you'll get it all, don't you trust me? It's all here." She displayed a wad of hundred-rupee notes.

The girl lowered her eyelids.

"Now, have some tea. It will give you a little lift." She poured out four cups. "One is for you," she said to Saladin in English. "A bit of my potion is in it. It'll make you last longer." She laughed. "Maybe even long enough so that there'll be something left for me."

Saladin took the cup silently. Outside the sky was darkening. Kamala opened the large casement windows. "What a superb spring evening," she said languidly. Then she turned, chucking the fat girl under the chin. "It is time for you to go to work now. Have a good time." She herded them out the door like so many school children, then lay down to relax and clear her mind.

But the American, Jeff, kept coming into her thoughts. Why was he bothering her so, she wondered, why was he disturbing her peace. Because no one treats Kamala that way, a voice kept repeating inside her. No one! And yet he had. That was what was irritating her and what intrigued her.

She reminded herself to phone Sundar. She must find out where Jeff had gone and track him down.

The room boy came and went, asking if she wanted food. After a time, lying alone in the darkened room, she drifted off.

§

She awoke to a persistent knocking at the door.

"It is I, Saladin."

She opened the door. The girls went directly to the bathroom.

A pokerfaced Saladin counted out the rolls of thousand-rupee notes. Five thousand each, that made fifteen thousand, one thousand each for watching, eighteen thousand. He handed them to Kamala.

"And for yourself?" she asked. "Did he give nothing for you?"

"Six thousand for me, and two thousand tip."

[113]

"Then I assume he had an orgasm?" Kamala asked dryly.

"Three times."

"Very good. Very good, Saladin."

The girls returned from the bathroom looking fresh and inscrutable.

Kamala counted out ten hundred-rupee notes for each girl.

"Well," she said in Hindi, smiling. "Take them. They're yours."

The girls refused. They wanted a tip.

"Aha, aha," Kamala cried, feigning rage.

"Bakshish, bakshish," wailed the girls in chorus. "We did good work. The customer was well-satisfied."

"Work," Kamala hissed, peeling off three more hundred-rupee notes. "You don't know the meaning of work." She knew that it was a formal ritual and that they would demand another round of hundred rupee notes. "That is all you are getting."

The girls stubbornly refused to take the money.

"Whores," she said, rolling her eyes melodramatically. "You agreed to one thousand. I have given as agreed, plus one hundred. Still you are not satisfied."

"But misstress," they all said together.

Kamala whipped out a second round of notes. "Now go, or Saladin will beat you. Saladin!"

The girls grabbed the money and giggling, beat a hasty retreat to the door with Saladin at their heels.

"May I return?" he whispered.

"As you like," said Kamala, stretching lazily.

§

"Eighteen thousand less three thousand six hundred makes fourteen thousand four hundred." Saladin sat lightly on one corner of the bed like a dog who does not quite dare to lie down on a carpet. "That's good."

"It's all right," Kamala sighed. "But I have made three times that amount in half the time."

"Of course," said Saladin modestly, "you are Kamala. We are only rabbits compared with you."

"And now you have learned a few tricks from me, eh?" She yawned and uncurled on the bed to reveal her magnificent breasts. "You will escort us to His Holiness in the morning?"

"As you wish."

Kamala gazed at him thoughtfully.

"I want to stay," he said, "is it . . ."

[114]

"That depends."

"On what?"

"On what you will pay, of course," she whispered carelessly, watching his face to judge the effect of her words.

He stood up, a tall bronze figure. "Is it enough?" He pulled the lining of his pockets out and laid his eight thousand rupee notes on the bed.

When she made no move at all he knelt on the floor beside the bed, and stretched his arms out blindly until his hands were resting on her warm thighs.

"Get up and let me look at you," she said, pushing his hands away.

He took off his sweater and shirt and stepped out of his pants.

"Have you had a bath since . . . ?"

He nodded, not daring to meet her eyes.

"Then come and lie down beside me," she commanded.

He lay down on the bed on his stomach, his lips on her breasts. She took hold of his hair, lifting his head up toward her. With her free hand she took the eight thousand rupee notes and brushed them over his body.

"Turn over," she said, scattering the notes on his chest, his thighs, and on his swollen penis, clutching at his hair, drawing his face close to hers. He watched like a mouse in the claws of an eagle as she gathered up the money. Then moving her hand over the candle of her bedside table she thrust the notes into the flame. They caught and burned slowly, one by one.

"Now," she hissed, letting go of his head, "let's see what you've learned in two years."

VII

§

EACH MORNING AND evening Indra waved to Laura at the rapids. She was happy to see that his jaundice was clearing quickly. Though she only saw him across the river, she began to feel a closeness with him she had never before experienced with anyone.

At first her fourteen-hour sessions seemed interminable. Her legs and back ached until she discovered that she could prop herself against the wall of the cell. And her mind wandered, relentlessly. She would go off on long mental trips, and forget to keep repeating the syllables. But after the third day she was able to stop most of her cerebral wanderings, and by the sixth was able to stay on track for the whole of the fourteen-hour period. But what track? Where was she going?

On the last day she began to hear a chorus of voices singing something like a Bach chorale. After that a blue field began to appear, as it had in the temple. Once, into this space, came the three-quarter profile of a man. He was looking at her out of his left eye. She thought it might have been Indra but when he returned at the end of the week and she told him, he only looked at her with his left eye and winked.

"Is that all?" he said.

She nodded.

"Good," he said, "and now I have a surprise for you."

She felt disappointed that he wasn't going to talk further about her experiences, but just then a barefoot man wearing a faded red cloth and an orange turban appeared from behind a tree.

"Alex, is that really you?" Laura gasped. "Whatever brings you here?" She wondered if anything had gone wrong with the acid distribution or with Jeff.

"Not too much conversation now," Indra said. "We have exactly twelve minutes to pack and eight minutes to reach the bus to Petoraghar before it leaves. Don't think, act."

[116]

§

On the long dusty trip Indra began talking with Alex in Hindi. Laura felt somewhat indignant over being left out of the conversation but supposed it was a test of some sort.

"Tell me why you have come," Indra was saying.

"Stan, the man I work for, has cancer."

"You mean some doctor has told him he has it."

"Yes, and he's gone to Ananda Baba hoping to get cured."

"Good. Ananda Baba can easily cure your friend if he wishes, but the cure will be very expensive."

"Should I have brought him here, to you?"

"It's hard work, the curing business. Takes a lot out that has to be put back. I always lose a bit of my hair when I do it. Let the Malayali Baba heal him if he will. So you have come to India to be with your friend?"

"And for other reasons," Alex said quietly. "Has Laura told you what she and her friend Jeff are up to?"

"No, not directly," said Indra. "But I put her to repeating mantra for a week, fourteen hours a day. Of course, the whole thing came out in my ear. Very interesting indeed. I have had this LSD, you know."

"Yes?" said Alex. "When?"

"Oh, perhaps two years ago."

"From whom?"

"From a servant who worked for some Irishman from America who was living about thirty miles from here."

"Do you remember his name?"

"The Irishman's name? It was Cleary or O'Leary . . . some such name, and the servant's name was Prem Singh. Which do you mean?"

"You answered my question."

"It's a dangerous poison," Indra said. "Very good and very poisonous. You've had it?"

"I've made it," confessed Alex.

"It's very dangerous. I took it, nothing happened. Then I took a whole mouthful, about twelve tablets, still nothing happened. But the ordinary local people who got it went mad and still are. One boy became catatonic, like a saint. It is equal to ten years of meditation. Imagine, ten years of meditation in ten hours. Should never be given except by an adept. Even then it isn't wise to open up the uninitiated to that extent."

"They put the Irishman in jail for telling people to take it."

"That was foolish. Anyway, this stuff shouldn't be passed out freely in India. And you mustn't remain involved. After you leave me, get out of India at once."

"But the distribution will happen anyway. Stan might agree to stop it if you saw him, but it's Jeff who has the stuff—and he's disappeared from Delhi. No one knows where he is."

"But Jeff will get in touch with this one, won't he?" Indra glanced at Laura who had fallen asleep beside him.

"Maybe, maybe not."

"Well, we'll see," said Indra thoughtfully.

After sunset the bus stopped for the night in a small village and the passengers tumbled out, hoping to find a place to sleep. Indra, Alex, and Laura walked along the empty main street. It was cold and damp. Gigantic cedars and deodars towered over the line of closed shops.

At one of the small wooden doorways Indra stopped and knocked loudly with his chimtah. There was bustling inside, then the door opened a crack. An old man's startled expression changed to one of wide-eyed incredulity when he recognized Indra.

"Babaji," he cried and fell to the ground at Indra's feet.

"Shut up and let us in quickly," Indra said.

The man scrambled to his feet and led them into the warmth of a tiny blacksmith shop where a small fire glowed in an open forge.

"Shut the door before anyone sees," Indra commanded, "and then prepare some tea." He turned to Laura. "I once practiced here in another time."

Laura looked surprised.

"My dear child," he said patiently. "I am a sanyasi, a yogi. I have all fourteen initiations and twenty-one past human lives that I know of. I am what is called a siddha. I play different roles in different places, sometimes at the same time. Let it suffice I once played out a play here which this man has not forgotten." Indra paused, watching to be sure their host was preparing the tea correctly.

"Let us have a chillum and some tea and after that more chillum and more tea," he said gaily, "because we must leave before daybreak, otherwise all hell might break loose here. We'll catch the bus on the road."

§

The cold bit into Laura's cheeks as they walked along the road before sunrise the next morning. It was a relief to come out of the

[118]

damp forest over a ridge and into the sunshine. Scarlet rhodo-dendron blazed everywhere against the blinding Himalayan snows that towered above them. Flutes echoed in the valleys below, where cows and goats grazed among bamboo groves. Soon they heard the grinding of the bus and minutes later they were squeezed inside like sardines.

"The yoga of the bus," Laura murmured to Alex. "How far now?"

"Far enough," said Indra, overhearing her. "Don't ask silly questions. When you get tired just repeat the syllables I have given you. And it's because of you we have to take these wretched wrecks they call buses. I would rather walk, but you two would not be able to keep up. Some day perhaps you'll buy us a limousine." He winked at Alex. "Better yet, maybe we could go speeding through the Himalayas in your mother's Rolls Royce. Then we'd crash and that would be the end."

"You want to go then," Laura said.

"Some day I will tell you how much," he said, "and why I can't. Tried many times this time around, but She won't let me."

"She?"

"Goddess—she keeps me here working for her. I'm tired of it. Will you go with me when I go?" He grinned at her.

The question frightened her.

"Ah, I know. You want to stay a bit longer—just a little bit longer. Thinking you might finally get the jam."

After half a day's ride on a road barely wide enough for the bus, they reached a tea shop where they bought supplies and set off on foot. For three hours they climbed steadily to the top of a densely forested mountain. On one side was a sheer cliff with a cave at its base. Around the other side was a large wooden temple with a pagoda roof and, attached to its eaves, deer antlers bearing tattered bits of crimson cloth.

"Alex, you show Laura what to do while I go above," Indra said. "This is the home of Durga, one of Kali's emanations, the Temple of Tigers. Have you ever seen a Kumaon tiger? They're as big as water buffaloes, bigger sometimes. I must do certain things now to protect us while we are here." He bounded up the path around the mountain.

Alex showed Laura how to make a twig broom. She swept the floor of the cave while he reconstructed a fire pit outside.

"Now for the wood," he said.

"The wood? Will someone bring it?" Laura asked.

"Yes. Us!" Laughing, Alex took an axe from his bedroll. "I'll cut and you carry. The experience might come in handy some day," he

[119]

said, looking at her intently. "Come on, you'll do all right."

After many trips they had a sizable pile of logs on the terrace in front of the cave.

"Enough," said Alex, out of breath at last.

"I should hope so," panted Laura.

They sat alone for a moment in the late afternoon sun. A chorus of locusts sang in the high pines.

"Alex, you haven't yet told me why you came to India," she said. "Has something gone wrong with the acid thing?"

"Not exactly."

"Then what?"

"It's Stan—he has cancer. He's gone to a healer, a famous saint in the south."

"And you came with him?"

"Me and Carlos," said Alex. "He got off the plane in Bombay while Stan and I came on to Delhi."

Laura looked worried. "I don't like the sound of that! Carlos and Jeff don't get along at all. There might be trouble."

"Maybe," Alex shrugged.

"But why didn't you bring Stan to Indra? He can heal, I've seen it."

"He wants to go to this other man, he's well-known."

"But can he heal Stan?"

"If he wants to, for a price."

"Oh. Well, I don't exactly like Stan but I feel sorry . . ."

Indra appeared on the path. "That is quite enough wood," he said, "at least until tomorrow."

Laura sighed and made a face.

"But this is what you need, dear child," said Indra, looking too young to be calling her a dear child. "You need hard work, seven years hard labor." He grinned and bared his teeth at her.

"I feel like Red Riding Hood," she said faintly.

"And I am the evil wolf." He ran down the steep hill, peered out at them from behind a tree, showing his teeth and howling like a wolf.

"You won't forget him soon," Alex said.

"Is he human?" Laura asked. "I mean sometimes he seems to be more than alive, not dead, but more than alive. I can't put it any other way, it's when he goes transparent and all that."

"So he has shown you that much, has he?" said Alex thoughtfully. "I know what you mean but I don't know the complete answer—only some of it. Does he frighten you?"

"At first he did, yes. Very much. But now I'm used to things happening. I suppose there's a lot more?"

[120]

"Yes."

"I thought so."

§

They were seated in front of the fire, about to begin evening prayers.

"Someone is coming," Indra said slowly, opening his eyes. He reached for the conch shell he normally blew in the morning and evening and put it to his lips. As the last sound of it echoed through the forest and receded into the evening vastness, there was an answering call.

"Halloo-o-o, Halloooooo."

Indra cocked his head like a bird listening for a worm.

"Jackals are rare here, this is the place of tigers," he said. "It must be some other animal."

"Hallooo—is Maha*rodgee* there?"

"Ah, a human animal. Who is there?" Indra called. "Who dares to disturb a sage meditating in the forest?"

A woman emerged from out of the darkness, crawling up the hill on all fours. She was big, bony, and wore a threadbare tweed suit and boy scout shoes. Over her arm hung a tattered alligator handbag. She crawled onto the terrace and started to get up.

"Are you the Maha*rodgee*?" she gasped.

With a wink at Alex, Indra jumped up and stood over her. "Get back down on your knees, woman," he shouted. "Don't you know where you are? Remove your shoes at once."

She fell back on her knees and gazed up at him, smiling inanely.

Indra burst out laughing. "Woman," he said, "you are at the cave of a witch." He narrowed his eyes, then snapped his long hair in her face.

Her smile faded. "Then you aren't the same one," she whimpered. "You aren't the one who healed Mohan Singh Shah."

Indra glanced at Laura. "Now you see why they tell us never to use power."

"You *are* him then," the woman cried, falling at his feet.

Without a word Indra resumed his seat before the fire and began preparing a chillum, which he lit and passed to Laura. She smoked and then passed it to the woman as he directed.

"Oh no, no thank you," she said politely, holding up her hand. "I never smoke, really I don't." She turned her watery blue eyes to Indra.

"Smoke it," he said.

[121]

"But I . . ."

"Smoke it," he insisted.

"But I'm allergic to tobacco," she said, making a face.

"Alex," Indra commanded, "show her how to hold it and do it until she learns."

"But I don't—"

"What is your name?" Indra said.

"Elizabeth," she said meekly.

"You are the wife of a Methodist missionary?"

"No, Quaker."

"Nevertheless you are a missionary's wife?"

"Yes."

"Do you know that I eat missionary ladies for breakfast?" he roared, crashing his chimtah against a burning log.

A shower of sparks flew out of the fire.

Laura was becoming frightened.

"Now you are coming here to me, a yogi, to do the work your Christian doctors cannot do. Either smoke or get out," he growled, dead serious. He closed his eyes and froze in a posture of meditation, fists clenched on his knees.

Elizabeth cast a sheepish glance first at Laura and then at Alex. Silently Alex took the chillum from her hands and showed her how it was held. She fumbled with it, sucking on it and coughing, but after a few tries managed to swallow several large gulps without choking. Then Alex held the pipe in front of Indra.

He took it at once, finished it, refilled it immediately and passed it to Laura, who smoked and again passed it to Elizabeth.

Indra watched as she drew in on it. Then he smiled.

"Bola shakti durbar a ki," he shouted at her across the fire.

"Bola shakti dorabara a ki," she shouted back in a reflex action as if something locked up inside her had been suddenly released.

"Huh," he muttered, "I saw you coming this afternoon."

"But how could . . ."

He shook his head as if to get rid of a gnat or mosquito, and turned to Alex. "She comes for me to do her work but doesn't believe I could see her coming. I will do your work, that might also surprise you," he said glaring at her.

"But I haven't told you what it . . ."

"Do you think, young woman, that if I can take away your tumor I don't know beforehand that you have it and are coming to me for that purpose? Really, this animal disgusts me," he said in Hindi, turning to Alex.

Elizabeth burst into tears. "I'm so tired," she wailed, "may I go to sleep somewhere?"

"Wrap her in my blanket," Indra said to Alex. "Let her sleep at my feet." He rubbed his hands together. "Let us all 'sack-out' as they say."

Laura and Alex bundled the large limp form of Elizabeth into the blanket.

"And more are coming, so get ready." Indra smiled wanly. "I see them . . . two first-class fools . . . It seems we cannot escape, even here . . . if one is kind they come and want to eat, if we are not they want to kill us."

§

The next morning before dawn Laura awoke to see Indra sitting in front of the fire staring at the coals. She lay under her blanket watching him through a small hole. He winced visibly as loud internal rumblings and farts issued from the lumpy heap where Elizabeth lay sleeping.

It was cold. Alex jumped up naked from his sleeping bag and ran toward the spring several hundred feet below. Laura shuddered at the thought that she too was supposed to bathe in the icy water, and burrowed into her blanket.

"Think what a hopeless wretch is lying there," Indra said as Alex dried himself before the fire. "But what to do? Who comes to this fire cannot be turned away unless he disobeys the rules."

Alex prepared the morning chillum and set a pot of tea, cardamom and milk to simmer on the coals. The spicy aroma attracted Laura and she sat up, holding her blanket around herself.

"Bonjour, Mademoiselle," Indra said with his warm morning smile, a proud naked warrior welcoming her to the battle of the day. "Have some chillum and some tea before venturing down to the spring. It will protect you from the cold."

He sucked on the pipe. Sparks flew and great clouds of pungent smoke drifted from the corners of his mouth, giving him the appearance of a young dragon god.

"To me it is all the same," he said. "Cold, hot, hot, cold. It doesn't seem to affect me. It is a boon passed on to me by my mother's guru—the one I sat with from the age of six . . . a great rishi, my first teacher."

He poured tea, first into the fire and then into the cups set out by Laura. The sun, though not yet visible, had set the edges of the snowy peaks ablaze. Alex and Laura sipped their tea in silence. Indra took up his instrument and chanted to the sun as it rose.

The pale face of Elizabeth emerged from under the blanket. Fumbling for her purse, she extracted a tissue and blew her nose loudly, then tossed the wad of tissue into the fire.

Indra dropped his instrument and grabbing his chimtah extracted the tissue from the coals before it caught fire.

"Never do that," he said, throwing the tissue back onto her lap. "It is against the rules."

"But it's only a fire, Maharodgee," she croaked in the broad accent of Midwestern America, smiling at him as if he were putting her on.

"Wipe that smile off your face," he said with a sinister look. "Don't Maharodgee me, and remove those loathsome shoes immediately."

Elizabeth fumbled with the laces, and removed her shoes grudgingly.

"Now give them to Alex," Indra said, "along with the stockings. They must be removed at least one furlong from this place."

"But, Maharodgee," the young woman objected.

Crash came the chimtah, inches from her hand. "How dare you!" he cried. "Give this bitch her shoes," he said to Alex. "Now, get out!"

Then he fixed her with his eyes. "But before you go, feel your left breast. You will find the tumor is gone."

Quickly Elizabeth turned away and reached up inside her sweater. The disbelief on her face turned to joy and she burst into tears, her large white bony hands over her eyes, the big clumsy body shaking involuntarily.

Indra jabbed the chimtah into the ground in front of him and leaned on it, staring at her disdainfully.

"You'd better bathe now," he said quietly to Laura who jumped to her feet and ran down the hill in her blanket.

Alex appeared worried.

"Let that animal cry," Indra said, glancing at Elizabeth. "She needs it, she needs beating. Even now," he said after a pause, "she will lapse into forgetfulness and will say that the Surgeon General made a mistake and that really there was no tumor."

"How did you know about the Surgeon General?" wailed Elizabeth.

"She thinks I can heal her and not know the whole story," he said, laughing. "What a low type of animal you are. And take a bath," he added. "Walk down that path about two hundred yards to the spring. You can't eat until you bathe—that's another rule."

"But my shoes . . ."

"You must learn to use the feet God gave you," he said, grinning.

§

That afternoon they had just finished eating when they heard voices below.

"As I warned you, more are coming," Indra said. "Two of them, first-class fools both. And we will have to cook for them and feed them. I'm sick of it!"

A few minutes later two men, panting and out of breath, struggled onto the terrace. One wore a sloppy tweed suit and spoke with a Scottish accent while the other had adopted local dress and was wearing a kirta and dhoti. On seeing Indra, they removed their shoes and bowed deeply.

"See you made it," said the one in the dhoti nervously to Elizabeth.

"You are friends then?" Indra asked.

"We met in the village," said the Scotsman. "She told us she was looking for you. We'd heard of you and since we were passing this way we decided to take the opportunity to meet you. I am Dr. Reginald D. Long, and this is my friend, Dr. Albert Loeb. We are in psychology."

Indra nodded politely. "Very interesting. But why come to see me?"

"You are somewhat of a legend in these parts," said Dr. Loeb in a sharp American accent. He had gray hair and a withered left hand.

"You want me to heal your hand?"

The man smiled. "Never thought of it."

"It's possible," said Indra. "Just takes some time."

The Scotsman cleared his throat. "We came mainly to hear your opinion of certain Western theories of psychology."

"You mean Freud, Jung, Pavlov and so on?" said Indra. "They are correct as far as they go, but it is all too theoretical and parochial—in fact, they don't go very far at all. I have read them and burned their books long ago. . . . I think you want to be yogis or sorcerers, eh?" He laughed maliciously.

The two men looked at each other.

"In any case, this is not the hour for me to tell you anything. If you want to remain until after dark, then we may talk. Just now these dishes need cleaning. Take them to the spring and clean them with mud and ash. After that, I will have done what I have to do and will be glad to help you if I can."

Having spoken, Indra stood up and walked away toward the temple, leaving the two new arrivals staring into the fire.

[125]

"What does he mean?" Dr. Loeb asked Laura.

"He means go down to the spring and do the dishes if you want to stay." She disliked psychologists and was enjoying herself.

"We don't even know whether he's worth staying for. Why should I wash dishes for someone I hardly know?" said Dr. Long irritably. "It's ridiculous."

"Doesn't he realize we aren't fools, that he might even learn something from us?" said the American. "It's possible that we too have valuable information."

He glanced at Alex. "Say—don't I know you from somewhere? I mean, your face looks real familiar. Were you ever friendly with Tom? Of course, now it all comes back! Aha!" He glanced at his companion meaningfully. "He's the one I told you Tom was telling me about. Of course, Tom thinks you've gone mad, you know." He smiled patronizingly at Alex. "I guess you realize that though." He continued. "Reginald, this is Alex, you might remember him—he was at Harvard about the same time you were."

"He's quite serious about the dishes," said Alex evenly, trying not to betray his feelings of disgust. "Otherwise, Laura and I . . ."

"I'll do them," said Elizabeth.

"You'll do nothing of the sort," said Alex. "If he'd meant for you to do them, you can be sure he'd have mentioned it."

"Well," said Dr. Loeb, getting to his feet, "I suppose if we're going to stay we'll have to do them. Shall we get on with it?" He turned to his friend.

"You mean you want to stay?" exploded Dr. Long.

"Don't you?"

"I'm not sure, if it means I have to do dishes. Really, Albert, I didn't come to the Himalayas to start doing the dishes of every yogi we run across. And you're the one who has all the questions—I should really leave and let you stay and do the dishes."

"I could have finished them during the time you two have been discussing it," Laura said.

"It's not the work, it's the principle," said Loeb.

"After all," Long added, "we're professionals. We usually don't sit around cleaning up after yogis, you know."

Alex went pale with rage. "It's time for me to rest," he said quietly, then disappeared up the path.

Laura put two more logs on the fire and curled up in her blanket.

"There's always a test," she said to the two psychologists. "But I can see you don't believe in buying unless you've read the label or there's a Good Housekeeping Seal of Approval. I can assure you it's impossible to do that here."

[126]

"But if none of the potions have labels one might get poisoned," said the Scotsman, thinking himself clever.

"Yes, you might," answered Laura. She smiled. "Anything might happen to you."

§

When Indra returned, finding that the two men had indeed washed the dishes, he decided to reciprocate by preparing a banquet. He spent the last hours of the afternoon with Laura, grinding herbs and spices and cooking.

By sunset the food was ready. After Indra had prayed, Alex held the chillum out to him. He drew deeply on it and handed it to Laura.

"Sorry, but we're off the dope trip," said Dr. Loeb, his hand raised as Laura passed him the pipe.

"It is our rule," Indra said wearily. "One chillum after evening prayer. It is prasad of the Goddess, not what you call 'dope.' You cannot refuse it. After that we make music and then we eat."

"What's prasad?" Dr. Long asked suspiciously.

"It means gift. Ganja is one of the plants of the Gods. The sap of it is taken as an offering. It is given to the temple and returned as a gift—prasad. It must never be bought or sold. Your people have misused it."

"If you don't mind I'd rather eat," said Dr. Loeb, looking greedily at the food. "Be a shame to let it all get cold."

"There will be no eating until after the chillum. If you don't wish to smoke, then leave at once." Anger glittered in Indra's eyes.

"If that's his rule, Albert, then shouldn't we observe it?" asked Dr. Long.

"Unless you would care to leave?" said Indra hopefully. He began to tune his instrument. "I should warn you that this place is called The Mountain of the Temple of Tigers and often they sleep around the temple just above here."

The two professors looked at each other.

Laura held out the chillum again to Dr. Loeb.

"Well I don't see much point in discussing important theoretical points after taking dope but . . ." He took the pipe, managed to swallow some smoke and then coughing, passed it to his colleague. "You see what it does, Reggie? Terrible stuff!"

"It is prasad," said Indra darkly. "It might even heal your hand, how do you know?"

Dr. Loeb glared at Indra and Elizabeth tittered, then hastened

[127]

to cover her grin. When the Scotsman had smoked and handed the pipe to her, she handled it like a veteran.

"I didn't know that wives of missionaries smoked," said Loeb facetiously.

"She's just showing off," Indra said.

Loeb rubbed his hands together briskly. "And now for some of that good food you've been preparing, eh, Baba?"

Indra ignored him and continued to tune his instrument. He tuned and tuned while the two men fidgeted, and Laura and Alex stared into the crackling fire.

Suddenly the silence was shattered by a deep roar just below them.

"What's that supposed to be?" said Dr. Loeb loudly.

"Shhhh," whispered Dr. Long.

"Tiger," said Indra, continuing to tune his instrument. "If you will look to your extreme right, you will see the beast's eyes."

Everyone stared. Laura saw two burning orbs so far apart that it was difficult for her to imagine they belonged on the same animal. Then a sudden breeze brought a terrible stench that smelled to her like rotten meat.

Indra's face shone with a furious light. "Lovely, isn't it Doctors?" he said, baring his teeth. Then flinging aside his instrument, his hand clenched, he grabbed the chimtah, and rattling it yelled into the darkness: "Harr Harr. Hut Hut Hut."

There was a low growl followed by a crashing sound as the tiger retreated through the underbrush.

"If I'd been alone, I'd have sung to it and given it some supper," said Indra. "Female, most dangerous." Then he signaled Laura to serve out the food.

§

After dinner Indra prepared another chillum. "Now," he said, "let's have an after-dinner smoke."

"Oh, no," said Dr. Loeb firmly. "You said only before dinner."

"But this is an exception, Doctor. It isn't every day I receive visitors from the ... uh, medical profession. We must have more chillums. I insist. Unless, of course, you and your friend would like to leave. It's much faster going down, shouldn't take over an hour to reach the bottom. I can loan you a flashlight."

"Power tripping," muttered Dr. Loeb.

"Ah, you are beginning to understand."

Laura sensed something brewing. The chillum went around.

Indra had the same bland expression as when he had exorcised the spirit of the Moslem sadhu.

"Now," he said softly to Dr. Long, "you were saying something about schizophrenia."

"Why, oh, yes . . . what was it? Ah, we think there are two kinds of schizophrenia," he said, clearing his throat nervously. "One which seems to be caused by the environment, and another which seems to be genetic. Maybe both are chemical in the end . . . ah, a chemical imbalance. I would be interested in knowing . . ."

"There is only one kind," said Indra, who had taken up his instrument and was strumming randomly. He caught Laura's eye and smiled at her like a juvenile delinquent.

"Only one kind," said Loeb.

"Yes, only one kind . . . Another one jumps inside."

"What?" said Loeb sharply.

"Another personality—it gets inside. There are hundreds of them everywhere." He waved his hands through the air. "All personalities without bodies . . . waiting to get new ones. When there is shock from the environment, of a proper order and so on, they can squeeze in. The chemical imbalance is just a sign that it is happening."

"Well, of course, that's an interesting folk theory," said Loeb patronizingly, "but it's not scientific. We're scientists!"

"What does that mean?" said Indra indifferently.

"What does it mean? It means we give credence only to events which can be measured and observed in a cause and effect relationship."

"I am giving you the cause," said Indra.

"But we have no instruments to measure the personality, or whatever it is that's disembodied or embodied. It's hypothetical."

Indra slapped his chest vigorously. "This is the instrument by which we measure."

Laura could see that while he was talking Indra was making himself transparent. She glanced at Alex who was also seeing it. She thought perhaps the Scotsman was seeing something too. Loeb, she was sure, saw nothing. She wondered how far Indra was going to go.

"Confound it, Baba," said Dr. Long, "there was something in that last chillum besides ganja."

"Mixture No. 77," muttered Indra.

"I am interested in these, uh, personalities floating around," said the Scotsman, rubbing his eyes as if something had gone wrong. "There was a mathematician called Leibniz."

"He was quite correct, that Leibniz, as far as he could go given the world he lived in," said Indra. "When the monad goes out, unless it has become free it follows its whims, the same as its

[129]

attachments when it was embodied. It is attracted toward the attachments of its previous embodiment in the desire world. It may even fragment itself altogether in some cases."

"What's your cure?" asked Loeb.

"We usually scare it out," said Indra. "It gets in through shock, so it must be shocked out."

"Like electric shock?"

"That doesn't work . . . too mechanical. Right theory but wrong practice."

Indra strummed softly on his instrument, fixing the Scotsman with his eyes as he grew increasingly transparent. Dr. Long now gaped openmouthed at what he saw.

"But my dear Baba," continued Loeb, "we are scientists, we must have proof—"He turned to his colleague for confirmation. "Reggie, why are you staring like that?"

"Can't you see," he whispered to Loeb, "can't you see?"

Laura was frightened and began repeating her mantra. Elizabeth had fallen asleep. Alex remained erect and still.

"Can't you see?" shouted Dr. Long. "He's not there! He's talking but he's almost not there!" He rubbed his eyes, a look of terror on his face.

Loeb's eyes went to Indra. Laura saw Indra flash out entirely.

"What's going on here?" yelled Loeb.

Indra's form reappeared. He was smiling vaguely and strumming his instrument. "You wanted some proof, Doctor, a demonstration perhaps." Then he flashed out again.

Dr. Long jumped to his feet, pointing to where Indra had been and from where the music now issued wilder and faster. Then he began to dance, laughing and struggling to remove his clothes.

Elizabeth woke up, saw Long dancing, and started to giggle.

"What's going on here," Loeb stammered, pale with fear. "Stop this nonsense at once!" he yelled toward the place where Indra had been.

"Shut up," said Alex. "Don't interfere."

Dr. Long was now dancing stark naked around the fire, his eyes rolled back in his head.

"But he's a married man, he has a wife and children," Loeb shouted. He lunged forward, grabbing at Long's leg, but was kicked back. "Reginald!" he screamed. "Sit down . . . sit down right now!"

Laura could hear Indra's laughter over the sound of his instrument as he materialized again before them.

"You have put some drug into that pipe," Loeb accused him.

"Oh," said Indra politely, his eyes blazing, "then why aren't you also dancing and the others?"

"But he's going to fall off the . . ."

"Nothing is going to happen, Dr. Loeb," Indra muttered. "Your friend is what you call schizophrenic. You didn't know that, did you. . . . That's why he is so interested in it and has become such an authority. I am merely giving you a demonstration. The 'other' inside him has taken over. The one you call Reggie is in a state of shock. If this other can be coaxed or scared out, your friend will be, as you say, cured. Perhaps he'll·write another best seller about it."

Suddenly there was a roar at the edge of the encampment. Everyone stared speechless as an enormous white tiger with black markings crept along the ground toward Dr. Long.

"Reggie, watch out!" screamed Dr. Loeb. But the now fearless Scotsman began dancing in front of it, arms flailing, his skinny white body bouncing up and down in time to the music.

"Ah ha, miro Baba. Ah . . . ho. Nameste, nameste duragé," Indra sang as Dr. Long danced like a wounded butterfly before the huge cat.

Grabbing Elizabeth, Loeb dashed frantically into the mouth of the cave. Laura and Alex found themselves frozen in place, speechless.

"She's been attracted by this 'other' one's dancing," Indra whispered. The beast's tail began to twitch, her ears went back.

"Ahhhagrrr," he shouted, and flinging down his instrument, he knocked Long out of the way and threw his chimtah at the beast's head. The tiger rose up on its hind legs, growling, and bounded into the night.

Dr. Long, sweaty and covered with dust, crawled on all fours towards Indra, leering, his tongue hanging from his mouth.

"Bathe him in warm water and wrap him well in blankets." Indra said to Alex. "We'll all sleep in the cave tonight. Are you all right?" he whispered to Laura, smiling. "Remember, it is all illusion, don't get caught up in it."

§

In America, Dr. Albert Loeb was a huge success. He was considered brilliant and extremely advanced in daring to combine the techniques of psychiatry with those of yoga, and had been one of the first to introduce the ideas of Patanjali and Astanga Yoga to the psychological elite of the West. He even had an ashram of sorts called The Institute, high in the mountains of New Mexico, where distraught victims of a society without values paid seventy-five dollars an hour for his counsel, and where with an inner circle of initiates he imagined he was exploring the mysteries of Raj Yoga.

Now, his face haggard, his beard coming out white in patches, he was beginning to fear for his own sanity. Crisis mounted inside him; concepts had been shattered, theories set to crumbling by this naked yogi who made wild claims and had somehow managed to throw his colleague into a trance.

"Raj Yoga," Indra said disdainfully the next day during one of Dr. Long's worst fits. "Nothing but a name, some methodism made up by all those Anandas to make money. If you really knew what it is, what they call the Raj Yoga, you would be able to lift the trance!" He laughed in Dr. Loeb's face.

Dr. Long, still naked, was alternating between periods of wild excitement and long periods of immobility. Dr. Loeb had tried to get through to his friend but Dr. Long had only stared at him. Now his freakout had progressed to the sexual level and he had spent most of the afternoon chasing Elizabeth from one spot to another, cornering her and masturbating wildly in front of her. It sent Indra into gales of laughter.

"See," he said to Dr. Loeb, who stared grim-faced at the antics of his associate. "What an old monkey is inside your friend, a lecherous old monkey. In a few days I will be able to talk to it, find out who it is. It will be interesting, no? Right now it is so crazed from having been suppressed all these years by the other inhabitant—the one you call Reggie—that it is going mad from wanting. I must let it have its way for a while; if it is suppressed now there will be little chance that I can lure it out later."

On the third day Dr. Loeb awoke to see his friend on all fours eating dirt.

"He said that he was an expert on schizophrenia," observed Indra, who was already sitting before his fire. "Let him see what it is, from the inside—take the taste."

It was then that Dr. Loeb realized he must get away and return with Reginald's wife. As a scientist he found Indra's theory most interesting, but as Reginald's friend and colleague his sense of duty demanded he bring up reinforcements. What disturbed him most, however, was a voice inside him that he usually ignored, which was telling him he really didn't give a damn about Reggie, that it was just a way to get out.

After the morning meal he took Elizabeth aside. On the pretext of washing their clothes at the spring they would escape to the road, where Elizabeth assured him they could catch a bus. They would find Reginald's wife and return by car.

"So you are leaving to bring up reinforcements," said Indra scornfully as he noticed the two hobbling off down the path toward the spring.

"Oh no, Maharodgee," squeaked Elizabeth, as if anything of the sort were furthest from her mind. "We're only going to the spring to wash our clothes."

Indra brought his chimtah down hard on the fire like a sword. "You are lying," he said to Elizabeth. "How quickly the cure is forgotten once the patient is well. I had to spend two days on the mountain getting your lump off my body."

Then he raised the chimtah in a gesture of dismissal. "Go!" he yelled. "I can't stand the sight of either of you! Especially you!" He glared at Dr. Loeb. "Leave these things alone, find some compassionate Swami in orange who will fleece your pocketbook while he fills you with theories to take to your following back in America. Go! If you stayed I might trick you into going out into the forest with me—alone—and you might have an accident and never return, ha!"

He turned to Alex. "Let these two animals be gone," he said. "I am tired of seeing them."

§

On the third day after the departure of Elizabeth and Dr. Loeb, Indra came down from the temple. "They are coming back today," he said. "Prepare for the worst. They may bring the police . . . yes, I think so."

Laura looked surprised.

"You don't believe me," he said, "but it happens. I raised a man from death once and had to hide in a cave for seven days after. His family called the police."

"You what?" exclaimed Laura.

"Forget it," Indra shrugged.

Reginald Long was awake now. He'd spent most of the time asleep but now he was talking and yelling, frothing at the mouth, and farting. Alex had told Laura it was the poison trying to come out.

"What is to become of him?" she said anxiously. Dr. Long was swaying back and forth catatonically, naked except for the blanket Indra had thrown over him.

"If his wife shows up he might get worse. What can I do?" Indra sighed. "These things take time. That Moslem sadhu you saw was simple. This animal is complex. His patients have driven him mad. Another soul came in through one of them—the sickness of the patient always rubs off on the doctor if he's any good."

The voices of Dr. Loeb and Elizabeth could be heard, quarreling, then a third voice, harsh and businesslike.

"The wife," Indra whispered. "Don't be surprised at what happens. Don't interfere. That's an order. It will work out. If things get out of hand just repeat the mantra and shift into neutral."

Minutes later the three stood at the edge of the clearing catching their breaths.

"Well, we've come back," said Elizabeth.

Indra said nothing.

"This is Reginald's wife, Florence," said Dr. Loeb.

She was an extremely attractive blonde Englishwoman with a good figure and very large breasts.

"I had an English nanny named Florence," murmured Indra, a faraway look in his eyes. "She was very nice."

"What was that?" said Dr. Loeb nervously.

"I said you must remove your shoes and stockings if you wish to remain in this vicinity."

Florence removed her shoes and stockings and sank to the earth where she sat quietly for some time, observing her husband huddled in his blanket.

A "heavy," Alex was thinking.

Elizabeth and Loeb continued their argument in whispers while Indra began filling a chillum. "Why don't you have them come up?" he said. "It makes no difference."

"Who come up?" asked Elizabeth.

"Why the two police officers you have brought with you, of course."

Florence turned her gaze from her husband to Indra. "Just *what* have you done to him?" she asked throatily.

Before Indra could answer Dr. Long got to his feet threateningly, gurgling and babbling incoherently at his wife.

"I don't think he likes your being here just now," said Indra. "Maybe you should leave and let him finish what he came for."

"How long would that be?" she said. "We have two children and commitments. Reginald is supposed to . . ."

"Could be three weeks . . . or three years," Indra said nonchalantly.

"Look here," she said, "you aren't my guru. I don't even know who you are and I'm not interested. I'm only interested in getting my husband off this mountain."

"Then call the police officers," Indra said. "Let them carry him down, unless you think Dr. Loeb can manage. Let them come and smoke a chillum and then carry him down. I don't think that animal is capable." He gestured to where Dr. Loeb was huddled sullenly with Elizabeth.

"Elizabeth, could you go down?" Florence asked. "I mean, you speak Hindi and all that . . ."

Elizabeth was thinking of the tigers. "Florence, really—my legs just won't do it." She laughed nervously. "It's almost dark and I just don't think I . . ."

"I'll go. Give me the flash," said Dr. Loeb.

Indra took the first draw on the chillum. "I doubt you'll have to go far," he said, letting the smoke come out with the words. "The officers will be closer than you think. They know the reputation of this mountain."

The pipe had barely gone around twice before Dr. Loeb reappeared, followed by two young police officers.

"Please remove your shoes and be seated," Indra said.

Dr. Loeb removed his shoes and sat down but the two officers remained standing.

"Remove your shoes and sit down," Indra commanded in Hindi. "This is a holy place."

One of the officers fell to his knees and began untying his heavy boots. The other caught him by the shoulder and pulled him up defiantly.

"Do you not intend to respect the sacred precincts of a sanyasi's fire?" Indra said, his voice like a cold wind.

What they answered or whether they answered at all no one could tell. Faster than anyone's eyes could register Indra sprang upon the two men and flung them to the ground. The officer who had tried to untie his shoe sprawled unconscious, between Elizabeth and Dr. Loeb who stared speechless, too frightened to move. The other lay doubled up and screaming. "It's time someone taught you some manners," Indra was yelling in Hindi. With his chimtah he laid one damaging blow after another on the man's back until bloodstains covered his shirt.

"Stop! Stop! You're going to kill him!" shouted Dr. Loeb.

"I may just do that!" Indra shouted back. "Shut up—it's not your affair."

"But it is my affair . . . it is everyone's aff—"

Loeb never finished. With one blow Indra sent him reeling down the hill.

[135]

Laura, trying to stifle the fear that rose inside her, began repeating her mantra.

Florence was now standing over her husband, who was on his knees frothing at the mouth like a rabid dog and making obscene gestures at her.

"Reginald, get up right now and come with me," she screamed. "Help me, Elizabeth, for God's sake, help me get him up."

By this time Indra, shaking himself like a lion after battle, had sat down again in front of the fire. The man he had beaten lay with his arms outstretched. Alex, his face pale, dragged the other, still unconscious officer nearer to Indra, who placed his hand upon him.

"Can we get him up?" Florence was saying to Elizabeth. "Reginald, GET UP!" she shouted. The two women struggled with Dr. Long who had gone limp. Just then Dr. Loeb reappeared, brushing himself off, his face livid and sweat beading on his bald head. "Let's get the hell out of here," he urged. "This guy's crazy!"

"Stop," said Indra quietly, without looking at them. "You are all crazy. You'll get hurt going down the mountain at this hour. Lost or hurt."

"There are tigers," Elizabeth said, her blue eyes watering.

"I don't care, you think I'm going to spend a night here?" screamed Florence, her eyes bulging. "He's the one who's crazy. Look what he's done to my poor husband. Where I come from you'd be locked up," she said, glaring at Indra.

"Then have it your way," he said calmly, smiling at her. "But take this." He held out a tiny newspaper package.

"What is that?" she said disdainfully.

"If he should get worse, give him some of this on his tongue. It will bring him around."

"What is it?"

"Never mind, woman, do as I say!" Indra commanded, his eyes ablaze.

Unwillingly, Florence thrust the small package into the pocket of her coat.

"Alex," said Indra quietly, "see that they get to the teashop. You might sleep there yourself and return in the morning. Take my flashlight."

Sagging under the weight of Dr. Long, the three of them started cautiously down the mountain behind Alex.

"Jai Ho," Indra called after them, muttering something in Hindi under his breath. The officers at his feet were coming to. The one whom he had beaten whimpered with pain.

"Maharaj, forgive us," they stammered in Hindi. "It was all the fault of the foreigners."

"Pigs," Indra snapped. "It was not the foreigners who kept you

[136]

from removing your shoes and showing due respect." With the chimtah he hit the ground near the men so that they cried out in fear.

Laura winced.

"Always remember," he said to her, "if you want to win any contest, you must put your opponent off balance. Go for the feet first."

"What will happen now?" she asked timidly. "Won't their superiors come—and arrest you?"

"They'd have to kill me first," he said.

"No! No!"

"Yes, yes. That is what I want. I want to go. But I cannot myself cause it to happen. That would be what you call suicide—against the rules." He gazed at her. "You see," he said, "I am not afraid of death as you are.

"Listen," he went on, leaning toward her. "I am sanyasi. When you become sanyasi, you die. Legally I am dead and under the direct protection of the government of India and the ancient body of Indian law." He motioned to the two men. "These people have no jurisdiction over me, but nowadays they are getting fresh. The government wants to secularize the country and also there are many false yogis and sanyasins disguised for their own ends." He paused, raking the coals of the fire.

"As a sanyasi I have no past, no future—but in fact, I have had many pasts and hopefully not too many more futures. I will tell you of this life, of a few acts in the play I am playing now, because I think it may make me more believable to you. It is important, you see, that you believe what I tell you because—although you didn't know it—your soul has, shall I say, been placed in my hands. I myself didn't know it until Dorje's aunt told me. She is—or was—a foremost oracle in Llasa. It was she who summoned me. It is because of her that you are sitting here now."

Laura stared in confusion.

"I cannot say more, someday you'll understand it all, although maybe not in this life. But I shall tell you something about my recent past going back to the beginning of this life, my twenty-second on this earth. The twenty-first life was four hundred and seventy-five years ago, and the first was about three thousand years before that. Someday perhaps I shall tell you of the others. But remember it is all a play—maya—illusion. Don't think it's so important."

Both the police officers appeared to be asleep. Indra stroked the head of one with his long fingers as he spoke.

"My main purpose in disclosing to you these things is to show you that it is impossible for you to control your destiny in this world. There is a way of acting in accord with it but it cannot be controlled.

"I was born into a princely family from the state of Patalia, my father was a Gurkha, a follower of Guru Goraknath. When Alexander the Great invaded India, my father's family had already recorded five or six hundred years of history. My mother, an extraordinary woman, was of the royal line of Nepal and her particular family had carefully preserved and handed down much of the ancient wisdom.

"At the time I was born in 1910, the British ascendancy in India was at its height. My father was very much involved with them but my mother kept apart. We lived in a grand house, I suppose you would call it a palace, and had other homes in Delhi, in Shrinagar, and Simla. From birth I showed certain signs of clairvoyance and so on, which disturbed my father but delighted my mother.

"When I was six, against my father's wishes and only successful because I was the third of four sons, my mother took me to these mountains and placed me to sit with an eminent siddha who was then one hundred and three years of age. With this old man I remained until I was twelve. He was able to tell my mother a great many things about my past lives and he gave me the instruction proper to reawakening the talents of one who we say is 'twice born,' or in my case, many times born. For six years I saw almost no one. I wandered these hills with a cow, reporting to the guru only at certain times. I learned many things and all came easily, for of course I was really relearning them. My guru sent me to other sub-gurus for certain specialized teachings as was the custom.

"There are two kinds of gurus, you see. If I can teach you something you don't know, well and good, I am your guru. But a real guru is more than that: he must have had a guru, who had a guru, who had a guru and so on. Why? Ah—that is the greatest of secrets and I shall tell you. Because the real teachings are not written, in fact they are not even spoken but are communicated in a certain manner beyond even speaking or writing.

"But I digress. In my twelfth year I was given the initiation which is supposed to determine whether the student will go into the world or will, then and there, become a sanyasi. It is a very difficult and strenuous ordeal and all the years from six to twelve have been a preparation for it. It is given in one and one place only in India and has been given there since before the time of Gautama Buddha.

"Well, after the initiation of course I wanted immediately to take sanyasi and begin the twenty-five year period of austerities that is required. But my father suddenly stepped in. He was the sort of man you had to have an appointment to see, and I hadn't seen much of him. I was extraordinarily big for my age and strong. He wanted me to be in the Army. What could my mother do? She couldn't go against him. And so I was sent to Simla and educated there at the schools of the British Raj with other boys of noble birth, many of whom are, at this very moment, generals and so on in the armies of both India and Pakistan."

Laura noticed Indra had a faraway look in his eyes.

"I cannot say I disliked it. We had good times. I was an excellent athlete and won many awards, also I was a good scholar. It was all easy for me—except I knew it wouldn't last. During this period and in the summers and long holidays, my mother also had her way. My old guru left his body during my first year in school when I was thirteen; from then on I was taken by my mother to an even older guru, a woman, one hundred and thirteen she was when I was thirteen. Can you imagine? She lived not more than ten miles from where we are now sitting. I went to her for six years. She had connections in Tibet and sent me to Lhasa three times during those six years. Once I even missed three months of school as I was late getting back. Later on I went for several years. It was this woman who drilled me in the methods my first guru had only hinted at, and correctly foresaw most of the events of my life. I was with her when she left her body in 1941 at the age of one hundred thirty.

"To go on: my father got wind of my mother's doings and after I finished prep school at Simla he sent me to the British pre-med in Delhi, determined that I should become modern and scientific. I found it very interesting indeed, especially as by that time I already could heal people by touch. It amused me to learn all the Western medical theories and I excelled in all of it and became an intern to the then Surgeon General. During this period, from 1928 to 1936, I spent almost all my time with my third guru, a Moslem saint to whom I had been sent by the old woman, who was a Hindu. He taught me how to become invisible—as you have seen—and other things.

"Many people think there is some line between the fundamental practices of Moslems, Hindus, and Tibetans. That is all trash. There is only one wisdom. It is most ancient and he who knows it, knows it whether he is Moslem, Sikh, Pathan, Mongolian, Japanese, or whatever. It depends on the unbroken line of gurus.

"Then came World War II. I had graduated and was serving under the British Surgeon General. My father's regiment was Gurkha—very ferocious—and he had me put into the medical corps of the Royal British Army proper, not the Indian regiments. The Queen's Own Regiment it was called."

He stopped to throw blankets over the two officers and to bring logs to the fire. Then he continued.

"One day an order came through for volunteers to report for paratroops. 'Ah ha,' I thought, 'at last my chance to get out of my body. Once and for all out of this nonsense.' Of course, I had been well trained by my gurus in all the proper ways to go out correctly when it happened so I thought this might be the answer. I kept the order in my hand and reported the next day.

"I went into training immediately, near Agra under General Wingate. We would go up in those noisy B-27s and our parachutes would be attached to a wire. You had to jump, Pushing hard with your left foot. Then just as you got past the tail, the parachute would open and you would float down, ever so nicely."

Indra smiled to himself. "Once mine opened only partially and then gave out at eighteen hundred feet. 'At last,' I thought, 'I'm on my way out,' and immediately went into the proper dhyan. But nothing happened. I hit the ground, sprang up, rolled over and over, and nothing happened. I was furious.

"One man under my command fell twenty-four thousand feet and lived. We found him in a village later, playing in the mud with the children. He'd 'crossed over' on the way down out of fear—he was already halfway out of his body when he hit. When he didn't go all the way, he stayed in like a child. He was exactly like a baby. They wanted to institutionalize him, but I said no, let me have him. I had learned acupuncture in Tibet. I wanted to try it on him. As long as the needles were in he came back to himself, to his correct age, when I took the needles out he went back to being a baby. Then I opened up his head and applied electrodes directly to the brain. Slowly, after several treatments, he recovered. Nice English boy he was. After that he returned to England. He never had gone beyond the Eighth Standard, but after that he went to college and is today an eminent professor of biology. All that knocking about made him smarter."

He smiled, glancing down at the policeman. "I forgot to treat his back. We must get his shirt off before the blood coagulates. Get some water and boil it and we'll wash and bandage him up."

The man attempted to move. Indra put his hand tenderly on his head and spoke in Hindi. The man groaned but remained still.

"Where was I?"

"Paratroopers."

"Ah, yes. After that training we were to drop into Burma. I requested leave and took my men into some jungle land on one of my father's estates in Terai. I taught them JuJitsu, Karate and Lathi fighting which I had learned from masters under my father's direction. Those English boys got a real taste of the jungle. Then

[140]

we were flown to Burma and we jumped. Jumped right into a swamp."

He laughed, looking at her, and then proceeded to dress the policeman's wounds.

"It was a vast swamp with massive trees—absolutely poisonous, septic. In the center of it was a low sort of mountain and in that mountain was a Japanese bunker, an underground fortress. We were supposed to take it. It took me fifteen days to collect my men in that swamp. We lived mostly in trees, built tree houses and so on. We couldn't see where the openings of the bunker were as the mountain was covered with undergrowth. One morning I decided to make a dummy out of bamboo and cane and grass. It took me all day. We put a helmet on it and in the dark I carried it out to where they would see it. They knew we were there. When morning came—rat tat tat tat—they emptied round after round into it. Then every day we made a dummy and every morning they used up more and more ammunition. And their supply line was cut off."

He cleared his throat, resting his hand on the dressed wound of the policeman. "Don't worry about these," he said, noticing Laura's concerned look. "They'll be gone by morning.

"After six weeks, our rations were finished. The men started eating snakes and frogs and big turtles!" He laughed.

"Did you eat?" she asked.

"I tried some," he answered, looking embarrassed. "Horrible!

"Then came successive days during which no shots were fired. I decided to go in. I was a crack shot . . . give me a pistol and I'll shoot the ash off a cigarette at fifty paces. Like to try it sometime?" He raised his eyebrows. "Lovely—you'd enjoy it.

"So I told the men I would take red and green flares. Green flares meant come, red flares meant don't come, no flare meant I'm finished, don't come." He chuckled. "I went in the night, got to one of the bunker holes and lay there looking in. It was easy for me, I'd spent half my life in jungles. There was a big five-gallon kerosene lamp. Sitting around it were emaciated-looking Japanese. Two others were sleeping and there were stinking unburied corpses near them. I went in and let the bayonet do its work. They were so starved they had no energy to resist. Then I let the green flare go. My English boys came fast. When they got there, they started hacking the dead bodies into pieces, then they hacked at the putrifying corpses . . ." He paused. "It was a really strange sight," he said. "I learned a lot of Western psychology during that war." He sighed deeply.

"After capturing the bunker we got out fast. There was a walled village nearby and we stayed there for a time. The people gave us plenty of good cow's milk, wheat, rice, plenty of vegetables.

[141]

"But I knew the Japanese would be after us. So I had the villagers make an escape tunnel about twenty yards long through a hill on one side of the village. One night about a month later Japanese machine guns started blazing in the night. I told the men not to respond—it was a trick to see whether we were there. Minutes passed and when there was no sound from them at all, I knew they wouldn't come in until morning. I collected about fifty or so villagers and all their cattle and made them go through the escape passage. Then I sent my men through and then blew the whole thing up with dynamite.

"The following morning we found ourselves surrounded. I told all my people to run, that I would cover their escape. I thought it might be my chance to get out again. They ran for it and got away. I got hit, but the bullet struck a black obsidian medal of Goddess Kali that my mother had given to me. It was about three inches across and was swinging on my chest. When the bullet hit, it dropped into my lap—huh!

"I got captured. The Japanese knew me. The officer saluted when he arrested me and they were very courteous and polite at the beginning. Then I was handed over to their secret police for examination and questioning. They stuck needles under my fingernails and electrodes on my genitals . . . My hair still stands up when I think about it. Somehow I went into dhyan and stopped the pain. They wanted Wingate's strategy for Burma, but I never talked. The English were my friends.

"The second night I escaped by killing three guards with a large kitchen knife. I beheaded them. I had to behead six more on the way out. Kali did it, I didn't—I hadn't the strength. After that, I walked to Gauharti and did puja to Kamakshi Devi. Then I walked to India. They decorated me and at last I went home to Patalia.

"I had wanted to become a monk at twelve, to leave this world. After these experiences I came back and took up medical practice again but it was useless. My mother then produced written instructions from my second guru, the old woman. In them she foretold exactly what would happen to me. In 1940, a year before her death, she wrote down everything—including that the medal of Kali would save me from a bullet. She also gave detailed instructions for the twenty-five years of austerities I was now to perform.

"So I said good-bye to my mother then and my father and brothers and sisters—little did I know they would be wiped out in the unrest of 1947. I was never to see them again except one brother who managed to hide himself when the local Moslems ransacked our family residence.

"It was a fine spring day, I remember it well. I had loaded all my worldly possessions—books, surgical equipment, everything—on twenty mules. Only my mother saw me off. My father thought I was mad. As an officer and a war hero, I had been offered a high rank, Lieutenant General, even a British passport if I'd wanted.

"I took one servant and walked with the mules east to the Ganges below Hardwar. There I burned the books and chucked all my possessions into the river, stripped naked, and swam the Ganges. I then walked to Nepal where I spent twenty some years living naked following her instructions."

He laughed softly, gazing down at the sleeping policemen. "You think this low trash means anything to me? I should kill and bury them right here and now, but it is too good for them; besides She has commanded me not to take action. I cannot even get out myself unless She commands it—makes it happen."

"You frighten me," Laura said quietly after a long silence. "You're so final, so pure. It makes me feel so polluted." She shuddered.

"Only *it* feels polluted," he murmured dispassionately, grasping his own flesh with his large hands. "*It* feels polluted, not you. You cannot be polluted. You are pristine, uncreated, stainless, indestructable. Sometimes if this is realized strongly enough, you can manifest your former body after you've left it."

Laura looked incredulous.

"You want to prove it?" he whispered, staring at her. "Get some dynamite. Get some dynamite and tie it onto my head thus." He demonstrated. "Then put a long fuse and light it. Ah, you are wondering. No, yes, is he serious? Just do it and see. Just light the fuse, a long fuse. Sit and watch. Boom! You will see an explosion. Then again you will see me. I will be here looking just the same, and speaking as I am now."

For a long time she sat looking at him helplessly, assailed by her own confusion.

"Try it," he said smiling. "Try it and see. All you need is some dynamite. It's easy to get. You won't know till you try it."

[143]

VIII

§

"I TRUST YOU GOT a good rest?" Stan said to Kamala as the rented car sped along a dusty road on its way to the ashram of Ananda Baba. "You look especially fresh and glowing."

"I feel marvelous, all ready to see His Holiness," she purred, adjusting her silk sari. "And you also are looking well."

"It is the healthful air of the Deccan, Madam." Saladin flashed a dazzling smile from his seat next to the driver.

Stan scrutinized the young man, wondering what his real connection with Kamala might be. "But really, there was no need for you to come," he said to Saladin, "I'm sure it must be a bore to you."

"On the contrary," said Saladin, "I too am a devotee of His Holiness. I take every opportunity to visit Baba and this is a great chance, especially with the high cost of car travel. I also promised Mr. Sundaram I would look after you. It would not be correct for me to let you go off alone."

"I'm sure things will go smoother with Saladin out front," said Kamala. "Sundar has such reliable people."

Just then there was a small explosion, like the report of a pistol.

The driver pulled the car to the side of the road, then confirmed that the tire was flat.

"Very sorry, sir." Saladin turned around. "Would you care to get out while the driver is making repairs. I have brought coffee in a thermos."

Stan and Kamala got out and Saladin unrolled a straw mat. They sat drinking coffee under one of the gnarled old trees lining the road.

"The last Maharaja's father planted these trees on every road in Mysore," he said proudly, "so that we could have shade and fruit."

"The food!" Kamala cried out suddenly, pointing to the car.

[144]

A monkey had jumped through the window of the car and was rummaging inside. Saladin yelled and drove her out, but she made off with the lunch basket, perched above them in the tree, and began eating.

"No matter," Saladin shrugged. "There is a good eating place in the next town, Madam."

Kamala glared at him.

"Yes, it is . . . well, not too clean," he admitted sheepishly. "But very good food. Delicious biryani."

"I don't eat mutton," she said disdainfully. "And neither should you when you are going to see His Holiness."

A number of people had by this time gathered to give advice to the driver and gape at Stan and Kamala.

"They think you are cinema stars," Saladin laughed.

They continued on after the tire was fixed. Toward noon the road became crowded with oxcarts, cyclists, pedestrians, and animals.

"Must he sound the horn continuously?" Stan covered his ears.

"Otherwise it is not possible to drive, sir," Saladin yelled over the noise. "How would the people know when to get out of the way?"

Nervous over the flat and anxious to make up for lost time, the driver sped along oblivious to the potholes in the road, darting out from behind bullock carts piled high with sugar cane and narrowly missing the oncoming traffic. Inevitably, at the outskirts of the next town, he hit something that scraped ominously along the underside of the car.

Stan looked out the rear window. "Something's leaking," he warned.

"Stop at once," Saladin shouted in Urdu. The driver jammed on the brakes and sent them flying forward.

The sun was high in the pale blue sky and heat waves shimmered over a parched landscape dotted with mud huts and palms. A terrible stench rose from the side of the road, where the sewage of the town was carried off in open ditches to a bog alive with pigs, buffaloes, and diseased-looking children. No one seemed to notice either the smell or the children. The passersby appeared locked in the oblivion of their own separate worlds.

Kamala turned to Stan. "In India nowadays everything is breaking down," she sighed. "No matter how much money one has, one sometimes gets stuck."

The Quality Hotel and Restaurant was not exactly Stan's idea of a place to lunch. Skinny half-starved young men in dirty drawers and aprons served the food. The floors had a patina of filth and flies descended in clouds over everything. They were given a cement cubicle with a bathroom on the second floor of the noisy building. Kamala fluttered like a butterfly in a den of cockroaches as she extracted cloths from her bag and spread them over the soiled mattresses of the beds.

"You see what we have come to?" She stretched out on one of the beds and batted at the flies. "Before we never had these problems. A hotel was a hotel, clean and pleasant, none of these people existed. Now the government robs the rich to make all of us poor. These low people are procreating like flies, running about everywhere in public buses, leaving their filth everywhere. As a woman I should be more charitable, but really, sometimes I think a gas chamber is the place for these Congress Party people—in fact, it is too good for them. If I were ruler, I would have them trampled to death by elephants for what they have done to India in only twenty-five years." She smiled. "But India will survive, it has survived everything else."

Saladin successfully bribed a local politician for the use of his car and driver, and after a lunch was brought which no one ate, they started out again.

Stan fell asleep. Some hours later Saladin woke him. They were approaching the ashram.

"But I see nothing," said Kamala, parting the curtains, "it looks like a desert."

"You will see, you will see." Saladin grinned. "It's just ahead."

The car rounded a corner and a hidden valley came into view between rolling hills covered with palms and other lush tropical foliage. Green paddies alternated with large tanks of lotus and fields of flowers. Thousands upon thousands of pale yellow and deep orange marigolds were blooming. Nestled against a cliff were a series of terraced gardens and white buildings, some, Saladin explained, cut out of the rock itself. The car stopped at a huge blue tiled gate where a guard stood, holding a walkie-talkie. "What is the name?"

"Saladin. His Holiness is expecting us. I am bringing Mr. Stanley and Miss Kamala."

"Mr. Stanley," said the guard into the walkie-talkie.

"Do they think we are going to assassinate him?" muttered Kamala irritably.

After they were cleared the guard opened the gate and they drove through groves of giant fan palms, rose gardens, and then past meadows where deer and llama grazed among peacocks and flamingos. Here and there long low structures were visible behind carefully tended shrubbery. A hospital, crematorium, and library were pointed out by Saladin.

Stan wondered grimly which he would visit first.

In the parking lot they were greeted by a young blue-eyed blonde in a long saffron robe.

"Will you step this way?" said the girl in a midwestern American accent. She sounded like a receptionist at some large corporation. "We would like you to sign the register and there are a few forms to fill out. Your luggage will go to your quarters. Of course, you understand that men and women stay separately here." She smiled at Kamala.

"I am familiar with the procedures of ashrams," Kamala replied good-naturedly.

"I believe His Holiness has arranged a separate cottage for you. For Mr. Stanley and Mr. Saladin, let me see." She thumbed through a small notebook. "You will have adjoining rooms at the hostel. It's very nice, you'll be comfortable. But you are late—we expected you hours ago."

"We had a breakdown," Saladin explained.

"Oh, too bad. Sorry to hear that. Anyhow, run along now and don't take too long unpacking and all that. Just take a bath and I'll pick you all up in half an hour. It's almost time for His Holiness to make his evening appearance. Then I believe the program is that he would like to see Miss Kamala this evening and Mr. Stanley tomorrow morning at five-thirty." She caught Saladin's eye. "And of course Mr. Saladin too. Okay?" she said cheerily to Stan.

Stan nodded. "Okay."

§

The broad terrace jutting out over the valley was filled with people. At one end were the quarters of His Holiness, designed it was said by a famous French architect who had been an early devotee. Here His Holiness lived with the chosen few of his inner circle. There were pools under marble porches, raised gardens and sunken ones, water everywhere splashing in stone conduits and disappearing only to reappear in fountains on lower terraces.

"Have you seen Fatephur Sikri?" whispered Saladin to Kamala as they stood waiting for Stan.

"Yes."

"It is like that place, is it not?" His eyes glittered. "It is too wonderful. A real palace. Is it not truly magic how the Baba gets all the money to do these things? Yes? They say foreigners come every day, showering him with it."

They were joined by Stan and the prim American girl whose

[147]

name turned out to be Jai Devi. "It's almost time," she said. "See, they've lit the fires."

On the highest terrace of polished white marble there were four fires lit at the four compass points. Seated before them were naked yogis chanting and throwing offerings into the fire. A fifth fire burned in the center of the terrace on a raised square. Huge logs sent yellow and gold flames high into the sky and another yogi attended the fire there, throwing herbs and incense into it. All five men chanted in unison. Among the select group permitted on this the highest of terraces, many were on their knees or flat on their stomachs, hands outstretched toward a single doorway in the massive windowless marble wall. It was through this door that His Holiness would come.

Just as the sun touched the horizon, the yogi at the central fire blew a series of high-pitched blasts on a long silver trumpet. An expectant hush fell over the crowd. Then His Holiness appeared, a large figure in a calf-length cloth of shimmering scarlet silk, his hair frizzed out and falling to his waist. He wore wooden sandals elevated at the toe and heel with five-inch pieces of wood. His face was inscrutable, dark and intense, his form androgynous. All eyes were on him as he glided across the polished marble, holding his right hand palm outward in the gesture of blessing.

"See the milk coming from his hand?" Saladin whispered. A trickle of white liquid seemed to be spouting out of the palm. "Try to catch some and drink it, but be careful—here he comes."

As His Holiness approached, Stan's mind flashed to San Francisco; he had the strange impression that he was watching a female impersonator in one of the drag joints on Turk Street. He dove under the dripping hand and landed on the floor. Both Saladin and Kamala knelt with outstretched hands. His Holiness moved on, then as if picking up a vibration stopped and retraced his steps to Kamala.

"Rise, daughter," he said in Hindi, extracting from his mouth an enormous gold locket and chain which he dropped in her open hands.

Saladin gasped.

His Holiness moved on past the select group to the edge of the terrace to give benediction to the masses below. Then he retired to the central fire where he flung off his cloak and seated himself, naked except for a scarlet loincloth, upon a slab of basalt facing the fire.

Various groups of devotees now vied for the honor of singing to him. Strange wind instruments pierced the night air as drums beat out the message of the Divine Spirit. A famous film star,

[148]

accompanied by her own musicians, swayed and chirped in the high-pitched style of the Hindi Talkie.

Stan was thinking that someone could make a fortune booking this at the Paris Opera, or why not the Coliseum in Rome for a few weeks?

After the music, an Indian in white with a Western girl also in white knelt in front of His Holiness and presented him with fruits and flowers. The girl then lit a series of camphor lamps which the man waved in His Holiness's face while bells rang and echoed through the valley.

"This is the puja," whispered Jai Devi, who had come up behind Stan. "It is the greatest honor to be allowed to do puja to His Holiness."

Stan wondered if the Baba cured him whether he would have to stay here all his life waving lights. He decided he could think of worse places. But what would he do for sex? Everything seemed so pure—at least on the surface. Did he want to be pure? "Really, when it comes right down to it," he thought, "I suppose I dig my own hang-ups." He watched the mountain of dark flesh that was His Holiness glowing in the firelight. And what went on behind the scenes?

There followed a ceremony at which all those of the inner circle were allowed to kneel or prostrate before His Holiness, to receive on their foreheads marks of holy ash from his sacred fire. To the hundreds on the lower terrace able to watch but not participate in these sacred rites, subordinate ashramites distributed ash in small packets, like sugar, printed with a colored photo of His Holiness and the words ANANDA BABA LOVES YOU embossed in gold.

When His Holiness had finished the blessings, he was dressed in his scarlet cloak and sandals, the silver trumpet sounded again, and he floated back to the small door.

Jai Devi sidled up to Kamala. "If you are ready, you can follow me and go in," she said, sounding now like an airline hostess. "His Holiness is expecting you to dine with him."

"I shall have to return to my cottage first," said Kamala. "I have something for Baba and I would like to change." She smiled a haughty smile. "Is that all right?"

"Yes, of course, I will come with you," said Jai Devi.

"But what will Mr. Stanley and Mr. Saladin do?" asked Kamala.

"We have three canteens: one for invited guests like yourselves, one for devotees on pilgrimage, and one for the general sightseeing public."

"I think I'll just go to my room," yawned Stan, "if I'm to get up before dawn. I'm lost though—this place is so . . ."

"I will show you the way, Mr. Stanley," said Saladin. "I too am tired. But not too tired to eat," he added, flashing his teeth. "Will you not have something at the canteen first?"

§

Jai Devi paced the small drawing room of the cottage while Kamala bathed, oiled herself, combed her hair, and dressed. She had thought of asking the American girl to help her, but she suspected that although she looked it, she might not be of the servant class. In fact, Jai Devi was from a rich family out of Des Moines, Iowa, who had visited Ananda Baba in the 1960's before he was too well-known and had decided that he was God. It was Iowa corn that had paid for the magnificent setting erected in darkest India.

"We should really be moving along, you know," Jai Devi said to Kamala as she was putting on her eye make-up.

Of course Jai Devi wore no make-up but then, as Kamala sensed, they were on different paths. Kamala at last entered the room swathed in a scarlet sari embroidered with small emeralds, topazes, and cats' eyes. On her bare feet toe rings sparkled, gold jangled on her wrists, and her neck, ears and nose were afire with diamonds and rubies of incalculable value. It was evident that the girl was taken aback by her appearance.

Jai Devi conducted an amused Kamala through the maze of paths and gardens and a mirrored tunnel that led to the private entrance of the Baba's quarters. At a small gate she stopped and turned around. "We disciples must stick to our rigorous routine. I only see Him when my parents come." She smiled, robotlike, then looked somewhat sad. "He will conduct you to Baba." She pointed to a white clad young Indian just inside.

Beyond the gate there were more terraces surrounding a central courtyard where a baby elephant swayed from side to side, munching at a large pile of the tenderest palm shoots. The young man conducted her to an open terrace on the rooftop of a low building overlooking the courtyard.

Here Ananda Baba was reclining on bright orange silk cushions, while a young boy kneaded the muscles of his outstretched legs. An extremely handsome middle-aged man sat to his left. Torches burned. Puffs of amber cloud hung limpid in the night sky.

Kamala prostrated herself, careful to reveal the sumptuous curves of her buttocks as she went down. Slowly she inched her hands forward, to place an offering under the Baba's right knee. His

[150]

strong hand came down on her forehead leaving the ash mark and signaling her to rise.

"It was so hot today," he said lazily, gazing at her, "we thought it would be best to dine outside.... Here there's a breeze."

A second boy waved a large peacock feather fan. The Baba was appraising her. "It is very nice," he said after a pause. "Nice of you to come see us at last ... we have been expecting you for a long time now."

"He has the power to melt you," thought Kamala, lowering her eyes and sitting in perfect lotus position. "You are too kind, Baba," she answered.

"It is a most auspicious moment," he said thoughtfully. "The meeting of two souls like ours."

"We have many friends in common," she said, smiling.

"Yes, and may I present Major General Chatterji, retired. We call him Baji for short." He indicated the man on his left, who bowed.

"Will you smoke with us?" asked the Baba, withdrawing a small ivory chillum from a bag. Kamala nodded, still smiling.

The chillum was lit by one of the boys, who brought a glowing coal from a fire in an ornate box. Ananda Baba drew in deep draughts of the smoke, then passed the pipe to Baji, who was bare-chested, dark, and muscular. He wore a white dhoti of sheerest cotton bordered in gold, with gold jewelry and a gold earring.

"Did you know, Baji, that next to our illustrious Prime Minister this creature is perhaps the best-known woman in India? At least the most desired," the Baba whispered loudly.

The pipe was passed to Kamala. The Baba noted her skill in handling it. "You have sat with sadhus then," he said.

"Often," she replied, "at Kamaksha, Nepal, Varanasi—so many places."

"We have to be so careful these days with this," he nodded at the pipe as he took it from her hand. "The Westerners have gone crazy and spoiled everything. We do not smoke with them. We only smoke with our friends."

The General undressed Kamala with his eyes. He was reported to be one of India's great lovers and, if not one of its most illustrious generals, certainly its richest.

"How fortunate, General, that our stars have crossed here on this beautiful night," sighed Kamala. "I came here quite by accident, a friend—"

"You mean by design," interrupted the Baba, and launched into a discourse geared to impress the rather humdrum mind of the General that there was a divine plan already laid out and

[151]

decipherable only by the Baba. "That is the meaning of Karma," he said, then motioned to a servant who brought an oblong drum called a dholac and placed it on the General's lap.

"Baji is an excellent drummer, good rhythm." The Baba bent toward Kamala. "Sometimes I sit for hours just listening to my Baji play." He arched his eyebrows.

With an air of self-importance, the General hit the drum several times, upended it, tuned it and tightened the skin. Then he began to play, and then to sing softly.

Baba stretched, moving his pelvis like a woman, and lay back on his pillows. His dark skin glowed with a pale purple aura that contrasted with his bright teeth and glittering eyes. The General had been switched onto automatic. Now he could relax and drink in the woman before him—so voluptuous, so sensual, the very essence of desire. He would enjoy her, that was certain. Perhaps he would even suck out her energy: he knew the ways and had the physical prowess. He wondered if she knew the secret tricks of yogis. Ah, what delight . . . but also what a formidable partner.

"Alas, tonight must be short," said the Baba, after the plates of fruit and nuts and glasses of almond milk had been cleared away. "I am to see your friend tomorrow, am I not?" he said, staring at Kamala intently.

"Really, he is Sundar's friend."

"Sundar? Ah yes, but of course."

"He could not leave Delhi," said Kamala. "But he sends you his pranams, nonetheless. Mr. Stanley is Sundar's friend from school days. Some Western doctors have told him he has lung cancer."

"I have so many of these," said the Baba, turning lazily onto his stomach so that the boy could rub his back. "It has become a problem for me. What I have to find out first is whether a man or a woman is willing to change, bend—something like that." He sighed. "Otherwise, they can't get healed. I must find out what they are attached to and pry it loose, take it from them, then the disease comes off too. With the Americans, it is usually the money thing. They are most touchy about it."

"But don't we all need money, Baba," said the General, who was obviously sensitive on the subject too.

"I have no money," replied the Baba wearily. "What I get goes out, gets spent. I hardly eat. All this show is my illusion." He gestured out at the valley. "I am prepared to leave it tomorrow. Will you come with me?" he whispered suddenly to Kamala, then laughed. "Money must be kept moving, that way there is always more. But then she knows that." He eyed the General. "Don't you, Kamala?"

She nodded.

The handsome General was trying to think of a way to get Kamala alone. He had heard tales about her and wanted to find out if they were true, even at the risk of getting involved. He had heard it could be dangerous, but this excited him.

"You have a room in the hostel?" he asked politely.

"No, Baji, she has a cottage," the Baba answered, blocking the General's move.

"I am tired now," said Kamala, bending to touch the Baba's feet. "I must retire."

"Yes, by all means, I will see you to your cottage," said the excited General.

"Sit down, Baji," the Baba said, as if to a pet dog. "She is not a child, after all, she will find her way. Good night, beautiful lady." He held out his hand for her to kiss. "And how do you like the slave I have given you?"

"Slave?" asked Kamala.

"Jai Devi." He smiled. "Do you not think it is interesting that we have rich American slaves these days? Very interesting phenomenon, I think."

§

The following morning Stan woke up to music echoing through the valley. "If you call it music," he thought, listening to the strident sound of a woman repeating the same phrase over and over again like a broken record. He decided it was a bad dream and buried his face in the pillow.

Then he heard Saladin's voice too. He came out from under the covers. Saladin was in shorts, his hair tousled, looking very handsome and holding out a cup of tea.

"What is the awful racket?" Stan asked.

"Oh, that is the thousand names of the Goddess. It is always sung by Hindus at sunrise." Saladin disappeared into the bathroom. Stan heard the shower going. He got up and went in. "Your turn," said Saladin, "better you should hurry. Baba will not like it if we are late, it is four-thirty already. And watch out, the water is too cold."

"What, no hot water?" yowled Stan.

[153]

"Not here." Saladin laughed and pushed Stan in. "His Holiness does not approve of it."

Thoroughly chilled, Stan emerged wrapped in a towel to find Saladin holding a long piece of white cotton yardage. "A dhoti," he explained. "It's just as well you learn to wear it now. His Holiness doesn't like people to wear pants when they visit him."

Reaching under Stan's arms and around his waist, Saladin showed him how to fold and tie the dhoti. "There," he said, "you look like one of our Brahmins, I think, eh?" Saladin stood back, putting on a dhoti of his own.

"Now what?" said Stan. "Do I wear a shirt or . . ."

"You will wear only a shawl. I have bought one for you," said Saladin, producing a magenta cashmere shawl. "Let me see . . . Yes, you are ready now. Do you have an offering for His Holiness?"

"Yes, I have." Stan rummaged in his bag and found an IBM pocket calculator. "Don't you think he could use this?"

"What is it?" Saladin seemed unimpressed.

"An electronic calculator—addition, subtraction, and so on."

"How much did it cost?"

"About four hundred dollars."

"But you must also give him something to calculate."

"Oh."

"Yes, yes, you must," said Saladin. "Give, that you may receive."

"How much?"

"Say about ten thousand dollars," answered Saladin unblinking.

"Say that again?"

"Ten thousand dollars," Saladin repeated.

"I see," said Stan. "But isn't that a bit high?"

"Do as you like then," said Saladin, feigning disgust. "You get what you pay for."

Saladin's behavior made Stan very nervous. "Yes, of course, let me see." He rummaged in his bag again and withdrew his travelers checks. "How do I make them out?"

"Just sign them and leave them blank . . . then slip them under his knee when you greet him." He wondered whether His Holiness would appreciate what he, Saladin, a Moslem, was doing for him. He would have to find some way to let him know. He turned to Stan who was nervously adjusting his dhoti.

"I keep having the feeling it's going to fall off," Stan said.

"Don't worry, come, it's almost five-thirty."

They stepped out into the clear Indian morning and walked through the cool shadows of the park. Peacocks screamed and mynah birds whistled in the thickets as they neared the entrance to the Baba's compound. Once inside they passed through a dense grove of yellow bamboo beneath which bloomed hybrid hibiscus, the sensuous flower of the Gods, in dazzling combinations of colors. Soon they reached a lawn that sloped to a small lake, where they saw the Baba playing with his baby elephant.

Saladin approached and fell flat on his stomach, reaching for the Baba's feet. Gracefully the Baba, naked except for a large crimson hibiscus tucked into his hair, bent down and touched Saladin's forehead.

Then it was Stan's turn. Was he expected to go down in the dirt too, he wondered. His mind went to the elephant and elephant shit and that he had just had a bath. "Never mind," he said to himself, "just do it."

He fell down, fumbling with the checks which he managed to shove under one of the Baba's enormous toes. It seemed an eternity that he lay there, waiting for that press of the thumb on his forehead. The wide legs and thighs of the Baba flashed before him. Then the trunk of the elephant swayed back and forth and touched Stan's forehead lightly with its pink tip.

"I am teaching him to put the ash on the foreheads," the Baba chuckled. "Do you not think that amusing, Mr. Stanley?"

Stan stood up. The Baba squatted in the grass country style, his knees bent up, legs spread wide. Although his body was large it was solid and full of juice, Stan thought.

"Sit down Mr. Stanley, and you Saladin."

"I should go see to Miss Kamala's needs, sir," Saladin said.

But the Baba motioned for him to sit, a great honor for Saladin.

"Just watch the trunk swaying and swinging, Mr. Stanley," he said. "Is it not beautiful . . . like a great pendulum? Tell me, can I do something for you?" He smiled.

"I have the feeling you could do anything you wanted," Stan replied.

"And what would you say if I told you I could not, Mr. Stanley?"

"I wouldn't believe you," Stan said.

"Ah, you would be quite right, but would you go away if I told you to?" The Baba fastened his eyes on him, frighteningly dead eyes.

"Yes . . . I would."

"And stay away?"

"Yes."

Slowly the Baba extended both arms, palms forward. Before

Stan's eyes milk or something that looked like milk began to bubble up out of the centers of his palms and drip down.

"Incredible!" whispered Stan.

Saladin moaned and fell flat again on the ground. He crawled on his belly, hands outstretched to receive the milk, which he smeared on his face.

Then the Baba's neck tightened, his mouth opened, and a black stone came out of it.

"This is impossible," Stan thought. "A man delivering himself of a stone through his mouth like a chicken laying an egg!" The stone, a black cylinder about two inches wide and nine inches long, rounded at both ends, fell out onto the grass.

"Take it, Mr. Stanley," said the Baba's voice hoarsely, "it's yours."

Stan took the stone; it was warm and slippery.

Saladin's jaw dropped. He had heard that Baba produced these lingam stones out of his mouth from time to time. He had never believed it, but here was the proof. They were extremely valuable too, worth far more than ten thousand dollars. Mr. Stanley has made money on this one, he thought sourly.

"Will you have the time to spend here with me?" the Baba asked Stan softly.

"Yes." Stan's reply was serious.

For a long time the Baba seemed to look through him as if making a decision. "Very well then, you may leave now. I will see you tomorrow sometime."

Saladin stepped forward and knelt. The baby elephant dipped its trunk delicately into a brass container filled with red powder and then touched the tip to Saladin's forehead. Stan followed, clutching the stone and hoping his dhoti would stay on.

Both men were unnerved when they reached the small gate through which they had entered.

"Fantastic," Stan was saying under his breath, "really fantastic. Someone should book that act . . . to see that stone coming out."

"What?" said Saladin.

"Incredible to see this coming out," Stan said, fumbling in his shawl for the stone. "But where is it?"

"What?" Saladin cried.

"The stone—it's not here."

"You . . . you didn't lose it?"

"Why no . . . no . . . I—don't know, I—I must have left it on the grass. Maybe the elephant took it. . . . I'll go back and have a look."

Saladin was disgusted. What a commission he could have got if Mr. Stanley had decided to sell it.

Stan returned panting.

"He's gone—the Baba, the elephant ... Nothing—no stone, nothing!"

"Ha!" Saladin thought. "Baba is playing tricks. He got it back."

Outside, the park was bustling with devotees. They met Jai Devi who stopped.

"I'll be seeing you in about twenty minutes. I'm supposed to start some breathing exercises with you, Mr. Stanley. We'll be doing them for about two weeks," she said smiling. "And Mr. Saladin, please arrange to have a massage table from the dispensary. Mr. Stanley is to have massage, with hot and cold baths. You will assist."

Saladin nodded, eyeing her. Could he seduce this blonde, blue-eyed devotee and how long would it take? At least she might be able to have sweaters and other luxury import items sent to him if it worked out.

"I will have everything ready," he assured her.

§

Kamala was just stepping out of the bathroom. She too had been awakened at an early hour—by Jai Devi who brought bed tea and gave her a few pompous tips on breathing and exercise. "She imagines she can teach me breathing," Kamala thought. "She should live my life—then she would know something about breathing!"

But in a way the girl amused her. She had sipped her tea and tried to act good-natured, though it was certainly not her habit to see any but servants before lunch. How she missed Hassan. She wondered if she stayed on whether she'd be allowed to send for him.

Then Jai Devi left and she had decided to shower. As she was drying herself dreamily in front of a mirror, there was a knock on the door.

"It is General Chatterji—Baji. May I come in for a moment?"

Kamala put down the towel and threw on a filmy sari.

"I'm dressing, General," she called, letting her breasts and one thigh appear around the door.

"I have a message from Baba," said the General, coming in. "He would like to see you as soon as ..." He stared at her body open-mouthed.

"Oh, yes?" said Kamala, fidgeting with her sari. "Then I had better put on some clothes, hadn't I? Please sit down."

[157]

She retreated into the bathroom but made sure the General could watch as she combed out her hair. She made sure he saw the rise and fall of her breasts, a bare expanse of thigh as she slipped into her sari and drew it tightly across her buttocks. She even bent over and pretended to examine her toe rings so that he could have a really good look.

She emerged minutes later the essence of purity: white sari, white hibiscus in her hair, white cotton shawl. "Shall we go then, General?" she cooed.

Kamala could feel that he wanted to grab her. But then she thought how much more interesting the Baba would be, with all that solid flesh, the throbbing energy under the skin, his pectoral muscles nearly as big as her breasts. And she had heard he had a gigantic penis, almost like a stallion, and that he could do many unusual things. It would be better then not to seduce this General unless the Baba willed it—better to direct her energy toward His Holiness. Which was an exciting prospect: although she had been tempted many times, she had never yet made love with a holy man.

The General conducted her through the park to His Holiness's private quarters, where she found him seated in the shady corner of an open veranda, cheerful with songbirds and the faint sound of splashing water. A boy in a red-edged white dhoti and a dark red turban with a pink plume held a purple silk umbrella over him, while another fanned and a third massaged whatever part of the Baba's flesh was available to him from moment to moment.

The sight of his huge body and dark face set off by the glowing colored silks was enough to bring even Kamala up short. "How powerful!" she thought. "But we shall see—Kamala is afraid of no one."

"And so, you had a peaceful night?" he asked, as she prostrated before him.

"Yes, Maharaj," she murmured.

"And Jai Devi?"

"She brought me tea and demonstrated some . . . exercises she thought I might need." Kamala smiled faintly.

"It is important to give these people duties to make them feel they are doing something constructive—they think there is something to learn," he said, laughing uproariously.

The General was just seating himself. "You may leave now, Baji," the Baba added, still laughing. "I must speak with Miss Kamala alone for a while." A disgruntled Baji left the room.

"All must serve, even Generals. That is the price of living with me," sighed the Baba, rolling onto one side. "And who is this dreadful American," he said, suddenly getting to the point, "that I am supposed to heal him?"

[158]

"He was a classmate of A. K. Sundaram's abroad," Kamala answered, "and once a U.S. presidential appointee. He is very bright. A self-made millionaire from some pharamaceutical enterprises he owns. We believe he is the head of a group that has a new secret drug and that his associates are distributing it in India. He may not even have cancer—we do not know."

"What is the drug?"

"It makes you very suggestive, produces visions and hallucinations—they say it is used for brainwashing. His associate gave some to Sundar and Sundar has given some to me for you to try." She handed him a small envelope.

"Such tiny pills, and so many." He looked at her. "You have taken this?" Kamala shook her head. "Then we shall take them together, you and I alone. . . . Let us see what tricks this foreigner brings, yes?"

She nodded.

"Ah, and now this Mr. Stanley wants me to save him so he can continue to enjoy his millions." The Baba narrowed his eyes. "And I suspect he's a pederast too—highly oversexed."

"Not quite," said Kamala smiling. "He enjoys both sexes."

"A Moslem then," the Baba snorted. "He's just given me ten thousand dollars." He withdrew the checks from a bag and thrust them in Kamala's direction. "Shall I keep them, or would you like them?"

She played for higher stakes.

"No, no, dear Baba . . . I couldn't take them. If I did I would probably throw them into a fire."

"That would be wasteful," he said, smiling gently. "Someone will take the burden of them before the day is over, you will see. Not all are as wise as you, dear lady. But the question is—should I demand more from him?"

"Perhaps you could let time decide that," Kamala suggested. "Keep him here for a while and see whether he really has cancer."

"That is exactly what I had planned," answered the Baba. "I will test him. First, he seems to be constantly breaking wind and must be full of poisons. So I have decided that your Saladin will give him a purge, along with hot and cold baths and vigorous massage. Then he will have to go to the kitchen. He needs kitchen work, although nothing near food. He can scrub floors, clean the burned pots, and so on."

"But will he?"

"We will see how frightened he is of dying and if he is indeed a dying man we will find out! Meanwhile, Saladin must make his life as interesting as possible during the evenings and so on."

He handed her a small packet. "This is the medicine for the

[159]

purge. Have Saladin put half in a glass of tea today and give the other half in twenty-four hours."

Kamala was sitting with one knee up and had slowly let her sari part in such a way that only the Baba could see she wore nothing beneath it.

"Can you stay here with me for some weeks?" he inquired, looking down inside the sari between her open legs.

"I have no other plans at the moment," she answered.

"Good." He gazed at her. "Then return to me this evening after the public audience. You can find your way here yourself? Meanwhile, be sure to deliver the small package for the purge to Saladin. I will see Mr. Stanley after a week. By then, I hope he will have stopped breaking wind."

§

Loud cries of protest echoed through the hostel corridor as Kamala arrived at Stan's room. Several young boys were bringing buckets of hot water. She entered behind them to find Stan laid out on a table. Jai Devi was massaging him like a white demoness, pounding her fists into his flesh.

"She is strong, eh?" Kamala whispered to Saladin, signaling him to step into the next room with her. "I have just come from the Baba. He gave me this packet—it's for a purge. You are to give him half in some tea now, and the other half in twenty-four hours. Mr. Stanley will be very sick for one week, but the Baba asks you to see that he has an interesting time." Saladin looked puzzled. "Those are the instuctions," she whispered, "now I must go."

Saladin prepared some tea on a hot plate. In the next room Stan pelted Jai Devi with verbal abuse as she massaged him.

"Come on, baby," he yelled, "ah ... oh, this pounding, let's fuck ... ah, oh, no no ... Love to eat that healthy American pussy. Ah, no ... no, don't ... too hot ... water too ... ouch!"

Actually, Stan was having a terrific time. The pounding from the attractive young blonde and the alternating hot and cold baths stimulated him, made him want to yell. Yet although he was only pretending to be crazy, he wondered from moment to moment whether this might be the real beginning, whether he might not, after all, go mad. There was a lot of real craziness inside him. Insanity, he thought shuddering, dying of cancer ... if he had any sense he'd be in the Sloan-Kettering Institute. But something kept saying that would finish him and here he might have a chance. He was crazy, he decided, no doubt about it.

[160]

When Saladin came back into the room he noticed Stan's penis was erect beneath the sheet and that Jai Devi was pretending not to notice it.

"You can have a rest now," he said to her. "Sahib," he said to Stan, helping him to sit up, "have some tea, special ginger tea from His Holiness."

Stan sat up and gulped down the tea.

"You rest now," Saladin said, in a tone like a prison warden. "Jai Devi and I will just go into the next room for a while. Then there will be more exercises and baths."

"What a terrible man he is," Jai Devi whispered furiously to Saladin once they were alone in the next room. "Just terrible . . . Did you hear the dreadful things he was saying to me? And did you see that his his *thing* was sticking up?" She glanced at Saladin and then sat stiffly in a chair.

"The things I go through for His Holiness." She sighed. "I suppose it's good for me, but him . . ." She nodded toward the closed door with her big eyes. "Why he's almost a sex maniac."

"Yes, it is quite true what you say, Miss Devi," said Saladin softly. He sat down opposite her on the bed. "But it's a problem for all men."

"What's a problem?"

"The penis, the man's penis." He fastened his eyes on her. "It is the abode of the Devil, that is what we call it. . . is it not true?"

She nodded timidly.

"Yes, it is so. Take me for example," he whispered confidentially. "I have done everything to chase the Devil out of mine—prayers, diet, exercises, even cold baths. But still he is in there. It is a hard burden for us men to bear, this muscle of the Devil. It is a strange muscle you know, not like any other."

"Oh?"

"See," said Saladin, "I will show you." He stood up and whipped out his large brown penis.

Jai Devi jerked back in fright.

"Don't be afraid," he said smiling. "I hate it. It was getting me in so much trouble, I'll tell you. . . . But no more." He struck his penis briskly. "Now I am controlling it with yoga."

She looked up at him nervously.

"See," he went on, digging in his pants and extracting his testicles, "the muscle that controls it all is down here." He lifted his testicles up and pointed to a spot just behind them. "Here," he said, taking her limp hand, "put your finger there . . . don't be afraid . . . yes, there, yes." He twitched a muscle. "Can you feel it? Yes? Ah!" He withdrew her hand. "You felt it? That *is* the home of

[161]

the Devil; when he begins to twitch it is hard to stop him, I'll tell you."

"Mr. Saladin," warned Jai Devi, "I think it's getting bigger."

"When it gets big, that means the Devil is taking over."

He moved closer to where she was sitting. "I will do some yogic breathing and muscle exercises and it will go down." He sucked in his stomach muscles and pretended to do complicated breath control, while letting his erection come on. He could see she was hypnotized watching it.

"It's getting so big," she whispered, "I've never seen one that big before."

"Then you have seen others before this?"

"My brothers, mostly." She laughed nervously. "I mean, well, Mr. Saladin—it's too embarrassing, I . . . ." She was beet-red by now.

"Take it," Saladin said.

"What?" She almost fell off the chair.

"Take it. Take hold of it with your hand. You will feel how hot it gets. I am letting the Devil come out, the yoga didn't work. Sometimes it happens that way. So I will let him come out just for your sake, so you can see what happens."

Saladin closed his sphincter muscle, causing his erection to stand up straight. "Terrible, isn't it?" he said, looking down at himself and then at Jai Devi. "Take hold of him, feel how hot he is."

Jai Devi locked her hard hand around Saladin's penis.

"Not quite so hard, he will get worse if you hold him too tight. Now see, hold him up a bit more, hold up the testicles and look underneath," said Saladin. He knew that by this time Stan must be watching through the keyhole. He had positioned himself so that anyone looking through it would have a good view. After all, had not His Holiness commanded him to make Stan's stay interesting?

He contracted his sphincter muscle. "Don't you see it? Can't you feel it?"

"Yes," Jai Devi said frantically, "it's jumping like everything. Oh, Mr. Saladin, I think you'd better put it away. It scares me."

"Put it back then, if you like. Just take him and stuff him back in my pants."

She took hold of his penis and tried stuffing it back into his pants but each time she had it in it would pop out.

"I'm afraid it has become so large, Mr. Saladin, it just won't go in." She giggled apprehensively, almost at the breaking point.

"Then," Saladin turned around, "there is a knife in my back pocket, take it out. That's right, take it out and hand it to me."

He opened it and returned it to her. "Now cut him off."

"What?" cried Jai Devi.

"Cut him off!"

"But Mr. Saladin!" she wailed.

"There is no other way, Miss Devi, can't you see? I have tried everything. I have come to the end of the rope. Still the Devil, he is there inside!"

"But I can't!" Jai Devi pleaded. "It's living!" She burst into tears. "How can I cut a living thing?"

"But it's destroying my life, Miss Devi. The Devil is in it. You *must*!"

Jai Devi reached out hesitantly.

"That's it, hold it in one hand then . . . here." He took her left hand and placed it on his stone-hard erection. "Now with your other, whack it off."

Jai Devi began sobbing again. "But Mr. Saladin, I can't—oh, please don't make me."

"Then suck," said Saladin abruptly.

"What?"

"Suck him," he repeated. "The only other way to get him out is to suck him out." He guided the tip into her open mouth before she could speak.

Suddenly there was a falling sound on the other side of the door.

Jai Devi jumped up, wiping her mouth with her hand. Saladin, taking his time, replaced his penis and zipped up his pants. Then he yanked open the door.

"Oh, ah," groaned Stan, who lay in a heap on the floor. "Ah . . . ugh."

"Just what are you up to?" Saladin demanded.

"I think I'm going to be sick," Stan said.

"Mr. Stanley, please go back and lie down like a good boy," said Jai Devi firmly. "You need more rest, you'll feel better after—"

A loud flatulent sound pierced the air. Suddenly the room reeked.

"Mr. Stanley!" said Jai Devi, scandalized. "*What* is happening?"

"I don't know!" screamed Stan. "Can't you see I'm sick?"

"I think he's going to be sick," said Saladin. "Let me handle him, Miss Devi."

"But really, I—"

A fart exploded again and Stan began to vomit. Saladin pushed Jai Devi to the door.

"Poor Mr. Stanley." She looked back over her shoulder. "Should I inform His Holiness?"

"Yes, you may do that," said Saladin, shoving her outside. "Go and tell him what is happening if you like." He took her hand and rubbed it on his crotch. "The Devil will wait for you."

"Oh, goddamn," wailed Stan from inside.

"I will go then," said Jai Devi breathlessly, "and report back."

"Be certain you do that."

"Goddamn, I feel so ... ugh ... ah ... oh my God. Saladin, Saladin, what is happening? My God, what ... Saladin!" Stan looked up through bloodshot eyes. "Please, get me to the bathroom—I think I'm going to die!"

§

When the evening had turned into night and she was certain he would be alone, a carefully bathed and powdered Kamala threw on a sari and unobserved made her way across the park to the quarters of the Baba. She found him sitting by himself in the dark.

"I have dismissed the others," he said. "Come, we will go inside, it is more private." In one quick movement he lifted the great hulk of his body off the tiled floor. Then he took her hand and led her into a dark windowless room, painted red.

The room was small, about twelve by twelve feet. In the center a fire smoldered in a pit, the smoke curling up through a hole in the ceiling. On one side, oil lamps flickered in front of an ancient statue of a yogi sitting in meditation, his lingam erect.

"It is the Lord Shiva," the Baba said. "A rare example—very old, very rare. Most like this have been destroyed." He eased himself onto some cushions near the fire.

Kamala stood in front of him and for a long time he gazed at her through half-closed eyes. "Such beauty should not remain covered," he said at last. "I think you must remove your sari, eh?"

Kamala let her sari fall from her breasts and unwind itself about her.

"Now come here." He lay back on the cushions, extending his left leg. "Let us see how good you are."

Kamala knelt before him and massaged his foot, marveling at its enormous size.

"I have the chemical the American gave you," he said, producing a silver box full of the small yellow tablets. "How many do you think we should take?"

"They say one is enough," she murmured, moving her hand up

to his large calf muscle. "But perhaps two would be better just to be sure."

"Then here," he said, "put out your tongue, let us see what this Western magic is all about. Ah, that is good. Now I shall take." He popped two pills into his mouth, staring at her full breasts bouncing between her arms as she massaged his thigh. "If it works out, I will show you maithuna tonight . . . you know maithuna?"

"I know of it, but have not practiced it, Maharaj." Kamala smiled. Maithuna, a type of yoga using sexual intercourse, was something she had always wanted to learn.

"You do not know until you have practiced," he said. "It is a very complicated ritual to raise the shakti and should be performed with many offerings and mantras. If we should do it we will do the form of it, just the thing itself. I want to train you in that first, eh? The full thing we will do another time. I will have you perform it with the General later perhaps, eh? It would be a great help to me in . . . uh . . . keeping him on the path. He is very much in his body. Do you know the prana, the breathing?"

She nodded.

"And perhaps you then know the bhands, the locks, eh? And the Shiva mantra?"

She nodded again.

"Very good," he chuckled, extending his right leg so that she could massage it. "You must repeat the Shiva mantra mentally, continuously closing the locks on the inhale of the prana, and on the exhale, slowly opening them. When the exhale is complete, close out all the locks and inhale, holding your breath for fifteen seconds. Do you understand?"

"It is not quite clear," Kamala said.

"Like this." He squatted, sucked in his huge diaphragm and then breathing in and out, expanded and contracted his stomach muscles, holding his breath and locking his chin to his chest. "The sphincter you cannot see but it is opening and closing along with the stomach and neck."

He let himself fall back on to the cushions. "When the time is right," he said, "if the shakti comes, I will show you." He thought about telling her of the orgasm part but decided against it. "If she has orgasm so much the better for me," he thought. "Later I will show her there is another way. For the moment, I'll get the benefit."

She massaged his broad shoulders, pressing them with her thumbs.

"Ah, that is very nice," he said softly. "You have the good touch. The boy doesn't have that touch."

He seemed to puff up as she reached under his arms from behind and let her body rub against his back as she squeezed his large pectoral muscles.

"You are Kama Devi," he whispered, "you are desire." He let himself go limp against her body and reached behind with one arm to catch her hair as he lay back, pulling her head down onto his smooth chest.

Kamala felt a tingling sensation inside her, a loose, careless dreaminess she had never before experienced. "You have been looking at it." He glanced down at his loin cloth.

"I have heard many tales about Baba's lingam," she murmured, "and what he can do with it."

"Then fetch my lota," he said, his eyes glittering. "I have something to show you." He pointed to a small brass vessel about the size of a quart jar. "Fill it with water from that brass bucket and bring it here."

Kamala brought the lota and squatted in front of him.

"You desire to be a first class yogini now, I think," he said. "You have gone through sex, you can give up whoring. You want more interesting experience I think. If you stay with me you will learn."

He stretched himself out and opened his legs. "Remove the longote," he commanded. She bent over him, removed the scarlet loincloth, and stared at the jet black penis of the Baba, her lips parted.

"You will enjoy," he said, nodding slowly at her and getting to his haunches. "Now watch, you will learn something." He inserted his penis into the open mouth of the lota. "See," he said, beckoning her closer, "it will drink up the water." He began expanding and contracting his stomach muscles quickly in a fast rhythmic motion, as though an electric motor had switched on inside him.

Kamala's eyes were riveted on the swelling organ while it drank up the water in the vessel as though it had a mouth. "I have heard of this but have never seen it done," she murmured, amazed.

When he had emptied the lota he took a small hourglass-shaped drum off a shelf, and with a wrist motion began to vibrate it. Then, kneeling in front of the statue, he anointed its lingam with flowers and sandalwood paste, offered incense, waved lamps, and finally prostrated himself before it.

Then he arranged Kamala opposite the statue in the lotus position, tucked flowers into the crevices of her body and hair, and marked her forehead with ash as well as sandalwood paste and red and gold color. Then putting his hand under his penis he let the

[166]

water out. "Holy water," he said sprinkling her with it. "It got great shakti now, drink!" He held up his hand and let the water trickle into her open mouth and down her breasts.

Kamala groaned. The Baba's glistening skin had turned transparent so that she could see all the blood vessels and bones inside him and the fluids pumping through his body.

He saw the expression on her face.

"It is beginning to work, that American magic. Is it not good?" He waved a lamp in front of her eyes.

Kamala felt a rush as though she were taking off in a plane. Through lavender and blue clouds she saw the Baba replicate himself, many-headed and thousand-armed, through a prism of waving lights.

"Now you must do puja." His voice reverberated inside her. He lay on the floor beside the fire with his legs apart, rattling the drum in his upraised fist.

Kamala dusted his body including the erect lingam with ash from the fire, until he looked like a pale gray statue. Then she lit incense, waved the lamps, and finally, after decorating the lingam with flowers, let coconut water trickle over it like sperm coming out and down over his testicles.

The Baba began to see Kamala glowing pink and filled with juices. "You are the Kama," he said, shaking his drum wildly in the air. "Come, you have finished the puja, now lower your body onto the lingam. You are the Goddess Kama, let your yoni embrace the living lingam. Take it all inside you, oh Goddess!"

She seemed to hover over him a phantom form, then slowly lowered herself onto him.

"Ah ah, grhrr," he roared, then rose to a crosslegged sitting position.

Kamala wrapped her legs about his waist, her arms around his neck, and stared into his wide-open eyes. "Ah grhrr . . . that is it," he purred. "Now begin the breathing and the locking."

Her face shattered into a thousand mirrors as he watched her concentrate on her breathing, her eyes closed, her lips parted, groaning and chanting the Shiva mantra.

"You are mine," he said softly into her open lips, "you are to think only of my lingam, the Shiva lingam inside you . . . you Kama . . . you the shakti."

Kamala felt as though she were falling through space. He took her buttocks in both hands and moved her up and down as she continued to breathe. Her whole body tingled.

"You must anoint my lingam now, oh daughter of the Gods, anoint and worship. Together we shall rule as Raja and Rani. We

[167]

shall rule India, America, the world!" He took her head in his hands roughly, forcing her to stare into his eyes. Her orgasm mounted and discharged in spasms, flowing hot around his organ.

The moment he had been waiting for had arrived. He held her in his tight grip and slowly, rhythmically, began the pumping movements, directing all his concentration to his penis and sucking up her seminal fluid exactly as he had drunk up the water in the lota.

"See me," he said, "here between the eyes, oh daughter of Bharata. Let yourself flow into me. Let your thighs and womb open . . . open and flow into me."

She could feel a sucking motion deep inside her as she let go over and over again. Before her eyes his form expanded to gigantic proportions. She felt like a doll in the lap of a god.

He leaned down as though from a great height and began sucking on her breasts. The softness of his large lips brought her to the verge of collapse. Frozen in space and time, she watched as he held up his arms and began to make the milky liquid spurt from the palms of his hands.

"Ah," he moaned, "drink, spouse of Shiva, drink the elixir of immortality from my hands. You are mine, ah ah, grhrr," he growled again, his throat contracting in spasms as a long black stone came up and out of his mouth. "Take it," he cried out hoarsely. "Ah ah grhrr ah, yet another is coming!"

§

For seven days Stan purged. Bouts in the bathroom alternated with hot baths and rubs from Jai Devi. He wished he were strong enough to make it with this sexy Iowa blonde but when the rubbing was over he felt weak and was told to rest. Jai Devi would disappear through the door into Saladin's room, and although Stan resented Saladin's having this affair right under his nose, so to speak, he was so fascinated by the clever seduction of the uptight girl that he forgot to be angry.

Finally on the seventh day he felt better.

"Mr. Stanley, you really look like a new man today," Saladin said, slapping him on the back. "I have news for you. His Holiness wishes to see you. You must bathe and put on fresh clothes. The Baba is waiting."

§

The Baba was sitting in his favorite corner under the purple silk umbrella, being fanned and massaged.

"You are feeling better now, Mr. Stanley, is it not so, eh?" he muttered as Stan went down on his belly to touch the large bare feet.

"I've been very sick," murmured Stan.

"I know, it is I who ordered it, Mr. Stanley. It was important to clean you out first, eh . . . inside? That is always the first step before we clean out the disease." He chuckled, then surveyed Stan with his glittering eyes. "Your poison is coming out now, I can see that."

"You mean you *made* me sick?" said Stan astonished.

"But of course, nothing happens here that Baba doesn't control. You know how important control can be sometimes, eh?"

There was a long pause during which each waited for the other to speak.

"It is very beautiful here," Stan said finally. Watching the young boy rub the Baba's flesh was making him nervous.

"Ah yes, but it is so expensive to keep it all going, Mr. Stanley, so expensive."

"Is he asking for more money?" Stan thought. He let the moment pass, saying nothing.

The Baba rolled on his side. "Now it is time, Mr. Stanley, for you to begin taking exercise—first some light work, then we will see. Of course, you will attend daily bhajan in the morning and in the evening on the first terrace. The other times you will spend helping out in the kitchen. You will meet some very nice devotees there, they tell me they really need some help. You don't mind helping, do you Mr. Stanley?"

He threw Stan a long seductive smile, then raised his hand in blessing, his eyes closed. "You may go now, I shall see you this evening."

"So it's the kitchen," Stan grumbled to Saladin.

"But it is the rule of all the ashrams, Mr. Stanley. If you don't pay you must work. I hear there are several bank presidents also working in the kitchen these days. You will have good company."

"It's not that I mind working," complained Stan, "but I came to get cured of a bad disease. Time is running out for me—why should I waste my time working in the kitchen of some ashram?"

"But then why not make a donation?" said Saladin cheerfully.

"You must be joking," said Stan. "I just gave him ten thousand dollars!"

"But Mr. Stanley, the Baba knows that is nothing for a man of your wealth."

"How would the Baba know my financial status? Even I don't."

"Ah, the Baba sees everything, Mr. Stanley. If you will give him a big donation, then of course he will cure you. I tell you, you must give money first, then he will heal you."

"And I tell you that I will give the money after I am healed," sputtered Stan.

"But don't you have to pay the doctor whether he cures you or not?"

Stan felt angry. Never in his life had he given before getting. It was not his habit. He remembered too well the cold dingy Bronx apartment where he'd grown up. Even though he was a rich man now, he hated parting with money. "And what if I give more and he still doesn't cure me?" he thought. "It could go on and on!" He cracked his knuckles. "Ten thousand," he kept thinking. "It would have to be at least ten thousand more." The more he tried to dismiss the thought, the more it obsessed him.

He was still looking morose as he followed Saladin into the kitchen where he was introduced to a Mr. Dutt. Mr. Dutt was a short stocky man with beady, slightly crossed eyes. Stan disliked him on sight.

"It is a very good thing for us that His Holiness has sent you," Mr. Dutt said. "We have not enough help and are so rushed. You will be washing up the pots, Mr. Stanley. We do them here." He led Stan to a long low depression on the cement floor at one end of the kitchen. There was a pipe with flowing water and a large bowl containing wood ash and coconut husks.

"Do I kneel or what?" said Stan contemptuously.

"You squat, Mr. Stanley." Dutt demonstrated how to wash the heavy brass utensils.

"But I've never squatted," said Stan, gazing down at Dutt. "I'm afraid it'll be impossible for me to stay in that position for any length of time. If you can fix something up so that I can stand, it would be better."

"But the water is on the floor, you see, sir. It cannot be changed."

"Why not pay another ten thousand," he thought to himself miserably. But the squalor of the Bronx was too close. "Then I guess I'll just have to learn to squat." He smiled at Mr. Dutt. "When do I start?"

As the days passed the skin of Stan's hands cracked and the cracks filled with grit. His knees ached from squatting and, as the loathsome pots and pans arrived in a seemingly endless procession from the kitchen, he lost his appetite completely. At the bhajans the Baba never ceased to smile at him, often stopping to ask if he was all right. He began to feel for the first time in his life that there might be a force beyond his reason. He had always won all his battles because they had been waged with reasonable men, but here he began to realize that other axioms were operating. The rules of the game had changed. They were unseen, psychic; he felt repelled, yet fascinated.

Evenings after he returned to his quarters exhausted from the scullery work, he would lie listening to Saladin make out with Jai Devi or other young Western devotees of the Baba he had managed to seduce. After Saladin had finished with them he would come into Stan's room, scratching his crotch suggestively.

Stan pretended not to notice but the whole business was wearing him down, and making him neurotic. His breathing had become more difficult and he noticed that occasionally blood came up with his spittle. The smile of the Baba, the scullery work, the sadistic behavior of Saladin constantly fucking in the other room and then trying to make him into a cocksucker ... It had all become a pattern—or at least he imagined it had. He was in a trap, their victim. "They're out to make me a slave, they couldn't care less whether I get well or not," he thought darkly.

But he was sure that the Baba could heal him. Sadistic and self-centered as he was, the man had power. That was the rub. But there were no assurances that he would do it, even if a million dollars were put before him. As Stan had feared, the forces with which he was now dealing were irrational. He felt love coming from the Baba and pain from Saladin. He was sure the two were working in tandem to freak him out.

Why not just pay the money? Would it not just be easier to give in and enjoy himself? Give ten thousand to the Baba or even more, put Saladin on salary as a pimp, and have boys to rub him and luscious prostitutes to sleep with him whenever he liked. He realized that there was something in his character that had always prevented him from involving himself. He had always been the outsider looking on and here it was no different. The play was the same, only the cast had changed. "I'm getting in too deep," he said aloud, "it's time to get out."

The next day he was on the phone to Carlos, whom he had located in Bombay. "Very good . . . you've seen Jeff? Yes. I'll check in at the same hotel. Make the arrangements and meet me at the plane, I'll call from Bangalore . . . I don't know the time, I have to get out of this place first . . . No, I can't just leave, you don't understand . . . just follow directions! Right. And send the cable in care of Ananda Baba so he will see it—yes, you'd better make it express, it must seem as though I'm being called away on business, yes. Good-bye."

Stan mopped his brow as he put down the receiver. The fact was the Baba's power frightened him and he didn't want to set off bad vibrations; they might be directed toward him if it seemed he was leaving of his own free will.

§

Later in the evening as he was washing the last of the pots, a boy came and said something to Mr. Dutt.

"You are called by Baba," Dutt said breathlessly. "Go at once, I will have another finish your work."

The boy escorted him to His Holiness, and after touching the Baba's feet Stan sat down opposite Kamala, whom he had not seen for some time. She lay curled up like a cat, looking more beautiful than ever.

"You have received a cable from Bombay." She handed him the sealed envelope with a searching look.

He took the cable and opened it. After a suitable pause he handed the cable to the Baba.

"It seems that business requires that I leave this wonderful place. Presumably I will be away only for a week or ten days."

Kamala was certain that the cable had been arranged.

"But we will miss you, Mr. Stanley," the Baba said, after glancing at the cable. "I hope you will return soon. Do you think you should travel when you are sick?"

"Oh I won't be gone for more than a couple of weeks," Stan said, trying to make light of the affair.

"Of course, Mr. Stanley," said the Baba. He didn't believe a word but admired Stan's playing a good game, especially for a man so close to death. "When will you leave?"

"Tomorrow, I expect. Saladin can drive me to Bangalore where I'll catch a plane. Will you come," Stan asked Kamala, "or will you wait here for me?"

Kamala gazed at him, trying to show him that she knew it was all a joke. "Naturally, darling Mr. Stanley," she answered finally. "I will wait here. I am so absorbed with His Holiness. He is teaching me many things . . . and Bombay is so very hot this time of year. But you must hurry back."

"By all means," Stan said, and in the Indian style touched his forehead to the Baba's right foot. "See you in two weeks." He backed away, trying not to trip over the exotic potted plants.

§

"Of course he is lying." the Baba grumbled after Stan had left.

"Naturally," said Kamala.

"Let him go then. His disease is too advanced for me to cure without making myself sick for months." The Baba's eyes narrowed. "But we must have more of this acid substance. It saves so much time. See how it has brought the General under our control? He got scared to death." The Baba chuckled. "It will be most useful for me. So many of the rich devotees need this kind of scaring. They will see me as a god. Then they will surrender and give more money." He wiped his nose. "They never take time to do the meditations required, and this will overcome that problem." He shot a glance at Kamala. "May I send you to Bombay after him? I give you leave to say no, it is not an order."

"Let us wait a few days," said Kamala. "I will go when the time is right. I hear they have a great quantity of the drug. They won't get rid of it all at once. I also have something to settle with one of Mr. Stanley's associates, a man named Jeff." She smiled a thin contemptuous smile. "Do you know of a man called Wasu in Bombay?"

"A big smuggler?"

Kamala nodded.

"He has been here. A very bad man. He has given us millions of rupees from time to time because he is afraid of us and thinks we are lucky."

"He will also do anything I ask," said Kamala. "I shall phone him and ask him to watch Mr. Stanley. At the proper time he will tell me when to go to Bombay."

The Baba nodded his understanding. "Come here," he said.

She knelt before him.

He took her head in his hands and then pulled it gently down into his lap. "If you are successful in this undertaking," he whispered, bending over her, "I will place all India at your feet. Wait and see."

[173]

Back in the hostel Stan noticed there were no lights in Saladin's room although the connecting door was open. As soon as he turned on his light and began packing, Saladin appeared in his shorts, rubbing his eyes. "You are late," he said seductively, stretching his arms over his head.

"I had to say goodbye to His Holiness."

Saladin woke up at once. "You are leaving?"

"Only for two weeks." He handed Saladin the cable.

"I see," said Saladin slowly. "Business calls you away. You are a dying man yet still you do the business, yes?"

"I'm not dead yet," Stan shot back. "Will you drive me to Bangalore in the morning or shall I engage someone else?"

"I will drive if it is your desire," said Saladin, smiling.

"Yes, it's my desire," said Stan, absorbed in his packing, "and I'll want to start before sunrise." He looked up. "And could you have them prepare the bill now so that we won't have a long delay in the morning when no one's awake."

Saladin sat down with his feet up on the bed, and called the ashram secretary on the phone. He scratched his crotch suggestively as he spoke with the secretary in Hindi. When he was finished he remained seated, hoping that Stan would make some sort of move toward sex. When he didn't, and instead asked him abruptly to leave, he knew that Stan was terminating their relationship.

"He thinks he is going without giving something to me," Saladin said to himself. "But after all I have done for him—he'll pay!"

The problem of what to do obsessed him through the night. "He will wait till the last to pay me off," he kept thinking. "At the airport in Bangalore where I cannot protest, he will give me some trifling amount."

He knew that Stan had ten thousand in travelers checks still on him. He also knew that if he took them and Stan complained, he could bribe himself out of it. Stan was a foreigner. He didn't know that even A. K. Sundaram could be bought for the right price.

The next day in a wild section of jungle stretching for miles among cliffs and dry washes, twenty miles from the nearest village, Saladin pretended that the engine had stalled. He jumped out quickly, lifted the hood, disconnected a wire, and then asked Stan to start the car.

Stan tried with no result. Suspecting that Saladin might have pulled a wire, he examined the engine himself. But Saladin was clever and the wire he had detached was buried in a tangle of old connections that would have misled even the best of mechanics. Just as he was losing all hope of making the plane, a cloud of dust behind them signaled the almost magical appearance of a car. It drew up beside them and the driver leaned out the window.

"My car has broken down," Saladin said in English. "This gentleman must get to Bangalore. Can you help us?"

"I am just now returning to there empty, you are welcome to ride."

"But what about your car," Stan said, as Saladin began transferring the luggage from one car to the other.

"I will lock it and come back with a mechanic tomorrow."

"But I can send a mechanic from the next town. There's no need for you to make the extra trip. If this man will take me, you can wait here with your car to be sure it's safe."

"How shrewd he is," thought Saladin. "But it is my duty—this man might be no good," he whispered. "It is best I come along."

Stan was relieved to find that the back and inside windows were curtained, even if the car wasn't air conditioned. Relaxing, he eased himself down in the seat and congratulated himself on his good luck. He was dozing when Saladin took his hand and pulled it slowly across his thigh to his crotch.

Pretending to be asleep, Stan let his hand rest there. He was tired of this young hustler and wanted no more to do with him if possible, especially in a car.

But Saladin unbuttoned his pants and rubbed his penis against Stan's hand. Stan withdrew at once, blinking up at the driver and then at Saladin.

"No, no," he whispered. "Put it away, he'll see."

Saladin pulled Stan's hand back. "Take it, take it," he urged. "He won't see."

After that everything happened so fast that it was only much later, after he boarded the plane, that he managed to piece it all together. Saladin pushed him onto the floor. The car stopped and the driver forced his arms behind his back. Stan bit at Saladin's leg but got kicked in the stomach and passed out.

The next thing he knew the driver was holding a long knife barely two inches from his throat.

"You sign the checks to me, eh?" said Saladin, waving nine thousand-dollar travelers checks in front of his face.

Stan squirmed and looked away.

"No, no, Mr. Stan," Saladin said coolly, "do not try to get loose. You will get your throat cut."

[175]

"You cut my throat and you're in trouble," said Stan, his voice trembling. "Sundaram . . ."

"A. K. Sundaram will do nothing. I am only asking for nine thousand, Mr. Stan, only nine thousand. If I cut your throat I will get ten. It is so easy to forge your name, it is nothing to dispose of your body here, and no one is going to be interested in you—you are a dying man anyhow and a foreigner. There would be no investigation. Even A. K. Sundaram would not make one, especially if he got fifty percent. Really, no one would miss you, Mr. Stan. You had better sign the checks. I am letting you off easy because I like you." He grinned.

For a few moments there was an ominous silence while Stan tried to penetrate the barrier of Saladin's face. Rage churned his stomach as the ludicrous nature of the trap he had fallen into became clear, and an inner voice warned him that if he weren't careful his stinginess would get him killed.

"How should I make them out," he said finally.

"Saladin Travels Ltd.," was the proud reply.

By the time he had finished signing, something inside Stan had broken. He felt cracked and used up, like a broken discarded vessel. He had no energy even to resist the driver as his hands and feet were bound roughly.

"You will be untied at the airport, Mr. Stanley," said Saladin. "I will have a knife at your back. Do not be foolish enough to yell. And do not report these checks lost or stolen. I am an Arab, not an Indian, and we have connections all over—even in New York. Most unpleasant things would happen to you."

Then he smiled condescendingly. "Would you not enjoy sucking off my friend? Abdul come here," Saladin commanded. "Show Sahib what you've got."

The driver unzipped his fly and stood in the half-open door, his arms resting on the top of the car.

"See, nice one, huh Mr. Stan, yes?"

He raised Stan's head and pushed his mouth onto the erect penis.

"Suck, pig," he said in Urdu, forcing Stan's head to bob up and down until with a groan the driver discharged into Stan's mouth.

"Now, me too," Saladin ordered, pulling Stan onto the floor of the car between his legs as the driver resumed his seat and the car sped along the road.

"We have two hours till the airport," said Saladin, grabbing Stan by the hair, his eyes glassy with triumph. "Do a good job, Mr. Stan, you'll never get good Moslem cock again, I bet!"

Saladin did not free him until they stopped beside the

passenger entrance. Then, just as the car was surrounded by coolies eager to carry the baggage, Saladin cut the ropes and dragged Stan out, pretending to help him.

"You'd better hurry, Mr. Stanley," he shouted in a loud voice, saluting and smiling at people he knew. "Remember when you return in two weeks, just phone ahead and I'll be here to meet you."

It was over so fast that there was no time for Stan to protest in any way. "Besides," he thought miserably, looking around at the bustling airport scene, "how could I explain it to anyone here?"

He made his way to the checkout counter through a mob of shouting coolies and excited passengers, his only thought whether madness or death would come first. For the first time he almost welcomed the idea of his own end.

IX

§

THE EARLY MORNING flight from Delhi arrived in Bombay toward noon. Jeff took a taxi straight to the Taj Mahal Hotel, booked a room, and bolted the door. Exhaustion overpowered him; he felt like a fallen warrior, a defeated invader. He felt like sleeping forever.

Fucked in the ass by a eunuch. He pounded the bed with his fist as he lay trying to rest.

The glimpses of himself he was beginning to catch were too much for him to handle. Was self-knowledge too deep a risk? India seemed only to reveal his weaknesses, to expose as ridiculous the revolutionary ideals he thought he had espoused, when only the bread had really interested him.

He felt filthy. He showered and washed his backside carefully, cursing Kamala. Must be how a virgin feels when she first loses it, he thought, disgusted with himself. Drugs! He felt like chucking the two suitcases of acid into the bay outside the hotel window. But the bread. The BREAD! Why did he always have to be thinking about that end of it?

After a couple of days in the hotel he was consumed by suspicion and paranoia. He was a virus in a strange body; antibodies were coming to attack him, a brown multitude to finish him off. Laura had always been able to cast these devils out; without her he was beset by doubt and unreasonable fears. Even the room boy who brought food and fresh towels seemed to pose a threat, to be spying on him and have some ulterior motive.

He grew nervous about the acid and decided to check it outside the hotel. Reserving five hundred tabs to give away as sales promotion, he found an old, reliable English storage company in the phone book, took the bags there, and stashed them in a locker. It was his first time out in three days and his first time on the Bombay streets. Yelling, grimacing, nameless brown faces—miles of them—stretched out hands to him, watched him, wanted him. Wanted to fuck him or suck him, or more likely he thought, to serve him up for dinner.

No matter how much enlightenment there might be here in the bays and backwaters of this continent, he knew instinctively it was a dangerous place for him. At every turn he was made aware that he was a foreigner. No matter how many friends he might make here, he knew that in the end they would let him down. He was sure of it. For him it was an impossible place.

He returned to his room and spent three weeks locked up in it, sleeping, reading magazines and long Russian novels he had purchased in the hotel bookshop. The Russia of Tolstoy seemed like the India he had seen. In the late afternoon he would put up the shades and watch the parade: peddlers, whores, male prostitutes, money changers, and tourists promenaded in front of the hotel, around the great Gate Way to India, as the sun set pink and gold across the bay. Was it the road to Mandalay? The flying fishes no longer played. The water that lapped the base of the stone arch was full of garbage, and the sailing vessels out in the bay had been replaced by destroyers and dingy tourist launches.

One Sunday evening after he had read all the books he could digest and had slept as much as he could, he decided to venture into the hotel bar. He found it an intimate sort of place, thickly carpeted, and smoke filled. He had barely got through the door before he heard a familiar voice calling him from across the room. The girl from Texas, last seen getting laid by the smuggler at Kamala's and—he had to look twice—Carlos. Jeff would have liked to retreat but it was too late, they had both seen him.

He pretended to be surprised.

"Hello," said the girl from Texas suggestively.

"I hear you met Angel in Delhi," Carlos was saying. "Sit down ... like you to meet my old friend Wasu and his friend ..."

"Hadji," the man called Wasu said, "his name is Hadji."

Jeff sank into a chair.

"I have been looking everywhere for you, my friend," said Carlos. "Stan's here."

"Why?"

"He has cancer in the lung."

"What?"

"Absolutely. The doctors found it. He is going to die." Carlos gestured dramatically. "Only one, two months left."

"Where is he?" said Jeff, thinking of the money Carlos would probably get.

"He is with some holy man," Carlos sighed, smiling faintly. "He

[179]

thinks the man can cure him. I have told him the only place for him is the Memorial Hospital in New York, but he will not listen. You just missed him in Delhi. We arrived the day after you left. He has been with the holy man for three weeks now, his name is . . . oh, they all sound the same to me . . . ah yes, it is Ananda Baba."

"Ananda Baba can cure him," said Wasu, a broad man who wore a tan silk suit.

"If he spends enough money," said Carlos. "Otherwise, he will probably let him die."

Wasu laughed. "That is also a possibility."

Jeff didn't like his looks. He had the proportions and bearing of a Mafia bouncer, his face was sullen, and although probably not over forty he had the old eyes of one who has seen too much.

The other man, Hadji, had a handsome tan face with a long aquiline nose. His hair was hidden by traditional cream colored Arab headgear and he wore a soft, sheer wool robe of the same color.

"Out of the Arabian Nights," Jeff was thinking as he finished his drink and stood up to leave. The last person in the world he felt like spending time with was Carlos.

Wasu, his face haughty, motioned Jeff down. "Sit, my friend," he said, bringing a large heavy hand down on the table. "You have only just arrived—why are you jumping up so soon? I heard so much about you from my Angel and from . . . my friend Carlos. I want to get to know you." He leaned forward. "I have tried the pills you brought." He rolled his eyes seductively. "Very good. I will buy a great quantity, yes? Do you have some?"

Jeff eased back into his chair. "Now?"

"Yes."

"No, I don't carry them around."

Wasu turned to Carlos. "And you. . . ?" he asked, as if talking to a servant.

"Now?" said Carlos. "You want more now? They are not to be taken with liquor."

"I did not ask how, I asked if," said Wasu coldly.

Carlos took a small envelope out of his pocket and passed it to Wasu who pulled it into his lap. Then he took five tablets and dropped them into his drink and dropped five more into Angel's glass.

Jeff winced.

"Whatsa matter?" Wasu said. "Is good stuff, no taste at all." He mixed his drink with a spoon.

"Drink it," he ordered the girl from Texas. "You need it!" He waited while she drained her glass.

"Tonight you will come with me," he said to Jeff, bringing his big hands firmly onto the table. "I will show you something you never seen before." He emptied his glass and signaled the waiter. "Now I take you all to dinner. When the stomach is empty, nothing goes right." He eased his heavy body out of the banquette. "The car is outside."

At the door of the hotel, a large gray Mercedes limousine pulled up as if on cue. Two hefty bodyguards wearing gray suits and dark glasses jumped out. After saluting Wasu and closing the doors on the passengers, they got into the front seat with the driver. Jeff noticed pistols strapped under their arms.

Wasu said something in Marathi to the driver and the car sped noiselessly through downtown Bombay. Turning south and then east they reached what approximated a thruway though it was full of potholes and bumps. On this they continued past the old city until they reached the sprawling shantytown where a room could cost a poor man half his month's salary if he was lucky enough to find one.

"Are we going to the airport for dinner, or what?" asked Angel in a bored voice.

"It is Sunday," said Wasu. "Always I go to my mother's to eat on Sunday. I don't take no one. Tonight I take all of you." He gestured expansively. "She always got too much food anyway."

They turned off the main road onto an unpaved dirt street paralleling an open sewage conduit. The stench was terrible and came in even through the closed windows of the car. Angel covered her nose with her shawl as the crowds of wide-eyed bystanders scattered before the driver's persistent horn.

"It is not good, eh?" said Wasu, a look of disgust and rage crossing his heavy face. "Breathe deep and it will not give the bad smell. After some time you get used to it. My mother lives here alone. We are all grown up here, my father is died here. She won't move."

The car stopped and the two guards jumped out to fend off a crowd of admirers, mostly teenagers.

"Come, we get out here," Wasu said, reeling out of the car.

"Wasu, Wasu, Jai Wasu, Jai Jai!" Children in rags, old people, thin young men in tight pants, some smiling, others overcome with awe, all shouted in chorus: "Wasu, Wasu!"

Outside the stench was worse. Jeff took a deep breath. On a treeless wasteland between the highway and a distant power plant, hovels clung to the dusty earth. Coal smoke spewed into the evening air. The only water he could see trickled in the drains and open sewers that connected the huts. There was shit everywhere.

[181]

Pigs, chickens, and goats were busy recycling the human shit into animal shit. Flies covered everything.

"It is the cauldron of Maria Ma, the cholera goddess," muttered Wasu. "Who survives the disease here is real Indian!"

The bodyguards muscled a path for them to the entrance of a low mud hut with a thatch and tin roof. Inside a handsome tough-looking woman nodded to them and hugged Wasu.

"My mother she speaks no English—sorry, she never had no time to learn. I got seven brothers, eight sisters, all living." Wasu chattered with her in Marathi as he lowered himself onto a straw mat. "I was wanting that she should move to a good flat somewhere in one of those buildings I am owning, or hotel. It is no use." He gestured hopelessly. "She won't, maybe it is good, eh? People who know me see that my mother does not move. They are not so jealous then. They imagine I have no money to get her fine place? I tell them the car belongs to Congress Party, ha!"

Wasu's mother moved about noiseless and deft, squatting on the floor, rolling out chappatis for a daughter who cooked them on a wood fire. A large pot of meat swimming in fat boiled on a portable kerosene burner. The smell of sewage blended with cooking meat made Jeff sick. He wondered how this Wasu could make it with five thousand mics of acid in his system. Angel sat grimly in one corner as the meat was served in chunks on large mounds of white rice.

Wasu ate with his hand, slapping meat and rice into wads which he gulped down, smacking his lips in appreciation. The mud walls of the small hut were covered with photographs, many of Wasu. He noticed Jeff looking at them.

"That is my father," he said, his mouth full of food. "After 1947 he made Corporal in the Army. When Wasu is born, he is sweeper, peon. We are low caste. Pretty good for us, eh?" he said, patting his chest arrogantly. "The Congress Party they raised us up. My father was one of six brothers, only him lived to have children. My mother, she came from Jaipur—all her family died. Now I got seven brothers and eight sisters, all living—all got good jobs making plenty money." He gulped down more food. "Eat, eat," he shouted to Carlos who was pushing food around on his plate. "You think you are some Brahmin, eh? If I don't know you are Mexicano, I think you act like bloody Brahmin." Wasu belched, then glanced at Hadji and slapped him on the back. "At least you are eating, eh? Moslems eat meat. We are low caste. All the low caste and Moslems they eat meat in Bombay—we have no quarrel."

"Your father was a very handsome man," said Jeff, glancing up at one of the photos.

[182]

"He's died last year," said Wasu, frowning. "But he's died a happy man, to see his son Wasu rich like Raj. Congress Party people give him fine funeral. He was a good worker for them, organizing so many people. Now they after me, me Wasu." He sighed and touched Jeff's hand. "Can you imagine that they have raised me up and now they are attacking me? Yes, it is true. They want to finish me—ME, Wasu, they want to finish me off!

"Last year police come and took me to the Government of India court. I'm having to get lawyers. The judge he say, 'Wasu, what you got to say for yourself? We got the goods on you, you big smuggler, selling the gold, the drug, the women. We know it, we got spies all over. We know all the rackets you have.'"

He wolfed down more food. "But I tell him, I tell the judge— Brahmin he was—'Listen to me, I am Wasu. I am low caste and black. You go ahead, you put Wasu in prison. The day I am going through the prison gate fifty thousand people will lose their jobs. Ha, yes it is so! Can you find fifty thousand people jobs? Can Congress Party find so many jobs? Not all can be doctor, engineer or judge,' I say to him. 'Bombay people they like gold, they like numbers and fucking. That's where the jobs are here.'" Wasu closed his eyes, his face expressionless. "The biggest customer for the gold is Government of India,' I say to him."

"What happened?" asked Carlos, who had managed to finish his food.

"He fined me three hundred rupees plus the cost and let me go free from the court. What could they do? It is true, it is true. Wasu does not lie. He has seen the world too much to lie. And I had something on that judge too, I will show tonight. Tonight I will take you to see where the Brahmin judge likes to go.

"This Congress Party is no good now, all crooks: socialism from books, big foreign cars to ride in. We peoples are not socialists, we are all capitalists. Let them come, these socialists, these communists. Let them bring the Russians, the Chinese, what do we care?" He laughed loudly. "We go on forever, yes, it is true, Mr. Jeff. See the mud outside, smell the stink. We can survive it. We are on the bottom—they cannot move us.

"See the Indian man, he loves money more than anything. He loves women, boys, jewels, gold, and babies. You give any man three hundred rupees, he will buy some trash, some cheap stuff in the big market. Then he will bring his cloth out of the city and start selling on roadside. Next time you see him, he is in some small shop he has builded over himself. Next year you will see bigger shop, then cement will come and he will build hotel. Finally he own whole street, driving in Ambassador car. That's the way it

[183]

goes." Wasu sighed. "Now Congress Party says pay taxes, put money in bank. Bank is just trap to keep track of the money so they can steal it later. I know them, my father all his life he work for them." He rolled his eyes.

Jeff managed to clean his plate by holding his breath and swallowing the greasy food in big gulps. This pleased Wasu who ordered his mother to fill up the plate a second time over Jeff's protests.

"Eat! Eat! Eat!" he yelled, "You peoples are too skinny." He glanced at Angel. "Her, I try to get her fattened up," he said. "She not gain any weight. Who wants to fuck skinny woman, eh, Hadji?"

He leered at the young Arab, then turned to Jeff.

"Hadji is prince, Dubai prince." He slapped Hadji on the back. Hadji flinched. "He is only baby, only twenty-nine years, but he got four wives and twenty-three babies, all fat. I have seen." Wasu nodded. "Eh Hadji, when you invite Wasu to Dubai again, eh? Some first-class women they got there. I ought to know, those sheiks they buy plenty of them from me." He winked at Jeff and licked his lips.

As soon as he had finished, Wasu got up and went outside with a jar of water. With loud gargling sounds he snorted water through his nostrils and spit out into the crowd as if they didn't exist. Carlos followed suit. Hadji held the water jar for Jeff as he washed before the wide-eyed children and old people hanging around the door. Angel, who hadn't touched her food, remained seated in the corner lost in acid visions.

When they came back in Wasu sat down in front of the fire with his mother. They had a long animated conversation in Marathi which turned into an argument, the mother gesturing wildly at Wasu and yelling at him. Finally he reached into his tight pants and with his big hands threw out wads of hundred-rupee notes onto her lap. Casting furtive glances at the visitors, she straightened the notes out. When she had them in a neat pile she locked them in a metal box, which she put in a large old-fashioned safe that was covered with a piece of flowered oilcloth.

"The bank," said Wasu, with a sardonic grin. He stood up and called in one of the bodyguards, who helped Angel to her feet. Her eyes were fixed.

"God knows what she's seeing," thought Jeff dismally.

They filed out. Wasu's mother stood at the door, her hands folded in front of her sari, her face expressionless.

In the car Wasu's big meaty hand came down heavily on Jeff's knee. "Now I take you to the 'theatre,' a place I own," he said, picking his teeth with his other hand.

Soon the sleek grey limousine was back in the teeming streets of Bombay central.

"This is prostitute section," Wasu was saying. "You have heard of Sukhalachi Street—the girls in the cages, yes?" He ordered the driver to slow down and opened the window. What appeared to be shops with small barred windows lined the street. Behind the bars girls were sitting.

"Not much different than Amsterdam," Carlos commented dryly. "There it's picture windows, here it's bars and more girls."

"Amsterdam?" Wasu asked.

"A city in Holland," said Jeff. "It has a quarter like this."

The car stopped on a side street in front of a nondescript cement building that resembled a small hotel or apartment house. The street was thronged with barefoot urchins, beggars, and cyclists. Wasu handed Jeff a roll of five-rupee notes.

"You please give to the beggars," he said, his eyes now bulging with visions.

One bodyguard opened the door and pulled Angel out while the other guard and Wasu bulldozed their way up some steps to the door of the building. Hadji and Carlos followed in their wake. Then Jeff got out of the car, holding the five-rupee notes. What seemed like a hoard of grey ghosts of every age materialized out of nowhere and engulfed him, tearing at his clothes, grabbing at his arms, hands, and legs, clawing at him with filthy hands and leprous stumps of fingers or arms. Children scuttled under the legs of the old people trying to trip them and knock them down.

"Ahugh, ah, ah, sahib, sahib, paisa, paisa," they groaned, clutching at him.

"Give to the older ones," Wasu yelled from the top of the stairs. "The younger ones don't need."

In desperation, Jeff threw the money into the air. At least two hundred people reached like a cresting wave and fell into the filth of the street, old and young alike clawing at each other for the money.

Wasu was roaring like a bull, his eyes inflamed. "Now my friend, you have felt the touch of hunger, eh? I don't think you will forget it soon, eh?" He slapped Jeff on the back and pulled him up the stairs to the door.

"It's Wasu's joke," muttered Carlos as they entered the building. "He does it to everyone. There is a bathroom upstairs where you can wash off."

"You've been here before then?" Jeff whispered.

"Oh, yes." Carlos sighed. "There is no place like it, you will see. Wasu invented it himself."

[185]

A big young man in a tight suit who looked like he might be one of Wasu's seven brothers saluted him.

"You are late," he said. "Everyone is waiting."

"Let them wait," said Wasu contemptuously, brushing the young man aside. "It makes more exciting for them."

He pushed Angel up a narrow stairway and down a long hall. The bodyguards stood by as he turned a key in one of the many doors that lined the hall and motioned them all through. They entered an air-conditioned, thickly carpeted dark room, a little larger than a motel room. Nondescript, overstuffed chairs and divans faced a series of wall-length windows. The windows opened into a brightly lit room, upholstered floor to ceiling with pink vinyl and lined with mirrors. Just in front of the mirrors was a network of heavy chrome bars. Jeff realized that what he was actually looking at was a mirrored room with a huge cage in it. There was a door at one end of the room that connected to the cage.

Wasu eased himself into one of the divans. Angel collapsed on the carpet beside him, holding onto one of his big legs with both arms. One of the guards came and removed Wasu's shoes and then stood against the wall with the other guard.

Hadji too stretched out on a divan while Carlos and Jeff sat side by side on another. "Are there more rooms that open onto the one with the mirrors?" Jeff asked Carlos.

"Six." He leaned toward Jeff, talking fast and low. "Listen, this Wasu is the biggest smuggler in India, maybe in the world. He digs the acid, digs the freaky scenes, wants to buy maybe the whole lot. You have it with you?"

Jeff nodded.

"Good." Carlos relaxed.

"And these?" Jeff gestured at the windows they were looking through.

"One-way mirrors," whispered Carlos. "You will see, don't talk too much at first, he gets angry if . . ."

"Carlos," Wasu commanded. "Give this to your friend." He turned to Jeff. "Why are you sitting so far from me? Come, move the chair here . . . I have some good kief for you, best hashish in Bombay . . . Come, we will smoke first. It's better." Wasu smiled, his broad nose flaring. "You must have the good look. Angel, she tell me you are quite a stud."

Asian Muzak drifted in over a loudspeaker system.

The lights in the room brightened, bouncing off the pink vinyl and chrome. The doors at the end opened and a young girl was pushed into the cage by a fat attendant wearing a towel.

"Singapore girl," Wasu murmured. "Nice one, eh?"

The girl ambled to the center of the room, her big breasts

[186]

covered with a see-through brassiere, her lithe hips and thighs rolling under black lace panties.

She stood before one of the mirrored windows brushing her hair back, and squeezing her breasts at the mirror.

Jeff thought she was very young to know so much. He was so intent on watching her he failed to notice that another girl, carrying a tray of drinks in small glasses, had entered the room they were in.

"Arak," bellowed Wasu, unbuttoning his shirt. "Goes good with the pills. Take. Drink."

"Made from palm juice," Carlos said to Jeff. "Like Aquavit."

When Jeff looked back at the mirrored room another figure had entered, a young, very muscular, male with an oversized neanderthal head. The attendant was locking the door of the cage.

Jeff sat bolt upright.

The ravaged face of an idiot grinned in the mirrors, masturbating slowly as he watched the reflection of the Singapore girl. One of Wasu's bodyguards cornered the girl who had brought the arak. He fingered her idly, standing close to her, watching the cage over her shoulders.

Jeff looked at Carlos.

"Interesting scene, yes, crazies!" He wagged his head.

Jeff felt sick.

Wasu took off his shirt. Beads of sweat stood out on an enormous stomach and breastlike pectoral muscles, firm as rocks. He was watching his bodyguard finger the waitress. He leaned over Angel and said something to her. She shook her head.

Wasu pushed her off his leg. "You do it," he said, knocking her with his knee. She got up and stared at him. "I give you another chance, bitch!" he yelled, but she only stared. "Cunt," he said in Marathi. He slapped her, then motioned to the bodyguard. "She thinks she make Wasu angry," he mumbled. "She needs some good lesson." He whispered something to the guard. "Now she'll get it, you see."

The guard muscled Angel out of the room.

"Srini," Wasu yelled to the other guard, who made the serving girl kneel between Wasu's fat legs. With difficulty, Wasu unzipped his fly and pulled her face down on his penis, then gestured to the mirrored room.

"See," he said. "Is good, no?"

The girl was backing away from the idiot. He followed her grinning, aware somehow that he was stronger and that it was only a matter of time until he got her. He lunged for her several times, grabbing at her panties, then stood swaying, flailing his penis at her. At first it was a game, but as his desire heightened, and the girl

[187]

continued to evade him, the idiot became angry and went after her in earnest. Tired of running, she climbed the bars of the cage and kicked at him with her spike-heeled shoes. The sounds of the struggle were piped in over the Muzak.

Wasu lay back grunting as the serving girl sucked him.

"What the fuck?" Jeff said under his breath. "Who runs this place?"

"Wasu own it," muttered Wasu, "and he run it."

"He owns it," Carlos whispered. "But is run by freaks—an international crowd, all freaky psychologists, they dig sex with crazies."

"Very humanitarian peoples," Wasu grunted, overhearing Carlos. "I give them plenty money for their crazy peoples."

"It's true," said Carlos. "They have these places—homes for crazies, morons you know—private, very high class. Very careful about things. All the doctors and nurses they dig making it with crazies or watching."

"Otherwise, who would look after them," said Wasu out of the corner of his mouth. "They have good program. Here in India, Turkey, some Western countries too, all are healthy. See the muscles." He pointed. "Get plenty of work in gardens, plenty sex."

Wasu, tired of the girl between his legs, pushed her away. "I go take shower," he said, disappearing through a door at the end of the room.

In the cage the idiot had pulled the girl off the bars and was sitting on her fingering her vagina, opening it and looking into it.

"Do they put on these shows everywhere?" asked Jeff.

"No, no," whispered Carlos. "Wasu, he got to know them. They started doing it at their place. Then he is bringing them here. Very dangerous. Only special nights for high politicians, civil service officers. They don't know he owns it. He has something on them then. It's not always the crazies. Mostly he has beatings, sometimes animals, sometimes prison inmates, this is nothing . . ."

Another male, about thirty-five and raving, had been pushed through the door of the cage. The first one grunted ferociously at him and gestured for him to go away.

"You sell much of the acid?" said Carlos casually, ignoring the cage where the two wretches had started fighting over the girl.

"Half of it," said Jeff.

"You got the money for it?"

"The money is in Swiss banks. Checks deposited to Stan's account. When they clear, the people will pick up their stuff."

"They trust you?"

"What else can they do?"

[188]

"What are you getting for it?"

"Twenty-five cents."

"You have it in your hotel?" Carlos asked, his eyes now following the fight. The second idiot had knocked the other out by pounding his head on the floor.

"Are you kidding?"

"Then where?"

"In a safe place, where it will stay until Stan comes or I hear from him." Jeff looked at Carlos, knowing he was nervous that Stan would die and he, Jeff, would have all the acid.

"What about cash deals?"

"Sure. But not in rupees, only dollars."

Wasu came in wrapped in a towel and followed by a young boy. He sprawled out on one of the divans while the boy massaged his back.

The second idiot lifted the girl into the air and then threw her to the floor where he pounced on her and ripping away her brassiere, bit at her breasts, squatted on her face, plunged his face between her legs. She screamed wildly and clawed at his back but he turned around and slapped her face until she kept quiet.

"Fuck her idiot, fuck!" Wasu yelled, propped up on one elbow. "He is so stupid he don't know how to fuck." Wasu snickered, turning to Jeff and Carlos. His huge body glistened with oil.

The young masseur stood waiting for Wasu to dismiss him. Instead, Wasu pushed the boy's head down between his legs.

"You like to fuck this Hejjera?" he rasped at Hadji, who seemed very withdrawn under his robes and headdress.

"No thanks," Hadji said. "He is too young, too tight for me."

"He'll stretch, you see." Wasu turned to Jeff. "Come, I like to watch you fuck him."

Jeff shook his head. He wasn't interested.

"He very talented," snorted Wasu, "see, very clean, trained for it." He fingered the boy's anus. The boy raised his buttocks in the air.

Wasu beckoned to one of his bodyguards. The guard unbuttoned his fly, spat on his penis, and let it slip into the boy.

"We train them from six years," Wasu explained. "From six he is sitting on wooden pegs to keep it open—very good boy, very clean." He lifted the boy's head by his hair. The boy smiled inanely and started sucking Wasu again.

"Fuck!" shouted Wasu to the guard.

The guard had an orgasm.

"Now you," Wasu indicated Carlos. "Hey you, Brahmin Carlos, you come now, you fuck, he hot now, wants more."

Carlos hesitated.

"You fuck him!" Wasu yelled angrily, starting to get up. "Wasu like see Carlos fuck fat young boy."

Carlos dropped his pants and walked behind the boy.

"Let him watch in the room," Wasu instructed, taking the boy from his crotch and turning him round on his hands and knees facing the window.

But the participants in the scene had vanished, the room was empty. "Ah huh," grunted Wasu, slapping the young boy's buttocks. "Slap him, Brahmin, he give you more action." Jeff glanced at Wasu who lay back, watching Carlos with the boy. Then he flinched.

Angel was being pushed through the door of the cage.

Wasu was talking to himself. "She think she say no to Wasu, ha? I am just dumb black bastard, eh? She will see . . . She got to learn some discipline."

A tall man with a scarred face, dark brown skin, and blue eyes entered the cage naked.

"Convict," Wasu said hoarsely to Jeff, "I get him out evenings sometimes. He very strong, like to rape women—eighteen times convictions Bombay courts. Can you imagine how hard up he gets in jail house!"

Jeff began to feel sick.

"I give him some of your pills tonight, see what he is going to do now."

When the convict saw Angel at the other end of the cage he smiled faintly, and licked his lips. He beckoned to her across the room but she clung to the bars unable to move, fixed on her image repeated over and over again in the mirrors. Then he came up alongside her, his face frozen in a smile, and slipped his hand under her dress from behind. She tried to push him away but he grabbed her arm and held it, forcing her to stare into his eyes.

Suddenly she began laughing hysterically. The convict slapped her across the mouth and she struck back at him, clawing and kicking. But he stood his ground, smiling ominously and letting her exhaust herself.

"Think what a chance for him, the black bastard," Wasu chuckled. "He never had no white woman before—he thinks she's something special." He called one of the bodyguards and whispered something in his ear.

Carlos had finished and lay stretched out on one of the divans watching the cage while the boy massaged his back.

Suddenly the convict caught Angel's clothes with both hands and ripped them from her body. She bolted away but he forced her into a corner and hovered over her, trying to kiss her. When she covered her face with her hands he moved down her body with his tongue until he reached her vagina. She closed her eyes, letting him go at her, swaying from side to side in the corner, hanging onto the cage.

Jeff wanted to leave. He rose from his chair.

Wasu pushed him back gently. "You no like see white girl and black man, eh?" he laughed. "Listen," he whispered, letting his hand go up Jeff's leg. "I got something special for you later, you stick around. Angel tell me you got big one, eh?" He groped at Jeff's crotch. "Wasu, he like to see you fuck young girl—virgin ... you fuck, eh?"

Jeff gave a start and Wasu turned his head.

A very large shorthaired black dog, almost the size of a Great Dane but heavier, had been let into the room. It wagged its tail excitedly, its penis glistening scarlet and poking out of the hairy foreskin. The convict turned. The dog bounded across the room and tried to climb on his back. He pushed it off but catching its collar brought it up to Angel's crotch where it sniffed and licked eagerly, while the convict stroked its penis with his free hand.

Suddenly he stood up letting go the dog and dragging Angel out into the center of the floor. The dog barked wildly. Straddling Angel, the convict caught hold of the dog and dragged it over her head, trying to force her to take the dog's organ in her mouth. She resisted, flailing her arms and legs, but he backhanded her across the mouth. Then, eyes bulging, his mouth open in a crazy grin, he lifted her legs up and entered her. He began to fuck and forced her mouth to take the dog. The dog stood still panting and drooling as Angel sucked.

"It is interesting place, no?" said Wasu. He stroked Jeff's leg again.

Jeff turned to Hadji, who sat, throwing SOS signals with his eyes. "But who is in the other rooms?" he said, hoping to distract Wasu.

"The other rooms?" Wasu jumped up, looking paranoid. "Who is in them," he said, lunging forward with a wild look in his eyes. Then he laughed and relaxed. "Customers are in the other rooms, of course. Ha, you think you fool me, eh? Customers, ministers, high officers, Brahmin judges. I stand in hallway sometime when they leaving, they not know I own it. After that they get scared to death of me. I got photos too, cameras hidden, got all that. They no touch Wasu. Watch, the dog going to fuck her now."

The convict had got Angel on her knees and was fucking her in the mouth while the dog mounted her at the rear, humping wildly.

"Sometimes the dog get stuck inside," laughed Wasu. "It is

[191]

very funny. The dog he gets four times bigger. Once he get in, gets stuck. See what a good bitch she make."

The convict played with Angel's breasts as she bobbed up and down on him.

"I think she enjoy, eh?" boomed Wasu, going off into spasms of laughter.

Jeff got up and made for the door.

"Where you going?" Wasu lurched around and gave one of his bodyguards the high sign.

But Hadji stood up and came between the guard and Jeff. "Wait outside, please," he said. "I too am leaving. I will just say something to Wasu."

Jeff waited in the corridor. A moment later Hadji strode through the door, his robes flowing, and unselfconsciously took Jeff's hand. 'Come," he said, tugging him past the fat guard who looked like Wasu. "This place stinks. I will take you home."

Outside, Hadji led him to a small sports car. "Jump in," he said, then stared straight ahead as the car careened out of the tangle of side streets into a wide boulevard paralleling the curve of the bay.

"I think you may be going in the opposite direction," Jeff said after a long silence.

"You are staying at the Taj, I know it, but I take you home with me." He smiled nervously. "It is no time for you to be alone in hotel room after such . . ." He turned to Jeff and shrugged. "I have not the words to say it. That Wasu is one very bad beast. He is so bad he doesn't even know it. He thinks he is a maharaja, but he is animal. He was raised up like an animal, he is an animal." He sighed. "India, it is too much. Too much poverty, too much of people, too much of sickness."

"Too much of nothing," muttered Jeff. "But your wives and children . . ." he said after a while, not particularly wanting to barge in on some family scene.

Hadji smiled. "They live in Dubai—you think I would let them come to this India?"

"How many wives do you really have?"

"Four."

"And children?"

"I have four wives and twenty-eight children—that Wasu he left out five. And I am twenty-nine years and I am happily married for seven years." He grinned, watching Jeff's face.

"That makes one a year for each wife for seven years."

Hadji flashed rows of perfect white teeth. "And what is your age?"

"Thirty," Jeff answered.

"Then we are brothers," Hadji said, extending his hand.

They followed an arterial drive on the shore of the seven bays, north of Bombay,

"Where are we going?" said Jeff quietly.

"Juhu," Hadji said. "It is a suburb of Bombay. It is like your Long Island."

"You have been to America?"

"Oh yes, several times. I don't like much." He smiled at Jeff. "No mystery. People too simple-minded."

"We will be there soon. At my house, you may have something to eat. I could not keep that man's food down. I vomit it up in bathroom . . . even I do not eat the beef and I am Moslem. Crazy, that Wasu. He is only business acquaintance, that is all. How he does dare to expect I Hadji will perform for him? Man!" He turned to Jeff. "Someday I kill him."

The car went through a gate in a long white wall covered with bouganvillea, bumped down a dirt road toward the beach, and came to a stop in front of a modern house. They got out. In the distance, Jeff could hear the roar of the surf. A bright moon sailed above palms that rattled in the wind.

Hadji went ahead, switching on lights. He pulled off his headdress and made for the bar at the end of a large room. He wore his hair short, like a curly helmet, and reminded Jeff of an Olympic swimmer from Munich he had once known—an acid head.

Relax," Hadji said. You like to have a drink? Comm'on."

"Quite a pad you have here," Jeff said.

"It belongs to the daughter of some Indian industrialist. She has gone to California to be free—to lead sane life. I rent it. I must come here for business. It is my prison home in India." He laughed, leaning over the bar. "What a terrible country, eh? Terrible and beautiful. From the animal to the saint—it has everything and every kind of persons. My heart breaks when I come here to see such suffering, to see what is happening to this country, day by day, rich or poor, all suffering . . ." He frowned. "And it is just beginning."

There was a noise in the kitchen beyond.

"Who is there," shouted Hadji sharply.

"It is I only, sir, Nazimudin."

"My servant has got up to see if there is anything . . . You needn't have gotten up," Hadji said to a young barefoot boy of fifteen or so who had come in rubbing his eyes.

"Nazimudin, this is Mr. Jeff. Nazimudin comes from my country. He keeps me from . . . 'freaking,' is that correct?"

Jeff nodded.

[193]

"From freaking out here in India." Hadji smiled. "Then, as you are now up, Nazimudin, get us something to eat. Some chips, some lobster curry, something before going to sleep."

"Only two, sir," said the boy.

"Only two," said Hadji.

The boy disappeared. Hadji came from behind the bar, drink in hand. "Come," he said, putting his arm around Jeff's shoulder, "we smoke some good hashish now, eh? Then we have swim, then dinner, after that sleep."

They walked into a hall lined with photos. "See," said Hadji, pointing to the pictures, "these are my wifes."

Jeff saw four extraordinarily beautiful women.

"Plenty cool, as you say, no? And these are all my children, and here eldest son by first wife, my heir.

"But come." He tugged at Jeff. "Come in here, this room is for smoking, just off pool." He took a mixture out of a box and filled a large hooka. "Nazimudin," he yelled.

"Sir?" The boy came running.

"Be a good boy, bring coals from kitchen for hooka."

The boy padded off and returned with a pan of live coals which he placed in the mouth of the hooka.

"Ah, that is good," said Hadji, dumping a large amount of the hashish mixture onto the coals. "Enough."

They smoked from separate flexible hoses. The sound of the hooka bubbled in the silence of the room.

Hadji gazed out at the sea, the whites of his eyes like gleaming moonstones in the half light. "The great Babur is said to have smoked hashish," he said. "Also Alexander—so why not us? The light in India has gone out. The spark is going, day by day. Even Moslem here is no good. My country is same. We are going to be finished. The oil, the gold, it is going to finish us. We believe in God but our greed is getting us. To know such things is no good. I know, it makes me unhappy. Man should be happy, is it not so? Is it not right?" He smiled at Jeff.

Was it something in his voice, or the smile? He couldn't tell, but suddenly Jeff realized that he had never before felt warmth from another man, or never allowed himself to feel it or been aware it could exist.

"Come, let us swim," said Hadji. "Hooka is finished. There are towels just there. You can leave your clothes anywhere, come!"

He stepped into the shadows, threw off his robe, and emerged with a towel. Jeff did likewise, following him out onto the terrace.

"What's this?" Jeff examined a rather fresh scar about a foot long that ran from Hadji's shoulder blades to the small of his back.

[194]

"Oh, some guy, he almost got me. A combination of love and politics," he answered casually. "Politics very stupid business."

The white surf rolled in on the beach beyond the pool.

"You dig surfin'?" Hadji asked.

Jeff nodded. "Got any boards, we could . . ."

"It is no good here, too shallow, too much garbage. These people they shit all over their beaches. When you come to Dubai we will go surfing, best you have ever seen—even as good as South Africa." Hadji threw his towel down. "Race you," he said, diving into the pool suddenly.

They emerged together at the far end. "Tie," gasped Hadji. He went down, tackling Jeff and dragging him underwater, then bobbing up like a porpoise. Then he was out of the pool, drying off and yelling for Nazimudin. "Here is djellabah for you. Come, let us eat. I am starved—stoned and starved. What a good thing," he said, shaking the water out of his hair. "What a good thing to wash off that creep Wasu."

Nazimudin had brought candles to a low table with cushions and stood by ready to serve the meal. As they ate, Jeff became aware of the large number of rings that Hadji wore.

Hadji saw him looking. "Jewels we think are very lucky. We like them." He laughed, eating his food quickly. "But I see you Western men you never wear—you don't wish to sparkle, eh?" He removed one. "Here," he said, tossing it casually to Jeff. "I give you this, then you will begin to sparkle. Wear it on left hand." Jeff caught the ring, a golden snake swallowing its tail, the head a large emerald. "It is just matching your eyes, man," Hadji said.

"It's too much," Jeff protested.

"If I give freely you cannot refuse. Please keep it. Really—I want you to have it."

Jeff smiled and then covered a yawn.

"You would like to get some sleep, I think." Hadji got up from the table. "Or another hooka, no?"

Jeff shook his head.

"No, then we would be up all night, hashish after eating is not good."

Hadji led Jeff into a bedroom that looked like a safari tent. "Pretty cool, eh?" he grinned, cocking his head boyishly. He flopped onto the big bed and banged on the mattress with his hand.

"Come, you will sleep here with me, no?" he said. "It is better, yes?" He banged the bed again playfully. "Come, lie down here."

Jeff lay down.

"There is another bedroom," Hadji said, rolling to face him, "but it is no good to sleep alone. I have never sleep alone in my

[195]

whole life." He frowned. "I would not sleep. When I am alone, Nazimudin he sleeps at bottom of the bed." He looked at Jeff and was silent for a long time.

Jeff smiled. "Everything O.K.?" he asked.

"O.K." Hadji nodded. "I am just looking at you in the moonlight. I think you are very good-looking guy. I am enjoying the sight of you . . . what to do?" He winked."Do you mind it?"

"Don't mind, I guess," Jeff replied, gazing at him seriously.

"I dig you . . . is it correct, eh?"

Jeff nodded. "Yes, it is correct."

Hadji took Jeff's hand, then moved closer and kissed his forehead.

"We believe men can love too," he said softly. "You don't understand it, I know."

Jeff rested his hand on Hadji's waist, feeling the lithe body under the cotton djellabah. He had never really touched a man's body before like this and was surprised that he was allowing himself to do it. He let his hand go up the fine long neck, a neck like a column. Then on an impulse, he pulled Hadji's head down onto his chest.

"I want to love," Jeff whispered, "but I don't know."

"Don't worry so much about it," Hadji said, raising his head.

Without stopping to think, Jeff found himself kissing Hadji full on the mouth. After some time Hadji lifted his face.

"Love will come," he said. "It must. You need not worry so, man."

"I want more, can I have more?" said Jeff, burying his face in Hadji's hair. He felt the muscles of his own body relax as he stroked Hadji's neck and shoulders.

"We take djellabahs off," whispered Hadji. "Too hot for sleeping."

§

It was three days later when Hadji returned Jeff to the Taj. They drove in early from the clear air of Juhu to the sweltering muck of Bombay.

"See you later this evening, man," Hadji said as they arrived in front of the old Victorian hotel. "I got business to take care of, then I come by for you. We can have some food at a place I know. It's going to be my last night in Bombay for a while. Yes?"

As he lay dozing in the early afternoon heat Jeff realized that

[196]

something inside him was different. Even the room seemed to have changed. "Strange," he thought, "how weird that it should be another guy."

After the years he'd spent making out with women. Now this. But something else had happened with Hadji. Never before had he been able to get his mind off his own body, his own cock, to let go and stop watching himself. He'd always used the women like mirrors. But Hadji had made him forget himself, he hadn't worried about how he was scoring. Hadji had relaxed him, acted on him like a balm neutralizing his aggression. He laughed. Was he going to turn gay in India? It was against all his instincts. Was he supposed to fight it or let himself go with it?

He thought of the stupidity of so many things he'd run after like the acid scene and money, the way he'd always treated Laura, the crazy scene at Kamala's. Kamala, he thought, disliking her even more than ever.

But Wasu had been the final downer, Wasu and his mirrored room. Look but don't touch. That had been a real eyeopener. The acid didn't liberate Wasu but made him worse, by merely amplifying what was there from the beginning, beneath everything. Jeff didn't even want to think about it. Everything seemed hopeless. He decided he wouldn't give out any more of the stuff and would talk to Stan as soon as possible, try to get him to give up the whole crazy idea. Turn on India—ugh! Certainly it was a real mistake to front acid to a man like Wasu. He shuddered thinking of all the Wasus in Europe and America who had got it.

The phone rang. It was Carlos.

"Where have you been, man?" he whined. "I been lookin' for you for three days, phoning . . . Wasu is all ready to move, man, he really wants it. He'll take all we have."

"I'll wait to hear from Stan first," Jeff said. "I want to talk to him."

"Come on, man, it's business. You're supposed to be doing business, let's do it!"

"I'll wait," Jeff said.

"Stan is supposed to call me any day now," said Carlos angrily. "I'll have to say you won't give out anything, won't . . ."

"Tell him to call me. I'm always here till noon."

"Don't you truss me, Jeff? I don't think you truss me."

"I have my instructions," Jeff said. "Don't give to anyone till the money is in Switzerland. Doesn't Wasu trust you?"

"O.K., O.K.," said Carlos, "I'll come over and see you in a few days."

"Be sure to call first, man," Jeff said briskly. "I might be busy."

[197]

He put down the phone and buried himself in the pillows, thinking he could chuck all the acid in the bay right outside the window. It would be easy. A bottle a night. Except Stan would be after him. He'd better wait. But where was Stan? And Laura? He suddenly felt responsible for her and began to worry. There was a knock on the door.

"It's Angel," said a faint voice.

Jeff got up and opened the door. She walked past him into the room, pale and sick looking, her hair tangled, reeking of brandy. She stood at a window fingering the curtain and gazing out at the street.

"What's happening," Jeff said. "You O.K.?"

"That bastard Wasu," she said, turning around, "he's always pulling things on me, always laying trips on me, spiking drinks and all that, getting me into situations like the other night . . ."

"Nobody's making you do anything you don't want to," Jeff said.

"Are you kidding?" she yelled. "You think I enjoyed it? You think I dig fucking with dogs and jailbirds while God knows who's watching?"

"You put on a pretty good show of it there," he said.

"That's how much you know, son of a bitch. I was fighting for my life. I saw that convict bastard kill a young girl in there a couple of months ago. He strangled her and fucked her afterwards. With all those creeps laughing and watching."

"Why'd he throw you in there?" Jeff asked.

"Because he wanted me to go down on that girl who was serving the drinks, that's why, and I wouldn't. Me, I'll do most anything if I get high, but not that lesbian shit—I'm no freak, ugh!"

She lit a cigarette. Her hands were shaking.

"Then get out," Jeff said. "Just get on a plane and go back to Texas. You need bread, I'll give you bread. Leave, get out of it, go!"

"Just like that, huh?" She smiled furiously. "I got bread—I could go myself. But it wouldn't be any better, shit. I know too much. He's got too much on me, he'd get me—besides I told you, I tried, I can't hack it."

"But Texas is Texas. It's a long way from India."

"You think so, huh?" She shook her head. "That's all you know, man. You'd be surprised to know he's very big at Vegas, got connections all over . . ."

"I'd be surprised," Jeff said.

"A lot of other places too." She seemed to drift off. Her eyes changed focus, as if she were looking at something far away.

[198]

"What is it?" asked Jeff.

"Nothing," she said. "I keep seeing things. Say, what is this acid shit anyhow? It sure ain't like anything else I ever had, I keep seeing things in corners."

"Like what?"

"Big snakes." She looked scared.

"You got the DTs," Jeff said.

"Naw," she said, "I know what that's like. This is different. I keep seeing real things in all the wrong places, ever since I got doused by your stuff in Delhi."

"Who told you I had it?"

"That Ismail. Say, that was a really far-out party, heh? That big snake and all that." She edged onto the bed where Jeff was lying. "You really put those creeps uptight when you stripped down naked." She gazed at him, her eyes going in and out of focus.

"But you never fucked me yet," she murmured, putting her hand on his leg. "I wanta get fucked right," she declared, and began fumbling with his fly. "Come on, lets ..."

"Cool it," Jeff said, "I'm beat. Been fuckin' three days solid since I left that place."

"I wanta get laid," she moaned. "I got to! I'm goin' crazy, I ain't had no good lay ..."

"I thought that dog was doin' a pretty cool job on you."

"Fuck you, too."

She hunched up on the bed, staring wide-eyed at the corner of the room.

"What is it?" Jeff asked.

"Can't you see it? Can't you see there's a big fuckin' snake? Look—somebody!" she yelled. "You gotta save me, I'm going crazy." She started sobbing and edged her face onto Jeff's thigh. "I want some love. These people got no love in their hearts, only money and frustrations."

"Then get on the fuckin' plane and get outta here," he said, getting up off the bed.

"Sorry." She stood up and brushed back her hair. "Guess you don't want me, huh?" Her face and mouth were twitching nervously. "Sorry I even bothered to come over here and see you. It won't happen again."

Jeff followed her to the door.

"Say," she laughed. "That acid? Maybe if I get enough I'll stop seeing all this. . . . Could you give me more?"

"I shouldn't, but I will," Jeff said, wanting only to get rid of her. "But promise not to bother me again for a while, O.K., and keep your Wasu away from me."

[199]

She nodded weakly.

He got twenty tabs for her. "Listen, don't take it like candy, or you'll wind up in the hospital, understand?"

§

About five the phone rang. It was Hadji.

"You are alone? I will come up."

Jeff had been half asleep, trying to forget Angel. Minutes later, just as he finished showering, Hadji was at the door.

"I am disturbing you, yes?"

"No," Jeff said. "You look very sharp."

"It's not often I wear a suit. Sometimes it is necessary to do business. But I do not like the pants, they are most confining, useless. Invention of your Napoleon I believe." He mopped his forehead. "It is really hot. You are O.K.?"

"O.K.," Jeff smiled.

"I thought you might be uptight about . . ."

"Not uptight."

"That is good. Very good." Hadji smiled mischievously. "Let us get out of here then, it is too hot. I will take you to a fancy air-conditioned Moslem restaurant."

"Sounds good," Jeff said. "Let me get dressed." He put on the suit he had bought in Delhi and the dark red turban.

"What?" exclaimed Hadji. "It is not you? Ha! It is very good disguise. I like it. You look like one of those Northwest frontier fellows, some Afghani or something."

Jeff let the turban unwind. "I wore it in Delhi," he said. "Fooled a few people too."

"It looks great on you, but not in a Moslem restaurant. You look too much like a green-eyed Sikh."

The restaurant had white tiled floors and a large courtyard full of trees and birds. Off long corridors were private dining rooms with swinging doors. The air conditioning was by fan.

"I see I am mistaken about the air-conditioning," Hadji said, removing his jacket. "But anyhow, it's a good fan."

There was a low table and cushions on the floor. The waiter came and Hadji ordered in Urdu. The music of Islam drifted through the air.

Hadji smiled at Jeff and reached across the table for his hand.

"You come to Dubai," he said softly. "I am loving you very much. It is most strange for me, I never expect. I hope it is not too strange for you? In Dubai I have many houses, I will give you one."

[200]

"Why is it so strange for you?" asked Jeff.

"Because I have all these wifes, if I want I have boys, anything I want but—but I am not feeling as close to them as I am to you."

"I think I would probably see you every other week on Thursday." Jeff grinned. "Or something like that with all those wives to look after, not to mention the children. What would I do?"

Hadji's eyes sparkled. "You would get married, of course. We Moslems, we can marry Christian or Jew, but we cannot marry Hindu. I find a good wife for you. After the proper time you get another, perhaps a third. Then you can be very independent. You can help me in business, take care of business with the West. I do not like to go there. My father he is gone. I am eldest member of family; everything is on my head. My uncles they are no good, jealous. My brothers are double worse. There is no one I can trust. All are cheating me."

"Our wives would probably poison us."

"No, no, there are no problems there. Mine would rather see you than another wife. They would say to themselves: well, at least he's through with women, now we can rest easy."

Jeff laughed. "How do you know I wouldn't be unfaithful in the end?"

"Because we have love for each other, my brother. You may go to bed with whom you like, but love does not come so easy. I know it. I know you know it too, eh?"

Jeff gazed at him.

"I can see," Hadji went on. "I know you might not understand, but I can see. I have bad feeling about leaving you here. You are alone here, many peoples are jealous of you on sight. It is most dangerous place for you." He nodded thoughtfully. "You don't know how dangerous. That Wasu, he can kill you anytime he likes, really. In a crowd . . . a knife . . . he has so many agents. Who would know, who will investigate? And who would tell me in Dubai, my brother—no one! I can tell you that."

The waiter came with steaming plates of biryani, pilaf, big round bread circles and tall cool glasses of beer.

"You come to Dubai," Hadji continued. "I will get a good Sheik—that is teacher. He will teach you Islam. Yes, you will become Moslem. Then you will come to your senses. You will have beautiful children."

"And boys to rub me?" Jeff smiled.

"Yes, why not?" laughed Hadji, clinking his beer glass with Jeff's. "You can have anything you want in this world but always you must use properly. Not to overdo, not to put down—not to

[201]

debase? I think, yes—not to debase, not to misuse. It is not what we have, it is how we use, not what we do, but how we do—is it not so?"

Jeff nodded.

"We will have separate place somewhere. I have very beautiful place in country. I never go there. In our world it is not unusual, two men. Nobody bothers. Anyhow, I am ruler—no one tell me, I tell them."

"But you don't even know me," Jeff protested. "I'm really not . . . Really I've been pretty no-good up to now." He shook his head. "Yes, it's true, I'm afraid."

"Don't say I don't know you. Ha! I know all about you, don't be foolish. To know, that is from the touch, not from words."

"I think you would get tired of me." Jeff laughed. "Want to leave me, have me poisoned."

"Now you are making fun," said Hadji. "Why do you make fun when I am wanting to be serious?"

"We'll grow old together then," Jeff said. "Two old lovers."

"Why not?" Hadji's expression was withdrawn. "If you go to bazaar in Arab country you will see plenty of old men sitting together. Many are lovers. Yes, it is true. And in Afghanistan, you will see they will even be knitting and crocheting.

"It is not the body we love. That goes. How can we love that only? But you are disillusioned, that is why. Islam is calling you infidel. It means *without faith*, in-fidel. A man without faith or hope is infidel. You must have faith in your own immortal spirit."

"You must know it is very different from our way of thinking," said Jeff thoughtfully. "In the West men who love each other are thought to be . . . well . . ."

"I know, that is all crazy," Hadji said, bringing his fist down on the table. "Who is to say man is not to love man? It is your women who have enslaved you there. All men in West are women's slave. That is why, even though they are acting so mighty with the muscles and the bombs and such, really they are soft inside. Brought up by women all—women teacher, ha! No wonder you all have no good army. No comradeship. If you had that you could win your Vietnams war. Your Western men cannot even defeat those little Communist bastards from Hanoi."

"Wait a minute," protested Jeff, " we haven't really tried."

"No, no," said Hadji. "You have tried like hell with your machines. But your men on their own, your men are too soft. Hand to hand you cannot win—too soft. But I could, any Moslem could. We do not allow our women to weaken us, only give us strength. We do not allow them to work outside. We treasure them in our house like dangerous dragon goddess. All women are that way, we make love to them, we feed them and make the babies with them, and they are very strong for us. Not against us like women of your country . . . not competing. All the time *with* us."

He took Jeff's hand again. "Listen, America is going to leave Vietnam. After that the whole world is knowing how weak U.S. man has become. That will be the beginning of the end. Russian and Chinese will divide Asia.

"But Islam will survive. It is strongest religion in the world. We believe in God, why should we not fight for God? Your Christians, they do not believe. There is much trouble ahead. We will die happily for Islam if that is necessary. . . . Would you die for Christ? You come to Dubai, we will try forget this bloody world—you will come, you must!"

Jeff shrugged. "I have things I must finish here. Business, just like you. I would like to go—even tomorrow—with you. I'm tired of this place."

"Ah, now you are making sense."

"There is a man coming," Jeff said, trying to think of a good excuse. "I must wait until he arrives in Bombay. He is the employer of Carlos."

"Then?" said Hadji.

"Then I will try to visit you. We can go on from there and see what happens." He smiled at Hadji warmly.

"Let us go back to your hotel then," suggested Hadji, breaking the silence. "I will say good-bye. My plane leaves very early."

The night air was heavy with humidity and pollution as they got into Hadji's car and drove to the hotel. There was no breeze. The streets were still crawling with beggars and hustlers, moving in slow motion past boarded-up shops, around and over clutches of the poor and starving who slept on sidewalks, against the buildings, and in gutters.

A few blocks from the Taj their way was blocked by a large crowd in front of a tall modern building.

"It is one of Wasu's hotels," Hadji said. "Probably he is giving out money. You stay in car, I will see."

He jumped out and elbowed his way through the people. In a few minutes he returned, his face grim.

"It is that girl," he said.

"You mean Angel?" Jeff opened his door.

"Stop!" Hadji exclaimed. He threw himself against Jeff and slammed the door shut. "You no go. She is dead. She has come off the top. It is not pretty."

Jeff bolted out of the car and pushed his way into the crowd.

Angel was spreadeagled on her back, her skull flattened. In falling, she had killed a leper, and a second leper whom she had also

[203]

hit sat seriously injured beside her body unable to get up. Flailing wildly with the oozing stubs of his arms, the man was demanding that someone in the hotel pay him the price of his broken leg.

"Falling from the sky she did not," he screamed in Marathi. "She is falling from hotel—hotel must pay!"

Jeff stared speechless, his hands clenched. No one was even looking at Angel.

The leper saw Jeff and directed a barrage of epithets at him. A police officer arrived and asked Jeff if he were a relation of the dead girl. He wanted to find someone to pay off the leper so that the crowd would go away.

Jeff shook his head silently and retreated to the car.

Hadji drove backwards along the street to an intersection and then screeched away towards the Taj.

When they reached the room Hadji exploded. "That Wasu has finished her off I know it. He was tired of her. Otherwise, you don't send dog to fuck her. After fucking by dog everyone knows it is over. Would you believe me if I tell you she really loved that Wasu?"

Jeff felt shaken. He stood looking out at the bay, unable to meet Hadji's eyes.

"Yes, I know," he said, turning at last. "But I think it's my fault. She took too much LSD. First in Delhi, then here in Bombay. This afternoon she was here raving, seeing things—wanted me to fuck her. I gave her more of the stuff to get rid of her."

Hadji looked thoughtful. "You should have given her your sex, not the drug."

"But I kept thinking of that dog fucking her and I couldn't."

"You see?" said Hadji, slumping into a chair and wiping the sweat from his forehead. "But what is this LSD? I have not had."

"You don't need it," Jeff snapped. "Maybe nobody needs it."

"Jeff?" said Hadji.

"Yes?"

"I implore you to come with me to Dubai tomorrow. This Angel, she is an omen. You must listen to me and do as I say. You must not stay here."

"But I have certain responsibilities, especially now. I've decided to persuade the owner of the drug not to sell to Wasu and if possible, not to sell any more in India."

"But cannot it be done in a letter? You are thinking you are too important. Do not think it. Just forget the whole business and disappear. Let them do what they will with it. When I went into the crowd I knew I was going to see death. It is the angel of death. She is very close. You don't understand, you cannot see, but it is

[204]

true, my brother." He stood close to Jeff, touching his shoulder lightly. "If I am leaving you here tonight, I am thinking I may never see you anymore."

"Believe me," Jeff said, "I'll come as soon as I can. But I can't give the stuff to Carlos, not now."

"Even if it would cost your life?"

"Don't worry about me, I can take care of myself. The man who owns it will come. I will persuade him and that will be the end of it. It's my duty," Jeff said, trying to appeal to Hadji in terms he would understand. "If I leave now, I'd just be running out on it, you understand?"

"And what will you do alone here, with those two wanting the drug from you?"

"I will sit here in the hotel. Not go out, give instructions not to let anybody . . ."

"Whew!" Hadji shook his head violently. "You don't understand, man, in Bombay Wasu gives instructions."

"Then it's a risk I'll just have to take."

Hadji paced the room.

"I see your mind is made up then. What can I do? Here," he said, handing Jeff a package. "I am so mad at you I almost forgot presentation. It is Arab robe and headdress, like mine. See—soft, like Kashmir wool."

He took Jeff's hands and held him at arms' length.

"If I may never see you again, is all right?" he said, smiling. "I know we will meet again in next world. Surely it will be so."

"Did you give me your address?"

"It is on that paper near the phone. You can phone easily from Bombay—very clear reception."

"I'll call you."

"Yes, of course," said Hadji from the doorway. He started to leave, then turned around. "My plane leaves at five-thirty. You *can* be on it. We can fly away together. I get you on board somehow if you are showing up. There is time still. Yes, you should listen."

X

§

THE RICKETY COUNTRY bus had taken them many miles through a jungle of dry scrub and thorn bushes big as trees.

"It's a 1928 Mercedes," Indra said. "Can you imagine how they are still keeping it together?"

Large areas of the side had been patched with odd bits of metal and in the front where fumes poured out past the driver, you could even see the road through holes in the floor.

Laura had no idea where they were. They had come out of the mountains by a different route, caught a night bus, and the next day were in Benares putting Alex on a flight to Delhi, where he would catch the London plane. Indra had even given him money. Laura wondered why he was so anxious for Alex to leave.

The landscape was a uniform dust color. Foliage on the trees was drying up or dead, and what green remained was covered. All day long the bus had stopped at pitiful dried-up villages, disgorging one full busload only to take on another. Except for three sadhus sitting up front, there were few through passengers. The upper caste sat in the first three rows, the middle caste in the center, and the lowest in back.

Indra insisted on sitting at the back, jammed between live chickens and cans of kerosene.

"When you are riding or walking with people, always try to stay behind them," he told Laura. "Your waves can be broken by anyone sitting or walking behind you—if they know how to do it."

Hour after hour the unchanging barren landscape slid by. Laura watched the people, absorbed with their relationships, admiring their grace, their forbearance, their fearlessness. At each stop those leaving would stage a sort of battle to get out, while at the same time those entering would battle to get in, pushing each other through windows and pulling children, tattered luggage, and animals along with them. Fifteen minutes later the driver would return to collect tickets. Beggars and lepers, crawling on all fours and led by small boys, moaned, chanted, and cracked obscene jokes as they solicited funds.

Outside youths in shorts and tight pants shouted in at the passengers, poking large cucumber slices through the windows, warm soda pop, or trays of candy made of sugar, puffed rice, stones, and a peanut or two. Lower-caste women traveled in gangs, wearing cheap nose rings and new machine-made saris with gold borders that never tarnished. They were tough and quarrelsome. Upper-caste women wore homespun rags and sat immobile, staring fixedly into space like the idols they worshipped. And everywhere from loudspeakers and portable radios All India radio blared with frantic music from Hindi films.

"The luxuries, the pollutions, the mysteries of the plains," said Indra.

Auk auk. The bus horn, like the cry of an aging goose, announced departure. Skinny ravaged villagers, their joints swollen with hookworm anemia, waved to friends and relatives while swarms of flies fought over bits of dropped food.

Now the dust swirled up behind them and the countryside was less populated. Women became sick and vomited out the window, splattering those in the rear. Though the sun was not more than an hour from setting, the wind that flapped the tattered canvas window curtains blew hot and dry.

Indra elbowed Laura awake and beckoned her to follow. The bus had arrived at a terminal point and the last of the passengers were collecting their belongings.

"From here we must walk five miles," he said. "We'll reach our destination after dark."

"But where are we?" sighed Laura.

"We are here." He smiled. "Don't ask foolish questions." Darkness had come rapidly. Fires were burning in the ramshackle tea shops where sweaty boys prepared bread and potato curry in large iron pots. An anxious commotion seemed to hang on the edge of the night.

They ducked into a hut with long tables at which were seated rows of tired-looking travelers, laborers, and children in rags. Outside Laura could hear at intervals the fast persistent beat of drums starting, then fading away, starting again and fading. "What is all the drumming about?" she asked curiously.

"This is the last stop on the way to the Gate," he said. "This village survives on transporting the dead and dying to the burning ground. You will see the bearers running on the path toward the fires at the other end."

Laura shuddered. "Is that where *we're* going?" she asked.

Indra nodded.

Tea came in brass cups, sweet milky tea and yellow balls of lentils stuck together with raw brown sugar. Flies crawled over everything.

"Messengers of Kali," Indra said, waving them aside so that he could drink his tea. "They are her thousand eyes, always watching and waiting."

Laura noticed the cook blowing his nose with his hands while he washed the utensils.

"Don't worry," Indra assured her. "You won't get sick as long as you are with me. It is impossible."

Laura marveled at how composed he always looked under the worst circumstances. "Like an echo from another age," she thought, "come back to catch the final act of a five-thousand-year-old play: humanity at the brink of destruction."

When she saw him perfectly calm and glowing with energy, it was like seeing a hero from the other side. "The other side of what?" she asked herself. And why did he still frighten her so when he radiated such strength and calm? She found it impossible to frame the unthinkable in the clouded mirror of her mind.

"This may be the last food for some time," he was saying quietly. "We will have fresh water to be sure, and I have a sack of lemons and some brandy. I may have to get you drunk." He chuckled. "But don't worry, you're stronger than you think. You'll come through, don't worry."

It was a test. She had agreed to come, but as the time drew near she began to doubt herself. She knew that here was a chance, that he was trying to awaken something deep inside her, maybe a still glowing spark of faith. But there were strong blocks, and although she hated them she strengthened them by trying desperately to hang onto what remained of her old self. "What will I turn into if I really let go?" she kept thinking. The unknown so terrified her that she felt as if she'd been kicked in the stomach.

Outside the tea shop it was night. A runaway donkey careened down the street as if mad. After it came naked bearers running with a corpse on a litter and followed by the relations of the deceased, all jogging along behind.

"We must hurry," Indra said, "otherwise it will be getting too late. There are too many wild pigs on this road, not to mention bandits."

A waning moon rose deep orange behind the thorn trees as they hurried along the broad foot path. The hot windy night was alive with mourners and mendicants passing in both directions. After a while a glow appeared on the horizon and moments after that the

[208]

smell. The ludicrous thought crossed Laura's mind that it smelled exactly like a barbecue she had once been to—a fundraising barbecue on Long Island. She wondered if all those people were still at it, buying diamonds from Harry Winston and having benefits.

"Ah, I see you can smell it. Like your American hamburger stands, yes? You'll not forget it soon."

How could she explain the associations crowding in on her? Would he understand "cook-outs" or McDonald's?

He gestured ahead. "The largest burning place left in the world. Also the most remote. Do you recall I told you about an initiation at twelve that changed my life?"

She nodded.

"Don't be afraid, I am with you. I'm going to give you the same initiation. It is a risk, but one you must take. Remember, you are going to see a gate. It has nothing to do with endings. There are no endings, nor are there beginnings. All that is just maya—illusion."

Laura noticed first the many small temples, some hidden in the undergrowth, some grouped in open spaces. Their walls were constructed of human bones cemented with mud. Row upon row of gaping skulls fixed their blind gaze on the travelers.

"You must cover your head now and follow exactly as I say and do. We are nearing our destination. If you feel faint or sick, repeat the syllables I have given you."

The sacred fires of holy men burned brightly here and there under ancient trees. Laura stared at a group of naked sadhus covered with dirt, their hair matted and filthy.

"These are Aghor sadhus," Indra explained. "They are in the third class. It is one of the main divisions: they use filth and degradation whereas we go right to renunciation. Don't they remind you of Dr. Long? You see, there are many paths all leading to the same place."

One of the Aghors beckoned them to sit down. "Let's join him for a smoke," Indra suggested. "These are the watch dogs here . . . it is well for us to treat them with respect."

Two other naked men were squatting in front of the fire. Large rings with chains attached had been inserted in the foreskins of their penises, weighing them down.

"Who are they?" Laura asked.

"They are Nagas, simple-minded ones. They think by weighing down the penis they can kill desire. It is stupid. Once I tried it. Delusion," Indra said, spitting on the ground. "He who eats dirt and filth becomes dirt and filth. He who chains his organ becomes chained to it."

He paused, then accepted a small packet from one of the men.

[209]

He noted its contents and took out his chillum. They were honoring him by an invitation to prepare the pipe, an act of homage paid to one of superior merit recognized on sight.

"In the end all must come here," he said seriously. "This place is itself a guru. Though very few know what to do here as they are without guru. But these men are not capable of higher paths just now. It is all the same. And it is better they come here while alive than as corpses. Yes," he said laughing at Laura's astonished face, "they will benefit greatly at the proper time."

"See," he went on, glancing up as he prepared the chillum, "there is a dying one having himself brought here before time. He has good faith." Indra indicated an old man on a litter whose bony arm was outstretched, pointing to the bearers to take him inside and place his body on the pyre.

"Jai Ho!" Indra shouted at him.

The old man moved his head around trying to see Indra. "Jai Ho! Maharaj!" he shouted in a cracked voice.

"You are blessed," Indra yelled back at him in Hindi. "Go now and enter the Gate."

He went back to preparing the chillum, rolled bits of herbs together and murmured a mantra. Finishing, he took from his bag a small cloth which he dampened in water. Then he held the pipe with his arms outstretched and chanted loudly until the mouth of the pipe caught fire on its own. A ripple of admiration stirred the sadhus around him as he inhaled deeply and passed the pipe.

The next man had no cloth and had to pass it on. Suddenly all were rummaging in their belongings looking for pieces of cloth.

"They thought I would let them use my soffie," he said, chuckling. "See how low they are, they were even testing me on that! They hang around outside here smoking chillum and getting what they can. They are not to be given any secrets or instruction."

"Don't take too much of this," he added quietly, handing Laura the chillum. "It will dry you up too much for what you have to do later. And it's early yet. Spread your cloth and sleep. We won't begin until later tonight."

§

When she awoke his hand was on her forehead. The warmth and a certain electrical tingling from it roused her at once. The fire was out but the glowing embers shone on the sleeping sadhus, themselves like dying embers, their saffron and red robes crumpled into strange forms. Once Laura had wondered how the Indian people were able to sleep any time at any place. Now with the fatigue of the past months mounting inside her, she understood.

Paco pac pacoo wakoo pacpac pacoo. The call of a night bird echoed through the teak and mahogany trees which towered above them.

"Are you all right?" he said, guiding a warm cup of steaming liquid into her hands.

She smiled up at him. "Yes, a bit sleepy but all right."

"It is lemon water," he said. "Drink! I will be giving it to you from time to time. It is very sustaining."

It tasted like hot lemonade. Laura wondered how long she would last at this experiment and what would happen to her—or what was left of her.

"Don't plan," he said, aware of what she was thinking. "Don't plan a moment into the future. It closes you up, spoils all the play and you'll not be able to get the cues, or the clues." He smiled and stood up. "Now we must begin. Remember, I will be with you, even though it may seem to you that I have disappeared."

The jungle became sparse as they entered the cremation grounds. Smoke drifted and hung in the branches of the trees, bare of leaves in this hot dry season, the Indian summer when men go mad. Night breezes whipped fitfully at the pyres, blowing hot coals across the dusty paths that separated them. Here was the activity of death: like the hustle and bustle, the sense of expectation near the entrance to a great city.

Laura felt release, a physical sensation of letting go, almost as if one strand of a woven rope had snapped under pressure. They paused as Indra, his brow furrowed with compassion, glanced down at the corpse of a young sadhu in a saffron dhoti lying atop a carefully stacked pile of logs. Flowers covered his dark body, bright red hibiscus buds, jasmine, and marigolds tumbled down his naked chest. Markings of white and crimson across his brow and on his hands and bare feet completed what seemed more an appearance than a reality.

Laura shuddered.

"Have no fear. Every act is an act of the gods. We do nothing," murmured Indra. "This place is a gate. His inner one has gone through but not completely, not yet. It is waiting total release by the fire."

"You are already dead," he said, gazing at her. "Or alive . . . There is no difference."

The Dooms—those in charge of burning the bodies—darted in and out of the firelight, pouring ghee and oil onto the blazing pyres or poking the dying embers with large sticks to make sure the

[211]

corpses were consumed. At one pyre an entire family of old men and women huddled together in grief while on the ground beside them two small boys played marbles in the light of the burning corpse. Few other mourners were left at that hour but there were many monks and sadhus meditating.

The smoke grew thicker and sweeter as Indra led her through more forest into an area so large its boundaries were lost behind distant hillocks. Here the corpses of the nameless ones burned by the hundreds—those unable to pay for a separate burning, those whom no one knew, who had no friends. The rickshaw wallah, the nameless beggar, the leper, the ciphers at the edge of life were burned here. Smoke drifted into the night, blue smoke that smelled like sirloin steak. Figures appeared and disappeared, the scene went beyond Laura's imagination. A hand jutting out from one pile caught fire and burnt to the bones like a flaming sign. Logs and stiff bodies tilted in every direction, some reduced to glowing coals, others only charred. A rigid corpse suddenly snapped into an upright position, its head in flames, the flesh burning away from the wide-eyed face to the skull. Then it exploded, sending bits of brain hissing into the flames.

"The master computer meets the master programmer, the mirror reclaims its image," she heard Indra muttering.

Laura felt sick and reached out for him but he had vanished. Wasn't he just there, hadn't she just now heard his voice? Looking for him she peered into the night through the flames and smoke. A feeling of total emptiness possessed her, deeper than anything she had ever known, beyond shuddering or crying out. But that was unnecessary; was it not an illusion? Something stirred inside her, a long neglected power. Her connections to it were strengthening.

Then she felt his hand on hers. "Are you all right?"

"I don't know."

"There is more to it," he said. "Come!" He made a crude broom of twigs and swept until the hard dusty clay was smooth and free of debris. Then he scattered water to settle the dust and swept again. After repeating the process three times he gathered green leaves and spread these on the earth, and then on top spread the skins of a buffalo, a tiger and a deer, soft and worn thin with age. Over all he placed three pieces of colored cloth: blue, purple, and red on top.

The night wind sang balefully in the scrub thorn trees and drove low clouds across the moon. With ash trickling in a thin line from his closed fist, Indra carefully drew three large circles around the place he had prepared and divided them into eighteen segments, inscribing each with a sign.

[212]

"Do not be afraid," he said casually, "it's a most auspicious place. You know it otherwise you would not be here. Sit down now on this seat I have prepared for you. You may lie down if you have to. The only rule is that your back should remain straight whatever position you are in." He removed the red cloth he was wearing and sat down on it to her left, his head cocked slightly toward her but not looking at her.

For a long time they sat silent, then he said: "Please repeat this group of syllables with me and continue after I have stopped." He lowered his voice and began repeating a very long mantra. She repeated it with him. Slowly his voice died away, and she was saying it alone with her eyes closed until it became automatic.

Then his voice came again in a monotone. "Now open your eyes and focus on one spot in the fire, anywhere in the fire. Do not take your eyes from the spot and keep repeating the syllables. You should, in fact, be saying them even now while I am talking to you." He looked at her. "You are," he said. "Good."

Laura picked out a point in the fire and stared at it. After some time everything began to whirl around the point on which her eyes were fixed. She lost track of time. Turbulent at first, her mind quieted as she continued repeating the syllables until she could feel their rhythm develop in her body, their vibration ringing through her.

Then she began to hear a vast chorus of voices, at first like the sound of a crowd in a large auditorium before the performance of a play. Then they became like singing voices and filled her with their sound, like a chorus from a Mozart opera. Just as this singing began she started to see something. At the point where she was staring into the fire of burning bodies, she noticed a brightness, expanding and contracting like the iris of some fiery eye. For what seemed like a very long time she kept staring while the singing became a great thunder in her head. When she thought about it the bright opening became smaller but when she forgot to think the iris opened wide.

Then all at once the voices became ringing bells, almost like an electronic simulation, high-pitched and lilting. Her eyes went blank, as though she had been blinded. An intense white light, brighter than the sun on the snowy Himalayas, replaced the throbbing eye. It was as if the eye had opened and she had gone through it. The white turned to blue, like the blue of a color television screen, pulsing with blue cells of light, and there was a tickling sensation up and down her spine.

When Laura regained her self-awareness the blue screen didn't fade or disappear. She knew where she was, she could feel her body,

[213]

she could feel that her eyes were wide open and that she was repeating the syllables he had given her.

As if on cue, Indra's voice came from far away. "Now you will see the syllables you are repeating," he said.

On the blue screen that had replaced her sight, she saw the Sanskrit letters of the syllables in gold, pulsating like neon signs.

"And now in the Roman," he said and a transliteration in gleaming Roman letters appeared.

Something inside her felt elated and excited. What she was seeing exhilarated her and seemed unbelievably beautiful. "At last I'm 'seeing,' " she thought. "There is a universal connection . . . to a bigger place."

"Good." His voice cut in as though it were transmitting on short wave. "You have got the hang of it, now. Very good." The voice faded and the fire crackled like static. "You will remain here for fourteen days. If you feel sleepy you may lie down. You may open or close your eyes, that will have no effect now. You will need less sleep as we go on. But be sure to keep repeating the syllables, and no matter what happens I will be here. I am always here."

After that she heard nothing, not even the fire; it was as though she'd become deaf. The syllables came and went on the blue field until all track of time or place or being seemed dissolved.

She was not able to calculate how long she'd been there when slowly in the field she saw, as if through blue mist, the corpse of a tall black man with enormous feet and a profile resembling an Egyptian priest. Astride the corpse was a naked yogi seated in siddhasan who resembled Indra. Was it he? She was uncertain. Veils of blue obscured the phantasm which shimmered before her. She felt her heart jump and knew she was becoming frightened but kept repeating the syllables Indra had given.

Then his voice came out of the image although the lips of the yogi did not move. Laura thought she might pass out. An emission of energy in the form of a black cloud, like a swarm of bees, seemed to be coming at her out of the fire, from the body of the yogi. Somehow it made her very ill, she felt like vomiting. She was sure that when it reached her something very unpleasant would happen. Then she heard his voice.

"Yes, yes. It is possible to be in many places at the same time, as many as you want. Now listen, this is a very dangerous thing we are doing."

The cloud vanished and she could see that it was his form sitting on the corpse although the voice originated inside her head.

"A most dangerous thing," he was whispering inside her head. "You require strong doses so that you will go right. You have got on the wrong track—it was not meant to be. You are already very far along although you do not know it. It is too dangerous to be open and not have proper instruction. Now you will be opened all together. Do not be frightened, be brave. There is *no thing* to be afraid of. But you do not understand the precarious position, you do not understand that there is something to be won or lost. It is in this body."

She saw him slap the corpse on which he sat.

"This body is like a battlefield and the stakes, my dear child, are very high. You get this body after a long time. It is just a jumping-off point, energy changing into spirit, a launching pad—a great gift after many other tries, other embodiments. Would you care to see some of them?"

"See what?" she asked, frightened by the sudden question.

"Would you like to see some of the other embodiments you have taken—to relive them?"

She nodded, too frightened to think.

"I will show you some."

At once the vision disappeared and was replaced by the form of a young woman. Laura started, it was her mother: she was young and beautiful, full of color and light.

"Now remember when you were five and she was laughing at your first attempts to maneuver your knife and fork."

How beautiful she was, Laura thought as she watched. She could feel tears welling up inside her.

"I am taking you back slowly." His voice was muffled.

The image of her mother vanished and there was a hall, a space so vast that its boundaries were outside the range of her vision. She could hear voices echoing in the halls, speaking a language foreign to her. "How odd," she thought, but somehow it was very familiar too. Then she felt a hand stroking her head.

"This is the place where everything is," said Indra's voice, "everything past and everything future, it is at this level, like a reservoir. I am only opening your eye so that you can see it."

"But what is this, where am I," she stammered, "I feel so small."

"This is Russia. In Russia some five hundred years back you are embodied in a female dog, a very beautiful and sensitive Russian wolfhound. You are being stroked by your mistress, see, look up now. See how she is stroking you, see how much she loves you and how good she is to you. But she is very old and will soon die. See now, who is this . . ."

The scene changed and a very ugly dirty hulk of a man towered over her.

[215]

"Ah," said Indra's voice, "this is her servant. Your mistress is dead and this man has been left money by her to care for you, but see, he takes all the money and the food for himself. And now he is going to hit you—duck!"

She felt her body jerk away. Then the scene changed. She felt cold and overwhelmingly alone. Snow seemed to be falling all around her.

"Yes, it is clear now," said Indra. "You are going to leave that dog's body; rather than put up with the cruel keeper you have come to the grave of your mistress. See, there is her name on the stone in Russian, ah, and it is very cold, is it not? Your dog's body will soon freeze, here at the lady's grave." He chuckled softly. "For this act of faith you . . . uh, got promoted."

He laughed uproariously and then her eyes went blank and again she saw him, seated on the corpse, laughing at her through the smoke.

"Aha, Uma—you are surprised, no? I am surprising you with my maya, my illusions. But they are not mine, not anybody's. Always remember the world of bodies is maya. Would you like to see some more!" he shouted at her through the smoke and flames.

At once she was in a different space, she felt strange and light and the giant head of a snake crawling toward her filled her entire vision. She felt terrified until the snake's head seemed to recede as if she were flying away.

"Ah, I see," he said, "you were sitting on your eggs." He laughed. "Yes, yes, it is you, you are a bird. Many times you have laid eggs only to have them eaten by the serpent. You are old now, and have become weak. You will soon be killed by the sharp claws and beak of the kite who lives in the rocky cliffs above and has been watching you, waiting to get you."

She felt herself screaming but there was no sound of it.

"Yes," his voice went on, "the fear of being eaten alive is very strong, is it not? So many times before it has happened."

The gleaming syllables appeared once more. She felt like a small boat at sea in a great storm. The syllables she kept repeating were like a rudder, she hoped they would prove strong enough.

"They are the keys," his voice murmured inside her, "and once the door is opened they are the rod and the staff. As I told you, this short path is a dangerous undertaking, but it is what the old Tibetan woman saw. It is your time for it. Your past actions have been spotless, your present birth is correct, the result of your accumulated acts. You need have no fear. But if by accident people who are unprepared by past experience are shown the things locked in the structures of their cells and in their genetic code, they will become mad."

[216]

She could hear the fires crackling now, consuming the corpse.

"Still, I know you do not believe me," he sighed. "You will think I have 'hypnotized' or 'mesmerized' you, and am putting you into whatever state I imagine. That's why you still become frightened. You think it is *my* power but that is wrong.

"It comes from another place, it belongs to no one though it is worshipped in many forms. You will know it . . . know that what is happening to you is correct."

Suddenly from deep inside, she felt sleep coming on.

"Yes," his voice said. "Lie down and rest for some time. There is plenty of time. But remember, remember to remember to keep your back straight and keep repeating what I have given."

§

After a long time Laura became conscious of warmth and could hear the syllables going on and on inside her—a deep throbbing, like a heartbeat. The blue screen was gone, and she lay warm and secure wondering whether to open her eyes. When she did, and raised herself to a sitting position, the corpse and the yogi had vanished. It was day, the sun glared through a high overcast sky.

The Dooms were stacking corpses and wood on a huge pyre. At the edge of her vision she caught a glimpse of Indra's eyes floating in space, but when she turned to look they disappeared and his seat on her left was vacant.

She sat erect and stretched, sipping a glass of lemon water that she found, freshly made, beside her.

Then his voice came through her exactly as if she were a radio set that had tuned itself in.

"Please remember when your eyes are open to focus on a point. Do not fail to keep repeating the syllables. Do not imagine that it is morning and you are waking up and that it is all over. You are just beginning."

"Where are you," she asked, finding a point in the smoldering ashes before her.

"I am in the tree over your head," the voice said casually. Without thinking she turned and saw him squatting in the lower branch of a large mango tree which extended over her sitting place. His eyes were closed. She stood up and put out her hand toward his. He put down his hand until she could touch it. But there was nothing there, her hand closed on thin air.

She started back and fell to the ground.

"Sit up," he said firmly, "you are not following directions. You are to stare at a spot. Remember. You are not advanced enough yet to let your attention wander here and there."

She nodded, resuming her position.

"Otherwise, it could be most dangerous," he said. "You see, we are doing these things so you may come to understand that there is more to things than you have been led to believe, than 'meets the eye' as they say." He laughed. "Don't ask how things work, do not try to discover the causes, that is the Pandora's box. It is what men call 'science' these days. Your people, the Western peoples, have become too simple. They want only a certain range of wavelengths to be considered 'real.' They wish to exclude all others for which they have found no measuring instruments. Your people will be gone through though, they are going to be destroyed because they cannot understand what is this existence, that it is thicker and more complex than they are willing to admit." Suddenly he appeared seated in front of her. "Gone through," he repeated. He thrust his fist toward himself as if to beat his chest, and his whole arm went through his body as though it were made of jelly. He grinned at her.

"In the West you suffer from the sin of pride. You think because machines serve you and you seem to make them that you are the creators of your world and that you are the operators. You think you have constructed a world free from the unpredictable.

"All the devils in the Christian religion—who are they? They are sadhus and yogis. They are dark, they wear red, they carry the trident. That means anger and danger. Anger and danger to the weakhearted—those without faith or courage. The slave religion of Christianity is so frightened by chance, by fate, that it has condemned as bad everything it can't explain. The yogis carry the tridents to kill you—that part of you who thinks he alone is the maker and shaper, the operator of this world—to kill the pride. For until you get killed, you cannot get across."

"Where *are* you," she said after some time.

"Aha, I am everywhere! Just now I am sitting beside you but you will not see me. Reach out and touch."

She felt his warm arm.

"But you won't see me—if you turned, which you must not, you wouldn't see me." He laughed as if it were a great joke, until she began to laugh too. His laughter calmed her and made her feel secure.

"I must do these confusing things so that you will believe this ancient wisdom once and for all. Otherwise, how could you be expected to believe? You cannot read what is unwritten, you cannot speak of the unspoken. Nothing of importance has been written, only passed down through dhyan.

[218]

"Whom you call your forefathers in the West, they were afraid of wisdom, deathly afraid of it. They had crusades, killed dragons, burned witches, sent missionaries—even opened schools for the public to stamp it out. All frightened hypocrites.

"Always remember that the Christian religion was made by slaves and former slaves. Christ was a great yogi, a great Master. He cannot be blamed for all that came after him in his name. The church councils, they made up a religion out of Aristotle, the first low-caste philosopher. They threw out the unseen truths which were passed on through the high castes, and substituted measurable appearances. In one stroke got themselves free of caste and changed the rules of the game—they thought. But the unseen truths do not change. How can truth change? It goes on working whether people know it or not."

"Christ did not die in Jerusalem, he is buried at Shrinagar, in Kashmir, where thousands, mostly the Sufis, worship at his grave in the Moslem section every year."

"Are you Sufi?"

"That is another made-up thing," he answered wearily. "I have studied with those calling themselves Sufis, but they are all branches. There is only one teaching. Its root is here, lost now in antiquity. Moses and Manu knew it but it is not recorded. Gautama knew it but refused to teach it. It is a very final teaching, a shocking one and shockingly simple—a hard pill for people to swallow, especially these days."

He sighed. "Once you know it, once it has been shown to you, your life in this body can become too difficult, too painful. You long to get out. That is where the duty part comes in. It is not for us to assume the role of creator or destroyer."

He sighed again. "That is why I have to give you these signs and shows. It is my duty to persuade you. It has become hard nowadays—things have gone too far toward the end. Certainly there are few of my own people I have found who wish to understand."

The Dooms were bringing in more corpses now and beginning a fresh pyre of wood and corpses right in front of the place where she was staring.

"Ah," he said, laughing softly, "here come some fresh victims."

She felt herself shudder.

"See what bad actions are etched on that face," he said, referring to the corpse of a middle-aged man which had just been thrown in front of her.

"And the woman beside him—would you believe me if I told you that hag's body was once beautiful, that she was a great prostitute desired by thousands. I could show you her life if you like."

[219]

Laura held up her hand, not daring to see.

Indra laughed. "Too much, yes? And too boring. See how she lies there now and watch closely as the flames are kindled under that once beautiful and expensive body which gave pleasure to so many. Watch as it melts before you." He paused. The blue space was beginning to open up again. She felt relief that she might be getting away from the scene before her. She hoped that the body of the old whore would vanish but it didn't; on the contrary, it appeared even more vividly than before.

"Fire is a gate," his voice said. "Fission. There are other gates. Pleasure is dissolved into them. The supreme pleasure is beyond them."

She could see the syllables of the mantra again, partly obscuring the scene. Some old men in white dhotis had come, their Gandhi hats in their hands. They were performing some ceremony over the old whore's body.

"They loved her so much they cannot even give the money for a separate burning," Indra chuckled from somewhere. "Her inner one is here now. It has become a ghost, what we call a Bhut or a Preat. It is so attached, even to that terrible old body, that it is hanging around."

"What can be done?" whispered Laura.

"Nothing now. For what follows, all the work must be done in this body. When the body goes it is too late then, the fate of the inner one is sealed. It will go back into another body, perhaps even an animal one, but before that the inner one will drift here and there according to its past actions. Eventually it will be attracted to like bodies and will go in, a letter looking for the proper envelope to be sent in, yes? Maya is endless, beginningless and endless. It just goes on and on until you are ready to get out, until you cease wanting to have a body."

The Dooms were pouring oil on the bodies now, trying to get the whole pile to start burning. As the fire caught she thought she saw Indra again through the blue, sitting on top. Then she heard his voice chuckling inside her.

"You can see me then," he said intimately. "Very good. At least now we know you haven't lost it, that you are getting better at it. The connection is getting stronger. You're becoming a better receiver."

"Why are you sitting on the corpses again?" she thought to herself.

"It doesn't matter where I sit," his voice replied. "I am having a conversation with the inner one of this woman. It is high time she came face to face with things. Don't be frightened, I am just trying

[220]

to do her a good turn, trying to get her to really see her own body there, while it gets burned. She doesn't want to see it, she loves it so much and now it is going to be burnt. There is no chance of her changing anything now. Now that is all over. It is high time she faced up to such things and stopped wandering from body to body."

The flames were crackling again.

She saw his fist come down on the stomach of the old corpse. Then she saw what appeared to be a young woman fighting with him. He was shaking a small drum in the air and the woman was grabbing at the drum and trying to stop him.

"I think I see her now," Laura said.

"You may. Her inner one is freaking out, as you say. Most intense. That is why you see it. She can't stand me sitting on her body—hates it. She still thinks it's her own body even when it's burning up right in front of her. She thinks she is powerful—it is a great laugh for me."

Laura watched as the form of the young woman flew out of the fire and landed in the dust a few yards away, curled up like a fetus. It seemed to be breathing. Then it caught sight of her.

"If you get a female body," it screamed wide-eyed, "try to hang onto it, try to hang onto . . ."

The apparition vanished.

"Enough." It was Indra's voice again. "She won't try any more tricks. What a bother these strong-willed people become when they are directed toward their bodies. Know-it-alls who never know anything. But fire is fire." He laughed. "It is there for them always the same, always burning."

Laura felt frightened again, too frightened to think of running away. Dead bodies were supposed to be sacred, weren't they? Or were they just garbage, just worm food? The thought flashed across her mind like a telegraphic signal.

"You are frightened because you have not seen. Not yet. You are not fully opened up."

"Then how can I see?" she cried out.

"Believe only in me," came his voice as though echoing down a mountain. "Believe only in me and you will see. I will vouchsafe to you the Divine Eye."

Then the blue screen opened again, shimmering, wider and more complete than before. In it appeared the gigantic form of a yogi like Indra. She seemed to be sitting by the toe of his left foot, which dwarfed her. Many others were standing and sitting near her.

She felt her hair stand on end.

"I'm seeing!" she felt herself shouting.

[221]

The face of the form floated far above, ageless and wise, decked with flowers and smiling down at her. The mouth was open, the large black eyes shining. Then she heard his laugh, like the roar of the wind, and saw teeth in the mouth and in the mouth fire. Hands came out of the sky and with fingers larger than bulldozers began to scoop up those around her and toss them into the laughing fiery mouth.

Then she was scooped up. There were others with her, some screaming, some praying. She hung on tight as the ground vanished, even though to have fallen off might have been a better course. Her life flashed before her and she felt ashamed. Then she blacked out.

When Laura again became conscious she was standing on a dark plain that reminded her of the Jersey meadows near Hoboken. Long rows of concrete buildings like apartment houses stood against a dark brown sky. There were no trees and no other vegetation except some mosses and fungi.

Then she saw people. The earth was covered with very small dark half-naked people, running in every direction. The tallest of them reached to her knee.

They took no notice of her. Some copulated on the spot where they met. Males with erections caught females, then threw them to the ground and fucked them. Others when they met began to fight. Those not fighting were eating. There were hand-to-hand battles everywhere, and murders. Dead bodies lay unattended.

Laura heard herself repeating the mantra. It was all that seemed to cut off the terror churning inside her. She looked around for some sign of Indra.

"Now you are seeing into the future of your cherished mankind," his voice suddenly boomed inside her. "Your beloved and cherished mankind to whom all of you are attached. In the desire world they turn deaf ears to Truth, and this is the result.

"Ah ha, Uma, is it not wonderful, is it not terrible? To see how the negative forces proliferate and spread like rampant weeds—mass communication, mass production. Jam today, jam tomorrow, jam all the time. 'Let it all hang out.' And here it is, two thousand years later you see it all *really* hanging out." His voice roared with laughter.

One of the small male creatures had spotted her and ran toward her, its penis erect and red. It fastened itself on her leg, and began fucking it like a dog.

His laughter mounted inside her. She kicked until the small creature, frightened, rolled into the dust. Others cringed seeing her now for the first time.

"There are only a few large humans left at this point. I have caused you to enter one of their bodies and you are seeing through its eyes."

"But how is it possible," she gasped.

"It is a great thing," he said. "You cannot understand yet. Space and time are just functions of instruments. Bodies are instruments. When you get out of them, you can look either way. You are nowhere. Really there is no 'where,' only 'that.' "

Then a strong hot wind began to blow and darkness covered everything. The syllables of the mantra flashed like lightning in the sky and it began to rain. A foul stench arose.

When it cleared somewhat, Laura could see ruins where the endless rows of buildings had stood. A fine hot rain like the spray of a shower fell over everything. After a while, she realized the earth was now covered with even smaller human forms about the size of rats. Many dead ones lay in the mud. Festering sores covered their hideous emaciated human bodies.

"Come," his voice said. "We will explore a bit."

Then she seemed to be flying low over the sodden earth, hovering here and there and floating on. Everywhere was the same heat, rain, stench, infection, and death.

On higher ground a few groups of small naked ones were desperately trying to stay alive. Without tools they had built shelters of bits of refuse and mud. There was nothing to eat but moss and fungi that grew in the drier places, and every morsel meant a life or death struggle.

In some of these colonies she noticed that the bodies of the dead or dying were being eaten by the survivors. Here copulation and birth seemed to be the main business, since everybody born might be a future meal. She guessed the average age of the creatures to be fourteen or fifteen but as they were so small it was hard to tell. Certainly no one was over twenty. Many were born dead and were eaten at once before they became diseased. Surviving children were forced outside the walls of the colonies where they fought children from other settlements with teeth and bare hands. Others dragged the dead back to be eaten. After the eating there was an orgy of fucking among the stronger ones, while the children and weaker ones looked on, masturbating wildly.

"Do they see me?" Laura asked.

"No," he said gravely. "By this time you are not embodied because you have finally come to your senses and have stopped desiring it."

"What?"

"Embodiment—when you cease to desire it, you get out."

The plain talk in the midst of the hideous apparition before her

[223]

made it seem even more real and frightening. She noticed she could even feel the rain.

"But the rain seems real!"

"Like an amputee continues to feel the limb that has been cut off. So when one becomes at first disembodied, the inner one continues to experience certain basic sensations. *Real* is whatever we imagine it to be."

"Can't we leave this terrible place?" she asked, on the verge of tears. "Why do you have to keep lecturing me . . . in the middle of all this . . ."

"Because you still won't believe it."

"Believe what?" she cried out.

"Believe me, understand! That the universe is moral!" he shouted back at her sharply. "It is not things, not bodies, not machines. Its form *is its content.* Not the action, but the *intent* of the action. I am the inflamed one!" he thundered, again assuming the shape of the gigantic yogi. "Time, the destroyer of the world, is in my left hand. All this you have seen, what you call future has happened many times before."

"But if I am seeing the future how can I be here?"

The smiling face towered over her. "I am showing it to the awakened one within you," it whispered. "The knower I have awakened in you looks both ways, has no location. You are not your body, never have you been nor ever will you be in any body but for brief periods."

"Why am I so frightened?" she asked.

"You think you are your body, this particular body you are now in. But it will end and you are afraid. Believe in me," his voice thundered, "I am beyond fear."

"Do you mean there is an individual soul that goes on?" Laura asked.

"Yes, once you discover it," the voice answered emphatically. "It goes from one embodiment to another, strengthening itself until it doesn't require embodiment. It cannot really be explained. The maker of the tool is changed by the way he uses his tool. Yet the tool cannot know its maker and every maker is a tool."

Slowly the vast form became transparent and dissolved into the blue field. Finding herself again in the comparatively "safe" territory of the burning ground, Laura felt relieved. The fires that crackled around her seemed almost friendly when she thought of where she'd been. She turned, expecting to see Indra beside her. Instead she heard his voice coming from the fire.

The smoke parted. He was standing naked on the burning coals amid bodies and flaming logs, his hair unbound and hanging to his

[224]

knees. "Look here between my eyes!" he yelled urgently, pointing to a spot on his forehead just at the hairline.

She obeyed at once. A dark spot appeared and as she stared began to grow and widen, engulfing his face, growing, threatening to swallow up everything. "Now jump!" he yelled again. "Stand up and jump! There isn't a moment to lose—jump toward the black hole!"

Automatically she felt her body rise and jump forward into the black hole widening before her. For moments she fell into darkness. Then an internal spasm shook her roughly into light. Daylight.

§

The early morning sun slanted pink through lingering smoke.

"Is it over?" she asked, not daring now to look either to left or right.

"Nothing is ever over, only different," his voice said quietly from her left.

A half shudder, half sigh rippled through her body. "I feel quite weak," she said, "I have been here . . . ?"

"Twelve days," he said. "I cut it short by two days."

"May I see you now—please—in the form that is familiar to me . . . I mean if I turn and look at you? Will it be .you?" She had difficulty saying it the way she wanted.

"I have shown you my true form," his voice said softly. "The form you speak of, the one you know as Indra by sight and touch, is only a manifestation. One of many. No amount of reading or praying nor doing of good works can bring you to my form. But yes, Indra is here. Turn, you can touch him if you like."

She turned and seeing him sitting next to her smiling, collapsed into his lap and cried.

"I'm sorry," she said after some time, wiping her eyes on her skirt. "I can't help myself. I feel so confused."

"You are," he said sternly, gazing down at her. "Your Western doubt is confusing you."

"It's very hard to shake off," she whispered.

"I know. They say you must die and be reborn on this soil to get rid of it. Do you believe that?"

She wasn't able to answer.

"We usually perform this initiation at the age of twelve or fourteen, rarely later. I have never given it to any woman, although a woman gave it to me. When you have passed puberty they say it

[225]

is too late. But you have seen," he said, shaking her shoulder gently until she looked at him.

"Yes, I saw."

"Then you will succeed. There is a time for everything. You may be late but yours will surely come."

§

The warm rain poured steadily on the metal roof of the northbound platform of the Benares Railway Station. They had taken their time returning to Benares, stopping at Bodgaya where he had shown her the holy ground of the Lord Buddha. Now they stood together, the tall half-naked yogi and the American girl, two among thousands who thronged the platform waiting for the train to Delhi.

The sound of his singing echoed through her. She felt close to tears, but after what she had learned, could she let herself cry? And why, if it was all true, should she feel so sad?

"You are running away," he said, standing close to her with his bare toes curled over the edge of the platform.

"I feel an attachment to you," she said simply.

"But it is of a different order."

"Part of me wants to leave, another part to stay."

"Part will stay. Your body is only leaving. It is running away from me. I have worn it down."

"I feel I am suffering from a kind of indigestion," she said. "Too much, too fast."

"*It* is suffering from the indigestion." He smiled. "Eat more and push the poisons out."

"I feel taken apart."

"And you wonder whether you can be put together again," he said, his eyes twinkling. "There's the rub, right?"

"I'd like to bring Jeff to see you," Laura said to change the subject. "I'm going to Bombay to get him."

"I think you want to bring up reinforcements, like Doctor Albert Loeb."

"Perhaps," she whispered, looking at the ground. "I hope I'm not like him."

"It is quite natural. It is difficult to change our ways. See that young cow," he said, turning his eyes in the direction of a heifer further down the platform, who was stealing garlic from a hole in a large gunnysack. "Watch her. You are exactly like her and I am the coolie. Watch."

[226]

A coolie came and beat the cow with a small stick and she ambled along the platform, pretending to go away while watching the coolie out of the corner of her eye. As soon as she decided he wasn't looking, she returned to the sack and again began nibbling the garlic.

"The cow is naughty by nature." Laura smiled. "And hungry."

"And the coolie is not too harsh," he replied.

The train arrived and the confusion of pilgrims, beggars, holy men, animals, and coolies exploded.

"It's really a form of athletics," he said, watching a group of youths dive through the window of a third-class carriage. The platform turned to grease under the imprint of thousands of wet bare feet.

"You will be in Varanasai," she asked.

"Don't know," he said shrugging, looking down at his feet. "Doesn't matter. I could be anywhere . . . don't make plans, you know. You can always reach me through the Delhi number. I let them know my whereabouts."

The third bell for the departure of the train sounded.

He pulled himself to attention and saluted, staring through her.

"Always at your service," he said softly. "Jai Ho!"

XI

§

THE SHORT FLIGHT to Bombay had given Stan a chance to calm down. "If I don't die of cancer, I'll have a heart attack," he kept thinking. But he'd always had a strong temper, and when he considered that this trip had already cost him well over twenty thousand dollars he found it difficult not to become even angrier. Ordinarily he didn't mind spending money. But when it came to losing it or spending it uselessly, he raged. His otherwise poker face would redden, and his eyes narrow to bloodshot slits, as if trying to see the unseen powers aligned against him. Now the forces seemed to be gathering on every side. He'd been having a recurrent dream ever since he'd worked washing pots at the ashram. He was high in the branches of a large tree. There were persons he couldn't see at the bottom of the tree chopping at the branches. After the branches they began chopping at the trunk. He knew the tree was going to fall and that the unseen ones, whoever they were, were going to finish him off. He wanted only to be a bird so he could jump off and fly away.

When the cabin door of the Viscount opened at Santa Cruz airport, the hot humid air that rushed in set him to coughing again. He put his face in his handkerchief and bolted out into the Inland Flight waiting room, an erzatz 1940's affair crowded with gift shops and soda fountains, where thousands of confused passengers tried to hear flight announcements over an obsolete loudspeaker system.

He was relieved to see Carlos but he was in the middle of a coughing fit when Carlos caught sight of him. They exchanged glances and Carlos could see that Stan was going through some heavy changes.

"You have a car?" Stan rasped through his handkerchief, trying to spit out the bloody phlegm that kept coming up.

Carlos escorted him to a limousine. "Get in," he said, "I'll get your luggage. Do you have your baggage stubs?" He watched as

Stan fumbled in his pockets and guessed that it might be the last act of the play for him. "I'll be right back," Carlos said grimly.

The car moved slowly in the heavy evening traffic of Bombay Central.

"I'm very sick," said Stan quietly. "I hope you have a good place for me to stay."

"The best."

"I want you to find out who the Surgeon General of India is," Stan went on, "tonight. If he isn't in Bombay then have him recommend the best cancer specialist he knows. We can fly him here if necessary. I understand the Surgeon General is a cancer expert himself. Tell him about me and say I want a check-up." He glanced at Carlos. "Is it possible that can be done this evening?" He tried to smile.

"I'll try."

"Not a bad looking place, Bombay," Stan murmured, peering out through the curtains of the limousine. "Looks like Hong Kong or Singapore, but a little threadbare, eh?" They pulled up at the entrance to the Taj Mahal Hotel and Carlos led Stan to the desk where he explained that Mr. Stanley was ill and asked that the registration forms be sent up to the rooms.

Once in their suite, Stan made for the bath. "Haven't had a hot bath since I last saw you," he said hoarsely to Carlos. "This is going to be great. Can you call room service and have some tea sent up?"

Carlos busied himself tracking down the Surgeon General. "This Indian phone system," he shrugged. "I go crazy juss trying to make the hotel operators understand me."

Carlos helped Stan into bed and then sat rubbing Stan's feet. "You look terrible," he said bluntly. "What happened to you anyway?"

Stan stared at the ceiling. How could he possibly tell Carlos what had happened to him in the past few weeks, or anyone for that matter?

"The cancer is growing inside me," he said matter-of-factly. "I'll probably choke to death in a few weeks."

"But what was Ananda Baba like? There are many people here who worship him. Is it so, is he a god?" Carlos paced the room while Stan tried to tell him about Ananda Baba and the ashram, omitting anything of a personal nature.

Carlos knew there was more to it. "The woman Kamala sounds interesting. Will you go back in two weeks' time?" he asked. "Maybe he will cure you yet."

"Let's see what happens this week," Stan said vaguely. He had in fact thought of going back, but only because he wanted to revenge himself on Saladin. If he had only a few weeks left, he wanted to buy Saladin like a slave, no matter what the cost, to exhaust him in a final frenzy of money and sex, and then hire someone to kill him at the proper moment. The driver of the car should be exterminated too somehow. It was a fantasy he'd been working on for the last twelve hours.

Carlos noted Stan's tightly clenched fists and his flushed face. "There's a lot he is not telling me," he thought. "He's lost some bread." He could feel the vibrations.

"And where's Jeff?" asked Stan.

"He is here, in the hotel," said Carlos, his face darkening.

"Then call him up, will you? Tell him I've arrived."

"You'll have to call him yourself," said Carlos dryly. "We're not speaking."

Stan closed his eyes, trying not to lose his temper. "What is it now?"

"I have a big cash deal lined up. . . . He won't give me the stuff. Has it locked up in some storage company somewhere. Says he has got to talk to you on anything other than straight deals through your bank in Switzerland. Iss really bugging me."

"He's absolutely right," Stan said. "That's exactly what I told him."

"Juss when it means a big sale?"

"Especially on big sales. What would we do with all those dollars—if they were dollars and not counterfeit. How would we get them out of or into anywhere? I don't think you're thinking too well, my dear Carlos." Stan began to cough again. "Whether you're speaking to him or not," he said, "get Jeff on the phone and have him come here at once."

Carlos glanced at him.

"At once," Stan repeated.

Carlos picked up the phone and asked for Jeff's room. Stan heard Jeff pick up. "He's here," Carlos said, "Yes, he wants to see you immediately. Yes, immediately." There was a click at the other end.

Carlos hung up. "He's coming right up. He's on the seventh floor."

Stan had picked up a current issue of *Time* which he was pretending to read. "Now go into the other room and see if you can't get the Surgeon General. Have the hotel help you. Tell them it's an emergency."

Jeff tried to hide his surprise when he saw Stan. He sat down on the bed and rubbed Stan's legs.

"Why don't you tell me I look like a dying man?" Stan said. "I can tell that's what you're thinking."

"Why did you come to this godforsaken country? You should be in New York Hospital, or Boston . . ."

"Because I prefer not to die in a hospital, and India's almost the only place you can do that. Doesn't seem too bad a country," he added, trying to keep things light. "How's the distribution going?"

"Half gone so far."

"The money is in the bank?"

"Yes, and the stuff has been delivered."

"Last time I saw you it wasn't finished," said Carlos. "You mean you finished it in the last week?"

"That's correct," Jeff said to Stan. "Can't he leave this room while I'm here? We really aren't getting along!"

"Well, you damn well better get along," Stan exploded. "At least respect the fact that I'm at death's door. Try. Is that too much to ask?"

"I'd like to ask more," Jeff said.

"What? More what? What do you mean?" Stan sputtered.

"I'd like to have your permission to throw the other half into the bay."

"What?" Stan thought of the twenty thousand dollars he'd just parted with. "No, absolutely NO! You can't do this to me. What's got into you anyhow?"

"You must be out of your mind," said Carlos.

"You stay out of it, pimp," Jeff snarled. "I've seen enough to know it's useless here. They don't need it—it just makes them more fucked up."

"That's your private analysis," said Stan. "Have you taken a survey or something?"

"An American girl jumped out the window a few days ago," Carlos said flatly. "Iss upsetting him."

"Well, people are doing that all over," Stan said, "When they can't stand what they see, they jump or do all sorts of things."

"I have a sale for the other half," Carlos said.

"But it's cash. I told you it won't work," Stan reminded him. "What can we do with all those dollars in cash?"

"Stuff them in your jockey shorts and leave," said Carlos. "That would work."

"The man who wants it is a creep," said Jeff. "You want to cause a lot of suffering, then go ahead, sell to him. But it's a lot to have on your head." He eyed Stan.

"I don't care who distributes it. Their morality is of no concern to me. It's the cash thing. It's too dangerous. So easy for us to get ripped off." Stan nodded to Carlos. "It just won't do. Can't he give us a check in Switzerland?"

[231]

Carlos shook his head. "He doesn't operate that way—he doesn't keep records, only cash deals."

"Isn't there anyone else we can sell to here who can give us the money in Zurich?"

"There's a friend of mine in Goa," Jeff said. "An American named Grey."

"Where's Goa?"

"It's south of here, overnight by boat. It used to be a Portuguese colony, now it's a sort of hippy hangout on the ocean. Supposed to be a cool place. I've talked to him. We can front it to him and in six months it'll be all gone. Anyhow he's honest. We can even stay there while he sells it. Some nice houses right on the sea, very relaxing."

"I met a lady who admires you," said Stan. "Her name is Kamala, she traveled with me to Ananda Baba. Seemed to be quite interested in you. I think she would like to see you again."

Jeff wondered how much Kamala had told him. Not much he guessed. "Very far out, eh?" He winked at Stan who closed his eyes.

"I hear we missed you by only a day in Delhi. Too bad, you could have gone to the Baba's with us."

"You made it with her?"

"Yeah, once or twice," Stan lied. "That's new, let's see," he added, changing the subject when he noticed Jeff's ring, the one Hadji had given him. Jeff held out his hand. "You buy it?"

"A gift," Jeff said casually.

Carlos came closer to look. "Not bad," he whistled, "real emerald, worth a lot of bread, I think."

"Who gave it to you?" Stan asked. "Kamala, I suppose?"

"Nope, an Arab I met who fell in love with me, wants me to go to Dubai and live with him."

"In the harem?" snickered Carlos.

"Why not?" Jeff smiled and took back the ring. "Might be interesting for a while. I'm fed up with this place."

"Trying to get a straight answer from you is like trying to pull a crocodile tooth," Stan complained.

The phone rang. It was Laura from the Santa Cruz airport.

"Interesting coincidence," said Stan, handing the phone to Jeff.

"Stay where you are," he said. "We have a car. I'll be right out ... near Indian Airlines counter ... O.K. Right, about an hour, I suppose." He hung up.

"Did she know you were coming in today?" Jeff asked Stan.

"How could she know—I didn't tell her. She must be getting psychic out there in the jungle with Alex's guru." He lay back on the bed and started coughing again. "The driver is downstairs with

[232]

the car. Carlos will show you. And when you've done that, Carlos, come back and start on the Surgeon General again." He turned to Jeff. "The Goa thing sounds good. We'll see what happens."

§

"Hello," Laura whispered huskily when Jeff surprised her by hugging her from behind in the crowded waiting room of the airport.

"Are you becoming a psychic?" he asked, as he led her through the crowd to the car. "Stan just got in a few hours ago. Is it true these yogis can see into the future? Perhaps he taught you a few good tricks!"

"Of course," Laura said, dropping into the back seat of the car. "Why else would one go to a yogi?" She smiled at him, trying to look vague.

"I'm supposed to take you very seriously now, eh?" he said, closing the window of the car against the sewage stench. "How come you're not wearing robes?"

"I really had some heavy experiences." She looked at him soberly.

Jeff could see that something about her had changed. Sitting there in the back seat of the car she seemed to have lost a lot of the old brittleness of Laura Weatherall. They had rarely been serious with each other.

"I suppose he wants your money," he said, turning toward her.

"He might, but he'd give it away or burn it up in his fire. He would only want it to get rid of it, doesn't need money, comes from an old family, was in the Paratroopers with the British in Burma."

"Does he understand trust funds—that they just keep producing income?"

"Of course, silly. I'd just have to keep disposing of it as it came in."

"Detachment, eh?" Jeff said.

"Mmmmm," Laura said, slouching further into the seat. "It's freaking me out though. He makes me feel weak, so temporary. He's so final, so uncompromising. After a while with him everything around you looks different, everything." She gestured out the window. "One thing begins to seem like another. One is just putting in time here."

"How about love?"

"Mostly attachment," she said.

[233]

"I can see why you're freaking," he said. "Stan's freaked out too."

"Did his Baba cure him?" Laura asked.

"Not yet. I think he had to give up a lot of bread though. You know the look he gets when he's lost bread?"

Laura nodded. "That's good. He needs it. If he could let go of all the bread, he could let go of the cancer too." She changed the subject. "Indra would like to meet you. He sent Alex home, made him promise to give up the acid thing. He'd like to persuade you to give it up too."

"Then he should see Stan, not me."

"Why?"

"I'm tired of the whole trip. I'd like to get out of it but Stan's insisting, wants to get his money out. And if he dies you can bet Carlos will sell it to the first creep that comes down the street. He already has a first-class goon who wants what's left. I told Stan I'd like to throw it in the bay, but to him it's money. The closer he comes to dying the more uptight he is about bread. You'd think it would be different. He's just holding on tight to everything now."

He studied her. "You really look different."

"Haven't seen much of a mirror for a long time," Laura murmured. "You've no idea what I've been through, what I've seen."

"Maybe you should be more careful."

"More careful?"

"These fellows know a lot about mind games—they're raised on them. They show you all these subtle tricks. You ooh and aah inside and freaky things start happening to you. But mind tricks are tricks—it's a matter of concentration. After the mind games, after you've been zapped, then they try to sell you their religion. You know—life after death, life before death, eternal punishment, eternal happiness . . . And when they've got you feeling really guilty then the money pitch comes in."

"But not for themselves," Laura said.

"Of course not. It's always 'give it to my favorite charity.' It's not the bread, it's the power."

"That's true in most cases," Laura agreed. "But the teachers with big scenes around them, lots of charities and so on, are fakes."

"Before you let your Indra burn it," Jeff said, "give it to me. I'll be your one and only charity case. You can live in a cave and I'll have a penthouse."

They both laughed.

"We'll ask Indra if that's a good idea—maybe he'll agree."

The car pulled in at the hotel and Jeff hustled Laura through the lobby and into the elevator.

[234]

"I'm too tired to think," she said as they came out on the seventh floor and Jeff showed her into the room next to his. "Bathroom," she sighed, turning on the water in the tub. "Would you believe I haven't had a hot bath since I last saw you?"

"I'm impressed," Jeff said, standing by as she opened her luggage. "Incidentally, your Sikh brothers are here."

"In this hotel? Harpal too?" She looked up.

Jeff nodded. "In fact I saw him just as I was leaving to pick you up and I'm afraid I told him you were due to arrive."

"Thanks a lot," Laura said, peeling off her clothes. "But I really don't want to see anyone tonight. It's too late for me, I'm used to going to bed at sunset."

"I'm afraid you'll have to see Stan," Jeff called after her as she made for the tub. "It's only eight-thirty, he's waiting to see you, really in a bad way. I think you might get him out of it."

§

Some time later Carlos opened the door of Stan's suite.

"We are very anxious to know everything that has been happening to you," he said to Laura stiffly.

"How is he?" she whispered.

Carlos shook his head.

"I think Alex's teacher could help him, the one I've been with." I've seen him cure people with my own eyes . . . one of cancer."

"He is just returned from one of these healers," muttered Carlos. "I think he has made Stan worse. He seems, er, so much rattled. Please go in, he is waiting for you."

Laura found Stan with his eyes closed and his face the color of old ivory. He was in his yellow silk pajamas, velvet robe and red slippers. He reminded Laura of a picture she had once seen of a mandarin king lying in state.

"For someone who's supposed to be at death's door," she said softly, "you look great."

Stan opened his eyes. "Death's door is supposed to be extremely narrow," he said weakly. "I don't think I'm going to be let in there."

"That's heaven," Laura said. "The only other one is plenty wide enough."

Stan grimaced. "What will happen, will happen, won't it?" Yet despite his fatalism he seemed to be asking for her help.

Laura sat down on the edge of the bed and began telling him about Indra. She knew if she sounded too enthusiastic he would stop listening. He had never been one to show emotion and she

[235]

wondered now whether he simply had no emotions at all, or whether his immobile face was simply a mask covering deeper feelings. Nor had he ever been serious: he'd either been busy making money or engrossed in planning his next fuck. Now as he told her about the scene at Ananda Baba's she thought she detected a change. Something had shaken him up. As Indra would have said, he was on the brink looking over. He told her about scrubbing the pots in the kitchen, about his purge, about the milk coming from the Baba's hands.

"You should really check Indra out," she said. "He told Alex that Ananda Baba could heal you if he wanted to but that he has healed so many people he may have depleted his energy and might just string you along. Now he's supposed to be building hospitals for advanced cases like you."

"To die in," Stan said. "Unless of course you give him enough bread. If you build him a hospital, chances are you won't have to go in it yourself." He grimaced. "And to have put me in the kitchen when I have so little time!"

She thought he might be going to cry. "Some doctors have told you you have little time," Laura said reassuringly. "How do you know? Cancer is a funny thing."

"I know, that's why I came to India."

"It's like inside each of us some other person is giving the orders," said Laura. "It can also give orders to kill the cancer, can't it?"

"Antibodies," Stan mumbled. "Listen Laura, I don't know whether I can take another ashram scene. I think time may be running out for me. I've got Carlos trying to locate the Surgeon General—he's supposed to be a cancer expert. After I see him I'll know. And we'll probably have to go to a place called Goa to get rid of the acid. Where is this Indra of yours?"

"I left him up north," Laura said, "but there's no telling where he is now, or where he will be. I have a number I can call in Delhi, they always know where he is, at least enough to track him down."

"A yogi with an answering service," Stan laughed. "How weird!"

"Not really," said Laura. "There's just an old servant whom he phones whenever he moves. I'll call him later after your plans are made. But why do you have to go to Goa? Can't you stay here and let them go?"

"No, because Jeff and Carlos are at each other's throats and I'm the referee. There's supposed to be someone there who can handle the deal properly, an American fellow named Grey. Carlos has a man here who wants to do a cash deal but Jeff says he's not to be trusted. In any case, cash won't work, it's too risky. I hope Carlos

[236]

hasn't got us all in trouble letting this smuggler friend of his know we have the stuff. Once we get to Goa I hope things will get lighter. But you look beat. It's nearly eleven, you'd better get some rest, eh?'

"I just had my first hot bath in four months," said Laura, "I feel pretty good."

"Ugh." Stan nodded sympathetically. "What a country."

§

Alone in her room after leaving Stan, Laura was having a hard time. She sat looking at the bay, trying to figure out why she felt so uneasy. The city, the hotel, the hot bath, seeing Carlos, Jeff, and Stan—all the old tapes she thought she had erased were beginning to play again. She wished there were some sort of psychic de-magnetizer that could erase them all at once.

She bit her lip, remembering that Indra had told her it would be hard. "Once you start getting out," he had said, "it becomes more and more painful to reenter until you've become completely neutral."

Do you want to spend the rest of your life living like a yogi? This was the question she couldn't answer and she felt guilt above her weakness. "It was the bath," she muttered to herself. "That did me in. I was all right until then."

She lay down and was dozing when the phone rang.

"Hello, I say, hello, Laura are you there?"

It was Harpal. "I know it's late," he said, "but may I come up just for a moment, on the way to my room? I'm just above you."

"It's almost midnight, I'm afraid I'm beat."

"Just for a moment. I really won't stay long."

His voice did her in.

"Then stop by. I'm just about to go to sleep, but I'll see you for a moment."

She had a pair of Jeff's old pajamas on. She thought of changing but decided against it. Changing was what she would have done four months ago. "Let him see me as I am, I won't go after him—at least that tape is gone."

When he knocked she opened the door and hid behind it.

"This is a stick-up," she said, coming up behind him after he had entered the room. "Give me all your jewels."

He spun around and caught her by the waist.

"Laura, Laura," he said. "Let me look at you." He held her at arms' length, smiling. "I was very angry at you," he said softly. "My brothers were ready to kill me."

"Don't think I wasn't angry at *you*," she said. "It served you all right. I should have thrown the things in the Jamuna River or something. It was Sundar who persuaded me to return them."

"But it's our custom."

"That's a line and you know it," she said, walking away.

Harpal sat down on the sofa looking sheepish. He folded his hands in his lap like a naughty child. She loathed playing games with him. She liked him but she knew if she was straight with him he'd take advantage of her. She had learned that much anyhow in four months.

"So," he said, slapping his knees, "Jeff told me you have been to see the Guru. That is very good."

"The Guru?" she asked.

"Your guru. All gurus are one Guru, it is all one teaching. Did you know that we Sikhs are known as the defenders of the gurus? We are the traditional line of defense against the invaders of India, we guard the Himalayas where the gurus sit. We are in the plains on our elephants, behind us is the army of naked sadhu warriors who are in the foothills, behind them are the gurus."

"You're telling me all these things, Harpal Singh, but you are looking at me like I'm a prostitute."

"I am not looking like. You are saying it. I am just enjoying you with my eyes." He grinned. "Even though you are covering your beautiful body with those disgusting men's pajamas. Your body has given me great pleasure. There is nothing wrong with pleasure. Some of our greatest sages have reincarnated themselves as prostitutes to teach men by giving them pleasure. If you don't experience love and pleasure, how can you ever get out of it. You will crave it forever in many lives. You have to go through it, not against it."

"But you can get trapped in it," said Laura.

"Not if you don't believe that you're responsible. God is also in your body, you know. Guilt is just another form of selfish attachment."

"But I am saying something much simpler and you know it. The trouble with you Indian men is that you think every unmarried girl is a prostitute, up for grabs. It's like a game you're playing."

"Ah, that is too deep," he said, sprawling on the sofa. "Woman, she is all woman. Man, he is half man, half woman. He's only got half as much as she has. He has to steal energy from her. That's why

[238]

he wants to make sure he's got at least one woman somewhere, keeping his fire going. He wants to connect with her as much as possible to keep stealing the energy."

Harpal was not used to intelligent discussions with women, especially beautiful ones. Sometimes in Chicago he'd had such intellectual exchanges, but they were exhausting to him. Some women would argue with you forever. He stood up and started pacing up and down in front of the windows, his hands jammed in his hip pockets.

"Food kills the urge," Laura said under her breath.

"What did you say?"

"I said food. I just remembered that I had forgotten to eat anything. Sit down, take off your shoes, I'll order something." She picked up the phone, dialed room service, and ordered a complete Punjabi dinner in Hindi. Harpal shot a glance at her, surprised to find that he had taken off his shoes. He grabbed the phone just as she was about to hang up, gave some additional instructions, and admonished the startled room service to be quick.

§

"You came for a moment on your way to your room. You stayed for dinner and now you're lighting your pipe." Laura smiled at him. "Remove your stockings please, and I'll massage your feet. Then you'll sleep better."

She squatted by the sofa and rubbed his bare feet. It was a sort of experiment for her. She was sure it was the last thing he ever expected her to do. When she had finished, he drew her up to his side.

"I see you have really learned something," he said. "To know enough to rub the foot in the evening, you a foreigner . . . that is very rare." He beamed at her. "But I see you are very tired, I shall go now, Madam."

"What did you call me?"

"It is what we are taught to call you in boarding schools here." He laughed. "I will see you again soon," he said, putting on his shoes. "I have a suite of rooms on the top floor—alone."

At the door he held her in his arms and kissed her neck. "Every moment away from you has been filled with remembering," he whispered. "I want to make love to you properly. I have thought about you now night and day for months. I am going to make up to you for that night, you'll see." Holding her head between his hands, he kissed her forehead, "I'll call you tomorrow in the morning, yes?"

She nodded.

§

Laura opened the window and gazed out over the dark bay dotted with the lights of anchored boats. How strange to be a part of it again. It makes you want to be part of it, she thought, it forces you. Perhaps Harpal was right—one has to go through it, not against it.

She fell asleep on the sofa and dreamed about the little man she had seen in the fireplace in England. He seemed surprised to see her. He was wearing some torn rust-colored rags and was sitting in front of a hut, his long white hair and beard blowing in the wind. He waved and she could see him yelling at her and laughing. She felt herself floating over the ground toward him. Just as she was close enough to hear him over the wind, she was awakened by someone shaking her arm. It was Jeff.

She looked up at him. "I was having a lovely dream," she said. "How'd you get in?"

"We have adjoining rooms." He pointed. "I guess you didn't notice."

He lifted her up and carried her to the bed, and then collapsed beside her on the soft mattress. For a long while they lay without moving. Then she turned toward him and brushed the hair out of his eyes.

"I have to look at you to believe you're here," she said. "Strange, isn't it, how we're not together much anymore . . . we aren't, are we?"

His green eyes glowed like emeralds in the dark. "That's because you're very good and I'm very bad," he said thoughtfully. "Now we're getting older, it's showing more." He got up, stepped out of his clothes, and kicked them into a corner of the room.

"All my life people have been attracted to this." He slapped his thighs. "This body. This." He grabbed his crotch as he slid between the sheets. "It makes everything too easy for me. People become wonderful mirrors; when I smile, they smile. What I want, they want. It's like jerking off. And I keep wanting to repeat it 'cause it makes me feel so good." He turned to her. "Hopeless, yes?"

"And when it gets old," she said, stroking his body, "then what?"

[240]

"When that happens," Jeff said, "I'll be done for. I'm hooked on it."

"Is this a confession?" She smiled at him.

He wondered what she would think about him and Hadji. "Confession," he murmured, "not even half a one . . . I think a lot these days. It scares me so I've been trying not to."

"Have you ever surrendered to anything?" she asked, staring into the dark.

"I tried to I think, to a very beautiful lady, friend of Sundar's in Delhi." He shrugged. "She turned out to be a witch—a sadistic witch. I'm never going to make it," he added. "I know it. I think I may be locked on a collision course. Think of all the acid I've taken, trying to get out of this." He slapped himself again. "It just got me locked further in, that's all."

"In is out," she said.

"Ugh. Just because you've met a yogi, now you think you have the answer to everything in words. It's not like that, it's not that simple . . . just in and out."

"That's why you should see him," Laura said.

He yawned and rolled over. "O.K, O.K."

She pulled the sheet up around herself and lay awake beside him. For a moment in the darkness she saw the burning ground, the smoke drifting above the fires. She reached over and brought his head close to hers.

"Listen Jeff," she whispered, "you're not alone, believe me. We're all going through it together and we're all connected."

"I know that," he said. "I really do, but it's all in my head. I don't feel it. Sometimes I wonder if I feel anything."

§

The next morning she awoke to find herself in his arms. He was asleep hanging onto her like a large child. It was good to feel him close to her. For a while she lay with her eyes closed, pretending they were together again, back in New York, safe New York. What irony, she thought.

The phone rang abruptly.

When she reached to pick it up, his arms tightened around her.

"I thought you were asleep," she whispered.

"I am," he said.

"Shouldn't I answer it then?"

"No."

The ringing stopped. He turned her toward him, guiding her

hand down between his legs. She closed her eyes and began letting herself go.

The ringing began again.

"Go ahead, answer it," he said, rolling over and out of the bed. "Might as well answer it."

"Yes," Laura said into the phone, with a smile at Jeff retreating crossly through the door.

"Oh, Harpal, yes, yes, good morning."

"I was hoping you would have lunch with me," his voice yelled out of the receiver.

"I was asleep," she whispered.

"Lunch," he said, "lunch!"

"Yes, yes," she yelled back, wanting to get his yelling voice out of her ear. "What time?"

"About one, I'll pick you up."

"Now I've done it," Laura thought, putting the phone back.

"Who was that?" Jeff said. He came back into the room, drying himself with a towel.

"I just accepted lunch with Harpal, shall I cancel?"

He smiled at her.

"I really mean it, I'm bewildered at myself. I thought we might spend the day together—go out maybe, see Bombay. Now I've accepted lunch with him."

"There's nothing to see in Bombay. Go to lunch."

"Will you come?"

"Three's not a good number. Besides I don't go out on the streets. I stay in my room. Sometimes late at night I walk around that silly arch out there, otherwise I stay put."

"We never seem to get a chance to . . . Something's always interrupting."

"Don't make a big deal out of it," he said, going into his room to dress.

"I love you," she shouted after him.

He returned a few moments later. "Don't," he said. "I love you too, but it's no good. I'm no good. I told you that last night."

He kissed her neck. "Don't think too much, you'll only drive yourself crazy."

§

There were numerous expensive cars lined up outside the entrance to a building that resembled a large flying saucer. It was perched on the edge of a cliff overlooking the Arabian Sea. A clutch

[242]

of doormen saluted as Harpal, with Laura behind him, strode into an elegantly appointed lobby. The lunch hour was in full swing, and the lobby was alive with the hustle and bustle of discreet assignations. Fat Congress Party politicians in Gandhi hats and fine cotton dhotis waddled off, attended by handsome male secretaries in suits and ties, to rendezvous with young girls working their way through college—or more likely just working. A group of Arab princes from Kuwait talked quietly in one corner with Bombay customs officers, the officers twitching at the thought of the hot female flesh the Arabs were about to produce for them before lunch, in return for certain "favors." Some young Parsee dandies talked in muted Oxford accents and waved grandly to Harpal while leering at Laura. Harpal walked directly to an elevator marked "Private" where a liveried operator waited to take them up.

"I suppose you own this place too?" Laura said.

"We built it," Harpal answered absentmindedly. "I don't know whether we still own it or not."

"What is it exactly?" she asked.

"Oh, I guess you'd call it a luncheon club, cum hotel—private one. There's a condominium attached."

"You mean brothel."

"Not exactly. You have to be a member and own an apartment. All cooking is done in a central kitchen and sent up."

He gazed at her with his amazing dark eyes. "I brought you here because we won't be interrupted. At the Taj my office may call, that's where they always look for me when I escape them. No one knows of this place, at least no one who works for me."

They got out of the elevator and Harpal opened a door into a large apartment overlooking the sea.

"Quite an engineering feat this was," he said, "cantilevering twenty stories out over a cliff. You like it?"

"It's very beautiful," Laura said, looking out at the surf as it pounded in on the rocks below.

"Why don't you move out of that hotel and come live here? I hardly ever use this place." He smiled, opening a bottle of iced champagne. "Perhaps if you were here I'd come more often."

She admired the strength of his long lanky body as he came from behind the bar with the champagne glasses. He was a different breed than most of the men she'd met: arrogant yet warm; extremely masculine, yet with certain characteristics that in other parts of the world might have been thought womanish.

They sat down on a thick blue Chinese carpet. "To you," he said, lifting his glass, "and to our future."

"Our future?"

[243]

"I have asked you to come here for a reason," he said. "I want to marry you."

"What?"

"I want to marry you. Five simple English words: I-want-to-marry-you." He sipped his champagne and gazed at her over the rim of the glass.

She smiled. "But I just came out of the jungle," she said lightly. "I don't think I have anything to wear."

"And now you are at the seaside," he said. "Please don't joke with me. I am serious. I want you. I want to marry you."

"But I . . . "

"You don't believe in love, but I will show you that it exists," he said, lowering his eyes. "I desire that you shall be the mother of my children. I want to give you everything. I am very rich, richer than you even." He took her hand. "And I am also very gentle, though you may have received other impressions that night in Delhi."

"Do your brothers get to marry me too?" Laura smiled.

"Only if I die," he said, "and only if you were living in India. But we will have to live in your country. I own a ranch in California, also properties in Hawaii. I'll become a cowboy. Why not? I've spent half my life on horses."

"Why America? You mean you would become an American citizen?"

"I'm not crazy too," he replied. "A Sikh like me can never really leave Punjab wherever he may go. But it would be necessary to go there. Our children would never be accepted here. They would be classed as Anglo-Indians, despised by everyone. The days when one could live life peaceably in India have drawn to a close. Whether you accept my proposal or not, all the younger members of my family intend to leave quite soon. We were swindled once by Nehru in '47, we will not make the mistake of being crushed again."

He pressed a small chamois bag into her hand. "I believe you call this an engagement present," he said. "For me it is a token of my love for you. The first of many, I hope."

"But Harpal, we barely know each other and now suddenly . . ."

"Suddenly, nothing," he interrupted. "Nothing is sudden in this world. It all happens right on time, you are just not keeping up with it. Besides," he said, a smile playing at the corners of his mouth, "we know each other in the most important way a man and woman can. When things happen, let them happen. Don't resist. Don't think. I've been thinking of you too long—four months now." His eyes narrowed. "I want you. I must have you. If you won't marry me, then be my mistress. I am very selfish, I know it, but I am also filled with love for you. We can get married today. Immediately. Civil marriage right here in this room."

He sipped his drink silently. "Otherwise who is going to save you, tell me that?"

"Save me from what? From whom?" said Laura indignantly.

"From yourself, of course. From your own craziness. You are too lovely to be acting so crazy."

"I'm trying to become detached," she said.

"You're going to find you have become deranged if you aren't careful. You'll have plenty of time for that after you have become a mother. That is the only real test for a woman. She must go through it. Only then will you learn true detachment."

"And what about men?" she asked.

"For men it is the same. For us the real test is when we begin to lose our strength to our sons." He leaned over and kissed her tenderly. "You feel guilty about the way you turned out because you don't fit any of the molds. Who is going to relieve that guilt?"

"I have found a great guru."

"That is fine," he answered. "I have no doubt that you have. Every wife and mother should sit at the feet of a great guru. Family and children must have a guru. But you don't have babies with him. Your guru can only advise you, after all you are a woman. That for us is guru in itself, ask him. He will tell you I am correct. We can even bring him to California if you like."

Laura sighed. "I can see it now. You'll keep me pregnant on a ranch in California—ten years of pregnancy. I'll become a breeder while you, the stallion, are off roaming faraway fields."

"You must breed. That is your function, your duty as a woman. You have to go through your function. You must breed, you must nurture and bring forth plenty. Woman has this power. She must use it and keep it pure, otherwise the world will go mad." He shrugged. "Like now."

She opened the bag and drew out a black walnut-sized stone cut like a diamond.

"Put it to the light," Harpal said, "and you will see what it is."

She held it up and saw that it wasn't black but deep blue.

"It is called a black sapphire. It is the largest in the world as far as we know. King Philip of Spain acquired one from the Portuguese which is now in the hands of some American, but it is second largest." He grinned.

"This has belonged to our family for generations. It was part of an ancient breastplate worn once a year by our forefathers. On that day the King had to walk through his capital naked except for the breastplate and with his penis erect to show the people that the fertility of the state was secure."

"What happened when he couldn't get an erection anymore?"

"Then his eldest son became King."

Laura held up the jewel to the light. "You think you can get me with glitter?"

"It's only for show," he said. "I don't need that to get you and you know it." He kissed her hand.

Laura gave way inside. His touch was warm and affectionate. Strength and calm radiated from him. She remembered his long hair falling over her that night in Delhi. Was she hanging on Sundar's imaginary Himalayan cliff she wondered, and was Harpal trying to save her?

He stood up, gathered her in his arms as if she were a feather, and carried her into a bedroom. The sea outside thundered in her ears like a heartbeat. Slowly he undressed her, kissing her body as he took off her clothes. She lay waiting as he undressed and removing his turban, let his hair fall to his waist. Then he lay down beside her.

"What you don't know is the secret of this body," he whispered, pressing his tall young body close to hers. "These muscles, these breasts, this womb, this lingam, they are all sacred gifts—all paths to heaven."

He kissed her lips, letting his tongue play gently over the corners of her mouth. "They are gifts—always remember—not your body, not my body, but gifts to enjoy and take care of. The body is not to be abused nor misused, either from greed or from guilt about it. It is the palace of the spirit, the temple of the soul."

She felt him slowly entering her and let her hands run down his long back to the firm buttocks.

"This pleasure is granted so that other holy bodies can be made for the souls who are waiting to come in," he whispered on her cheek. "Only when we make children, then sex is holy. Then the body will not be despised, nor the organs that are used be profaned or turned into objects of loathing."

His hair covered them like a tent. "Your body is perfect," he said. "There is a great temptation for you to misuse it unless you have a man who can satisfy you fully."

He moved rhythmically inside her. She felt as if she were a sand cliff and he the sea, and that she was caving in slowly, slowly sliding away in the rising tide.

She opened her eyes, meeting his as she gave way, opening and closing on him in waves of desire and fulfillment. He lay perfectly

[246]

still, holding back and letting go inside her, the warm sperm flowing out, filling her. She locked her legs around his waist as he paused to catch his breath, kissing her eyes, her neck and breasts. He wanted to go on forever connected with her, swimming inside. She was groaning under him, her eyes rolled back, her lips searching for his, her hands trembling on his thighs. He felt her going out of herself, her inner membranes vibrating uncontrollably on him, opening him, sucking at the root of his fecundity. A groan rose inside him and he began to cry out softly in Punjabi, his pelvis lapping against her, twisting and turning ecstatically until with a final lunge he overflowed again. Then laughing and crying, kissing her breasts he rolled over with her and slid onto the floor, pinning her hands down in a final fervent discharge.

A vast stillness engulfed her. Peace, she thought, peace, rolling off through the infinite spaces inside. Peace.

He fell asleep beside her, his warm body encircling her, the dark ringlets of his hair festooning her body. Suddenly from a long way off she heard a voice calling her name. It was so real that she raised herself up, half expecting to see someone on the shore below.

"Do not disturb the naked defender of the gurus," the voice said. "He is a very good man."

It was the voice of the old woman she had heard in the temple, speaking in broken English.

"We have made a compact, remember, yes? I begged you not to ask but you insisted. Now it cannot be broken. You must give back the jewel, do you understand? It is to me that you are giving. You have chosen to go out. How can you go out whilst you are busy making new bodies? You must give back the jewel. It is too late now for you to choose a path with him. You have already begun to cross over. . . . If you go with him now you will go mad."

She felt tears welling inside her.

"You asked to have your burdens taken from you. I did not ask it. I am only here to fulfill your most true wish. You are already in the crossing, it is too late now. Give back the jewel and forget him."

Harpal stirred beside her, then suddenly came wide awake with a frightened look. "I was dreaming that someone came and took you. I was . . ." He pulled her onto his chest. "Promise that you will never leave me," he whispered. "Please say it. If you leave me I cannot live, do anything with me, take everything. It is enough for me only to satisfy you hour by hour, night and day. I will do anything you ask."

She was unable to speak.

"Will you come with me to see my teacher?" she asked after some time.

[247]

"That is quite out of the question," he said as if she had made a joke. "I have my own guru. We do not jump around from one to another. Really, you must go to the husband's guru before the wedding. Some day, no doubt, after we are married I will visit your Indra."

"You said you would do anything I ask."

"Of course I did, but this—you must be joking. Come, let me call a Justice and we will be married now."

She sighed and turned her head away.

"What has come over you?" He turned her face toward him. "See, am I not good to look at? I am, I know it. Do you see any flaws? Am I not well endowed—more than enough to satisfy you and give you strong, healthy children?" He rose to his knees, stretching. "Fathers have offered fortunes in dowry for me. Even now, my older brother is entertaining over two hundred proposals of marriage for me."

"Is that why you are in such a hurry?"

"Yes, of course. I have been putting them off for four months. For four months they are harassing me, night and day. Because the memory of you haunted me I put them off, but they will insist soon and I will have to yield and it will be too late."

He leaned over her, touching her body delicately and staring into her eyes. "I beg of you. Save me. As I will save you. Otherwise my life will be hopeless—a hopeless idiotic frustration is all I can see."

But when they were dressed and about to leave Laura handed him the sapphire. "I can't take it. The burden would be too much for either of us to bear."

"What are you saying?"

"You must keep it for me, it's too risky with me."

"Are you saying 'no' then, is that it?" he said quietly.

"No, I'm not saying no."

"Then?"

"I want a month longer to think it over. Can you wait?"

"Yes, I suppose so."

"I'll probably be leaving Bombay soon—maybe even tomorrow. I have to take a friend who has cancer to see my teacher. I hope he will cure him. It should take about a month."

"Most women would do anything to get this," he said, bouncing the chamois bag in the palm of his hand.

"I'm not most women."

§

That evening while she was resting the phone rang. Laura picked it up sleepily. A laugh crackled through from the other end. She woke up fast at the sound of Indra's voice. "Where are you?"

"At a phone in the village of Kalpura about five hundred miles south of you. Near the sea. I hope you gave the gem back to that Sikh fellow," he said.

She sighed. "I thought you might have been there."

"Yes and no, I tuned in and out. Your waves were very strong."

"Yes, I gave it back. But he's really a lovely person. He even wanted you to come live in California."

"Lovely until after the ceremony, then see what would happen," said Indra.

"I heard the woman again, the voice at the temple, she . . . "

"I understand," he cut her off sharply. "But why did you call Delhi?"

"I must see you. Things are difficult here; I would like to bring Jeff and Stan." The connection had become weak. She found she was yelling. "Yes, the one with cancer. No, no, he didn't get cured there. May I, yes thank you. How soon? In ten days I think . . . Just go to that town? Yes, I can remember it. Yes, I'll call you there if there's any change of . . ." The receiver clicked at the other end.

"Jai Ho," she said to herself, and hung up.

Jeff came in. "Who were you yelling at?" he asked.

"It was Indra," she said. "He's in South India, not far from Goa I think. He says he's willing to see both you and Stan. How is Stan? Did he see the Surgeon General?"

"He recommended a specialist here who has his own hospital. He gives him six weeks to six months. Wants to do another biopsy. Stan won't let him."

§

They went down to Stan's. He looked better and was up walking around. Carlos sat anxiously by the bed.

"Guess I needed rest as much as anything," Stan said to Laura. "You look well I must say—I guess you needed a rest too!"

"I had a call from Indra, he said he would see you."

He looked at her. "Laura, tell me honestly. Should I go to New York tomorrow or shall I go see your Indra?"

"You're hanging your fate around my neck."

[249]

He smiled. "Maybe."

"What do you say, Carlos?"

"New York."

Laura didn't really want to be involved in this decision. She didn't like Stan and felt he was more or less getting what was coming to him. But the idea of bringing him together with Indra fascinated her and she knew if he went, Jeff would come along.

"What will happen will happen," she heard herself say. "If it were me I'd stay here."

"And go to your man?"

"As you like."

"Then it's settled." He looked at Jeff and Carlos. "We'll go to Goa and see this Grey fellow, and then see Indra. Have you located him?"

"He's about a hundred miles south of Goa."

"Good," Stan said. "Then it's settled." He turned to Carlos. "Did you say there was a steamer to Goa?"

"Right."

"Then book passage for tomorrow and we'll start to pack."

§

Jeff sat on the first-class deck of the Goa steamer and looked out over the glittering sea. Dubai was out there somewhere, he thought, remembering that he had forgotten to call Hadji before they left. Laura was in their cabin doing some sort of meditation and had asked him to leave, which had pissed him off. Not only an affair with a Sikh but at the same time all this guru business. India was such a downer. He felt stifled by it and wondered why he hadn't left with Hadji, why he was stringing along with Laura and this idea that he should meet her yogi. But he was dead set to see that Carlos didn't get hold of the acid. Jeff was sure he would try to pull something so that Wasu would get it. He drummed his knuckles on the railing.

From below somewhere he heard music. He went down to the third-class lounge, which was crowded with hippies dancing and smoking dope. Someone passed him a joint, and a girl gave him a snort of cocaine. It was crowded and dark; the vibes were comfortably Western. The girl faced him, hunched up on a bench so that her vagina stared right out at him. She was young and blonde, and spoke tough English with a French accent. She gave him another snort and he edged close to her in the darkness and let his hand go between her legs.

"Let's dance." He led her to the floor and they danced in the dark among four or five other couples. He let her bounce against him till he got hard.

"I'm too stoned to dance," she said. "Let's go outside."

They went out to the narrow passageway that served as the third-class deck. A number of Indians slumped against the steel walls.

"You have a cabin?" she asked.

"Sharing one."

"It's a shame to let the coke go to waste."

"How about one of the lifeboats?" Jeff asked.

She rubbed against him. "Too hard," she said. "I like soft beds."

The music stopped.

"Maybe I'll see you in Goa. I'll be staying at Anjuna . . ."

"Sure," Jeff said. "Hope so."

The girl drifted back to the gloom of the third-class lounge.

Jeff went above deck and tapped on the cabin door.

"Yes?"

"It's me, are you finished?"

"Yes."

He opened the door and went in. Moonlight filtered through the shuttered window and onto the bunk where Laura lay.

He took off his clothes and lighting a cigarette, sat down beside her.

"Beautiful night," he said, not looking at her.

"Jeff?" she said after some time.

"Yes?"

"It's all over between us, isn't it?"

"Seems to be." He turned to gaze at her, rubbing his cigarette out with his heel. "Either you're balling Sikhs or meditating. I suppose you'll be balling this Indra next."

She slapped his face.

Jeff didn't move. "I told you I'm no good," he said, "but I'm just warning you. Yoga is not for you. You should marry this Harpal fellow, take him back to America."

"You'll see," she said. "You'll meet him and you'll see."

"Meet who?"

"Indra."

"I know all about him. Sundar said he's a sorcerer. And you're fascinated. He's put you through some things. It's changed you. . . . But you're going to get in too far with him and you won't get out. This stuff is for the Indians, it's their thing, not ours." He paused. "He only wants your money anyhow."

[251]

Laura's hand landed on his jaw again. "Stop saying those things," she ordered angrily.

He caught her wrist and pinned her down on the bunk. "We've known each other a long time," he said, leaning over her. "I tell you this business is not for you. I feel responsible for bringing you to India. At least go back to New York and come back on your own, then I'll be clear."

Looking at her he wanted to go on, wondered whether he could arouse her. The coke was working, he wanted to fly with her.

"I don't even know you," he said softly. "I've lived with you all this time and you're still a mystery to me, a beautiful mystery." He let his hand rest on her thigh and stretched out on the bunk beside her. "It's like the first time with you every time," He slid his hand to her stomach, watching her relax. "Your Sikh is no good in bed," he whispered. "Admit it."

She sat bolt upright. "You monster," she shrieked, "get out of this bunk!"

Holding her by the waist, he put his head to her belly.

"You didn't hear me," she said, her voice shaking with rage. "I said to get the hell out of this bunk." She dug her nails into his back.

Jeff sat back on his knees, letting her see his erection.

"There's no comparison between you and Harpal," she said.

He looked at her hard.

"Yes, you heard me. He might not be as good as you in bed and he might be better, but at least he's not an animal."

She got up, wrapped a cloth around herself, and began pacing the darkened room. Something inside her was burning mad at him. "You freak," she hissed, "at least he's normal, he wants to have babies, not like you."

"Why are you on the pill then if you want to have babies so much," he said. "Come on, let's have babies, who said I didn't want to have babies?"

"I stopped taking it three months ago."

"Then come on, let's make a baby."

She stopped pacing and looked at him. "Are you ready to become a father?" she asked him quietly. "What can you teach your child? Can you do anything except press buttons and make up scams to get money? Your father wrote music, did he teach you how?"

"That was a scam too. What he wrote wasn't music." Jeff looked away from her. "But your father's a scammer too."

"And my mother is a button pusher."

"Are you ready to be a mother?" he asked.

[252]

"I don't know. I never had one to teach me how—all I remember were the nannies and the no-no's." Laura sat down on the bunk again. "I'm tired of just having sex," she said. "It leaves me so empty inside. You don't feel empty afterwards?"

"No, I only want more. Don't you know that's my problem?"

She lay back on the bed. "You're in love with your cock," she said. "That's why with you I always feel empty afterwards. You give it, you take it back. For you it's just a reflex action, like jerking-off. Instead of using your hand you use women.

"Don't get uptight," she added, seeing the dark cloud across his green eyes. "It's not only you. It's the chicks too—all using the pill, turning whore, mutual masturbation. I ought to know, I've done it enough myself."

"What can you do about it?"

"I think I just want to get out of the whole thing."

"Whatever that means." He got up and put on his shirt and pants. "I'm going out for a while."

"You can lie down here—do we have to fuck?"

He spun around. "God damn right we have to fuck. When I want to fuck I do it." He slipped on a pair of sandals. "And I'll have no trouble getting any here either, even on this goddamn boat."

He slammed the door and stumbled down the gangway to third class. It was later than he'd thought. The music had stopped. The lounge was dark and silent except for the sound of snoring. He went back to the first-class deck, lit a cigarette, and stood watching the moon go down in the west. To hell with Laura he thought, to hell with Stan and Carlos too. Why hadn't he gone with Hadji? The boat plowed steadily on while flying fish raced alongside, leaving phosphorescent trails in the black water.

§

They docked early in Panjim harbor. Goa looked more like Christianstadt or Montego than the dreary India Stan had expected. The morning sun splashed against the trim white and pastel stucco walls of the old colonial buildings. The citizens wore pants and the streets were clean. They breakfasted on the terrace of a modern hotel overlooking the harbor.

After breakfast they went in search of Jeff's friend Grey. The taxi sped down shady palm-lined avenues where massive houses, built in an era of splendor, lay decaying now behind bright hedges of bougainvillea and hibiscus. Across rice paddies that looked like magnificent green meadows, whitewashed spires of Christian churches loomed above the coconuts. Laura could have sworn she was in Mexico. Stan had started coughing again.

The car pulled up in front of a high wall with ornate plaster moldings and an elaborate iron gate. Some men were painting the grillwork. Jeff got out and spoke to them.

"This is it," he said, jumping back into the car.

Inside the walls a sprawling heap of stone and stucco, cast iron porches and shuttered balconies, had been rescued from a jungle of overgrown plantings. A platoon of workmen was putting the finishing touches on what Stan concluded must have been an expensive job of restoration. "The dope business must be awfully good," he said.

"Looks like it," Jeff agreed. They got out of the car and were led by an old woman past cool high-ceilinged rooms with new tile floors in exotic designs, then through teakwood doors into an octagonal room with old red- and blue-paneled windows. In a far corner a young man, naked except for some bracelets, was seated on the floor facing a woman, also naked. They seemed to be doing some sort of yoga. The young man rose and walked toward them followed by the woman.

"Hi, good to see you, man," he said cheerily to Jeff, extending a hand with painted fingernails. Jeff flinched, reminded of Hassan's red nails. He introduced Laura, Stan, and Carlos and Grey introduced his friend, whose name was Joy. Grey was fresh out of Princeton into dealing and Joy was fresh out of Santa Monica into Grey. Stan was impressed by their coolness at talking with four strangers while stark-naked.

"Looks like you're planning to stay for a while," Jeff said.

"Not sure." With a shrug Grey ambled to his stereo and put on a Bach chorale. "Just got here a few months ago. Bought this old place without thinking. Now we've fixed it up, looks like we might stay. Goa's a good place. Good Christian smugglers, not those Hindus. You can buy anything here: privacy, protection, immunity—you name it. It's a tradition or something."

After lunch Jeff talked with him on the beach beyond the house, in the deep shade of some date palms.

"Isn't it dangerous to show all this money?" Jeff indicated the extensive renovations to the house and grounds.

"Not here," said Grey indifferently. "They think we're all rich anyhow. It just makes them mad if we don't spend it. In Goa they just love money. They don't care where it comes from as long as you spend it here on them."

"You paying off?" asked Jeff curiously.

"A little. We had a party the other night, had the head of the Goa CID here, Panjim police chief, some local ones too. Spiked their drinks with acid and got them laid by a platoon of chicks—our sex shock troopers. They had a groovy time. Never had Western women, never had acid. They thought it was the chicks. Now they want more. Little acid, little sex. They'll do anything we ask them to do after a while."

"I got a half-million hits to get rid of for my friend Stan," Jeff said. "Can you do it?"

Grey whistled. "I don't know, man, that's a whole lot to move. The season's almost over here, you know." He doodled in the smooth sand with one long red fingernail.

"I'm really desperate, man. I agreed to distribute this stuff for him but I'm fed up. Want to get outta this fuckin' country."

"Some people don't like it, I guess," Grey said. "This is as far as I've been in India."

"Don't go anyplace else."

"Lots of people go up to Kashmir and Kulu."

"He only wants his cost back," Jeff said, getting back to his subject. "There's a guy in Bombay willing to pay cash but Stan wants it in a check in his bank in Switzerland. I know you can do it."

"Who's the Bombay cat?"

"His name's Wasu."

Grey laughed.

"You know him then?"

"Sure, doesn't everyone? But he can pay in Switzerland, he's got dozens of Swiss accounts."

"He told Carlos he wanted to do it in cash."

"Then Carlos is lying or Wasu was after some fishy deal. Cash!" Grey snorted. "Probably all counterfeit—or else he planned to steal it back before you got out of town. "What did you say his cost was?" he added.

"I didn't say, but it comes to about three rupees a hit," said Jeff.

"That's not bad, but it'll take some time." Grey looked up, smiling. "A few months, that sound cool?"

"You think Stan can rent a house here?" Jeff asked.

"Sure, easy. There's one down the road, some French cat's just leaving. Got a terrific electric kitchen: juicers, blenders, a freezer, the works—really far out for Goa."

Later in the afternoon Jeff had tea with Stan. Laura was swimming and Carlos had gone off to the local hippie hangout.

"It's all fixed with Grey if you say so," Jeff said. "He says it'll

[255]

take a couple of months but he'll do it. Also gave me a piece of interesting information: Wasu could have paid in Switzerland all right—he has plenty of accounts there. Grey seems to know about him, says the cash deal was a scam."

Stan looked pleased that he hadn't been tricked.

"Grey's got a house lined up if you want it."

Stan's cough had worsened although he looked better and had told Laura at lunch that the sea air made him feel good. But the pressure was there in his chest as well as a pain in his left side each time he tried to breathe.

"When can we move in?" he whispered hoarsely.

"Tomorrow if you like. Don't you want to look at it?"

"Not especially. Let Grey keep the acid locked up here. I'd like to go and see Laura's yogi, he's only a hundred miles or so down the coast. We'll leave Carlos in the house. I guess it has a phone?"

Jeff nodded.

"Good. We can reach him then in case anything happens. I'll see what the yogi says, then . . . Then I don't know what—what can I say?" He smiled defeatedly at Jeff. "I'm at death's door, I guess." Stan fidgeted with his tea, mopping his saucer with a paper napkin. Jeff noticed his small pink hands trembling. "Do you trust Grey, he looks pretty weird."

"He's just got his own style," Jeff said. "You know Princeton boys."

Stan nodded. "We won't tell Carlos what we know about Wasu. He's just to stay in the house and stand by. There seem to be enough chicks here for him to play with, that'll keep him busy." Stan sighed heavily. "You'll come along with us to the yogi, won't you? I'm not sure Laura could handle it alone with—well, with me. You know, I might fall apart altogether along the way. Carlos wouldn't know how to act with a yogi and I'm sure the yogi wouldn't want to see him, otherwise I would suggest you stay here."

Grey appeared wearing a towel. "Hope the tea's O.K.," he said to Stan. "Jeff tells me you're sick."

"They say it's cancer," Stan replied.

"Not much to say about that," Grey murmured, with a nervous look at Stan as though he might possibly transmit the disease. "Guess we all have to go some way, eh? Anyhow, they say India's supposed to some sort of a special place to die in." He managed a bland smile.

Stan ignored Grey's effort at conversation. "So you'll do the work for us," he said abruptly.

"Sure, I'll try anyhow."

"I'd like to rent that house and leave Carlos in it while Jeff and

Laura and I go south to see someone. I'll leave the acid with you. Is that cool?"

"I guess you trust me," said Grey.

"Is there any reason why I shouldn't?" Stan smiled. "But please, lock it up in some closet or something and don't give the key to Carlos."

"I understand."

"The coke business must be thriving," Stan said, changing the subject. He gestured at the house and garden.

"Can't complain." Grey shrugged. "We don't bother with the States anymore, too tricky. Just South America, here, and Europe."

Laura appeared on her way from the beach.

"Come, have some tea," Stan called to her. "Grey's found a house for us just down the road. We'll move in tomorrow and the following morning we'll go search for your yogi. Have you got the directions?"

"Where are you going?" asked Grey.

Laura repeated the directions Indra had given her.

"Well, you can get a reasonably good car to the Goa border, but then there's a river and a ferry and on the other side it's India again where I hear you have to take your chances with taxis."

"I was afraid you'd say that," said Stan, coughing. "The whole idea of traveling in this country is enough to make you forget about it."

"I dig what you mean," said Grey. "I use bikes and motorcycles. Otherwise, I don't go out much. Anyhow, one place in this world seems pretty much like another. I never was much for sightseeing."

XII

§

THE FIRST COCK WAS crowing as Laura and Jeff stood by the hired car waiting for Stan. Even though she was shivering in the early morning chill, Laura stood apart from Jeff.

"Certainly get started early in this country," muttered Jeff. He watched a group of pigs following a fisherman who had gone to the beach to perform his morning toilet.

When Stan emerged from the vast pinkness of the two-story colonial house, he seemed small and green.

"Even at a distance he looks sick," Jeff whispered to Laura.

She sighed. "I never liked him. I don't know why I'm doing this. I'm afraid I want to test Indra. Isn't it awful, what does that mean? It's terrible of me."

"Oh, it's just your practical side," Jeff said, smiling. "From all those generations of Wasps."

Carlos came out with Stan's luggage, obviously relieved not to be going. He handed the luggage to the driver and got Stan into a back seat that had few, if any, springs left. Stan's face went red with exasperation as he sank out of sight inside the sordid vehicle.

"Is this the best we could do?" he rasped, as the car made a screeching start down the quiet lane.

"The good ones don't like to get up early," Jeff explained from the front seat. "Nobody wants to make long hauls any more, there's no money in it. Gas is too expensive here."

The cool morning gave way to blistering heat as they traveled through groves of palm and mango. Oleander and hibiscus crowded the narrow road, which touched the sea and then climbed back to higher land.

They reached the Goa border at noon and paid off the driver, who insisted on treating them to tea and cookies in a grubby, fly-infested restaurant with piles of dead fish drying in the yard. When the antique steam-driven ferry arrived, there was a mad rush for seats. Coolies threw luggage inside and pushed passengers in through the windows. The boat moved away from the pier just as Laura got in, dragging Stan behind her. Jeff had to jump.

Across the estuary they were in Hindu India again, assaulted on all sides by beggars and food hawkers. Several drivers converged on them, yelling place names even Laura couldn't understand.

Stan got sick and began vomiting, which calmed things down long enough for Laura and Jeff to get him into a taxi. But once they were inside the car the crowd converged again, faces pressed to the windows. It was Jeff's first experience out in the country.

"Try not to get uptight," Laura said quietly. "It only excites them and makes them more aggressive."

Continuing south their discomfort increased. The taxi swerved from side to side, avoiding potholes and road repairs. The sun heated the bare steel roof of the car so that whenever they stopped, which was often, the heat and blowing dust became unbearable.

Stan slumped out of sight, coughing now and then. He was frightened, it was obvious to him he was getting worse. Curled up like a fetus, he tried to sleep but couldn't. He was sure he'd die in India, maybe even in this taxi. What was it, he wondered, that kept telling him to stay?

He had learned self-preservation early. Now a sense of guilt began to surface slowly, there in the dust-filled Indian heat, a feeling he'd never thought much about, or had quickly relegated to a remote corner of his mind. That, after all, had always been his power; he was like a computer: reliable, programmable, emotionless. What had guilt to do with him? But now nameless guilt arose along with his gradual awareness of something else, some quality beyond the poverty and suffering around him. It floated in the air outside, some higher value unknown to him that made him feel small and guilty.

He tried to put his finger on it. Was this the way the end was? Was his life going to pass in review—his utterly meaningless, unnecessary life? He had to admit it had been a sordid and maudlin affair, except for the few times when a sudden generosity had gotten the best of his judgment. An affair of greed, born out of . . . He tried to get it. Born out of fear. Yes, fear was the basic program. He felt guilty about that and he guessed it was the real reason he had come to India. He was here to throw his life into the lap of the gods. If it were meant for him to live he would be spared. If it were time for him to be snuffed out, that would also happen. Were there really people who could alter the course of fate?

Jeff handled a change of cabs in the early evening with a minimum of fuss. Then after a long sleep, Stan became aware that

[259]

the car had stopped, that it was cool, dark, and silent. He looked out the window at a small crowd of bare-chested young men dressed in white dhotis, holding flickering tapers.

Jeff helped him across a stone courtyard into a spotlessly clean cement building with small sparsely furnished guest rooms. The air smelled of the jungle. Outside the windows water rushed over rocks, bells rang at intervals. A dark, good-looking young man entered their room. He reminded Stan of a black version of John F. Kennedy.

"Oh, gentlemen," he said in clipped English, "it is the custom here to bathe in our river and come to the temple on arriving. We have very few foreigners as it is somewhat out of the way. You are most welcome." He bowed slightly, beaming.

"How do you come to speak such very good English?" Laura asked as several other young men crowded into the room behind him, peeking around and over each other like children.

"I am the eldest son of the Chief Priest of this temple. From British times the eldest son must be able to speak English. But you must bathe now—it will be most rejuvenating for you."

"We don't have any bathing suits," Stan said politely.

"We do not wear bathing suits, oh gentlemen," said the young man. "We have these." He produced some folded white cloths with red borders. "My sister will come for the lady. Here the gentlemen and ladies do not bathe together."

With the aid of several torches, Stan and Jeff found themselves awkwardly descending a flight of stone stairs toward the sound of bubbling water. Stan detested bathing in anything but a bath or shower.

"Remove the clothes and jump in," said the young man, waving his torch over the water.

"Is there anything in there?" Jeff asked.

"Only a few fish," the young man giggled. "They may nip at you but they are not dangerous—go ahead."

A crowd of men had gathered to watch the submersion. They tittered decorously as Stan and Jeff removed their lunghis and stepped timidly into the water. Surprisingly it was not at all what Stan had expected. It was warm, almost body temperature, and had a certain texture to it. He submerged himself over and over like a sea lion, feeling at once cleansed and stimulated, and almost enjoying the quiet laughter and applause of the watchers on shore.

"Do you think this is the sacrificial bath?" Jeff said to Stan as they paddled together out of earshot of their host. "I hear they still sacrifice strangers to their idols in these out of the way places, and bathe you before they do it.

[260]

Stan found himself regaining his sense of humor.

Back in the room they dried themselves and put on dhotis, which Stan showed Jeff how to tie. Laura came in dressed in a white sari. She seemed considerably cheered by the bath.

"Ah, they want you to wear dhotis," she said.

"Feels like a dress." Jeff fidgeted with the folds. "Do we really have to go to their temple?"

"He thinks they're going to sacrifice him—eat him for dinner," Stan said.

Laura laughed. "It's important to honor the local gods, rather like a toll fee. Come on, bring five hundred rupees and we'll go to the temple. I'm afraid it's something you'll have to go through with." She glanced at Jeff. "Really, they won't eat you! And they know Indra's out in the jungle somewhere. Unless we spend some money they won't tell us where he is."

The torches, the glint of the bronze and gold idols, their jewels, the beat of the drums and the music touched something deep inside Stan. "As though I've been here before," he thought. They entered through a gate encrusted with a writhing frenzy of gods and goddesses that rose out of sight into the night. In the courtyard a chorus of bells was ringing as hundreds of worshippers prostrated themselves on the pavement.

The son of the Chief Priest came over to them. "The first puja is almost over. There will be another in a few minutes. You would like to do puja?" He cast an eye at Laura, sensing she understood his meaning.

"Yes, of course," Laura answered. "We will do Maha Puja."

"Maha Puja!" The young man's eyes bulged. "That is five hundred rupees, ma'm."

Laura drew him aside and let him see the five hundred rupees Jeff had given her. "I understand you might be able to tell me the whereabouts of a yogi called Indra," she said. "Maybe you call him Indrajit here?"

The young man did a double-take.

"You are a friend of his?" he asked. He looked frightened.

"Yes," murmured Laura, fondling the hundred-rupee notes.

"I can take you to him in the morning." The young man smiled, his eyes on the money and his hand ready to take it.

"Then I think we will do the Maha Puja in the morning before going to see him. At the five-thirty puja. I think it is too late for us now, my friends are very tired and it takes some time for you to prepare for Maha Puja I know."

"Yes, yes, of course." His eyes followed her hands as she slipped the money back into her sari blouse. He realized at once that Laura knew more about India than he'd expected. For even if she gave him the five hundred rupees now it was too late to perform the expensive puja, which took many coconuts, kilos of ghee, and special herbal mixtures. She also seemed to know that once he got her money, he would most likely forget to get up so early in the morning. He narrowed his eyes at her.

"Yes, of course, as you wish. We will perform Maha Puja at five-thirty tomorrow morning and then I will take you to see the yogi of whom you speak. You must be hungry now," he said, smiling. "Will you take your food in the dining hall or in your rooms?"

"In our rooms," she said, trying to sound like a memsahib. These were after all very elegant Brahmins even though they lived in the jungle. "And we are extremely hungry so you won't forget us, will you?"

At three-thirty in the morning Stan was awakened by bells clanging in the temple. He lay in bed listening to the delicious sound of the water in the river below. Shortly after, the light was suddenly switched on, and Prakash, as he was called, stood at the door. Jeff, furious, dove under the blankets.

"It is time for the snana," Prakash said, grinning. "This morning you will snana at the main bathing ghat. Come, it is time. Otherwise, the Maha Puja will not be able to begin on time."

"For Christ's sake, what is this, some sort of a Cub Scout camp?" Jeff moaned.

"Not for Christ's sake, oh gentlemen," Prakash answered, "for Goddess' sake. We do not worship the Christ here, we are Hindus."

"Snana is bath, I presume," said Stan.

"The bath here is most healing, the water is filled with minerals and herbal tinctures. It is the jungle which is everywhere around us. If you worship here for forty days, all sickness goes."

"You think I look sick?" Stan asked.

"I think you have come from a long distance to get healed. You do not look sick, but there is something inside, yes?" Prakash smiled.

§

Jeff was cursing under his breath as the young priest led them down the red clay road from the temple to the bathing ghat. Mist hung in ancient banyans with roots like elephant trunks and pepul trees so large that twenty men could embrace their circumference.

The place was very old, Prakash explained, as they walked with dozens of other white clad worshippers all headed for the snana. It was recorded as having been an auspicious spot at the time of the Buddha and even before that, back into the forgotten past, people had come here seeking immortal wisdom and healing.

The bathing ghat was a wide turning of the river that formed a deep clear pool about one hundred yards in diameter. Rocks jutted out over it, orchids bloomed in trees, and the scent of wild jasmine was so strong it seemed artificial. Naked yogis and mendicants sat performing their morning prayers, and a group of widows with shaved heads and red saris immersed themselves in the pool, repeating mantras.

"Some scene, eh?" Jeff muttered to Stan as they stood at the edge. "What now?"

"Do get in, it is not cold," Prakash said.

"Do we go in with our dhotis on or off?" asked Stan.

"If you are wearing something underneath, then you may take off, otherwise leave on."

"Well as long as we're in our jockey shorts," Jeff said, throwing off his dhoti, "we might as well have a swim."

Much to the astonishment of the onlookers who bathed but never swam in the water, Jeff and Stan swam to the opposite shore and back.

"Oh, gentlemen, you are excellent swimmers," a grinning Prakash said when they returned. "I hear that people swim in your countries but I have never seen. We are much impressed. It is good, very good."

Laura had been bathing as Indra advised her, up the stream and out of sight. She was giggling as she approached them.

"What's so funny?" muttered Jeff.

"You two. Guess it's the jockey shorts in the middle of all this. They look so strange."

"You'd better put your dhotis on now, it is almost five-thirty," advised Prakash.

"Over these wet things?" Stan asked.

"It is the custom here to go directly from the bath to the puja. It is good if you are wet, then the Goddess is sure you are clean."

Jeff looked at Prakash as if he were mad.

Laura reached into her sari blouse and silently handed him the five hundred rupees she had promised.

The fresh air exhilarated Stan. As they walked back to the temple he felt something inside him being pushed out as though by some superior force that was entering him. The feeling wasn't exactly pleasant, but he was glad something was about to happen to him at last.

The deep bass sounds of the temple drums echoed through the

[263]

hills, summoning pilgrims to the sunrise puja. From every direction white-, red-, and saffron-clothed worshippers converged on the temple bearing offerings: coconuts, bananas, garlands of flowers on brass trays, mounds of rice and betel nuts. As they passed under the ancient gate the scent of burning ghee and wood sent Laura's mind hurtling back to the burning grounds. Priests wearing scarlet loin cloths darted in and out of the crowd, herding their devotees into corners for special pujas. Every imaginable form of devotion was going on simultaneously.

"Noisy, aren't they?" Jeff commented.

"No, just free," said Laura. "Each just doing his own thing. They don't have any group worship."

"Looks like a religious three ring circus," muttered Jeff.

"Don't you dig idol worship?" joked Stan.

At a sudden clanging of bells and a burst of drumming they were propelled by Prakash through a door into an inner temple.

Flaming tapers and oil lamps illumined the priests and worshippers. Coconuts were being cracked open on the stone steps to the shrine, and lights waved in front of a many-armed, big-breasted goddess astride a golden tiger. Prakash pushed them forward until they were directly in front of the idol, which was covered with garlands of walnut-sized rubies and diamonds. Laura watched Jeff with amusement as his mouth dropped open at the sight of the gems.

§

"Was that the Maha Puja?" asked Stan as they breakfasted later on. "It all went so fast and so much was happening, I didn't quite understand."

"I suppose those stones are real," said Jeff. "It's sort of like a Dorothy Lamour jungle movie, isn't it?"

"Prakash told me they'd been stolen several times," said Stan. "He says they always came back and the thieves died horrible deaths."

"Good thing Grey doesn't know about this place," Jeff said. "He'd figure out some way to rip them off."

Prakash came into the room. "When you are finished eating we should go. He is up on the mountain." Prakash pointed to a peak that rose like a vast green pyramid, ringed with clouds. "It is a good climb for us, over five thousand feet. I have arranged for coolies to carry your luggage. There are other temples there and a place you

[264]

can stay in. Himself, he is in a cave on the face of a cliff. It is covered by clouds, otherwise I could show you."

Stan found out at the last minute that it was possible to drive part of the distance to the top. He complained to Prakash.

"Oh, gentlemen," Prakash said, "the radiator of the car would boil over. It is not made to climb such a mountain. No, no—the car would blow up. It is a road for jeeps only."

"If a car can't make it, how can we?" persisted Stan. "What about a jeep?"

"There are no jeeps. Only the forest guards have a jeep and they are out of station. The walk will give you a lift," he said, slapping Stan on the back. "You will see."

Stan started coughing and choking.

"You must really look after that cough," Prakash commented, laughing. "You might be coming down with the grippe."

Jeff and Laura exchanged glances.

§

They left the village, skirting rice paddies, and plunged into the jungle. A forty-five degree incline started abruptly about a half mile out. Prakash strode ahead like an English athletic director on a Boy Scout hike, yelling mercilessly at the skinny undernourished coolies who ran barefoot ahead of him with hundred pound loads on their heads.

The pace was too fast for Stan. "Why must they go so fast and why do we have to keep up with them? Can't we just have a nice leisurely walk? Let them go on, I'm sitting down for a rest."

Prakash, seeing Stan sit down, dashed back. "Oh, gentleman, you must not sit down. You will get more tired that way, and we will also miss our lunch if we do not get to the top by one o'clock. It is not far now," he said. "Come!"

Stan got up and they started climbing again. After about a half hour the trail leveled out. They were on a high plateau of sparse jungle. The grass was burned gray and the black earth looked parched in the summer heat.

Stan turned to Laura. "I'm sitting down right now. Here. How much further?" he gasped, mopping his brow.

Prakash pointed to a small speck at the top of the green pyramid that loomed above them, shimmering in the haze.

"You don't expect me to go there? Look," Stan said to Jeff who had just caught up. "Look, he says *that's* where we're going."

Jeff stood panting. Sweat poured down his face.

"It's really only a few furlongs more," said Prakash, "Come, we must not delay or we will not get the lunch."

Stan could see that it was useless to argue with a man whose main preoccupation seemed to be food.

Laura realized that she was in much better shape even than Jeff. Well, all the trials of the past four months hadn't been in vain, she thought. "You go ahead, Prakash," she said. "Just leave one of the coolies with us and make sure he has water. We'll rest here for a while. Really, we're more interested in going slowly than we are in having lunch. You run ahead, we'll be all right."

"Then I will take my leave," Prakash agreed. "And this man is my own servant, not a coolie. He has a flask of drinking water."

After resting they set out again and in a few minutes were in thick jungle. Large stinging flies dive-bombed them. When they came out of the undergrowth the path rose steeply in hairpin turns up an almost vertical cliff. The heat was so intense that Stan was sure he would die on the spot. His eyes were blinded by sweat. Bits of rock that gave way beneath his feet could be heard bouncing far below.

"Stop!" he yelled frantically. "Stop at once! This is crazy, I can't make it." He clung to the dark red burning rock of the cliff. The servant came and doused him with water and they began to climb again until finally the path leveled out once more, follow ing the saddle of a broad ridge. At the higher altitude the air was miraculously cooler. They could also see their destination, a group of temples nestled in one of the clefts of the moun tain. Prakash and the coolies, white specks, were just arriving at the top.

The path, bordered by giant ferns, continued through groves of eucalyptus and palmetto. Small birds twittered in the tops of the teak and cinnamon trees. Suddenly the forest opened onto a broad meadow that sloped around the side of the mountain in a crescent of green waving grass. Just as they stopped to catch their breath, they were amazed to see an Arabian stallion bearing down on them at full gallop. Before they had time to think, the rider, a naked man with hair to his waist, had swooped down on them. He bent over and with one graceful movement caught Laura under the arm and lifted her onto the horse in front of him.

"Who was that?" cried Stan in astonishment. "He's really ter rific!"

Jeff shook his head.

"Far out," said Stan, as the horse jumped some bushes at the end of the meadow and scrambled up the side of a cliff. "Whoever he is, he can certainly ride!"

Jeff, who had always imagined himself a better than average

[266]

rider, could see that he had been out-classed. "Rides like a stunt man," he admitted grudgingly. "Pretty cool!"

For a moment the horse and riders stood motionless, silhouetted against the hazy sky. Then they turned, galloped across the field toward Stan and Jeff, and came to a dead stop right in front of them.

"This is Indra," Laura said into the cloud of dust that enveloped the two men. Grinning, Indra shook his long hair free. Then with a wild yell he raised his left arm, twirled a rope in the air, and lassoed Stan around the shoulders.

Laura dismounted. Indra walked the horse across the meadow followed by Stan, who, roped like a steer, half walked, half ran out of sight into the jungle.

Jeff watched in disbelief as they disappeared.

"What the hell is happening around here?" he said, eyeing Laura mistrustfully.

Once out of the meadow, Indra slowed his horse down. Even so, it was fast for the exhausted Stan, who had to trot to keep up along the narrow and tricky jungle path. He had not time to notice through the towering trees the splendid view of the valley below, or the sea beyond. Nor did he pay much attention to the white-clad pilgrims who stood grinning, their eyes sparkling with delight and curiosity as they watched Indra pull this foreign captive along the path toward his cave.

He felt like a bug in a spider's web being hauled inexorably to his doom. "What indignities I've suffered at the hands of these people," he was thinking. "Me, Stanley, one of the best brains in the West!" He thought of Sundaram and his Kamala, Ananda Baba and the despicable Saladin, and now a hooligan on horseback! He desperately wanted to live at any price, but what kind of number were they trying to pull on him anyway?

After what seemed like another endless trek, they arrived at the side of a sheer cliff. The path ended. A clear stream gushed out of the rocks into a pool before dropping a thousand feet into the jungle. Indra dismounted and removed the rope.

"You are tired, no doubt," he said calmly. "Sit down here by the pool. After you're rested, take a dip in the pool. I'll bring you a towel and some fresh clothes." He disappeared on a footpath over the face of the cliff.

It was the first time Stan had thought to observe closely the man whom he'd heard so much about, this huge naked brown man with his henna red hair and boyish appearance. The sight of him frightened Stan, struck fear at the deepest level of his consciousness, as if the mere existence of such a creature invalidated everything he had hitherto known or believed in.

[267]

"If I were a dog," he thought, "every hair on my spine would be standing on end!"

Indra returned with a towel, soap, and a cloth. "Here," he said, lighting a small brownish cigarette, "smoke one."

Stan hesitated for a moment. "Is that tobacco? I never smoke tobacco."

"Take it," Indra commanded.

Stan obeyed.

"When you have bathed, come and sit with me. The sun will be setting, from there you can see the whole thing. It's quite startling. But mind the path, it gets narrow and the wind can be treacherous."

Stan bathed in the small pool. The water bubbled out like a chorus of voices singing inside the mountain. It was soft too, and his skin felt as though it had been shampooed. Now that he had finally stopped moving he began to relax, and splashed around in the pool wondering what would happen next. What was fate, after all, that he should find himself in such a place?

After putting on the lunghi that Indra had left he made his way timidly and carefully along the path onto the cliff face. Rounding a corner he started back in fright. Over the precipice yawned a drop of at least two thousand feet. Vultures and kites hovered ominously off the rocks, floating on updrafts. From where he was standing he could see Indra's camp, nestled in a huge fissure midway on the face of the sheer cliff, where a vast section of rock had fallen and caused a cave to be formed between it and the mountain. Fifty yards of narrow path remained. Indra was sitting in front of a fire playing an instrument and singing. He had covered his brown body with ash.

"Are you all right?" he shouted across the chasm at Stan. "Don't think about it, just walk across. Nothing will happen to you."

Stan dared not look out or down. He kept his eyes glued to his feet as he put one in front of the other. He held onto the rocks with his hands and paused when sudden blasts of wind buffeted him. Finally, crouching, he clambered across the last few feet.

"You looked like an old monkey," Indra said grinning when Stan reached firm ground. "A lecherous old monkey coming to rape me."

He fluttered his eyelids and brushed back his long matted hair with a gesture that reminded Stan of Joan Crawford. "Welcome," he leered. "Welcome to the cave of the mad witch."

"Who?" gulped Stan.

"Me," said Indra. "Yes, it is true, I can tell by your face—you

[268]

were seeing me as a woman just now, a female, eh? Yes, ah ha, that is most auspicious . . . most auspicious." He picked up a drum and rattled it wildly. "Ho! Ho! Ha! Ha! Oay!" he yelled out toward the setting sun. "I smell the blood of an Englishman. Yes! Is it not true?"

"I'm not English, I'm a Jew."

"Don't be self-centered," snapped Indra. "It wasn't your blood I smelled. What is 'Jew'? I'm not sure I know. . . . You mean like Moses in the Bible?"

"It's a Western tribal group."

"Has had many troubles?"

"Yes—always has been on the move," Stan explained. "Specializes in communications: money, writing, newspapers, radio, now TV. But mostly money—maybe invented it."

"Ah," said Indra, "that carries very difficult karma. We have tribes like that here, two or three separate ones."

"Yes?" said Stan, interested.

"They are called Marwaris and Jains and Parsees. The Parsees are the Pharasees of the Bible, the Marwaris are big moneylenders, the Jains are merchants and puritanical reformers—Gandhi was a Jain."

Indra put down his drum. "As I was saying, I smell the blood of an Englishman, did some Englishman come with you? A rather young, handsome, ah—I see him, yes, he is with Laura. Very upset he is. Called Jeff, is he not?"

Stan felt a tremendous force pulling at him and realized that Indra's words were a screen for something else, some mental activity so strong that he had to look away to avoid being turned inside out.

"You are a very guilty man," Indra said slowly and firmly. Stan was surprised to find himself nodding in assent.

"You need not nod," he said. "There is no need for you to agree with me. But understand that I find you guilty."

"Of what?"

"You have a mother, I believe?"

Stan hesitated.

"Answer me," Indra said sternly.

"Yes."

"And she is your responsibility." Indra frowned.

Stan felt himself begin to shudder.

"Yet I see her in an institution of some sort. Very bad place. Very dirty—ah, I see. She is very unhappy about it, eh?"

"I put her in a very nice institution because she is getting old and she went crazy."

[269]

"She is not crazy," Indra snapped. "It is you who are crazy."

"That's not true!" yelled Stan.

"It is!" Indra yelled back at him. "She told you the truth about yourself and you couldn't take it so you had her put away!"

Stan felt a great rush of energy flowing into him.

Indra pointed dramatically to the setting sun. "You spend all this money on your desires and whims and on sex—don't deny it—and your poor old mother is locked up in a cheap old age home." Indra laughed uproariously.

Stan felt a chill envelop him as the red sun disappeared below the horizon.

"And you have come here," Indra went on, "because Laura has told you I can heal what they call your cancer."

Indra leaned over the fire and with his long forefinger beckoned Stan nearer. "You know what I should do with you?" he whispered over the smoke and flames.

Stan trembled as he leaned toward the naked giant, gray with ash, who was whispering spookily at him through the smoke. "What should you do?" he asked hoarsely.

"Kill you," said Indra. "Right here on this spot. So easy." He gestured to the precipice showing all his teeth in a skeletal grin.

Stan felt tears well up inside him and made no attempt to stop them. Soon he was sobbing openly.

Indra retreated into a corner of the cave and returned after a while with a cup of hot tea. He handed the cup to Stan. "Drink and cry—it is good for you," he said. Then he picked up his instrument again.

As Indra began to sing, Stan realized that he was in a situation over which he had absolutely no control. He couldn't stop his own convulsive crying, nor could he halt the flow of bitter memories of every sort that now flooded his mind.

The man seated across the fire from him seemed to change from one moment to the next behind the smoke. For a time Stan thought he could make out a beautiful girl—or was it a boy? Then when a gust of wind blew the smoke aside the youth became a haggard old woman, an ancient sphinx-like creature, barely human. At each change he noticed that a fresh set of memories would drift into his consciousness.

He wanted to confess his guilt!

The thought made him feel ridiculous and uneasy. He glanced at the path wondering whether to try getting back across the cliff while there was still some light.

"Don't think about escaping from me," said Indra, pausing in his song. "You will fall off if you go back now. I have waited a long time for you," he added ominously. "Now you are here, you shan't escape me. I owe it to your mother . . . to my Mother."

Stan fidgeted with his cup, unable to meet Indra's gaze.

"Do you want to confess everything to me here and now?" Indra said smiling.

"I can't," Stan mumbled. He burst into tears again, spilling his tea. "I can't, I can't. I want to but I don't know how."

There was a long silence. The fire crackled. From far away came the sound of water rushing out of the mountain.

Indra stood up. "Get up, rodent," he said. "Come with me."

Stan was startled but felt too weak to move.

"Come, get up at once—get up!" Indra prodded him with the tip of his chimtah.

Stan got to his feet, feeling weak in the knees. He tried nervously to secure the lunghi around his waist.

"What are you doing?"

"I'm afraid this will fall down. I mean, I'm not used to wearing . . ."

"Let it!" Indra said sharply. "Why are you all of a sudden so modest—you who pay for bodies, for flesh! Ha! Do you think I care what you are wearing or what you look like? I have seen everything under the sun. Yes, for centuries. Whether your cloth falls or not is nothing to me—here!" He reached forward and ripped the lunghi from Stan's waist. "Now you won't have to worry about that. You won't need it where you're going anyhow."

Indra grinned at the absurd figure of Stan standing in his jockey shorts. "What bumpy knees you Western fellows have," he laughed. "Come, follow me."

In a dark corner of the cave was a small opening, just big enough to squeeze into. "We go up through here," Indra said, "observe how I do it and follow where you see my feet go."

Stan struggled up the shaft after him. After a few yards of vertical ascent, the shaft opened into a small horizontal passage where there was room to stand. He felt the strong warm hand of Indra pulling him up.

"Follow me." Indra walked quickly and deftly along the passage. Stan felt as if he were going toward the center of the world. It was warm and he could hear water splashing somewhere ahead. They came to a large underground chamber, warm and slippery. Indra clicked on a flashlight.

"Look there—the water is bubbling up out of the center of the mountain into this lake. A lake inside the top of the mountain—is it not marvelous?"

The light shone over a good-sized pool fed by water splashing over a rock at one end. It was difficult to judge the scale of the place.

"Come," said Indra, "we'll go behind the water now."

There were footholds cut into a small cliff. The size of the cavern now became apparent.

"A whole herd of sheep could go behind this waterfall," said Indra, waving the light at it.

The rock was damp and slippery where mosses grew under the spray. Then they were above it, climbing steadily up steep steps cut in another fissure. Indra paused, feeling the wall of rock. They seemed to have reached a dead end. "Ah," he said suddenly, "yes, it is just here." He pressed his back against the rock. Slowly a whole section slid to one side and Stan could see a pale light. "Now, up through this opening," Indra said. "We have reached our destination."

Stan struggled through the opening and climbed onto what seemed to be the stone floor of a room. "Stand up!" commanded Indra.

He stood up. A strong wind sent him back on his knees. He looked around and saw a four-armed male figure, dancing, silhouetted by the pale light from a crescent moon. They were in a small temple, a pavilion with arched openings almost to the floor on all sides. "Are we on the top of the mountain?" he asked.

"Look for yourself." Indra had sat down in front of the huge stone figure and was lighting a fire. A supply of wood was stacked in one corner.

Stan walked around peering through the arches. Vertigo was a sensation he seldom experienced but with sheer cliffs falling away on every side, he felt very uncomfortable. He was also cold.

Indra gestured at the stone figure, whose four outstretched arms grasped battle gear and drums. Stone snakes writhed in its hair and around its neck. "This is Shiva," he said. He ground something between two rocks, mixed it with oil and poured it onto the fire. "He is destroying everything. See how he is stamping down on the body beneath his foot. See his necklace of human skulls!"

Stan moved closer. The flames seemed to infuse life into the deity, flickering over the polished black stone frozen in its fierce muscular dance of annihilation.

"It is Shiva Bhirava, we call him Kalabirava—the destroyer." He turned to Stan. "Lean closer," he commanded, then placed his outspread hand over Stan's head and skull, and dug his thumb into Stan's forehead. He held him motionless for some time and then released him.

"Now I must go," he said, standing up. "You will remain." He pointed to a large black stone, phallic in shape and highly polished, beneath the dancing figure. "Do you see this dot?" He indicated a red mark at the tip.

Stan examined the stone.

"You will stay here and stare at that dot. Remain sitting—it's too windy to walk around. If your eyes become tired from staring, close them and just listen to your own breathing." He started down through the opening.

"Is that all?" Stan said.

"Isn't that enough?" asked Indra.

"But it's cold here, I haven't anything on, not even my cloth."

"Don't worry, you won't freeze."

"You bring me up here and now you are going to leave me just like that?" Stan was furious. "I'm very sorry, I can't stay. I can't spare the time . . . I . . . ."

Indra burst out laughing. "You had better spare it if you want to go on living."

"But . . ." In all the craziness of the past two hours Stan had actually forgotten about the cancer eating away at him.

"No buts!" Indra bellowed. "I'm leaving. Come down if you like—if you can! Why should I care about you, rodent! I am only doing it because your friend Laura asked me. As far as you are concerned, I care nothing. You are trash to me." He ducked through the aperture in the floor and closed it behind himself, leaving Stan seated in front of the fire in his jockey shorts.

His first thought was keeping warm. He jumped up to look at the woodpile but knowing nothing about fires, he couldn't tell how long it would last.

He guessed it wasn't even nine in the evening but already the wind howled around the lonely rock pinnacle, gusting through the arches and bounding back and forth in the small space so there was no escape from it. The flames licked fitfully at the base of the statue.

"Sexy," thought Stan, noting the muscular body of the dancing youth. He wondered how best to spend the night and after an inspection noted that there was one corner that seemed to be less windy. Cautiously moving the fire into it, he edged himself onto the floor, curled up and fell into a fitful sleep.

He began to dream vividly about his childhood. His mother was there, beautiful and loving, her face luminous. Then he saw her scrubbing floors and doing menial work for neighbors. Her face and body began to age, grew older and older. He wanted to get rid of the images, to kill off the grotesque forms as she aged gradually before him.

[273]

Suddenly he woke, terrified, wondering where he was. The fire was out, he was cold. Outside he could see the stars glittering like ice in the black sky. The stars, he thought, the great spaces. Are we nothing then? Just specks in a vast chaos of equally meaningless specks? He began reviewing his life. It had never occurred to him to do this but now it was happening automatically, the events of his life rushing one after another into his consciousness. He had never really considered dying. His life had been so filled with money and machines that he had come to think of himself as a machine to be repaired and rebuilt indefinitely, provided one had the money to pay for it.

And now that he approached the end what had it all meant? Was there any meaning? Why was he sitting here in front of the image of destruction, the dance of death itself, in a strange land— while a microscopic community of organisms multiplied inside his body.

He was cold, colder than he'd ever been. He began shivering uncontrollably. He crawled to what he thought was the stone covering the passageway. If only he could get down there, he might be warmer. He clawed at the stone and dug between the cracks with a stick but nothing moved. He realized there was no escape except to jump. Yes, he could jump—and end it all. But would that end it all? Something was unfinished. . . . Oh what was it that felt so unfinished inside him and not ready to die, not ready to give up all . . .

Waves of self-pity engulfed him and he fell to the floor convulsed by spasms of crying and shaking, and aware of himself as a coward with not enough guts to bring the fiasco of his life to an end. He lay hunched in the corner, thinking how strong was his attachment to his body, even though it was diseased.

His thoughts were interrupted by a series of loud crashes, one after another, like stones falling on the roof. He looked up to see sizeable rocks hurtling through the open arches onto the floor.

Several stones landed near enough to send chips biting into his legs. Fear swept him, and he cowered like a frightened rat in his corner. It wasn't possible! It couldn't be possible! He clenched his fists and pounded the wall. How was it possible for rocks to come flying through the air like this on top of a five-thousand-foot mountain?

Just then a rock the size of a tennis ball hit the wall beside him and bounced into his lap. It was smooth and black, not unlike the rock Ananda Baba had brought up out of his mouth. Somewhere Stan had read of stones that fall in the night. They were supposed to be the work of poltergeists, but what were they? Now they were coming from all directions, big and small, pelting the roof of the temple like hail. He became numb with fright, his supply of adrenalin had been depleted by the "thing" growing inside him. His brain was too rattled to think clearly. A wailing assailed his ears until he realized it was himself, jabbering incoherently.

Then some deep instinct commanded him to follow Indra's directions. He listened to it as one attends a call far off in a valley. "I must sit up and do it," his conscious self then said. "As stupid as it seems in a situation like this I must." What else, after all, was there to do? He couldn't stand it. And maybe the rocks would stop.

He dragged himself to the place Indra had shown him and sat rigid, his face pallid with fear, staring at the red mark on the stone thrusting up from the floor. As he stared he became aware that his breathing was shallow and irregular. He tried to regularize it, directing what energy he could still summon, counting so many seconds in and so many seconds out, so many in, so many out, in, out . . .

As one trained to observe changes in phenomena, he noted that the more regularly he breathed, the warmer he became. But the feeling of reassurance that this gave him was soon shattered. While staring at the dot on the stone, he could see on the edge of his vision a halo of fire around the head of the idol. If he looked directly at it, it disappeared, but when he observed it with peripheral vision, the manifestation appeared again. He grabbed a stick and held it to the halo of flame without looking. When he withdrew the stick, it was blackened and smoking.

"So what?" he said, looking at it angrily. "So what?"

Just then the statue came to life, dancing ponderously to the rhythm of many drums, a bass like a dirge, a sharp clacking in the upright arm of the dancer. Two of the four arms disappeared. It was a frighteningly beautiful figure. Stan heard himself laugh and then yell, and he heard his own breathing as though through an amplifier. Never in his imagination had he seen or thought of such a being.

It began to dance in slow motion before him, its skin dark and taut over firm young flesh, its penis erect and hair a mass of curls with snakes slithering down across almost female breasts. The full lips were frozen in a sadistic tantalizing grin, dark eyes glittered between lashless lids.

Stan fell back on the floor as the figure advanced. "Who are you?" he stammered. "Get out! Get out!"

The figure's eyes opened wide as if in rage. A great roar, then yelps and screams filled the air.

Then it vanished. Stan sat up, oblivious of whether he was hot

[275]

or cold or breathing or not. When he regained his senses, he was in the midst of a fit of coughing. Large globs of phlegm were coming up, pieces of tissue and blood.

Enraged, he beat the floor with his fists. What was he waiting for? What power held him there, refusing to let him end it all, to be sensible—to jump!

Again he lost sense entirely and rolled on the floor, screaming and crying and clawing at the place where he imagined the entrance stone should have been. He hurled the stones that had fallen from the sky at the idol, hoping wildly to demolish it and somehow be set free of this place that held such terror for him. But all he did was tire himself out. Finally, his mind past reasoning, his body exhausted, cut, and filthy, he lay down on the stones.

§

The eastern sky had turned a dull pink. Low clouds, moving in from the sea, scuttled across the horizon. Indra was asleep in the cleft of rock near his fire.

"Hello, are you there? Hoy!" He opened one eye to see Laura, followed by a young man he supposed was Jeff, about to traverse the treacherous cliff path.

"On and on it goes," he thought to himself. He wanted no visitors but here they were. Pretending to be asleep, he watched through almost closed eyes as the two began their crossing. "The Englishman is coming," he thought, "so cunning, so unwashed, why do I smell blood when he is near?"

"You will please remove your shoes before stepping into this space," he said, opening his eyes as the two reached the edge of the cleft.

Jeff stopped to remove the special hiking boots he'd had made in Paris. Suddenly one slipped from his hand and went tumbling down the precipice, bounding into a bush fifty yards below.

"Don't go after it," Indra said, sounding like an English nanny. "If you do, you won't be able to wear it." He laughed as he always did when something got lost or stolen.

"They were new," Jeff said irritably. He stood holding the other shoe.

"Throw the other one overboard too," Indra said sternly. "I don't think you're going to need them." He pointed to his solar plexis. "It has bad feelings about leather."

"Sorry if I've offended you," Jeff replied coldly, seating himself to one side of the fire.

It was a stand-off between them.

Laura knelt and touched Indra's feet in the Indian manner she knew he understood. He placed his hand on her head and let it rest there a moment, gazing at Jeff.

"Quite a place you've got yourself here," said Jeff, trying to make conversation.

"I am smelling blood," Indra said, looking at him closely. Why is it I am smelling blood when you are near me?" He released Laura's head and she sat up and stared at Jeff.

"Where is Stan?" said Jeff, not wanting to look at Indra.

"Green eyes," Indra muttered. "Very bad. Very bad—Pathan."

"What was that?" asked Jeff uneasily.

"Very bad, green eyes," Indra repeated. "It is the rule, it is not my idea. It is the old teaching."

"I don't see Stan," Jeff said to Laura, trying to ignore the comment. "Didn't he come out here with him?" He looked at Indra. "Didn't . . ."

"Blood and green eyes," said Indra.

"What have you done with Stan?" Jeff asked loudly. "If something's happened to him, I'm here to . . ."

"Jeff!" whispered Laura reproachfully.

"You are here to *what*, me lad?"

"To find him!" Jeff shouted. "Where is he?"

"I pushed him off," said Indra quietly, gesturing at the edge of the cliff.

"You *what?*"

"Pushed him off," Indra repeated. "I couldn't stand him. I can see why the Malayali Baba wouldn't heal him—all the lying, the craftiness, like a weasel, and breaking wind constantly. Why prolong suffering like that?"

"Why prolong it!" yelled Jeff. "Why prolong it? Because he could've been with the best doctors in the world right now. . . . You have no right to push anyone anywhere."

"But I have pushed him," said Indra in his grandest English accent. "You forget that this is India. Even you could disappear here at this very moment and no one would come looking." He frowned at Jeff. "It doesn't matter," he went on. "He went to the place he would have gone to sooner or later."

"You had no right!" Jeff repeated.

Indra gazed at him with fiery eyes. "When a man throws himself in my lap, I must decide the cure. It was best, believe me!"

Jeff looked at Laura. "Let's get out of here," he said. He stood up and brushed off his clothes.

"You're not going anywhere, young man," Indra said. "Sit down."

[277]

Jeff sat down heavily.

"I see I have to give you a lesson." Indra put his hand into a pile of cloths and books near him and withdrew a revolver.

He uncocked it professionally to show Jeff and Laura it was empty except for one bullet. Then he snapped it shut and tossed it to Jeff.

Jeff caught it adroitly in midair.

"Now," said Indra, "point it to your head, twirl the cartridge chamber and pull the trigger."

"But that's Russian Roulette," Jeff said, his voice faltering slightly. "After you," he said, tossing the gun back to Indra.

"No! No! No!" screamed Laura hysterically.

Indra spun the chamber, put the pistol to his head and squeezed the trigger. Click!

"Your turn now," he said. Gazing coolly at Jeff, he tossed the gun to him again.

"I can't stand it," Laura burst out. "If you don't stop—both of you—I'm . . . I'm going to jump."

"Jump then," Indra said casually. "Jump if you like. It doesn't make the slightest bit of difference. You'll understand that some day. Go ahead."

Laura closed her eyes weakly. Jeff picked up the pistol, put it to his temple, and twirled the bullet chamber. But he couldn't bring himself to squeeze the trigger. "Why should I play this game with you," he said, putting the gun on the ground. "I came here to find Stan."

"It would cure you," said Indra.

"What!" Jeff laughed bitterly. "You mean finish me—like you finished Stan, I suppose."

"Ah," said Indra smiling, "do you really care about him? After all I know he is not really your friend. Neither he nor you has any friends, except her maybe—and she has brought you here to test me." He looked reproachfully at Laura. "Give me the gun then," he said wearily.

"Perhaps I should keep it a while," Jeff said coldly, pointing the gun at Indra.

"Jeff!" cried Laura. "Put that gun down." She grabbed for it but he jerked it out of reach.

"No, no, let him keep it," Indra said calmly. He got a box of bullets from his bag and tossed them across the fire to Jeff. "Examine them, please, and fill the other chambers up—five more bullets."

Jeff hesitated.

"Do as I say!" Indra roared.

Jeff felt his will beginning to slip out of him. He examined the bullets. They were real enough. He dropped them into place and closed the chamber.

"Now," Indra hissed softly, "aim the gun at my chest and empty it."

Jeff lifted the revolver and pointed it directly at Indra's heart. The smoke of the fire drifted between them as Indra went into his peculiar slump.

"Jeff, Jeff, no!" wailed Laura. "You don't understand, you don't know. Put that thing down, put it down!"

"Shut up," muttered Indra. "Pull the trigger. I pushed your friend Stan off the cliff. Eye for an eye. Pull the trigger!"

Jeff was angrier than he'd ever been in his life. All the frustrations, all his doubts and contradictions were being compressed into a moment.

"Shoot!" Indra ordered.

Jeff squeezed the trigger three times. The shots echoed out over the cliff.

"Again! Pump em all out, boy!" yelled Indra.

Again Jeff squeezed, this time until the chamber was empty. In the split second that it happened Laura thought she saw the bullets enter Indra's flesh and the flesh close behind them. Indra sat, slumped, veiled by the smoke of the fire.

"You see, it does not affect me," he sighed, holding out both arms grinning boyishly at them.

"It's some sort of trick," Jeff said, looking sideways at Laura.

"Yes, Indian rope trick." Indra laughed. "If it is a trick then reload and point it at yourself—or at her." He nodded at Laura.

Jeff realized that Indra had defined his limit for him.

"You see," Indra went on, "what you do not understand is that some beings are different. Your society does not allow you to believe that men are not all equal, or that you may make your soul or body immortal. It is your sickness.

"Go ahead—fill the chamber and empty it into your body if you think it is a trick. If you want to compete with me, then you must now do as I say."

"I came here to find Stan, not to compete with you," said Jeff.

"You came here to find yourself but you are failing," replied Indra. "As I told you, I pushed him overboard. He was a very bad case. Absolutely no hope for him to continue in that body."

"You gave him another body then," said Jeff cynically.

"He will have," said Indra matter-of-factly, "if I choose. Perhaps I'll let him seek his own natural level." He laughed wildly. "Some dog or goat, perhaps."

"You'd think you were God or something," said Jeff. "Are you a god?"

"No, just empty." Indra pointed to his forehead. "Here—feel," he said, extending his arm across the fire to Jeff. "Flesh and blood."

Jeff touched the large muscular arm pulsing with energy and warmth, then grasped the hand that Indra offered across the fire. A familiar feeling, like an acid high, came through into his body.

"Have you taken LSD?" Jeff asked, holding Indra's hand.

"Several times. It has been given to me by your countrymen. It does not affect me."

"You think it is useless then?"

"It is not useless. It is equal to ten years of meditation practice. Think of it—ten years—in twenty minutes." Indra cocked his head, smiling. "It is most dangerous to give people the result of ten years' practice in twenty minutes. It is like opening Pandora's box—you know Pandora's box? Very dangerous for the social fabric. Not everyone is ready for power, for knowledge. It will destroy many. Not everyone can get out at once, some must stay. That is a Christian mistake, saying everyone can be saved. It was a political ploy—simplification for the masses. Rome had mass media, the prize was Rome in those days."

He dropped Jeff's hand. "But I see you do not even follow the teachings of your Christ. If you had his faith, you could pick up the pistol and aim it at yourself."

"Without his training?"

"Believe me, my dear boy," Indra said patiently, "training is not at all necessary. Salvation comes in one moment. You can get there by training too, but people get sidetracked by too much training."

"Did Stan tell you about his project?" Jeff asked.

"He did not have time before I pushed," laughed Indra. "But I know it all anyhow. You are engaged in smuggling this drug. You must stop—it will do you no good."

He gazed at Jeff thoughtfully. "You could be a good sadhu," he said. "Come stay with me—I invite you, I will train you. You reek of garbage and sex craziness but that can be normalized. If you return to the smuggling business you might as well blow your brains out right now."

"But I'm not smuggling!"

"I know you call it distribution but you smuggled it into this country and our people think of it as that. They cannot believe anyone would ever sell for a loss." He paused. "Besides India does not need this drug. It is just another Western misunderstanding, thinking we need to be awakened. It is your country that is asleep and wishes to put to sleep the rest of the world with computers and

[280]

servo-mechanisms. Yes," he added softly, "I know everything that is going on.

"What India needs is to give up all outside drugs, all medicines. Let epidemics rage, let our armies go back to horses and elephants. Let our warriors attack naked with spears. Let our widows jump onto funeral fires and widowers walk naked into the jungle. That is the way to save India. Then we would be impregnable. Out of fear, no one would attack."

"I'm leaving," Jeff said to Laura. He got up and threw the gun across the fire to Indra.

"You're *what?*" said Laura.

"I'm leaving. If you want to come then come now, or I'll probably be at the guest house until tomorrow morning. If you want to stay, then stay. I have to get back to Goa. There's all that acid. With Stan gone, Carlos will try to sell it to Wasu."

"Let him have it," pleaded Laura.

"No."

"You're thinking of a couple of million bucks, right?" said Indra in American slang.

"You shut up."

"Jeff!" exclaimed Laura. "How can you talk that way after what you've seen?"

"I've seen nothing," Jeff said with bravado. "Just a few tricks. Your problem is that you believe all this—this bullshit. Houdini could do the same thing." He brushed off his pants with a show of unconcern although he was disturbed and frightened.

"What will you do about Carlos?" Laura asked. "Will you tell him about Stan?"

"No." He shifted his weight fretfully. "Well—are you coming?" He looked at Laura. "At least if you have to get involved with these bla—" He caught himself about to say blacks. "If you must get involved with Indians, then marry that Sikh. He's certainly better than this one."

"Jeff, you don't know what you're saying." Laura felt waves of rage coming from Indra and was afraid for Jeff's life. "Please leave."

"He wants killing," Indra muttered.

"What?" said Jeff.

"Killing," said Indra aloud, tossing the pistol back to him. "You may need this where you are headed. Not for your friend Carlos. There is another, a woman—very dangerous."

Jeff was unnerved. How could he know. It was impossible. "You mean Kamala?" he said incredulously.

Indra smiled, nodding.

Laura looked surprised. "Who's Kamala?"

[281]

"He knows," Jeff faltered. "Ask him."

"Yes, Kamala. You know what Kamala means?"

Jeff shook his head.

"It means desire. Desire with the big D as you say. Take the gun," he said. "You may need it."

"But who *is* she?" said Laura.

"A friend of Sundaram's," Jeff snapped. "Why should I be afraid of her?" he asked Indra.

"Because she is the mirror of your own actions, bouncing back to you, catching you up." He gazed at the fire, tapping a log lightly with his chimtah. He looked suddenly old, like an old woman. "There are certain people who should never come to India and you are one of them." He paused, frowning at Jeff. "I can see that you do not believe me."

"What if I kill her with this?" Jeff said, bouncing the gun in his hand.

"Yes, you can try it," Indra answered, "but she is your mirror. I think you will not be successful. It does not balance out."

"We'll see," said Jeff, slipping the revolver into his belt. "Maybe I'll see you later?" he added to Laura. Then, crawling across the ledge he disappeared into the morning mist that enveloped the mountain.

Indra sat motionless at the fire, his eyes closed and his face full of pain.

"Why did you try to do anything with him at all?" Laura asked.

"For the same reason I took away the tumor of that ridiculous Elizabeth. It is my duty. But your Jeff is not ready, he cannot begin to get out this time. He will go backwards for some time now. Anyhow, I tried. It's my duty to try to help anyone who comes to this fire. That is the rule. I'm not to go out, not to proselytize in any way. But I cannot turn anyone away."

"Even a 'low-caste rascal'?"

"Even an outcaste," Indra replied. "The caste business is all my immersion in this particular life—I was born in a high-caste body. But for us sanyasins there is really no caste, just as there is no world." He laughed. "Simple, isn't it?"

"Should I go with him—with Jeff?"

"No!" said Indra emphatically. "You cannot help him. He is far more powerful than you. He would destroy your soul—what you have built up so far."

"Who is this Kamala?"

"She is his *fate*. He has come all the way to India to meet his fate. See the play—is it not wonderful to watch?" He leveled his eyes at her. "Don't get mixed up in his fate. You have more important work."

[282]

"Shall I stay here?"

Indra gazed at her and sighed. "Relax. Stop thinking you're doing anything. We will do morning prayers. Then I will prepare food."

He stood up, stretching, and gazed out to where the sea shone like a silver blue ribbon on the western horizon. "You can almost see the breakers rolling in on the beach. It makes me want to go," he said.

A warm breeze brought the scent of wild flowers from the jungle. They watched a leopard crouched on the cliff below, waiting to attack, its tail twitching.

"How beautiful this place is," Laura said.

"Nothing is beautiful," Indra replied. "It only seems that way. It is neither beautiful nor ugly. The sea appears beautiful from here, but if you drink it you will die and in a storm it may drown you. The smell of the flower seems lovely, but it goes away. The flower will die, you might get asthma from it or a rash. The leopard is watching the monkey. It is hungry. When you call something beautiful, it is a function of your own desire." He paused, gazing at her. "Now do you understand? It is the same desire which is catching up now with your friend in the form of a high-class Malawa prostitute." Indra laughed. "She has even been given the name Kamala!" He laughed again. "If he had known Sanskrit, he would have been warned."

After morning prayers Indra prepared a breakfast of tea and hot bread made in the fire.

"Did you really push Stan off?" Laura asked while they were eating.

"No," he said, "but I'm going to have to do it. It's the only way. There's no time for him to learn. And it's important for us that he be cured." He chewed his bread thoughtfully.

She didn't know whether he meant literally or figuratively. And the way he lived, it was impossible to separate the two. For her, his very being was a commingling of impossible opposites.

"He's too bright," Indra said. "He's a genius, a siddha—a man of power—like me. All your Western scientists—your Einstein, your Oppenheimer, your Max Planck—they are all siddhas. But because they do not follow the rules, because they are impure, because they use their powers, or worse, hire themselves out to politicians . . . Because of these things, they are the worst devils. We call them asuras. Asura is a greatly gifted siddha who has gone wrong. Like your Satan. They are the black magicians of our time. Especially that Oppenheimer, he should have known better, he knew the rules. He had received plenty of training from us. Unfortunately, his guru, one of us, did not know how to persuade him, to make him understand. He used words. You have to know how to make magic shows, to frighten them to their senses." Indra sighed. "Otherwise, no one will believe."

"How can I stop desiring then?" asked Laura.

"By worshipping," he said.

"Worshipping what?"

"Anything. Everything. Different things have different results, take you on different routes. But they all lead to the same place. *It* shines through everything—diamond, mud, rich, poor, animal, vegetable—you just have to see the many faces of *It*. They are neither good nor bad nor beautiful nor ugly.

"And remember that the world which you imagine is so real, is created by your own desire—the desire to keep this." Indra grabbed at his flesh, then yawned. "You must go now, but do not leave the mountain, and return to me in forty-eight hours."

She looked at him quizzically.

"Sit back and watch the play, dear Uma, sit back and watch the play. You are not to become involved. Your path is in another direction."

§

He had to be alone. These Westerners tired him with their endless questions, always so serious, no sense of humor or feeling. Besides he had work to do. That animal above should be about ready.

When he reached the end of the passageway under the temple, Indra moved the stone up a crack so that he could observe the patient unseen. Two motionless columns of flesh were all he could see—two white hairy legs and two pinched feet. The sight disgusted him. "Leave this animal to his own fate. Why should I intercede?" he thought. But he knew that it was not his doing, what he had to do he did. The voices of his guru and his guru's guru backwards in time were directing him. They had trained him to watch the signs. The signs told him. This was his training and it was correct, the best, since he was six years old. Everything at the proper time, from the most secret and the highest. His mother had seen to that. It was not his desire to save anyone. As a matter of fact, he preferred cultivating roses above all else. But it was his duty to be kind, even when kindliness might take a drastic form. The man had come to be cured. He would cure him.

He pushed up the rock. "Are you all right?" he asked of the frightened form before him. "You have had a 'rough night' as they say, eh?"

Moaning, Stan collapsed at Indra's feet. "I've had a terrible night," he said, not daring to look up. "Terrible!" He could feel tears surfacing again.

"So, you have seen what a hopeless animal you are, yes? You have seen it?"

Stan looked up at him.

Indra could tell he was ready. "You want to confess to me," he said, "like they do in that Roman Church. It's not necessary for you to do that. I already know."

"But my life," Stan said grimacing, "what I call my life. This series of stupid actions and reactions . . . I have seen it and more, I . . ."

Indra raised a hand to silence him. "I know it, all of it. I know all your life, you needn't tell me. You need not explain to me."

Stan smiled weakly. He recognized for the first time that this barefoot, naked man might be his equal and more. "This world—is it all nothing then?"

"It is all nothing," replied Indra. "No Thing."

"Then why can't I end it here and now?"

"You can," said Indra casually.

"But I can't, I'm too cowardly. I wanted to last night. It would be suicide—and that's wrong."

"You cannot end it because you are attached to it. Suicide is a relative notion. You are afraid because you believe it is something. You believe your desires.

"You Western people always oversimplify. Your teachers lost touch with the real thing centuries ago. They were made to lose touch with it by bigots like Aristotle."

"Is that so?" said Stan, realizing the implication.

"Yes, it is so. The secrets were too final for them, too final for the suppressed masses of the time. Aristotle even sent spies to watch his pupil Alexander when he came here—to see that he didn't get it."

"Get what?"

"The Truth."

"You mean our science doesn't give us Truth?"

"No."

"What is it then?"

"A Pandora's box of cosmic dimensions," sighed Indra. "You people are just wizards of a new order, manifesting illusion and more illusion by different means. You have the secret of mathematics but it is a cul de sac."

"And our instruments and all the inventions?"

"All mirrors—they do what they are designed to do."

"But what about this?" Stan pointed to his body.

[285]

"An instrument too—*the instrument* of instruments. Did you not see last night how it can be tuned, how it can receive?"

Stan nodded, unable to meet Indra's glance.

"You people who go by the name scientist are all second-class sorcerers. You need tools to perform your manifestations, exterior aids. Mind you, there is nothing wrong in it. What is wrong is that you have power and none of the training that *must* go with its use. And that you can learn only from a teacher of the first class." He laughed. "You only get it through tapas."

"What is that?"

"Austerities."

"What do they do?"

"Was your last night not somewhat austere?" Indra smiled.

"Yes."

"Austerities reveal the truth and lead to kindliness. No man should be empowered until he is kindly. That is one thing that separates first class from second. For us it is a prerequisite. For you that element of the teaching was lost centuries ago."

"And so?"

"See what is happening: Hiroshima—and birth control. Extremes, destruction of balance."

Stan looked up. "Can nothing be done?"

"Nothing!" replied Indra emphatically. "It has already been written."

Suddenly, lying there in his jockey shorts, Stan was revolted by the scratched and dirty crumpled mass of white flesh and hair that was his body. He could smell poisons discharging from all its openings. "I wish I could jump," he said, gesturing outside.

"You can," said Indra simply. "Why not?"

"I told you, I have no courage."

"I will give you the courage," Indra said. "Nothing will happen to you because I am here. That is why you have come."

Stan felt something pour into him and fill him up—a sort of happiness and energy he had never known before. Trembling, he reached for Indra's hand. "Will you take me to the edge?" he asked.

Indra gripped Stan's cold and perspiring hand and pulled him to his feet.

"Do not be afraid," he said. "I am with you."

"Then I am going." He felt flooded with energy. With a smile he released Indra's hand, went to one of the arches, and looked out over the precipice.

"Go," said Indra. "You are not going anywhere."

Stan paused, gazing at him. He felt his whole system now

[286]

operating with a kind of super clarity. Indra was smiling warmly, like a mother watching her son's first few steps.

"Oh my God!" he heard himself cry as he jumped out into space.

§

As soon as Stan disappeared, Indra bounded across the parapet. He could see the limp form lying on the rocks about fifteen hundred feet down the face of the cliff. He sighed to himself. Why had he allowed himself to become involved with these people? It was all the trick of that old Tibetan witch, Dorje's aunt. Why had he let her complicate things with this girl and let the girl bring him two more. He knew why he had to, yet he felt vexed and put upon. And now, so much work, a work he had performed once as a young man with his first guru. He had been given explicit instructions in it again by his second teacher, the old woman, but he had only done it once more since her going. It would be a gamble and a fight.

Quickly he lifted the rock and made his way down inside the mountain. Just above his cave he squeezed through an opening in the cliff and started climbing down a steep path leading to the place where Stan had landed. One vulture had already spied the body and was circling. He shouted it away. A great hornbill, like a giant bat, interested in the possibility of a meal, soared nearby. He threw some rocks at it, while continuing to clamber down the cliff face as fast as possible. There was no time to lose—a tricky business this, especially in the south, with the heat. Usually it was possible only in cool climates, where the cells didn't rapidly decompose.

In moments he had reached the crumpled form. Stan's fall had been broken by a bush halfway up the cliff and so there was no blood, which was good. After finding no pulse he examined the body thoroughly, recalling all the knowledge at his command: multiple concussions, compound fractures, etc.

Then he lifted the body onto his back. (What a stench—these meat eaters, he thought, disgusting practice.) Quickly he scrambled up the face of the cliff to his cave and placed Stan on his own sitting place. He removed the jockey shorts and washed the entire body carefully, prepared a place opposite his and transferred the body to it face up. He then covered Stan's body and his own with ash.

Then he sat in front of the fire following the ancient practice until the energy flow inside him reached an effective level. He built up his fire and made offerings to it. Noting the angle of the sun, he

[287]

judged not more than one hour had passed. There was still time. Another hour and although he might still bring him back, the memory would be gone.

Taking up his small two-sided drum, Indra stripped naked and began moving around the body in the way he had been trained. After about ten minutes he jumped onto the body with both feet, pressing gently at first, and then letting himself go until he was dancing with full force on the limbs and torso. After a few minutes he could feel the breath coming back. Through his feet he could feel the slow rhythm as the body began to breathe again. Color was returning. Now was the crucial moment. The head was his biggest worry because there had been concussions.

He knelt beside the newly breathing body and grasping the head between his large hands, charged now with a superhuman energy, he pressed the skull lightly with his palms. After about an hour, the mouth began to twitch, working its way into a smile.

Then the eyes opened.

"Are you all right?" Indra said into the eyes that stared at him as if from another place.

"Ah, ah, I, I . . ." Stan's voice faltered. "I . . . Ah . . . Where am I?" A look of disbelief spread over his face. "I . . . you . . ."

"Yes, is it not as I said it would be?"

"But I'm here," Stan whispered. "Didn't I . . . I did jump, didn't I?"

"Get up," said Indra gruffly. "I want to see if my work is finished."

Stan got up at once but his legs crumpled. Indra caught him, held onto him. "Do you have much pain?" he asked.

Stan shook his head. "Only numbness and pins and needles in the arms and legs."

"Good," said Indra. He let Stan down gently and covered him with a blanket, then threw a cloth around himself. "Do not try to move just now. You must remain perfectly still here with me for thirty-six hours. Then you will be all right. You may have more aches and pains, we will see."

"Am I dead?" Stan whispered.

"In a manner of speaking," said Indra coolly, smiling at Stan's radiant face. "You were an extreme case. I had to use extreme measures. And . . ." He paused, looking at Stan. "There are certain conditions that are now imposed upon you."

Stan nodded.

"First of all, your cancer is gone. Your body is new again. Although you may be only dimly aware of it, you've been blown clean of all the old things, but . . ."

"But . . .?"

"You are wedded to me."

"Wedded?"

"Or welded," Indra said smiling. "Whatever you like. But you are in my power—totally. That is not a boast or a threat, it is simply a fact. It is what happens."

"It's the price I pay?"

"If that's the way you want to think of it." Indra sighed. "But you must understand, otherwise . . ."

"Otherwise?"

"I'll snuff you out."

Stan nodded. "And what are the other conditions?" he asked.

"Second, and just as important, you must never *never* reveal to anyone the details of what has happened here. This is not for the average person to know; if you reveal anything your cancer will return. I will now be able to teach you how to do what has been done through me.

"Third, you will return to your own country. You will dispose of your wealth anonymously in some trust arrangement to be used to better the lot of aged women—direct gifts."

"Like my mother you mean?"

"Correct."

"And then . . ."

"Aha, and then my friend you will change your name and get a job—male nurse, I think they call it—in the cancer ward of a big hospital. You will work as a male nurse for some time." He paused, tapping the fire with his chimtah. "These things you will do. I will be in touch with you later with further instructions. You are being led now toward liberation."

"And will I see you again?"

"Yes."

"Do you know when that will be?"

"Yes."

"Can you tell me?"

"When the time comes I will be in touch with you."

Stan was filled with awe, exhilarated by a clarity and happiness he had never known. Everything he looked at seemed to sparkle and shine.

"Why did you save me?" he asked. "Because Laura Weatherall asked you to?"

"We are given our directions in strange ways," Indra answered. "But I didn't save you. I'm only an agent. You are saved it is true, and more than you know. You became fearless, that is half of it. Perhaps you were saved so that there will be someone of your kind, some 'scientist,' who understands, who has crossed over and come back.

"There is another point I have forgotten." He looked at Stan. "Before, you had no feelings—not that you were neutral—you just had no feelings at all. You were outside of everything. Now, you have to go through your feelings to get across, to have them and go through them. And so I am requesting—in fact I insist—that you marry now and have children."

Stan gulped.

"Yes, yes, you must learn that attachment and go through it." Indra grinned. "Am I too hard on you?"

"Is that all?"

Indra looked thoughtful. "There is still time to save that animal, the one you caused to come here."

"Jeff?"

"Yes. It is my personal wish that you destroy the LSD you brought. It gives too much perception without preparation, too much empowerment without tapas. It will only harm. And if you intercept Jeff in time, you might be able to save him."

"You want him back here?"

"Yes. No. Yes, no. I am undecided. It is not clear to me at this point."

"One other question," Stan said. "Can I be killed now?"

"Just now it would be quite easy. In a few days, next to impossible—except, of course, by me." Indra smiled.

XIII

§

CARLOS WAS SURE they'd all gone crazy. He paced the house like a caged lion, trying to figure out where they could have stashed the acid. He hated them all—so much money and so stupid about it, especially Jeff with his superstar complex. He had no soul, was no good. And now Stan was going to die. Stupid. Always thinking he's doing so much, always busy with some project. Whew! Now the project was cancer. He, Carlos, would need money now. Here was the chance—all that acid in three suitcases. But where?

Then it dawned on him. "Ah, Carlos, you are being very stupid. Of course, it's at Grey's." He sat down on the porch and lighting a joint stared out at the sea. He remembered seeing the bags loaded. Then he didn't see them again. When they stopped at Grey's house, what had happened? Nothing. That meant Jeff had left them in the car until he could talk to Grey. But how to find them. Grey was a dealer, a smuggler; if he could get Wasu to Goa before they got back . . . He could tell Grey.

That afternoon he saw Grey on the beach.

"They weren't so crazy as to take that acid with them, were they?" he asked casually.

Grey was busy making out with a chick, flashing his rings in the sun. "Don't worry, it's safe at my place," he said over his shoulder.

His guess confirmed, Carlos went for a swim, ambled back naked to the house enjoying the looks he got, sat down at the phone and booked a call to Bombay. As he finished his shower the phone rang. He lit a cigarette and answered.

"Hello, Wasu," he said into the phone. "Carlos, yeah man."

"Yes, Carlos, yes, it is me."

"How are you? Yeah, I'm in Goa, yeah . . . I think I can sell you that stuff. Yes, you want to come? You were just getting ready to come? Coincidence, eh? Bringing who? A female friend, yes. O.K., tomorrow. Jeff? No, he isn't here. No. Gone south with Stan, but he's coming back. Yeah, O.K. See you soon."

Carlos hung up the phone. When he saw Wasu Grey would shit. He would have to give up the acid. Otherwise anything might happen to him—he was too vulnerable. Wasu could just take it and Grey would owe Stan a lot of bread. Carlos sat smoking, his hand still on the phone, weighing the possibilities of a showdown with Grey.

§

Two days later Wasu, Kamala, and Wasu's two bodyguards arrived by Mercedes-Benz. Kamala was feeling ragged. The drive from Bombay had been tiring. Though she knew him well, she had never thought she would find herself traveling with Wasu, a thoroughly disgusting person. Such noises he was always making, she thought, so much spitting and stopping to piss all the time drove her mad.

"Goa always depresses me," she said out loud. "All these pigs, everywhere you look, dirty pigs eating shit!"

Wasu was lying half-asleep. He grunted.

"Wasu, creep of creeps," she said under her breath. She had recently learned the word creep from Sundar and found the sound of it to her liking. It exactly fitted many of the men she had been forced to deal with in her life. This one was the worst. Creep of Creeps: it was a good title.

Wasu batted flies from his nose.

She was trying to assess her twin motives for making this horrible trip: the first to revenge herself on Jeff, the second to get some or all of Mr. Stanley's drug for the Baba. She must make them work together so that both ends were achieved. It was not her style to plan. She willed things and they happened. She thought of Jeff's body which still held a strong attraction for her. "But he is too filled with pride," she reflected. "No one will ever be able to harness that wild horse; something not nice is going to happen I think."

She had told Wasu that Ananda Baba attached great importance to her mission, trusting that he would get the point. The Baba was the only person in the world Wasu feared: when the Baba prayed for him things went well, if the Baba was displeased with him bad luck came. On this fear depended the negotiations she would have to make over Baba's share of the acid. She had been trained to act on the moment—then let the moments come! She hoped it wouldn't be a long stay.

The car stopped in front of the large pink villa. Wasu woke up, the two bodyguards got out and opened the doors. They were hoisting Wasu out of the low car just as Carlos came out on the front porch bare-chested and wearing a bright green lunghi.

"Hello Carlos," Wasu said, taking Carlos in his arms like a woman and hugging him. "This is Kamala," he added over his shoulder.

Carlos saw at once that Kamala was miffed at the casual introduction. He broke away from Wasu and bowed formally to her. "A great piece of ass," he thought. "Wasu has pretty good taste. It is a big house," he said to her warmly, "I have prepared a special room for you." He looked deep into Kamala's eyes before turning back to Wasu. "You'll be on this side of the house—there is a separate suite." He motioned the bodyguards ahead with Wasu's luggage. "You follow them—I'll just show Kamala to her room."

Kamala admired his lithe walk as he took her up the stairway of the central hall and along a corridor to an old-fashioned room with polished teakwood floors, campaign chests, and a brass four-poster bed with a canopy.

"I hope this will satisfy your needs," he said, smiling graciously at her. He strode into the bathroom. "You might like to freshen yourself after such a long trip—I will start the bath." He scanned her body. "Is there anything more I can do for you?"

"So you are Mr. Stanley's friend," Kamala said. "And how is Mr. Stanley?"

"Oh, he is not too good." Carlos tried to sound stupid. "He is very sick, you know."

"Yes, I know, I was with him at Ananda Baba's."

"I will see you later," he said, leaving the room hastily before she could ask him any more questions.

Wasu took a bath and sprawled out comfortably on a big bed. Both bodyguards had stripped down to lunghis and one was on massage duty, pressing the dark robust flesh of Wasu who grunted appreciatively, puffing a long Havana cigar.

Carlos came in and sat down. For a while Wasu was silent while he glanced through a newspaper. Mentally, Carlos compared himself with Wasu. "How could this stupid man have learned to read," he wondered, "while I, Carlos, have been unable!"

"So where's the stuff?" said Wasu all of a sudden, hoping to get the truth that way.

"I have it, don't worry." Carlos smiled blandly. He wanted to talk to Grey first. "But who is this Kamala?" he asked, to take Wasu's mind off the stash.

"She is a most high-class bitch," Wasu whispered. "Very, very expensive prostitute—famous all over Hindustan. She is devotee of Ananda Baba, I am also Ananda Baba devotee. He brings Wasu plenty good luck. I give him plenty money."

"But why she is coming?" Carlos asked.

"To see your Jeff—something she has against him," he said disinterestedly. "Also, the Baba he wished to possess some of this LSD. Your Mr. Stanley, he is giving to Baba. Baba has tried and he likes, he is sending this Kamala to me."

"She's a very beautiful chick."

"I don't like her," Wasu muttered. "She is too smart for a woman, she is like a witch. She treats Wasu not very good, like a dog." He paused, studying Carlos. "You like to make friendship with her, eh? Well you can try. She is too stuck-up, one very hard to get lady, very expensive. She might do with you for fun though, you do not know. Me, I won't pay her price. Anyhow, she don't want me—I'm too low-caste for her and too dark."

As soon as he could, Carlos left Wasu. He found Grey lounging on his front porch. "How ya doin' Carlos," he said as Carlos sat down.

"Not too well. It is so hot and now a friend has come with a woman and two servants and I will have to feed them. Do you know someone who can cook?"

"I saw the car," said Grey. "Who is this guy?"

"His name is Wasu, he is from Bombay."

Grey's face changed color.

"You know him?" asked Carlos.

"Yeah," said Grey, "if anyone can really know him. You mean *the* Wasu, big Bombay rackets?"

Carlos nodded. "He is very interested to buy the acid. I think you are keeping it for Mr. Stanley. If you will just give it to me then the deal will be finished and I won't have to feed them. He eats a lot. Did you say you knew a cook?"

Grey remembered Stan's warning about letting Carlos have the stash. He had to play for time.

"I'd like to see him," he said, getting up. "Come on, let's go see Wasu."

Carlos remained cool. "Sure," he replied.

Wasu was still reading the paper while one of the bodyguards prepared food for him on a small camp stove.

"You are cooking for yourself?" Carlos said as he and Grey came in.

[294]

"I am always cooking for myself. It is an old habit. You can't trust people's food, too many poisons. He has to eat everything he cooks in front of me, from my plate—Ha!" He smiled at Grey. "My friend Grey, how are you? Come and sit beside me." Grey sprawled over the edge of the bed. "I have not seen you for a year. Why you not see Wasu when in Bombay, eh?" He slapped Grey's leg. "How's the cocaine business?"

"Slow right now—end of the season," Grey answered, fishing in a pocket of his pants. "But I have something for you." He extended an ornate silver box toward Wasu. "Here."

Wasu took the box and opened it. It contained an ounce of pure cocaine.

"Tank you, tank you wary much," said Wasu, obviously impressed. "Carlos, see," he said rolling his eyes with pleasure, "tonight you bring me two, three, these hippy girls, see? Eh, Grey? You tell em big Bombay smuggler, big cock, with two big bodyguards, he got good cocaine, wants freakie time, give good money too."

Carlos was annoyed. He wanted to finish the deal quickly in case Stan returned earlier than expected. Wasu had agreed to a price forty percent above what Stan expected. It would not do for them to meet.

Grey looked pleased. "There are some far-out chicks here," he said. "I'll put out the word for them to see Carlos at my house. Then he can bring them over." His gamble had worked, he'd got another day. He'd have to hand the acid over if Wasu started demanding it. He knew it wasn't cool for him to go against Wasu, and he had to think of himself first. Anyhow, he was biding time.

§

Of the six girls who showed up at Grey's Carlos picked three, dropped some acid on them and took them over to Wasu. All night long grunts and groans, curses and sighs floated through the gardens of hibiscus and jasmine around the house.

The next day Wasu was completely knocked out and Grey, who had expected some sort of showdown with Carlos, was relieved when night fell and no word had come from the house next door.

The following morning one of Wasu's bodyguards arrived with the message that Wasu was waiting for him.

"Very good coke," said Wasu with a wink, extending the empty silver box to Grey. "You got more?"

"Sure. Guess you had a good time, eh?"

[295]

Wasu didn't answer. He leveled his eyes at Grey. "I had deal with Mr. Stanley for some of the drug he is distributing. Now Mr. Stanley is away and Carlos says you are keeping it for him?"

"Me?" Grey said. "No, I don't have it. Carlos, what gave you the idea I have it? It must be in this house."

"I have searched the house," Carlos said menacingly.

"I thought Stan was here for some cure. I don't really know him—Jeff is my friend. You say you had a deal with Stan?"

"He's lying!" snarled Carlos.

"Now, come on Carlos, do me a favor and drop dead, eh?" Grey got up. "I got enough hassles without you laying trips on me. I don't keep track of other people's luggage. You're sure they didn't leave it in Panjim?"

"I saw the luggage come here," Carlos said emphatically. "It is a big house and I have searched, nothing is locked up, the bags are not here. You even told me they were with you."

"I did?" Grey said blankly.

"Yes."

"I must have been stoned."

"Don't fight," grunted Wasu. "It's too hot. Grey?"

"Yes?"

"Get more coke, eh? I have so many friends here. My friend Gonzales, Chief of Police—you know him?"

"Yeah," said Grey, "he comes around the house sometimes."

"I have called him," Wasu went on. "He is coming tonight with two of his men. I need more coke and six girls—you can do?"

"O.K." Grey nodded. "How about some nice French ones?"

"Anything you say." Wasu leered. "I like anything!"

When he left Grey felt nervous. Wasu could blow the whole scene if he didn't get what he wanted. He had to get the bags out of his house. But it wouldn't be that easy. He was sure the house was being watched.

Carlos caught up with him outside. He had decided to share his profit with Grey. "Listen man, Mr. Stanley is going to die," he whispered confidentially, "he's going to die for sure. He may never come back from this trip—spitting and coughing so much blood when he left! Wasu has too much cash—dollars. He can't get it out of the country now, this way he can turn it into rupees. Our part would be twenty percent. It is something to think about, no?" He grabbed Grey's arm. "If Wasu gets mad he will juss come to your house and take it. Then nobody wins, eh? He is very strong with police here, good friends. They are always the biggest crooks, right? We should look out for ourselves."

[296]

Jeff hurried over the mountain path. Despite his agility he hadn't gone barefoot in years. The stones cut at his feet and the bandsaw fronds of the cane plants ripped at his shirt. A warm mist rose from the steaming jungle and the gnarled trunks and limbs of the stunted oaks, green with moss and vines, seemed frozen in some crazy dance meant to scare him away.

"So you have been out to see the Tapas Rishi, so early in the morning is it?" shouted Prakash, sighting him from a pool near one of the temples, where he had been saying his morning prayers. "That is good, very good to see the guru first thing in the morning. Very good. And in the barefeet too, very good. That way you get the shakti," he added, rolling his eyes.

"My boots went over the cliff," Jeff said.

"Oh ho," smiled Prakash, "that is the shakti also. She took them away from you. What a pity. I noticed them, they were very expensive I think. But of course leather is not worn here on the mountaintop as it is holy ground."

"Ho hum," muttered Jeff under his breath, not interested in Prakash's preaching. He turned, headed for the room he had been given in an old stable.

"And where are you going now?" said Prakash. "Come, they are going to serve breakfast. It is time to eat."

"I'm leaving, I'm going," Jeff said over his shoulder.

"So soon?" Prakash's eyebrows shot up.

"It's important I go back to Goa—I have some business there to take care of."

Prakash's face took on a conspiratorial look. "Oho, gentleman," he whispered, "I think you must be a big smuggler then. I like the smugglers—they give the large donation for the temple. Then the goddess She gives plenty good luck. They bring good foreign wash-and-wear cloth for the first-class pant. I wear the pant when I go to visit my cousins in Bombay," he said proudly.

"My business is real estate," said Jeff coolly, not wanting to get involved in Prakash's inner movie production.

"Oh, what a pity," Prakash said sadly. "But you must not go now. First eat. You can't go without eating. I will go also after taking the meal."

Jeff wasn't exactly hungry. He was running, he had to keep going.

"I'd like to start before it gets too hot," he said. "I'm planning to leave immediately." He went to his room and gathered his things together as Prakash watched from the doorway.

"You must give these people a few rupees each," he said, realizing Jeff wouldn't understand that he, Prakash, was also supposed to receive a good sum for his services. He would collect double from the red-haired woman then, he thought. "So, my friend, have a good walk down, perhaps I'll see you at the bottom." He waved cheerfully and disappeared.

On the path Jeff soon realized that it was harder getting down than going up. The coolie he had hired to carry his bag bounced ahead from rock to rock while he stumbled along behind, tired even before he began. To make matters worse leeches, dormant in the dry season, had been awakened by a recent shower. Hungry for blood, they attached themselves in numbers to his legs and feet. As he descended the heat increased. He began to sweat and had to fend off huge tropical hornets and ticks that dropped from the trees and burrowed into his skin. After about four hours he reached a red dirt path where the coolie, having arrived much earlier, lay asleep in the shade of a giant fern.

By the time they arrived in Kalpura the evening had come on even hotter and more breathless than the day. Jeff asked about onward transportation and learned that there were no more buses until morning. A taxi, however, had brought some pilgrims in from the coast. They would be leaving after the evening puja, which was in progress. The driver asked him what his destination was.

"Goa," Jeff said. The driver rolled his eyes as if Goa were the moon, but after Jeff reached into his pocket and extracted a ten-rupee note, the driver decided to take him.

"But it will be past ten when we reach the coast," he warned. "No cars will be traveling north from there—too many bandits these days." He hoisted Jeff's bag onto the luggage carrier and when the others arrived wedged him into the front seat beside two men. No one spoke to him.

When they reached the coastal town the taxis had stopped running: all the drivers were asleep in their back seats. He would have to go to a hotel, the driver said, and took him to a dirty Victorian affair overlooking the sea, a relic of a bygone era when people with money had once traveled in India. Now it was a brothel of sorts for local politicians, Army and police officers, and various traveling businessmen. They sat stolidly drinking whiskey under bare bulbs, in a green dining room with peeling paint. Simple-minded fat girls, trying to act fancy, waited to be taken into the rooms.

[298]

A waiter in a soiled white uniform brought some fried fish and rice covered with hot curry sauce the color and consistency of vomit. Jeff went to his room without eating. The cement walls smelled dank and there were cigarette burns and water marks on the furniture. The wooden doors separating the rooms had peep holes that had been filled up and painted over. The bed was a slab of wood with a soiled foam rubber mattress. He took a bath from a bucket, spread a lunghi over the mattress, and lay down under a creaking ceiling fan. Through the thin walls he could hear the slaps and squeals of the girls and their men. Like so many pigs, he thought.

Here in the south the woman was the aggressor and was supposed to jump around on top of the man to excite him until he humped her like a sow as quickly as possible. Immediately afterwards they got dressed and he treated her to a big dinner, which was half the reason she had come.

After a while Jeff fell asleep, only to be awakened from a dream by a horde of bedbugs. After throwing the mattress onto the floor he lay down on the board and drifted back into his dream. He was riding somewhere on an elephant. The elephant was going at breakneck speed and he, Laura, and Carlos seemed to be tied onto the animal. Like pieces of baggage they were wrapped up in sheets and blankets and tied so they couldn't move. He remembered thinking later how odd it was that Carlos was along—Carlos whom he so disliked, a fellow passenger on the great lumbering beast careening across India.

At cockcrow he woke up, his muscles aching. Washing again, he examined his various bites and cuts, hating the fact that his body had been attacked. Then he dressed, paid his bill to a sleepy boy at the counter, and carried his bag a few blocks to the center of town. The taxi drivers, just getting up, rolled out of their cabs to piss in the stinking open sewers and then stumbled into the tea shops scratching their heads. Jeff had some tea and then sat in an old taxi while the driver waited for more passengers. After nine more people were stuffed in, they started. The sun beat down mercilessly. As he stared out over the sea, Jeff made his plan: he would pick up his luggage and the acid at Goa, throw some of it into the sea, and get on a plane for Dubai. If there was enough bread in it and if Hadji wasn't too crazy, he might even get married there—who could tell?

When he arrived late the next morning he wasn't surprised to see Kamala having drinks with Wasu and Carlos on the porch of the pink villa. Though Jeff had disliked Indra, he hadn't been so stupid as to be blind to the man's power. He remembered the warning and was prepared for—whatever. When Carlos saw Jeff, he realized with resentment that his plan would have to be changed.

"Ah," said Wasu, "the Big Man has arrived." He stood up as Jeff entered, extending his beefy hand.

"I'm bushed, long trip," Jeff said with a faint smile and a glance at Kamala. "Let me just clean up a bit, I'll be right down."

"He doesn't want to talk," grunted Wasu after Jeff had gone into the house.

"Leave him to me," put in Kamala wisely, "there is something between us. Have no fear, Wasu, I will see that we get what we have come for."

Wasu rolled his eyes and smiled broadly. "I see. That is good. You make him understand, eh? You tell him Wasu's offer is benefit to everyone, is fair offer. That he should agree. Otherwise . . ." He spat noisily into the sand.

"We will see," answered Kamala vaguely.

Carlos could see that Kamala was going to cut him out. She would do business directly through Jeff. He had to go to her side so she would give him something when she was finished. And after all, Wasu was his friend.

Jeff showered and smoked a joint in his room. When he returned he wore only a cotton lunghi and looked cool and relaxed.

"Have a cold drink before lunch," Wasu invited. "Your friend Grey, he is asking us to lunch at his house."

"How's Stan?" Carlos asked.

"He's there with Laura, sitting on top of a mountain. I think the yogi might cure him—he's seeing him now. We'll know any day. Laura said she'd phone."

Carlos could tell Jeff was lying. He was sure something else had happened. "How come you didn't stay?"

"Not my scene," replied Jeff. "I didn't get along with the guru, it was just a waste of time there for me." He gestured at the glittering sea. "Much better to sit here. . . . nice beach, good company . . ."

"Too many pigs," muttered Kamala.

Wasu stretched his big body and got up grunting. "Then we go to lunch—you will come?" He poked Jeff.

"Think I'll go up and rest, I'm beat," Jeff yawned. "I'll see you later in the afternoon, O.K.?" He looked directly at Kamala.

A pang of jealousy struck Carlos. Why did Jeff always get all the women? When he thought about this it put him in a black rage.

§

In the quiet of the afternoon Kamala slipped into Jeff's room. She found him awake, lying in bed.

"So you've come at last to get me," he whispered, taking her hand. "You look more beautiful than ever, if that's possible."

She sat on the edge of the bed and gazed at him. "I could have you killed for what you did," she said after a while. "I still have the marks."

"I know," he said. He was excited by her anger. No woman had ever been able to stay angry with him for long. He played gently with her sari until her breasts were exposed.

"You still have the feeling for Kamala, yes?" she said, letting herself relax against his body. He took her hand and guided it onto his erection, then drew her up to him, stroking her soft skin.

"Why were you so bad to me? It was not nice of you. See, there is still a scar," she murmured, displaying her voluptuous buttocks. He let his hand go across it, turning her slightly so the tip of his penis rubbed against her.

"You are too big for me," she said, holding him back. "You will hurt me again when you get excited."

"Suck it then," he said softly.

"Don't be crazy," she retorted, staring at him. "How could I get it in my mouth? If only I had some of that, what you call it—that acid, it relaxes me."

"You've taken acid?" Jeff was curious.

"It is a long story." She smiled. "Don't you have some? The Baba, he would like to have a large amount of it."

So she was after it too—whew! Jeff thought. He didn't want to talk business now. "Stan stashed it somewhere after we got here," he sighed. "I think Carlos knows where it is."

"Carlos has told us you know where it is," she said, fingering his nipples.

"Carlos is lying," Jeff said, pulling her close to him.

Kamala straightened up. "I must go, it is time for my nap."

He caught her by the waist, thrust his hand between her thighs.

"No, no," she said, getting up and pulling her sari about her.

[301]

"Do not try to force me—if you get rough with me again you'll regret it."

She stood by the bed, looking down at him. "I find you so sexy, it's too bad you are so stubborn. Perhaps you can refresh your memory about where Mr. Stanley put the drug. This Wasu is a terrible man and he's getting impatient."

Later Jeff slipped quietly out of the house and went to Grey's. He found him alone in the kitchen feeding vegetables into a juicer.

"Looks like they're after it," said Grey, handing him a glass of juice. "Can't you get it out, or can't you let Carlos sell it to Wasu?"

"And never see any of the bread ourselves?" Jeff planned to appeal to Grey's greed and not to reveal that he intended to throw most of the acid into the Arabian Sea. "They're watching me like hawks," he added, "but the first chance I have, I'll get rid of it."

"They're watching this place too," Grey said, frowning. "Wasu could have me searched at any time. He's tied into the police. All he has to do is give the word. If they find it here, there's a big hassle, then I get kicked out of Goa and the cops give Wasu the acid for less than Carlos would charge him. I think you should make a deal with Carlos."

"You don't know Carlos, he's a shit," Jeff said darkly. "Don't worry, I'll have it out soon."

"But how?"

"It's full moon isn't it, or almost?"

"Day after tomorrow."

"Don't you usually give a party?"

"Yes."

"Then have a big party. Invite all the cops, Wasu, Kamala, Carlos. Get everybody stoned, have lots of girls. Put the Chief of Police and Wasu in a room with five or six girls, plenty of booze and coke, and douse the whole place with acid." He paused, then continued thoughtfully. "There'll be so much coming and going, cars driving in and out that no one will notice me leave. But someone must watch Kamala. That sound O.K.?"

Grey nodded. "It should work."

§

Sounds of amplifiers being tested at Grey's house floated through the palms on the sultry late afternoon breeze.

Jeff could hear the twanging in his shuttered room where he lay in bed going over his plan. He had packed his bags and Grey had given him the key to the closet in the servants' quarters where the

[302]

acid was hidden. It was time for him to go down the beach and engage one of the drivers that hung out at the bar there. The man had to be reliable and fast. He stretched, thinking about Kamala who hadn't spoken to him in two days although he had seen her twice. He thought of Indra's warning and fingered the butt of the pistol the yogi had given him. She might have plans for him, he didn't trust her. But he had his own plans, and if he let himself worry he would lose out, he knew it. The party would be a cinch. He could drop the bags out the low window of the servants' quarters and walk a short distance to the service yard. There, all sorts of crazy people would be coming and going. He'd hardly be noticed, especially if the driver parked his car with the trunk toward the house. He would have to find one that spoke good English.

The surf pounded on the far off reefs as the full moon rose over the palms. The air was heavy and still, sweet with the odor of jasmine and incense. The smooth sounds belting out of the big amplifiers carried far down the beach, calling all who could hear to come and boogie at Grey's, where the amenities of a brothel had been coupled with the perverse delights of a madhouse.

Grey stood in what he called the study: restored Spanish Victorian with a heavy dose of Tibetan thrown in. There were furs on black tile floors and expensive tankas on the walls. In one corner a massive Chinese screen enclosed a bar.

He was hoping Jeff would get the stash out of the house before Wasu blew the whole scene with a search. For himself, he had hidden his coke supply in an Ajax can in the refrigerator. That was what he cared about: it was pure crystal and worth a fortune. His whole lifestyle depended on that coke. But his scene was cool: himself, his friend Mike, and six girls. The cops would be cooled out on acid and chicks. Three of the girls were delegated to watch Kamala and three to watch the refrigerator.

People were coming now, wandering across the courtyard to the study. He saw Wasu followed by Kamala, sparkling with rubies and looking very grand among the strung-out hippy girls in their made-up outfits. Wasu's two bodyguards brought up the rear, eyeing the chicks hungrily. With them came the local Chief of Police, Gonzales, in a tight leather jacket, shades, and high leather boots. He dug the Western chicks Grey always had for him. He liked zooming off with them on his bike, taking them to out of the way places he knew where he could struggle with them in the warm sand.

The girls Grey had ordered for Wasu and Gonzales were arriving too.

"Hey Gonzales," roared Wasu jovially, "how you are liking these Western smugglers, eh?" He slapped Grey on the back. "I think I come here, live near Grey. He got good women."

Grey produced a silver box filled with coke and gave Wasu a straw.

"I don't take through the nose, I rub into the gums," Wasu said, taking a liberal pinch with his big fingers. "It works better on the gums—don't destroy the smelling."

Grey turned to offer Kamala some but she waved him away smiling. She was admiring him; he was the first Western man that puzzled her. She had never seen a Western man with painted nails. Yet if he wasn't a hedjara, what was he?

"Can I give you some punch," he said politely.

"Water," Kamala replied, "I can get it." She was certain that something was going to happen tonight. Instinct told her she might have to think fast and she had been well trained to take only water on such occasions. She saw Gonzales take a healthy snort of coke but noticed that Wasu's bodyguards didn't.

As soon as Grey was out of earshot, she spoke to Wasu quickly in Hindi. "Have your bodyguards leave one by one—stand at opposite corners of the house so that each can see two sides. Do not let them be seen, have them hide in the bushes. If anyone asks, say you have sent them home, that you see there is no need for them here. Do you understand my meaning?" Wasu nodded slightly. "Tell them to apprehend anyone attempting to leave with luggage."

After a while, Wasu called the two young men one at a time, instructing them as Kamala had ordered. The guards disappeared casually.

"Now we will see what happens," she murmured.

Jeff walked into the room wearing white flannels and a cream colored silk kurta. He knelt beside Kamala. "Thanks for a wonderful night last night," he whispered.

She frowned.

"In my dreams you came to me. We made love all night long."

She looked into his eyes wondering about him: so beautiful—so devilish! "And such stupid pride," she thought. "I could give him everything if he would let me."

"Why do you not return with me to Ananada Baba's," she asked suddenly. "He would like you. I cannot remain here much longer. We could slip away together, you and I."

He smiled at her.

"You are in danger here," she continued. "That Carlos and Wasu—they want what you've got. If they do not get it, something not nice might happen." She looked around the crowded room. "You are all foreigners for them, sitting ducks as you say." She gazed at him seriously. "With me you will be safe. What do you say?"

Jeff looked at her searchingly. It was a proposition he hadn't expected. Indra had warned him. Was she warning him too?

"I can't stay in India," he said with a shrug. "It's not my cup of tea."

"You are leaving soon then?" she asked.

"As soon as Stan gets back," he lied. "Shouldn't be much longer."

"I see," said Kamala, sensing the lie. "He will never listen to anyone or surrender to anyone," she thought. "How sad, how troublesome—what a pity!"

The evening wore on: Wasu and Gonzales got high and went off into a bedroom with some girls. The electric strings whooped and twanged, whipping the dancers into a frenzy of self-expression. Carlos came in and sat near Kamala. Jeff could see that he was high on coke and thought it was a good time to leave. He began talking to one of Grey's girls and after a while asked her to dance, smiling and nodding at Kamala as he left the room.

As soon as they were out of sight, the girl split to the dance floor. Jeff made his way unseen to the servants' quarters at the opposite end of the house, where he unlocked the closet and removed the bags of acid. He looked cautiously out the window he had opened earlier. It was quiet. About fifty feet away he could see the car he had engaged. He let the bags drop into the shadows, then climbed out the window and jumped to the ground. He picked up two of the bags and had started for the car when a sharp blow landed on his neck. He felt his legs buckle under him.

§

Carlos sat staring at Kamala. He wanted her, couldn't she see that?

"Where has Wasu gone?" he asked.

"Off in some room, I think," she said coolly.

"You are going to sit here all night?"

"You think I should go out and boogie?" she said, making the word sound ridiculous.

"You come—I show you," said Carlos. "Is not hard." He wanted to move with her, feel her big tits and her belly rubbing against him.

[305]

One of the bodyguards came into the room. "We have him," he said quietly to Kamala in Hindi.

"And the bags?" Kamala yawned.

"Yes."

"Lock them in the trunk of Wasu's car."

"What do we do with the fellow? He is unconscious now but he's got a gun."

"Drag him to the other house. Strip him and leave the clothes there. Then throw him in the ocean. If he wakes up and gives trouble, shoot him," she said coldly. "Then return the gun to my room and wait for me there."

The bodyguard nodded and left.

Kamala sighed and turned to Carlos. "That Wasu is becoming so difficult, now he wants *me* to come to him! I will not. He wants more cocaine. Ugh." She gazed at him listlessly.

"You want to boogie?" he asked eagerly.

"No, no, you go boogie," she answered disdainfully and yawned again. "I may go back to the house shortly, I am feeling rather tired, the heat you know."

Grey had come back to the study with two local police officers, big tough Goan boys. He was introducing them to his girls, the ones who had been watching Kamala. He'd just been to the servants' quarters, and was relieved to find the stash was gone. He offered some cocaine around to everyone. When he came to Kamala she held up her hand.

"No thanks," she sighed lazily, "I think I will go to sleep now. The sea air, you know—it makes me too sleepy."

Grey's eyes traveled her body. She caught the look. "I see you are a very interesting man, Mr. Grey," she said, smiling seductively as she got up. "I would like to see you again sometime. Perhaps you should come see me. I am at Ananda Baba's ashram these days."

Carlos got up too and stood beside her. "Do sit down, Carlos," she said. "Enjoy yourself. I am quite able to get to the house myself. It is a short walk. Good night, Mr. Grey, it was a fine party. We will meet again, I think."

Grey nodded, watching her disappear across the courtyard in the moonlight. Carlos was pissed. He wanted her. "Everybody is having her, why not me?" he thought. He ambled outside where he boogied himself across the dance floor and disappeared under the palms. He wanted one more try at Kamala, one more; if that failed he'd see what Wasu was up to. He was high and felt like fucking. The night was bright. As he neared the house he saw something that caused him to jump into the shadows.

Wasu's two bodyguards were hustling Jeff's naked body off the porch. Carlos stood staring, unable to believe his eyes. Almost automatically he began to follow them, darting from shadow to shadow the way he had learned as a child in the slums of Bogotá. They crouched on the path to the beach like animals, trying not to be seen. He followed them to where the trees ended and watched while they pulled Jeff's body toward the glittering blue-white light of the sea. It was like an apparition. Suddenly, Jeff was up and struggling. Carlos heard a shot and saw Jeff fall. Forgetting himself, he ran forward onto the beach. The guards saw him and ran away, dragging Jeff's body along the beach. Carlos ran after them. Another shot rang out. The guards stopped. Carlos stopped too, staring, his mouth wide open. Jeff's body lay limp on the sand. Why had he let himself be sucked into this scene? "What the fuck am I doing here?" he thought. He didn't want it. He wanted Kamala, not this.

The two bodyguards started back toward him. Had they recognized him? To run would be suicide. He waited. "So you have got rid of that swine, yes?" he grinned, trying to fool them, afraid for his life now as they closed in on either side of him.

§

It was days since she'd had a really good meal. "I've got indigestion," she thought, listening to the sounds inside herself as she walked beside the sea. "But nowadays, my only real pleasure is in eating. My desire is for food. I want food." She thought about all the milk her children drank, the ugly things, sucking her dry.

She'd heard that sometimes pigs eat their young by mistake. "Ha!" she thought, "it is probably no mistake." This had been her first litter. She hadn't known what she was getting into, she wanted to experience giving birth and didn't count on what came after. "If I have any more of them I might eat them by mistake, this baby business is terrible, always squealing and biting my tits."

Her social activities had been confined to the evening hours. Late at night after the little ones were asleep she would manage to escape. Then she would walk up the beach to enjoy the evening air and try to catch the tiny stalk-eyed phosphorescent crabs that darted in and out of holes at the edge of the sea. She was heading now toward the far end where the wild boars lived in the low deserted dunes. She wanted to get fucked roughly by the wild ones there in the moonlight. "So what if I have babies," she thought, "I'll eat them! There are too many pigs now anyway and not enough food for us."

[307]

She passed the rows of houses and shacks where the hippies lived. A few were still up, dancing. She paused, listening to the music with one of her large hairy ears cocked forward.

At the deserted end of the beach she was surprised to see three men, two in suits and one wearing a lunghi. They were walking quickly. "They must be running away from something," she snorted instinctively after they passed her. "Maybe they've left something worth eating." She hurried further up the beach, following their scent, and came upon another human. He was lying on the beach moaning. The sand was all kicked up. She sniffed him, grunting with nervousness. She knew that he was bleeding because she could smell it. Her stomach jumped when she realized the human was watching her. His body trembling and his face covered with sweat, he tried to get away from her by rolling onto his side. She could see blood streaming from his back and felt sorry for him. But what could she do, she was only a pig. Sooner or later every creature goes dead. She'd seen many die, especially fish; they flopped around in the sand until finally they got very stiff with their eyes staring straight out at you. She had seen these humans kill pigs too, like herself, and she knew that someday she might be killed by them. She saw shit coming out of him and nuzzled between his legs for it. He kicked at her groaning but the smell so intoxicated her that she nuzzled him again. Just as she was nipping at him with her tiny sharp front teeth she heard loud grunts and the sound of hooves and then two of the wild ones arrived. They remembered her and knew she had come back for more but pushed her aside and grunting savagely, sniffed at the dying man. Then the biggest one lowered his head, caught the man with his tusks, and tossed him several yards away.

"My body, my body," she heard the man scream in a language she didn't know. "My body, get out . . . fuckin' pigs!"

She waddled to where the screaming man now lay crumpled making gurgling noises. The wild ones were sniffing at her vagina, trying to lick it. Before she could stop him, one had mounted her and jammed his thing in all the way. She lifted her head snorting at him. She wanted to lick up some of the blood that was coming out of the man's back. Watching her across the man's body was the leader of the wild ones, the biggest in the herd. She stared into his dark brown eyes as he watched her getting fucked. Then he nuzzled his snout into the body and turning it onto its back, rooted between the legs and bit off the man's thing.

She was surprised when she saw him gulp it down. He must be really hungry she thought, eating something still alive, especially a man.

[308]

The man screamed, reached up and hit the wild one behind the ear with his fist. Blood was spouting from the place between his legs where his thing had been. The smell excited her. She dipped down, licking at him furtively. She had never before tasted hot blood but it was delicious. The one who had been on her got off and came around to see what she was up to, sniffing greedily at the blood. She snorted angrily and gave him a good nip on the snout. After all, there might not be enough.

Suddenly the human, who had been lying as if dead, opened his large green eyes wide, managed to stand up, and staggered away from her.

"Hadji! Hadji! Hadji!" she heard him scream as he reeled toward the sea, blood shooting out from between his legs. "Hadji! Hadji! Mama! Mama!" he yelled as his body sank and then, caught by the surf was sucked under and swept into the phosphorescent tide.

They ran to the edge of the water, watching for it hungrily. After some time a big wave came and washed the man back up again. His eyes were wide open now. He had the staring look of a dog she ate once after a car had hit it.

The wild ones ripped at the stomach with their snouts and gulped down large pieces of the warm flesh. They let her eat as much as she wanted. It was better than anything she had ever tasted. After they had finished she went with them behind the dunes where she let them all fuck her one by one while the others watched, licking their lips and gnawing on the bones that were left.

§

When they got down the beach, Carlos started casually in the direction of Grey's house and safety.

"No, no," one guard said, pushing him, "we go to other house."

"Wasu this way, Wasu at Grey's house," protested Carlos gesturing.

"No, no," they said in unison, "we go to other house—not Wasu."

He felt a gun in his ribs and obeyed. They reached the house and marched him into Kamala's bedroom, the room he had prepared so carefully for her. Kamala was lying on her bed in a sheer nightgown. "Tell these two goons to lay off," he said angrily, shaking the two men aside.

"He saw us killing the other one," they said in Hindi. "What to do?"

"Strangle him and throw him into the sea," Kamala answered. "Leave the room. Stand outside the door. When you hear me groaning you must come in and do it."

Carlos watched as they left the room, wondering what had been said. "Anyhow, it's good they have got that Jeff out of the way," he said. "Is no good man. Did you find the stuff on him?"

Kamala smiled, not answering. "How unfortunate for you to have seen all this," she murmured, gazing at him through half-closed eyes. "Come here, you must be so tired."

Carlos slumped on the bed, feeling more stoned than ever. He could see her big breasts, her creamy body beneath the chiffon nightgown. She pulled him to her with one hand, lifted her gown, and let him go down between her legs. She watched as he felt blindly for her breasts, masturbating himself with his free hand while he buried his head in her. She opened her legs wide and holding his head down, groaned. One of the guards darted silently through the door, grinning and flexing his big bare hands.

She gave a sigh, and nodded. The guard leaped on Carlos, grabbed him by the neck and threw him onto the floor. Then he sat on him, squeezing his neck and beating his head on the floor until the body went limp.

"Now you'll have to get rid of this one," she said. "There is no time to lose. Do you think you can get him down to the sea without being seen?"

"There are many people wandering around," one guard said.

"It's pretty risky," said the other doubtfully.

"Well, you'll have to risk it. One of you walk out and check to see the coast is clear. The other carry the body out quickly.

"After that," she said, smiling provocatively, "you may come back here."

They picked up the lifeless body and left. "What a lot of trouble tonight," Kamala thought. "Always so much trouble with these no-good Western people! Why don't they stay in their own countries?" She went to the window and watched the guards disappear beyond the trees. A few minutes later she saw them hurrying up the path and soon they presented themselves nervously outside her door.

"You can take showers if you like," she said pointing to the bathroom. "You must feel hot and dirty."

After they had bathed they came out in towels carrying their clothes. "We will go down to Wasu's room, we have fresh clothes there," they explained.

"Come here," she said to one of them. The guard stepped forward one pace. "Don't be afraid, I won't bite you. Come here!

Sit down beside me." She let the other one stand. They were young Marathi wrestlers she guessed, and eager to please. She had to get them in her power to keep them quiet. It was something she was good at.

She ran her hand over the heavy shoulders of the young man beside her, then grasping his hair pulled his face gently to her breasts while she motioned the other to come to her, and slid her hand under his towel to stroke his stiff penis. Then she groaned dramatically and lay back, closing her eyes. She let them take turns fucking her until they both came.

Afterwards they got up smiling and took another shower. "Now," she said sternly, "one of you get Wasu. The other pack the car. We are leaving tonight." They made for the door. "And if you remain faithful to me, there will be other times." Kamala let her languid eyes follow them out of the room.

She got up, dressed, and packed rapidly. Soon she heard Wasu bellowing as he came from Grey's house. One of the guards appeared. "He is here," he said. "Went to his room."

"Take my bag then," she said. "I will go down and talk with him. We must hurry."

"Wasu, are you ready? We're leaving," she said entering his room. She could see he was very high.

"Leave now?" he said, slumping into a chair. "What has happened?"

"I have the bags of LSD," she said. "They are locked in the trunk of your car. While you were having those girls, I was doing your work." She looked at him disdainfully. "Now get your things together and get in the car."

She stood on the porch in the dark. The moon had set and the first pale light of dawn shone in the east. Over at Grey's everything seemed quiet.

Wasu came out of the house, yelling impatiently at his bodyguards.

"Shhh," Kamala hissed. "Not so much noise, we must leave quietly!"

The guards opened the trunk of the car to put in the luggage.

Kamala motioned to Wasu. "See, here they are." She unzipped one bag and Wasu peered for a moment at the bottles of small yellow pills before she closed the suitcase and signaled the guards to shut the trunk.

"So, we have it," said Wasu, grinning slyly.

"No help from you."

"How did you get it?"

"They caught Jeff throwing the bags out a window. He had a

[311]

gun. I had them take him up the beach and shoot him. Also your friend Carlos happened to see all this. Now they are both in the sea."

"Who has the gun now?" snapped Wasu.

"I do."

"But only Wasu will be suspected of murder when the bodies are discovered," he said, coming sharply awake and squinting at her.

"They will not be discovered," she said smiling. "This is Goa. If the tide does not take them out where the sharks are, then those bloody pigs will finish them off—they eat anything. Grey will think they have gone with us. And if by chance some trace of them is found, who will identify it? Don't be silly. After all, the Chief of Police is your friend."

Wasu looked relieved. He slumped in his seat as one of the guards backed the car slowly out of the drive. "Now where are we going?" he asked. "I must have breakfast."

"You will drive me to His Holiness," she said, folding her slender hands and looking out the window.

"But that is two days' drive!" Wasu exclaimed.

Kamala's eyes blazed. "Is he not *your* guru?" she said angrily. "And you did nothing! If I left things in *your* hands we would still be there. The least you can do is drive me to the Baba's—after all, I have done this thing for him only."

§

Santa Cruz airport in Bombay was a mob scene. Several planes had been grounded and nervous passengers overflowed the waiting room. Stan sat with his briefcase on his lap. He had just called Sundaram in Delhi. There was no word of Jeff or Carlos.

After three days on the mountain with Indra, he had seen Laura briefly. She knew immediately that something had happened but as he was sworn to secrecy there was little to talk about. She told him Jeff had left before she could talk with him and that she was worried about him.

"I'm going to Goa immediately," said Stan. "Indra says he is in danger."

"I know," Laura said, "he told me that too. Then what will you do?"

"Destroy the LSD, leave India, give my fortune to charity, and disappear into an anonymous life." He smiled. "Funny, no?"

Laura smiled back. "You're lucky, the price is cheap."

[312]

Stan eyed her. "It wasn't all that easy."

She nodded. "So I may never see you again?"

"That's quite possible," he replied.

"Please try to send Jeff back," she said. "He might be difficult but Indra could handle him I'm sure."

Stan nodded. "I'll do my best."

He arrived in Goa to find the pink villa locked and apparently deserted. He went over to Grey's. The place was a mess and at noon no one was up except the servants. Grey had had a party—but where were Carlos and Jeff?

Not wanting to disturb anyone Stan walked down to the beach. The sea sparkled, the water was clear and cool. Hot from the long journey, he swam far out and cooled off, floating in the waves. Then, letting himself be pulled in, he rode the surf onto the beach. As he got out of the water he noticed something sparkling and picked it up.

It was Jeff's gold snake ring with the large emerald. "How lucky," Stan thought. "He'll be very pleased to learn that I've found it." He dressed and went back to Grey's.

Grey was in his modern kitchen. "Well! Did you just get here?" he said sleepily. "We had a full moon party last night—it lasted late. Too bad you missed it."

"My taxi had two breakdowns coming from the ferry," Stan said. "Otherwise I would've arrived yesterday afternoon. Where are Jeff and Carlos? The house is locked."

Grey was surprised. "So they all left?"

"Who?"

"Wasu," Grey explained. "He came here with a woman called Kamala—you know her, I think? Wasu was going to have this house searched but Jeff got the stuff out and disappeared. I'm afraid I gave him the key. Then I don't know what happened. You say the house is locked?"

"Yes."

"And there's no car?"

"No."

"Then Carlos must have taken off after Jeff with Wasu and Kamala."

He was too late then. He watched Grey making his breakfast, and knew he felt nervous about having given Jeff the key. A profound wave of boredom swept over Stan. He was out of it now. He had jumped out of it once and for all up there on the mountain. Grey's scene, all the scenes, all the actions of his own life, seemed remote and silly.

[313]

The feeling of unreality persisted and grew stronger. The world about him seemed mechanical, dead. He was able to look at people and know what they would do next and to his astonishment, if he looked long enough, he could know their past as well. At first he was disgusted and frightened by what he saw but after a few days the disgust turned to sympathy. He found himself wanting to help people if he saw they were about to lose something or to speak out to them when he saw through the mirror of their lives. But Indra had warned him about do-gooding. He was to keep to himself, not go out of his way to take action. If someone came to him, however, he could help.

At the Bombay airport his Paris flight was announced and there was a great crush at the check-in counter. An Englishwoman with two children was just in front of him, accompanied by an American with a withered hand, dressed in the Indian fashion of kurta and pajamas. They were arguing about a passport with the immigration officer.

"Her husband is sick," the American was saying. "He is being taken out on a stretcher."

The officer eyed the man suspiciously. "But where is he? I don't see him! The man must be with his passport or the passport with the man. Otherwise, how are we to know who is going or who is not?"

The American became frantic. "Look," he said, "her husband is a sick man. I am Dr. Loeb of Boston—his doctor. He is being taken out through another door."

Stan could see that Dr. Loeb of Boston was close to a nervous breakdown. "Can I help?" he said to the Englishwoman.

"Well I don't know," she said. She was on the verge of tears and her two children huddled against her. "What a terrible place this India is. What unfeeling people! My husband has been driven crazy here by one of their yogis. He's in a strait jacket going on first class. They're taking him out the side door. But this man won't let us through unless he is with us."

Stan drew his dark glasses out of his brief case. He remembered Indra telling him Indians were afraid of glasses.

"Can't you just send one of your assistants with the passport to make sure it is the right man?" Stan whispered, sliding over the counter to the official a twenty-dollar bill folded in his own passport.

The officer looked at him and called one of his minions.

"Give this man your husband's passport," he said to the Englishwoman. "He will take care of it. You may pass."

"I can't thank you enough." The woman smiled at Stan after they'd gone through. "My name is Florence Long and this is my friend, Dr. Loeb from Boston. We've been waiting two days to get on this plane—this place is so chaotic, so inefficient!"

Just then a stretcher was rolled out toward the plane.

"There goes Reginald," the woman sighed.

"Is that Dad?" the boy said, looking disgusted.

"Yes dear, it's your father."

The little girl started crying.

"It's all right, darling, don't cry. Daddy will be all right as soon as we get him home to England, you'll see." She glanced nervously at Stan. "This terrible country," she said shuddering. "I could tell you stories that would make your hair stand on end. The things that have happened to us—you wouldn't believe!"

Stan smiled. "Let me help you with your parcels," he yelled over the jet engines. "It's time to board."

XIV

§

Laura stood on the terrace of one of the Brahmins' houses watching Stan disappear down the mountain path. She hoped he might find Jeff and somehow talk him into coming back. But somewhere inside she knew it would never happen; Jeff had been too frightened and Indra too uptight. "What awful problems men have with each other," she thought. She went to her room to collect her things. Indra had decided that when Stan left it would be better for her to come to him. She paid for her food and lodging and walked out to the cave.

It was a very grand place, two thousand feet above the jungle, five thousand above the sea to the west. During the day kites circling in the air gave dimension to the space beyond. It was like riding through the sky in a chariot, especially when clouds rolled in from the sea. At night the warm breeze blew salty and strong, whipping up the fire and blowing coals onto the floor. There were strange moanings in the rock and the delicious sound of water somewhere inside it.

"So now you have had your wish, Uma," Indra said. "I hope that will be the last time you test me. One has been cured, which I must now bear for a while." He sighed. "The other wasn't ready. It is a pity, the young strong men like him are almost never ready, unless there is a severe shock. For a man the training must begin at birth, otherwise it is most difficult to separate the inner one early in life without the proper training. The delights of the body are too strong."

"What is the proper training?"

"Austerities. By performing voluntary austerities you break your way into the control room."

"Where is that?"

"Not in this time and space." He smiled. "They say it is behind the sun, on the other side of the fire. What they mean is it exceeds the speed of light, it is below the most static things like rocks, beyond protons. It is called the black fire by some, the place where the intent of the universe is stored, behind the mouth of Ma Kali. The fire is her mouth, the gate . . . any fire anywhere."

"A cigarette?"

"Yes, of course, I said any fire."

"Do you mind my asking how you cured Stan? He seemed a new person."

"No, I don't mind," Indra said. There was a pause. "You may ask—but it is not for me to tell. Like all cures, he did it himself. I was only the catalyst."

Laura's mind wandered. She was aching for some flesh contact. Indra's translucent body seemed even more beautiful, more perfect than she remembered. She longed to touch him but was afraid, for he was sacred to her. She felt guilty about these feelings, trapped by skin. The man trap was her main trap, she thought.

"Why do I have this desire for touch, for skin? After all you have shown me I still have it." She gazed at him steadily.

"Because it is natural," he said. "It is what makes the world go. Kama is what moves nature. You should have had children long ago, at fifteen, fourteen, then desire is transmuted. Everything is energy. If you keep on satisfying your physical desire all the energy goes out, and if you suppress desire it will turn against you. It must be transmuted." He stared at her sensually. "If I desire to make love to you and sublimate that energy, then I can use it to get in touch with your inner one, to take you across. Not using energy uselessly, that's the gag."

"But shouldn't I go to Harpal and have babies—or is it too late like the old woman said?"

"By all means go, if that is what you want. Go to America with him. It is the greatest of tests for a woman and man to have children. I have had them in other lives," he said seriously. "One must teach children courage and selflessness, and finally one loses one's own attachments that way.

"But this Harpal—he cannot see, at least not this time. He is too busy satisfying himself, too greedy. He is into the skin thing very heavily, more than you. Once you have seen past the skin to the bones, then you begin to get out."

"Can't you show him?"

"You don't know India. He is a Sikh and has too much pride. He wouldn't take advice from me. And it's too much to break that kind of pride. There is a different time for every soul. Chances don't come too often, and some keep missing them. When you miss a chance the body starts freezing up and getting old. You can see it in people. They get frozen into distorted shapes. The body passes up a chance for the soul to get out, the soul gets even by strangling the body. Then the body freezes and when the inner one is finished, everything freezes and disintegration takes place."

A cloud drifted across the cliff face below the cave. "It must be very warm down below," Laura said. "Here it's very pleasant though."

"Neither pleasant nor unpleasant," he murmured, smiling at her. "If we were down there it would be the same. We would be there where also it would be neither pleasant nor unpleasant."

"But aren't some places better than others for sitting?"

Indra shook his head. "There are certain places for certain practices, but no generalizations. Water and wood are required for certain practices where long isolation is necessary. To tune your instrument first you must learn to hear it, to use and read it. For that isolation is necessary. Sometimes we fast; sometimes we eat meat or fish, drink wine, and have women. For courage, dangerous elements are sought out: snakes, wild animals, precipices, diseased areas, rot, slime, fever, burning ghats, Piccadilly, Hollywood." He grinned. "The only proof of the success of the practice is in action: how well you manage to spar with this desire world until you can get out—even though you have 'seen' and know that it is all made up. 'Life is the stuff that dreams are made of and dreams are the stuff that life is made with.' Your Shakespeare, he was a great yogi, like Kalidasa . . . better.

"After seeing, some stay out as much as possible—become hermits, eccentrics, yogis like me. But it is equally possible to be involved in action as long as you remember it is all a play directed from elsewhere. When you can keep out—no matter what you are doing—then you go further beyond, you start going across. You begin to get the power to manipulate events. What you wish, that you will see becoming a reality. It can be frightening. You may only think something and it will happen even at great distances. These are signs of power. It is a dangerous period because it becomes easy to play around, healing this one and that one. But that is also desire and action."

"Is it wrong to use your power to heal then?"

"Healing the body can prepare the soul to get out. The paradox is that when the soul finds itself the body usually comes right on its own. Really there is no right or wrong. As long as you use power you will be linked to flesh through action. When you stop using it, one more cord gets cut."

"What's the goal?"

He shrugged and smiled, a far-off look in his eyes. "That is not

[318]

for us to know. Wave strengthening mostly. All we do know is that there are worlds in which embodiment is no longer necessary for the soul."

"You mean spiritual?"

"That is another made-up thing. Dualism. Spiritual and material. All made up. Everything is spirit and matter, spirit and matter are the same. the worlds are superimposed, not strung out like railway cars. They exist simultaneously. In certain practices we learn to slow down the rate of manifestation in the desire world so that we get into other worlds."

A fog had now enveloped the mountain and wisps of it floated through the cave. Below, the towering cinnamon and teak trees reached up damp and dripping. Far away a barking deer ran in the forest.

"See how fear traps us," Indra said. "The deer is so afraid of the leopard that when it catches his scent it becomes frightened and starts barking. Then the leopard knows exactly where to go. Fright always attacts the mortal enemy, it sets up a vibration in the other worlds which must be balanced. It commands the object of the fear to manifest itself through a series of events which usually seem accidental. That is how some doctors create disease in their patients if they themselves are frightened of disease. But fear can also be used to cure."

He looked at her. "You have more fear to get rid of. You need more training in that department. You need more wisdom teaching for a good rudder."

Laura knew it was a big decision. He was asking her to go further out. He gave her a lopsided smile, revealing his perfect teeth. He looked like an eighteen-year-old hustler with the eyes of the Mona Lisa.

"How long will it all take?" she asked.

"I dunno." He laughed. "It could take a few months, it could take a few years. You want to go on?" He looked slightly surprised.

She thought of Harpal. In her heart she already knew what it would be like to spend her life with him. What she didn't know was the path Indra offered. The unknown. She realized she had always been looking for the unknown.

"Should I want more?" she asked the Mona Lisa.

There was no answer, just a smile.

"Then what must I do next?"

"You have decided?"

"I'll go on," she said. "To see what happens next. Once I danced on the tables of a nightclub in Rome just to see what would happen."

"What happened?"

"I got kicked out."

He chuckled.

"What must I do now?"

"Now I must send you away," he said. "I am getting too fond of you. If I am fond of you, how can I teach you? You can go to Nepal though if you like."

"Nepal!" she exclaimed, thinking of all the strung-out people she knew in Katmandu.

The barking of the deer had stopped. Indra turned his nose into the wind. "Leopard—what a stink. He's having a lovely feast now in the moonlight. Souls who torture animals or humans become cats later on—they go into those kinds of bodies."

"What will I do there?" Laura asked.

"Where?"

"In Nepal?"

"Ah yes, Nepal." Indra slumped over and gazed into the fire for a long time, rattling his chimtah and rapping it on the logs as if knocking on a door somewhere inside the fire. "In Nepal there is a very old soul who is going to leave his body soon. Only one person looks after him. His disciples have all been sent away. But he will let you stay although it will be tough for you—it's a violent place."

"Cold?"

"Not cold, although the snow peaks are all around. It is warm but very rainy, a deep valley fourteen days east of Katmandu, south of a river called Arun."

"And what will I do there?"

"Help the servant. For three years he has been looking after the old man without assistance or relief. The old man is a genius. The servant is a simple soul, and very devoted. He doesn't understand the old man but he worships him like a god, so the real meanings come through to him.

"The old man is half here and half across. He is a siddha who never uses his powers, a great jiana yogi—that means philosopher, wise one. He is a siddha of wisdom. You need this grounding in the wisdom side. You don't need books, just contact him. It will all rub off on you."

"Can't you give me wisdom? Haven't you already?"

"It's not my cup of tea to teach that." He smiled. "You forget, I threw all my books into the Ganga in '47. I know it, like I know the Hatha Yoga from birth, but neither wisdom nor Hatha Yoga will get you out. You must know them," he said, "but I can't teach them—it's too boring for me."

The wind had come up warm and soft. "You'd better get some

[320]

sleep now," he said. "Tomorrow is Sunday. On Monday you must go."

"So soon?"

He gazed at her seriously, his lips full and pouting. "There is no time, always remember that," he said, leaning toward her across the fire, his muscular arms resting on his knees. He looked like a young Sioux warrior in the old photographs she had seen. "I could keep you with me, I would like that," he added. "But if you stayed I would find myself using your attachment—it can be used, I know how. After all, it is desire. Kama. I could use you like a battery charger. It would be fine for me, but you would be hopelessly trapped in your body then, in the skin thing."

Laura looked into her lap, not able to meet his eyes.

"Do not fret. We *will* be together again. Now it would only send you backwards. As long as you have the desire for this—"He stroked his shoulders and chest, puffing out his pectoral muscles almost like breasts. "As long as this interests you, your association with me would be fatal for your inner one. You need more power to be with me, more detachment. You have to shift into neutral. Then we can be together again.

"Staying with me or going to Harpal are both traps for you right now. If you can understand this you will save years in the crossing."

She had to admit she desired him. Physically he was the most perfect man she had ever known; his beauty, neither masculine nor feminine, surpassed reality.

"Could I bear your children?" she asked hesitantly, feeling like she might be walking the plank.

"Ah Uma, how I would like that!" He smiled and reached across the fire to take her hand. "But it is too late for me—you must know that. I am neither here nor there. Do not think I am abandoning you or throwing you out. Trust me, I can see ahead. I know why you came and what will happen. For certain I can tell you that fate has not brought us together for nothing. We will be together. It may be sooner than we both imagine. You will come to me again as flesh and blood, but . . ." He gazed through her as if seeing something far beyond.

"But what?" she asked. "Is there more?"

"You will see when the time comes. Do not imagine we are separate. I will be with you always. There is a great work which we are to do together. I cannot say more. You know how to reach me, that I can be anywhere. All you need do is practice."

He stirred the fire and put on two big logs. "That should see us through the night," he said. "Let us sleep now."

The next day it was drizzling. Clouds ringed the mountain and the whole world seemed damp and gray. During the afternoon he took her through the passage to the temple where Stan had been. When Indra pushed up the floor stone, the sun was shining brightly.

"You see," he said with satisfaction, "we thought because there were clouds below that it was a gray day. To us the whole world was dull and gray. Now that we're on top, it's sunny." He helped her out of the passageway.

"This is a strange place," she said. "It feels very old."

"Ruins and ruins on ruins and more ruins. Hindus, Buddhist and Jain ruins, and before that, Egyptian. Everyone has fought over this mountain. From the sea it looks like a perfect pyramid. Yogis have been sitting here since forever." He sighed, pacing around the edge near the arches. "And now tourists come. We are lucky it is not the season. . . . Vat iss your name, lady?" he hissed, mimicking the schoolboy's questions. "Vat is your native place?"

They laughed together. "What trash! What trash they are teaching in these schools. I am too tired of it, I pray to be taken but She won't allow it." He gazed toward the horizon.

"Why not jump off?" Laura peered over the precipice.

"That would be *my* desire then and *my* action. It doesn't work that way. I would just go into another body again." He stared at her.

Suddenly the clouds below them parted and Indra pointed to a grassy meadow for below on the mountainside. "See there, near the stones?"

"You mean the monkeys?" Laura asked.

"Watch!"

An enormous spotted leopard was leaping after the monkeys. "As a boy I could have picked that one off from here in one shot. See how it moves." He shielded his eyes against the sun.

"You shot animals before?"

"I was a crack shot—my father had me trained. All that is wrong but I was too young to know. I'm paying for it now." He turned. "Shall we go?"

"Can't we wait to see the sunset?"

He grimaced. "Must we?" He sounded like a tired husband trying to be polite. "I worship the sunrise, not the sunset."

Laura got up to leave but he saw how much she wanted to stay. "Let me just do some small puja then," he said, sitting down. He lit some incense and mumbled under his breath as if talking with the dancing god. "Shiva, lord of yogis," he said aloud.

Then he pointed to one of the arms, which had been knocked off the statue and restored incorrectly. "A fellow called the Tipu

Sultan did that," he said. "He was famous for destroying temples as he was a Moslem. He came from the east, the Deccan, and he got to here, but he got no further. The priests from the temple at Kolpura healed his ailing war elephant, restored its sight when it went blind. He had his cannon trained on the temple—he wanted the rubies and the diamonds. But when the elephant was healed he went away."

"What was his name?" asked Laura.

"The Tipu Sultan. He used to go out raiding, would catch the British officers, take their wives, and make the husbands jump off a cliff like this one. He lived on a mountain some two hundred miles east of here. Tipu's Jump they called it. When he was tired of the wives of the British officers, after he'd worn them out having intercourse with them day and night, he would force them to jump too." He paused and lit a small chillum. "Imagine the scene: Tipu raping and tantalizing the sex-starved blue-eyed girls who had come out to 'heathen' India to be with their husbands. And when finished with them he pushed them off—personally!" He laughed. "The British went crazy and sent out a young fellow called Wellesley who finished Tipu off in a bloody battle. After learning a few tricks in India, Wellesley went back and finished off Napoleon and became the Duke of Wellington." Indra paced around the small room, looking out impatiently at the setting sun.

"Oh Ma, oh ma, oh ma," he yelled suddenly, as the sun melted into the sea. The sound echoed down the mountain. "Oh Ma, ma, ma, ma, please please please take take take me me me . . ."

She was to leave at dawn. Getting down the mountain was a problem because of the jungle heat; every activity had to be finished by eleven in the morning.

At three-thirty he was shaking her awake. "Take a cold bath from the bucket and come to the fire," he whispered, stroking her forehead. At the fire he gave her ash which she dusted over her shaking body while he prepared bread and tea. Over tea he gave her instructions on how to find the old man. She was to go first to Benares and then to Katmandu, where a schoolmaster named Lal would help her.

Indra fussed over her like a grandmother—or a lover—as she prepared to leave. He gave her several amulets, a jewel, and a tin of dry food that he'd prepared. "Eat only this until you have reached the old man," he said. "It is very sustaining and will keep you from getting ill. If you eat the food served nowadays in these places they call hotels, you are likely to get very sick."

She touched his feet, then got up to leave. He looked sad and thoughtful on the way to the cliff path.

"Don't look back or you might fall off." He smiled. "Always remember, 'never look back.' Now go—I'll see you on the other side."

§

When Laura arrived in the Delhi airport two days later, she felt stronger and more alive than she had in years. But it seemed as though she were moving through a world of dead machines and almost dead people, and the brightly lit sterility of cement, plastic, and steel made her uncomfortable. She had difficulty focusing on the simple business of the pushbutton phones recently installed at the airport. On both sides of her coins jangled and voices croaked. After two wrong numbers and one busy signal she finally reached Sundar.

"Is it really you?" his voice chattered on the other end. "Where are you?"

"I'm on my way to Benares and then to Nepal. Yes, Nepal!" she shouted. "I don't know exactly where Jeff is. If he gets in touch with you, will you have him write me through Poste Restante, Katmandu?"

"Yes, of course, dear girl, I will find him. But can't you at least spend a night here and rest up? There are always planes to Benares. I can get you on one anytime."

"I have to meet someone there," she lied, not wanting to see him and be barraged with questions about what she'd been doing. "One more thing," she added, "if you see Harpal or hear from him, tell him I will write. *Write.* To his apartment in Delhi. The same, yes, O.K."

"You will return in how many days?"

"A few weeks, maybe a month."

"Have no fear, A. K. Sundaram is here!" he yelled.

"Yes, of course, I will stay with you then." She heard her flight being called. "Yes, thanks. *Thank you.*"

She landed in Benares early in the morning, took a taxi to the ghats on the Ganges, and had the driver wait at some distance while she bathed in the holy water. Then she drove to the bus depot, spread her cloth on the floor like everyone else and went to sleep. The next morning in the pink dawn she was on the bus rolling out of Benares toward Nepal. Flowers hung over pictures of the gods mounted in the front of the bus. The driver had done puja and incense floated out the window as they sped across the Ganges plain.

[324]

Laura felt solitary but not lonely. After her experiences with Indra it was hard for her to imagine that she would ever feel lonely again. She fell asleep with her head propped against the half-open window and woke later to the gears grinding and cool air blowing in. They were in the foothills; the first monsoon rains had fallen, turning the dry jungle green. Mango trees were crimson tipped with new leaves and flame trees were in full bloom everywhere. By late afternoon they reached Daveghat, where the Buddha was supposed to have been born at the junction of the Kali Gandaki and Marsyandi rivers. Daveghat was a peaceful village more or less untouched by the jangling hustle of the plains. She got a room for the night in the house of a poor family. The next day, following Indra's directions, she took a rickshaw a few miles out of town. There in the jungle she found the ruins of a temple he had described and spent the day repeating a mantra. In the evening she returned to Daveghat and did puja in the temple. The next morning before sunrise the bus left for Katmandu. All morning long they crossed the Mahabharat mountains and by late afternoon the peaks of Annapurna loomed golden in the blue sky. The bus reached Katmandu after dark. The brightly lit streets and bazaars were thronged with tourists. Chinese soldiers brushed elbows with hippies and bank presidents from America. Drums sounded from Bodanath temple and from Swayambunath came the peal of bells.

She'd thought about spending some time in Katmandu but when confronted with the tawdry tourist attraction it had become she found nothing much that interested her. It too seemed dead, part of her past that was over. She was afraid if she stayed she would inevitably run into old friends who had settled there to pass their days in a fog of hashish and opium.

WE ACCEPT FIRST NATIONAL CITY BANK CREDIT CARDS the signs read everywhere. Laura wondered if any of the beggars pretending to be holy men could credit your account to First National City? She had a credit card and decided to use it at the most expensive hotel in town. At least there she would see no one and could have a last hot shower before going off to find the old man. Her destination was a remote area near a small village on a tributary of the Arun river. She was supposed to get a travel permit for this section but Indra had advised her against trying; the man called Lal would smuggle her in if necessary. He turned out to be very likeable, a schoolmaster in his forties. It was fortunate that she had come just then, he told her, because school was out and he would be able to take her himself, at least to the village nearest to where the old man was sitting. It would be a two week journey. The oddest thing to Laura was that he said he had never heard of Indra,

[325]

although she showed him his address written by Indra, a photo of him, and the directions to the village. He also had no information about the old man. Nevertheless, he was willing to go. He would hire three horses and two extra men, he said, one to cook and one to care for the animals. Laura protested that she could cook but Lal explained that she would be too exhausted after long days of riding or walking at high altitudes.

Three days later he came to the hotel to tell her that everything was arranged and that if she agreed they could start the next morning. The last night she took a long hot bath, finished packing, and wrote a letter to Harpal. It was a long letter; in it she told him that she loved him but that she had to have time and was going off treking for a month to think things over. Later she found she had put the letter into her bag but had forgotten to mail it.

§

They followed the great central valley eastward, keeping the white peaks of the Himalayas on their left, until the rim of the valley had narrowed to a deep gorge. Lal pointed out Everest and on the far horizon the great snow mountains on the border of Sikhim. Miles below, the valley's narrow floor appeared various shades of green threaded with silver ribbons of streams and rivers. Dark canyons of pine, oak, and deodar rose above them. The air was like fine crystal, the ancient caravan path paved with massive gray slabs. Flutes in the mountain meadows mingled with the sound of temple bells and the bells of cows and goats. Evenings the conch horns of holy men echoed across the valleys, saluting the gods and demons of the eternal snows. Everywhere they went they met smiling faces. Some offered milk or ghee, many offered a smoke on the chillum. Laura felt exhilarated and relieved to be away from the sullen plains of India, where it seemed that grace and good feeling among strangers was only a memory.

They crossed the Arun on a bridge constructed of homemade rope and wood, precariously suspended at least a quarter of a mile above the gorge. On the other side they climbed a high mountain range and then descended into a protected valley. Pine forest gave way to teak jungle, where hidden villages appeared, built on stone terraces. The sound of water was everywhere, the orchards ripe with lemons and apricots. Further down the landscape was tropical: bananas flourished, bamboo and mahogany trees roofed out the sun.

Late in the afternoon on the fourteenth day they arrived at

their destination, a village built around a hot spring, hot enough to boil an egg, that bubbled out of a pale blue hole the shape of a morning glory. The people of the village were friendly and excited by the unexpected arrival of a foreign visitor. Soon Laura was taking a hot bath in the home of the village head man. Fresh hot water flowed from an ancient central system to every house in the village. The place was said to be two thousand years old, the air was sweet with flowers and the lazy smell of hay drying on the rooftops. Holy men mingled with bright-eyed children and townsfolk in a small stone temple complex near the spring. Inside there was a monolithic black stone with two gleaming mother-of-pearl eyes, a primitive statue representing the ancient guru whose descendants still lived in the village. Laura, bringing flowers, knelt before the statue to pay her respects. When she opened her eyes she had the feeling Indra was somewhere just behind her at the edge of her vision. She turned but the image had vanished.

The head man with whom Lal had arranged her lodging was a poor but robust barefoot Brahmin, about forty, who spent most of his time smoking chillums with cronies around the temple. His wife was a beautiful woman in her twenties, who prepared delicious food and smiled a toothless smile as she tended her fire and cared for numerous small children.

After a long conversation with their host, Lal informed Laura that the villagers held the old man in considerable awe. Although many of them had never seen him, there were all sorts of stories about what went on at his forest ashram, about seven miles by foot up the deep gorge of a tributary of the Arun. Lal had to return to Katmandu and couldn't accompany her further, but he made arrangements with the head man, who would take her up the river and have her luggage and provisions carried by his servants.

The Brahmin, communicating in broken English, explained that it was a very difficult walk and that Laura ought to rest for a few days before they started. The path lay in the riverbed itself. It would be tough going, over boulders and rocks, and they might even have to spend one night on the way. He scrutinized Laura wondering, she knew, whether this foreign lady was aware of what she was getting into. Nevertheless, two days later after a hearty breakfast and a few last words to Lal, Laura found herself with the Brahmin and four servants climbing a high path cut in the wall of a cliff overlooking the gorge. After about a mile the path dipped precipitously over a series of steps and landings, and ended in a washout at the edge of the dried-up riverbed.

The Brahmin jumped onto a boulder, trying hard to find the semblance of a path up the gorge, which was closed in by sheer cliffs covered with lush tropical foliage and alive with brightly colored birds and butterflies. When located, the river proved to be a small stream that wound along the floor of the gorge. Some places water had collected in pools, where bright green snakes lay waiting to eat frogs, and scorpions backed away at their approach, seeking safety under boulders big as houses. After about five miles Laura was too exhausted to go on, and let her guide know that she wanted to make camp. He seemed delighted and sat down at once to smoke a chillum. After a few puffs he handed it to her and darted up the stream where he bathed, singing and making loud noises. Later he returned to cook a simple meal of rice and dal.

In the high-walled gorge evening came early. Laura climbed into her sleeping bag while the Brahmin and his servants took turns sitting up with an ancient rifle, to scare away the wild pigs and leopards who were the real owners of the place.

Next morning the Brahmin woke her just as the first shaft of light filtered through the jungle. The servants were already having their tea and after a bath and breakfast she was ready. A few hundred yards after they started the gorge opened. The heat was intense. About two miles further the valley broadened and the path ascended out of the riverbed, following a low bank bordered by a grassy meadow, beyond which lay the jungle. The Brahmin signaled his servants to put down their loads and remain there.

Laura started to speak but the Brahmin put his finger to his lips.

"Servants stay here," he whispered. "Old man he is not liking visitors. If he see you with luggage he send you away. Shhh." He beckoned Laura to follow as he made his way stealthily through the tall grass. There in a clearing carved out of the thick jungle were three mud huts with pointed thatch roofs, surrounded by a low bamboo stockade. A strange grinding noise, like *rddd rdd rddd*, came from one of the huts.

They walked up to the fence and slipped in through a half-open gate. The strange sound continued, *rddd rdd rddd*. The Brahmin opened a rolled grass mat he had been carrying and motioned Laura to sit down on it next to him in front of the largest hut.

"A witches' lair," she thought as she looked around at the neatly kept gardens and the smoke curling up from the eaves of the hut. Above the cliff of the river gorge the tops of the snow peaks gleamed gold in the afternoon sun.

The noise stopped. Suddenly there were two voices arguing. They got louder and louder. Then a fat jolly looking young man backed out of the hut, his arms raised against a barrage of objects being hurled at him from within. He almost backed into Laura.

Stumbling to one side, he stared at her in wide-eyed disbelief, his hand clamped over his mouth. He stood perfectly still until the noise began again, *rdd rddd rdd.* It went on and he was just tiptoeing to the door when again it stopped and a high squeaky old voice began cursing in a language Laura didn't recognize. "Tunzing," the voice inside said, "Tunzing!" There were more curses. The young man remained motionless.

After a few minutes of silence a tiny fat man peeped out of the open door.

Laura gasped. It was the little old man she had seen dancing in the fireplace in England, and in India once in a dream. He looked, as he had then, like a tiny brown version of Santa Claus. Masses of matted white hair and beard made his face seem like a seed in a ball of white cotton. He was naked except for a mud colored rag tied around his waist; his fat little stomach stuck out like a pumpkin as he stood eyeing them, as surprised to see Laura as she was to see him. Then he walked a few wobbly steps to a nearby mat and with a sigh sat down. Fiddling with his cloth he withdrew from somewhere a pair of thick glasses. Huge magnified brown eyes suddenly fastened on Laura.

"We are making butter today but the rope keeps breaking," he muttered in a cracking voice, looking at her like a college professor about to expel a truant student. He gestured at the fat young man. "This fool forgot to bring rope on his last trip. Do you by chance have some?"

The Brahmin fell flat on his face in front of the old man and after receiving a perfunctory blessing, whispered something to him and went off in the direction of the baggage.

"And who might have sent you?" he said sternly to Laura after the Brahmin had returned with the rope. "There are instructions that no one is to come here, and no one stays here except Tunzing. I roam around out of my body most of the time." He smiled knowingly. "I'm making final preparations for leaving it altogether."

"Indra sent me," she said simply.

He removed his glasses and pushed the hair out of his eyes. "Young lady, please do not tease me in such a manner, it might be dangerous for you." He wiped his glasses and put them on again. "Do you by chance have a photo of this person you call Indra?"

"Yes, a photo and a note," Laura said, delivering the packet which Indra had prepared for her into the trembling hand of the little old man. He tore at it, trying vainly to open it.

"Tunzing," he muttered. "Please open this." His voice was barely audible. His eyes were slits in his old wizened face as

Tunzing broke the seal and cut open the stitched-up cloth with a knife.

Then he handed the opened packet to his master who held it in his hand for some time before looking at the contents. After he looked at the photo of Indra and read the note, the old man grabbed a bamboo stick and got up, waving the stick wildly in the air as if he might strike her. "Young lady," he said, "where and when did you get these things?" His voice was shaking with emotion.

"About three weeks ago on a mountain in south India," answered Laura.

There was a slow-motion pause during which the old man let the stick descend. He resumed his seat. Laura became aware that they were sitting beneath an ancient pepul tree. In the warm wind the leaves rustled like falling water. The old man sat looking at her through his lenses, and after a while a smile of satisfaction spread slowly across his face. Then he sighed and began laughing in a high tee-hee-hee giggle.

"Tunzing," he blurted out, still laughing as he removed his glasses and wiped away the tears that streamed from his deep-set eyes, "Tunzing—bring me something to give this young lady! And my red bag . . ."

Tunzing disappeared inside the hut and returned moments later with tea in a battered brass pot, four equally battered brass cups, and an old Benares sadhu bag. The old man fumbled in the bag, extracting bits of this and that—small newspaper packets yellow with age, a few gem stones, an old shriveled lemon.

"The twice born can read the book of Brahma . . . does that mean anything to you?" he asked.

"You mean going backward and forward," Laura answered.

He smiled at her over the top of his glasses and held out a small tin box decorated with a crudely stamped picture of the Taj Mahal against a deep blue sky. In one corner a pink airplane was flying.

"Well, aren't you going to open it?" he spluttered. "Open it— what do you see?"

"Ash," she said smiling.

The old man grunted, put on his glasses, and looked at her again. She reached out to return the box. "No, no, it's yours. Keep it carefully," he said, stroking his forehead with the tips of his fingers, palm out, looking through her into another kind of space.

"I suppose you have come prepared to stay?" he grumbled good-naturedly.

"To be honest, this man's servants are waiting with provisions and luggage across the meadow," she replied.

[330]

"Yes, yes, yes," he said, pulling at his nose. "Tunzing, have them bring her luggage." He leaned forward, squinting. "Now tell me, young woman, where did you meet Indra and what were the circumstances?"

"At a cocktail party in Delhi about six months ago."

"At a what?"

Laura smiled. "At an evening party in Delhi."

"And what was he doing in Delhi?" The old man seemed irritated.

"He was staying in his old family house which was deserted and in ruins. When I first met him he was dressed in a suit and wearing a turban."

"He looked young then?" the old man inquired.

"Yes, quite young. The next day I went with him to the Himalayas. Later we went to a large burning ghat where he gave me an initiation, then to the top of a mountain overlooking the Arabian Sea."

"Hmmmmm," he sighed. "Did many people seem to know him?"

"A few. He was reputed to be a rather dangerous character."

"Tee-hee," the old man snickered, "I should think so."

The afternoon was turning into evening. "And where will you sleep tonight?" he asked.

"Just here, where I am sitting. Will that be all right?"

"It gets chilly late at night—do you have blankets? I think perhaps we have an extra one." He paused, his hands trembling slightly in his lap. "It is time for me to have a bath and retire," he said. "Tomorrow we will see about more permanent quarters for you. You are welcome to stay, but you must keep to yourself a good part of the time." He smiled. "I trust you are more or less used to this life by now. Of course you will have to do your own cooking."

§

For the next three days the old man decided to remain silent. He wrote out orders for Tunzing on a small slate and for the servants of the Brahmin, who stayed on and in record time built Laura a small hut of mud, bamboo, and thatch.

On the fourth day, Tunzing shook her awake. She glanced at her watch—three in the morning!

"He will see you now," Tunzing whispered. "You must have a splash from the bucket and I will take you to his hut."

Laura lay half-awake listening to Tunzing noisily performing his ablutions outside. He seemed to be carrying on a multiple conversation by himself, taking various parts and changing his voice to fit each character, interspersing the lines with loud coughing, blowing, and spitting. She splashed herself from the bucket at the side of her hut, dried off, and put on a fresh cloth.

When they entered the old man's hut they found him sitting on a charpoy covered at one end with a thin torn cloth. Two candles on either side of him illuminated the hut, which was well constructed, paneled with large pieces of split bamboo, and lined with shelves containing many ancient-looking books and scrolls. There was also an altar containing a bronze statue of Kali and other objects.

"Do you not find that there is a materialist elite at work in the world today?" he asked when she had seated herself. He looked bright and scholarly. "And do you not find that they are generally pretty trashy people?"

Laura wasn't quite used to launching into heavy discussions first thing in the morning.

"I'm supposed to be one of them, I guess," she said.

"I know you think that, but you are not," exclaimed the old man emphatically.

"I'm not?"

"Of course not—otherwise, he wouldn't have sent you." There was a long silence. Laura felt as if she were on a precipice. Tipu's Jump maybe.

"Just now I have been meditating on the Katha Upanishad," he said suddenly. "Do you know it? I think out loud to myself every morning and Tunzing pretends to understand. I suppose you will also pretend to understand. But do not imagine that you can fool me. Words are all drivel. If *I* don't understand them after all these years, then how can you?" He chuckled. "You know the story of Natchiketas? Of how his father did sacrifice to the gods with all his old worn-out cattle? So many cattle he gave all the time because he had big herds, but never the good ones, always the old inferior ones. The gods became irritated and sent Yama the god of death to take his son Natchiketas to the realm of death where he was instructed in the secrets concerning immortality."

"I have read the translations," Laura said hesitantly, "but I never understood the instructions, just what it was that Yama was teaching."

"No one does," said the old man. "That's what I mean about words. Only the keys are given, not the details. It is like a secret shorthand for teachers; the jumping-off points are there, but all the details are left out. It is that way with most of the important texts, the words are just a reminder."

After three more days the Brahmin and his servants left for their village. One day began to melt into another. Each morning Laura would be awakened by Tunzing to sit with the old man. They sipped tea and ate hard biscuits until the sun came over the rim of the gorge. Then there would be puja and he would give her something to read which they would discuss the next morning. The old man had a vast storehouse of knowledge inside him, and seemed delighted that someone had come who was interested and could understand at least part of what he had to say.

Laura never knew what he did during the day. Late in the afternoon he would come out, take a bath, and sit. Sometimes he spoke to her, but more often he would remain silent in front of his hut, his eyes closed, his body erect and still. A great calmness seemed to radiate from wherever he was.

Tunzing taught her how to milk the cow and afternoons she would accompany him to the edge of the jungle where they would cut special vines, wild banana and dube grass that the cow liked. The weather was unusually dry, the rains almost a month late. The whole jungle seemed to be waiting for them to begin. At first Tunzing got on her nerves with his incessant speeches, his grunting, and compulsive body noises. She could understand why the old man threw pots at him from time to time. Slowly, however, as she watched his devotion to the old man—a devotion that never seemed to exhaust itself even though he might be awakened at any hour—she began to feel humble and inadequate by comparison. She even began singing to herself, something she had never done before.

"If you get tired cooking for and feeding that body you are burdened with," the old man said one day, "then just give it milk. That's all I'm taking. There is plenty of jungle fruit hereabout. We have lived on it for years. Milk and fruit are enough for this season. We have two kilos of milk a day, that is more than enough for all of us."

Laura was tired of cooking, she had to admit it. "It's these things that tie us to this world," he said, baring his teeth and pointing his finger at them. "Teeth always want to chew." He grinned. "I have been trying to lose mine for years but they won't go. Perhaps we should file them into sharp points and send Tunzing out to catch some wild game: we could dine on delicious partridge or quail, deer and wild pig—I hear they are great delicacies in the West." He went off into peals of laughter.

"Would you do it?" she asked.

"If you cook me wild pig, I will eat it," he said, his eyes twinkling. "Would you do it?"

[333]

Laura pursed her lips.

"I thought so—too much chewing, isn't it?" he giggled.

He was fond of poking fun at her but he was never sarcastic. She felt that in some ways, for the first time, she had found the father she had always looked for. "Maybe that's why Indra sent me here," she thought. Slowly she found herself looking after his needs until after a while she had relieved the harried Tunzing of part of the burden he had carried for so long. After the morning puja she would sit with Tunzing in his hut while he stirred his fire and prepared milky tea for her, grinding cardamom and other spices according to the mood of the day. He never spoke except to give directions although he knew English well—he had been taught some by the old man and had learned more listening to the English lessons broadcast in the evening on Radio Ceylon, which he just managed to pick up on his portable shortwave radio.

One day he asked her a question. It was something of an event. "Will you stay during the rainy season? It is coming soon, you know?"

Laura smiled. "I am not supposed to plan," she said. "Would you like me to stay? Would *he* like me to stay?" She nodded toward the old man's hut.

"He has become most fond of you," Tunzing said with a grin. "It is very good for him, you being here."

"Are you sure?"

He nodded.

"Then I shall stay."

"It is very hard though," he said, looking at her seriously. "It rains three to four inches each day. We may all get sick. The old man may go this time. He almost go—went—last rainy season."

"I'm not afraid," Laura said, looking directly into his eyes for the first time.

"He is getting weaker. If he begins to go there are certain things I must do for him, certain instructions to be carried out. You could be of great service to me at that time although you will not understand just what is happening. You will have to follow directions carefully."

"What about supplies?" she asked. "Do we have enough sugar, candles, oil, rice, and so on?"

"One of us will have to go down the river to the village. In the past I have gone but now he is weaker. I don't like to leave him—I have to help sometimes with the bath and the bowel movement. Will you be afraid to spend one night out by yourself on the way down? If so, I will go. When the rains begin the river rises. There is no way to go then except over the mountain. That way is very dangerous with snakes and the wild pig and leopard and taking one week to go and one week to return. I shall give you a spear and there is a shallow cave midway where you can spend the night. If you keep your fire going you should have no trouble. If the animals come just build up your fire and sing. I had two small bears sitting with me all night once."

"Ah," Laura thought, "Tipu's Jump coming up!"

"When shall I go?" she asked.

"Tomorrow," Tunzing said hesitantly. "Is it too soon? The rain could begin anytime. You must go and come within four days."

§

The trip down the dry riverbed was easier than she had expected. Near evening she spotted the shallow cave exactly as Tunzing had described it, about twenty feet up a narrow path on the side of the gorge. She hauled up enough driftwood to last the night, took a bath, leaned the spear against the opening, and fell asleep. During the night she woke; the fire was almost out. As she was putting on more wood she noticed, just out of range of the firelight, two large glowing eyes. She had seen eyes like those before and recognized the smell. Remembering Tunzing's words, she continued to build up the fire. She hummed a song she had learned from Indra and tried to repeat a mantra he had given her for just such an occasion, but to her disgust she found her knees were wobbling with fright. Finally the fire blazed up and she could see the leopard, a large young female, lying on the path purring loudly. She was surprised at how much it resembled a big kitten. After what seemed an eternity it yawned, got up, and leapt into the river-bed.

When she tried to go to sleep again she was sure she saw Indra standing below. She didn't try to look directly—to focus on him—and the image lasted for some time. Finally it saluted her and vanished. When she woke she found that she had overslept. It was full morning and the sky was overcast, with thunderheads piled up in the eastern sky against the Himalayas. She would have to hurry now. She ate some of the dry food Tunzing had prepared, clambered down the cliff path to the river and headed downstream.

When she got to the village she bought provisions from the list the old man and Tunzing had made and hired coolies immediately, determined to set out the next morning. She met the Brahmin head man on the street and returned with him to his house while the orders were being filled and packed into bundles. He persuaded

[335]

her to rest one day, all the time trying his best to dissuade her from returning.

"You are not knowing how much it rains," he kept saying. "You will not survive the damp climate. Send coolies back with supplies, you hurry Katmandu before rain is getting bad. You are foreign woman, not fit for rainy season."

She thought of Harpal but not like before. Living in the jungle with the old man and Tunzing was changing her. Things she once thought important were falling away. The old man was teaching it all to her now. How could she leave? It was a test, she was going through a door. It was her chance to go through once and for all.

The next morning after a hot bath at the temple, she had breakfast with the Brahmin.

"You *must* not return, memsahib," he said, looking very serious and sad.

"But I am one stubborn foreign woman," she said with a smile. "You've delayed me one day now. The old man will worry—that's no good for him. I am leaving tomorrow."

§

It was spitting rain the following afternoon and she was still three miles downstream from the clearing. She was just debating whether to make camp and give the coolies a rest or to push on, when Tunzing appeared around a big boulder.

"The old man sent me," he puffed. "He said you were coming, that I should go get you. If you stay in riverbed this night you might get washed away. Come, we must hurry!"

"Is he all right?" Laura asked quietly as they hurried over the rocks. She could tell by the look on the young man's face that something had happened. "What is it, Tunzing?"

"He could not get up today. He did not recognize me for nearly half the day. Now he has told me he will not take food, he will fast until—until his body lets him leave. The time has come." He was fighting back tears. "Let me carry the spear," he said, taking it from her. "He understands everything. I will just run ahead and tell him you have returned. Take the flashlight—it is going to get dark fast." He started ahead and then turned, smiling warmly. "We were afraid you might have run away."

When they arrived the coolies put down their bundles and left immediately, afraid the rain would block the way and leave them stranded.

They watched the light of the coolies' torches disappearing downstream, then Tunzing turned toward the old man's hut. "Come in now," he said. "He is expecting you."

The old man was sitting up. He put on his glasses and spoke softly to her. "This body has had a partial stroke—you know stroke, of course?"

Laura nodded.

He fidgeted with some manuscripts that lay in front of him, then wrapped them in a scarlet cloth. "There is so much more I want to tell you, after all. I have been following you for quite a time now."

"Then it *was* you in the fireplace in England?" she said.

He smiled, nodding his head. "Even before that. That was only the first time you were able to see."

He lapsed into silence and gazed at her over his glasses. "Indra was right," he said, clearing his throat, "it is better and easier to leave this body *before* it starts to go. In any case, now that I have been given the sign I intend to leave this one within the next ninety days. It is time. You must carry on as usual." He smiled. "Your trip to the village was O.K.," he continued, using the American slang. "Did you see someone?" He tittered slyly.

"Who?" asked Laura, testing him.

"I see you are testing me—a Western failing," he sighed. "Oh well, that is your problem. Whom did you see? Indra, of course!"

"How did you know?"

"He appeared here too, and told me he would stop and see you in the cave. He . . ." the old man's voice drifted off. Then he looked at her sharply. "That box I gave you, the tin box . . ."

"With the ash?" Laura said.

He nodded. "I burned the body of the yogi you call Indra on this spot almost nine years ago. He insisted on leaving his body before it began to age. He fasted and I carried out his instructions for burning the body just as he was leaving it. That was nine—no twelve years ago, before Tunzing came here." He cleared his throat again, smiling and watching her intently. "Now you know a great secret. What do you say?"

"I say it is a work of great art," Laura said earnestly.

"Indeed it is," returned the old man. "A lost art. Many have been given the opportunity but few take advantage of it. The work is too simple and too hard. Few can comprehend it. Most reject it. They don't see the possibility."

"Is that your path now," she asked, "or have you already done it?"

He looked at her seriously. "It is a possibility, one of many. You

[337]

flatter me—no, I have not done it before. You will help Tunzing?"

"Yes, of course."

Each morning about eleven the clouds would pile up against the great peaks visible above the river gorge and it would begin to rain. Fierce winds and electrical storms swept overhead, jumping the small valley which grew more humid every day. The river rose steadily. Tree frogs, crickets, and huge cicadas began to sing in the grasses. Orchids burst forth from leafy nests high in the trees and showered down sprays of white blossoms. The jungle was coming alive in a way Laura had never imagined possible. One morning she awoke to see a bright green eight-foot snake draped over the center pole of her hut, eyeing her cautiously. Each day she led the cow to the near slopes to graze on the new shoots of grass which seemed to grow several inches every night. Tunzing taught her to make curd, and ghee and butter from the curd, and to mix the whey with spices into a delicious light drink. Cooled in the spring it was good for the stomach in rainy weather.

One day Tunzing asked her to help him. Together they dug a pit about four feet deep, two feet wide and six feet long. She wondered whose grave it was to be, but there was no indication from Tunzing and she didn't ask. After they had finished he removed all his clothing except for his loincloth and got into the hole, sitting full length as if in a bathtub, his head just above the surface of the surrounding earth.

"Now please, you will fill the mud in around me," he said. "Take the shovel and cover me—everything except the face."

As she filled he removed his loincloth so that he was naked. She noticed that he was facing North.

"You are wondering about this, no doubt." He grinned. "We do it as a protection against the diseases of the monsoon. You will have to take over my duties for twenty-four hours. Do you think you can manage?"

"Yes, of course," Laura said. "But hasn't the monsoon already begun? It's been raining every day."

Tunzing laughed merrily. "This! This is nothing," he said. "You have not seen the monsoon. When you see it you will understand."

The clouds were black overhead.

"What will you do when it rains?" she asked, worried.

"Nothing. Only my face will get wet, and that is supposed to happen."

That afternoon it began raining and rained a steady downpour all afternoon. She stayed in the old man's hut, tending his fire. In the evening she milked the cow, who had been moved to a shed attached to the hut. Then she boiled the milk and prepared tea

[338]

and bread for herself over the old man's fire while he sat dozing. After eating she fell asleep.

About midnight the old man groaned and tried to speak but his tongue wouldn't work. She could tell he was having another stroke, she had seen her grandmother have one and knew the signs. His bowels had moved under the shock and she could see the fastidious little man was greatly upset.

She built up the fire under the large brass vessel containing the washing water, removed his cloth, bathed him front and back and put on a fresh cloth, then eased him onto the soft skins and got him to sip some lemon water. For the first time she realized what had been accomplished in her trip to the burning grounds with Indra. Everything was the same now. She had stopped discriminating between pleasant and unpleasant things. The desire world was going. Things she could never have imagined doing before now seemed easy. She was sloughing off being afraid.

After she had built up the fire she took the soiled cloths out into the rainsoaked night and by the light of her flashlight tucked under one arm, washed them downstream from the spring at the washing spot. The river had begun to sound like a freight train. She returned to the old man's hut just as a light gray appeared in the sky, but the downpour continued. The cow had to be fed and milked. She went into the lean-to and mixed the feed for the cow. The huge brown beast watched her with great limpid expressionless eyes. One ear was cocked back toward the wall where the old man was now snoring peacefully. The cow had been with the old man for over six years and she was very fond of him. Laura had seen her kneel down before him and put her brownish pink wet nose on one of his bare feet as he sat playing his flute. She thought about the steaks she had eaten at Sardi's and decided that it must have been in some other life, not this.

After milking and boiling the milk she lay down, exhausted. What had she got herself into, she was thinking, when she remembered Indra's advice to her. "Don't think. What you call thinking will drive you crazy. Repeat your mantra and don't think. Everything will go right. You will be in tune when you've erased all your tapes."

It was against everything she had ever known but it was the only thing that really made sense to her, now that such an incomprehensible chain of events had led her to this particular place in space and time.

Hours later when she awoke the sun was out. The old man was awake, blinking at her. She got up.

"I must see to Tunzing," she said. "He is buried in a hole outside."

The old man managed a garbled tee-hee but he couldn't wipe his watering eyes. She wiped them gently and went outside.

Tunzing's eyes were shut but she doubted he was sleeping. She got the shovel and started removing the mud. "The old man has had another stroke," she whispered as he got up out of the hole. "His tongue and left side seem to be paralyzed."

Tunzing showed no emotion. He bathed with rainwater from one of the buckets, put on a fresh cloth and went to the spring with the old man's brass bucket which he filled with fresh, clear water. Inside the hut he poured out a cupful and holding it to the old man's lips massaged his shoulders and arms gently.

"Now I will be very busy," Tunzing said softly to her. "You must carry on with the chores but be available. There are times I may need help in turning him over and so on."

Laura went to her hut and lay down, but was too tired to sleep. In the evening out of habit she went to see the old man. He was seated in the lotus pose, propped up by a board which Tunzing had placed against the charpoy. His eyes were closed. Tunzing was seated to his left reading to him from some oblong manuscript. He asked her to bring more wood and build up the fire. When it was burning vigorously he offered large quantities of all the supplies into the fire, muttering in Sanskrit while he threw handfuls of rice, sugar, and ghee into the flames, and then the personal effects of the old man, his prayer bell and flute—finally even his glasses.

The old man sat straight as an arrow now without using the board for support. His legs were crossed flat on the floor. In his right hand he held his prayer beads. Tunzing took them and dropped them into the fire.

Later, after she had gone to bed, Tunzing called her to sit on the old man's right. All visible signs of breathing had stopped. After he had taken the old man's pulse Tunzing began to read aloud again from one of the texts, sitting close to him and reading in a low voice into his left ear.

The reading continued for five days. It rained almost the entire time, day and night. Neither Laura nor Tunzing ate; they drank spring water and took naps between Tunzing's readings at three-thirty and eleven-thirty in the morning, three-thirty in the afternoon, and again at eleven-thirty at night. By the end of the fifth day there was no sign of life in the body of the old man, no pulse, no breath. Yet there was no rigor mortis, the body remained erect, and no decomposition had occurred.

The readings continued for three more days, during which Tunzing used a small drum and silver bells to accompany himself. Laura's job was to keep the fire going, the cow milked, and the ghee lamps lit. On the eighth day Tunzing laid down the drum and bell carefully.

"Get the shovel," he said. "It is time now. We must dig out the fire to a depth of almost eleven feet. It will be very hard work."

"Has he left his body?" Laura asked.

"Partly," Tunzing replied. "The total separation will come during the next twenty-four hours. We must dig fast. We will take turns digging and piling the earth in the far corner of the hut. It is important that certain things happen at just the proper moment."

It was impossible for her to tell whether the old man was dead or alive. What was dead and what was alive, really? By three the following morning, they had finished the hole. Five bags of salt were emptied onto the bottom. Then they lowered the old man's body, still sitting erect, using as a hammock the long cloth on which he was seated. Then Tunzing began alternating layers of charcoal, ash, and salt. Just before the head was covered, Tunzing asked her for the box of ash the old man had said was Indra's. He poured half of it over the old man's white hair and returned the box to Laura. Outside the rain poured down. The river rolled on like thunder. Tunzing went out and returned with a metal rod about as thick as a finger and two arms long.

"Please hold this carefully here, just where I am placing it," he said. Laura held the rod, which gleamed like gold. "Seven metals," Tunzing said, as he picked up a hammer and struck a swift blow on the top of it so that the rod was driven into the skull of the old man.

Laura started back.

"What are you doing?" she cried out.

Tunzing smiled calmly. "Oh, this is most important," he explained. "The last of his bodies, the subtlest, has gone into this rod which now is resonating with that vibration. It will continue to do so forever. There are ways you can get in touch with it if you know how. Now please hold the rod until I fill in the remaining space."

When the work was complete, cut stones were fitted on the top. The rod stuck up about nine inches above the surface. Laura sat exhausted, almost too tired to move after nine days with hardly any sleep. She felt like bursting into tears, but what was there to cry about? After all, was it not a joyful occasion when someone got out of his body? She went to her hut where she lay down wearily. Tunzing came in with some barley soup and some dry wood for her fire.

"Sleep for a while now," he said gently. "The rain is over for a few days. Sleep until you are well rested and I will complete the work."

[341]

Her sleep was fitful. She dreamed of Harpal, Jeff, and Indra all confused with each other, and woke up feeling tired and stiff. Tunzing was digging something. Wondering how long she had slept, she got up, made tea, and swept out her hut. Her back ached and although the sun shone brightly, it was so humid she could hardly breathe. Maybe the Brahmin had been right. "You are foreign woman, memsahib!"

When she went out she was surprised to find the old man's hut gone. Tunzing had removed the roof grass and piled it for the cow to eat. The poles were stacked neatly in a pile and he was leveling the mud walls to the ground. The bright sun made Laura feel dizzy and she caught hold of the corner of her hut to keep from collapsing. She wondered if Indra had known what would happen. Less than two months and now the old man was gone. She was to have learned wisdom from him, philosophy, so much else. Indra had said it would be a rudder for her. Now the rudder was gone. She felt a great loss, which seemed out of proportion to the length of time she had known him. He'd been so touchy about questions she hadn't even been able to ask further about his appearance to her in the fire or in her dreams.

Tunzing caught sight of her and leaned on his shovel. He was making a platform about a foot high. In the center the rod protruded above the stones.

"Why burial?" she asked. "I thought the body was always burned."

"Burning or salt, it amounts to the same thing. Two different methods for two different kinds of going out, one movable, one fixed. In a matter of days the salt will dissolve everything."

Thunder was rolling now in the west. "How long did I sleep?" she asked.

"About thirty-six hours. How do you feel?"

"Weak." She smiled faintly.

"You need food now. I will prepare. Go back to your hut. You'd better get in more wood, it's going to start raining again."

On her way to gather wood she looked in on the cow, whose hut had been moved next to Tunzing's. The poor beast knew that the old man was gone—or was he? Was anyone ever really gone? She kept thinking she'd been sent to this place for a reason. What was the reason? To learn, he'd said. What had she learned? She tried to think again but her brain was dull. By the time Tunzing ducked into the low door of her hut it was raining again. He placed a large plate of food in front of her with a cup of tea and left immediately, as quietly as he had come. She had no appetite but forced herself to eat, thinking she needed energy. There were things she had to do to help Tunzing and she had to keep moving to keep up her strength, otherwise she felt as if she would rot or turn to fungus. Her menstrual period was very late. Was she pregnant with Harpal's child she wondered, or was it just the general weakness that seemed to have come over her with the onset of the rains.

"After hunger is satisfied," she could hear the old man's voice inside her, "people think up all sorts of useless ways to pass the time—war, sports, games, 'the arts'. . ."

She felt sickish and drank the tea. It made her feel worse. She remembered she had some milk of magnesia pills in her bag and fished them out. She took three and felt better, decided not to eat and drifted off to sleep again beside the fire. In the dark of the night she woke out of a nightmare she couldn't remember. The night herons were screaming out in the rain and she became aware that she was lying in a pool of sweat. As soon as her eyes could focus she felt waves of nausea. She crawled to the hut door, pushed back the gunnysack covering and began to vomit. Even when everything had come up she still wanted to vomit more. Finally, so weak she couldn't even crawl, she rolled back into the hut and under her blanket. The fire was almost out. It was raining too hard for Tunzing to hear if she called. For the first time Laura considered escape, wondering whether she and Tunzing could make it over the mountain. But what about the cow? The tigers and jackals would eat her in no time.

The next morning Tunzing brought her a very bitter decoction of certain roots. She got up and gargled with spring water, scraping her tongue and blowing water out her nose. Then she took some stomach medicine Indra had given her and lay down thinking again about leaving. "When you've got bread, you can always run away from yourself," was one of Jeff's favorite expressions. Well, it had suddenly been made very difficult—maybe impossible—for her to run. Maybe this was what she'd been sent here to learn.

Her period still hadn't come. "If I'm pregnant," she thought, "at least it will make me healthier to live through this weather."

After two days it began raining again. In the morning about eleven it would stop for about an hour, giving her just time to run out and do her laundry and pick up some wood before the downpour started again. It would rain then through the afternoon and all evening without letting up, harder than any rain she had ever seen. The river was full. What had been a broad roadway of rocks and sand was now a torrent of boiling churning water carrying everything before it.

There was no break from this and Laura began to lose track of time. The fire was her main concern. Most of her energy went to

[343]

hustling wet wood and stacking it around the fire to dry. She had broached the subject of escape to Tunzing but he seemed not to hear her and had muttered something about the impossibility of twenty miles of mountain trails. For him it was just another monsoon, she supposed, and of course he wouldn't think of abandoning the place where his master had left his body. One day melted into another and she began some of the practices Indra had taught her on the mountain. It was all a matter of having the time and the solitude to turn off, once and for all, that part of herself so bound through past conditioning.

A few days later Tunzing came in and slumped down in front of her fire. His face was livid and he seemed hardly able to move his body. She felt his forehead and found it burning with fever.

"I think I have pretty bad jungle fever," he said softly, smiling. "Maybe I am going to follow the old man."

"Nonsense," Laura said, knowing it was not nonsense. "You stay here. I will get your bedding and whatever else you need. There is no sense keeping separate fires going until you feel better."

She felt adrenalin pour through her body; her whole system was now on alert. She began repeating the syllables Indra had given her at the cremation ground.

Tunzing told her what he needed and during a break in the rain she carried his belongings to her hut. By evening he was really sick. There was no time now to think, only to act: keep the fire going, keep things clean and boiled, milk the cow, collect firewood, nurse Tunzing. After a few days and nights he could barely move. He began having violent diarrhea and violent sweats. In three hours he could drink an entire pail of water. She had to clean and dry him every four hours. The rain poured down; none of the cloths would dry and she began ripping up what few extra clothes she'd brought so that some dry rags would be available.

"How much longer will the heavy rain last?" she asked him one night when he seemed to have regained his senses.

"Two more months," he rasped. "For two months you cannot get out."

"What about the mountain? Shouldn't I try to make it across, get to the village, bring a doctor?"

"There is no doctor in that village," he said weakly. "Mountain path is most dangerous. Do not worry about me, I am not afraid. I am going to follow the old man. I can see that he is needing me. When I go, then you must take the path you wish. It may be very hard for you here all alone."

The next night he became delirious. He woke up screaming for the old man to save him, repeating mantras and singing in a

[344]

childish voice between cups of water. During one lucid moment he gazed at her. "It is the cholera," he whispered hoarsely. He crawled to the hut opening and pointed to some bushes outside. "Chop plant, make stew, give to me," he said and rolled back onto his mat.

She dashed out into the rain and hacked at the bushes with a machete. Then she chopped them up and put them in a pot over the fire. The green mass gave off a bitter smell and tasted violently astringent. As soon as it was cool enough she spoon-fed it to him. His face was thin and haggard, his once plump body a dehydrated sack of bones. The decoction seemed to help him though, and he stopped needing water. For a few days he seemed to be getting better.

When he told her it was cholera Laura remembered that she had once had cholera immunization shots. She found her International Health card and looking on the page for cholera, discovered that her period of immunization had expired the week before she came to India. She had heard that sometimes the immunization effect lasted longer. Nevertheless, she had to face squarely the possibility that she might get sick like Tunzing. For some reason the thought didn't upset her. She had the strange sensation of being outside of it all, that things were happening around her. Even her own body was out there, while she, the observer, was somewhere else. "Though I walk through the valley of the shadow of death, I shall not freak," she kept saying to herself. This was it: Tipu's Jump!

§

Tunzing died two days later. Somehow she managed to drag the body through the rain to his hut. "Poor man," she thought, "he has been so faithful."

The poles and other wood from the old man's hut lay stacked in the hut. One by one she brought them and piled them inside Tunzing's hut as she had seen it done. Then she dragged the body on top of the heap, piled all his belongings around him, and poured ghee over the whole thing hoping the hut would burn down.

She gathered coals from her fire in a bucket and managed to get a fire going under the body, but the wood was too damp. Everything was too damp. She couldn't get the bamboo poles to burn. The hut was filled with acrid smoke.

She went back to her hut and lay crying for some time. When she returned to Tunzing's hut the fire had gone out completely. She knew she had to get rid of the body before it began to

[345]

decompose. Shuddering, she dragged the cold stiff corpse a hundred yards from the hut to the edge of the jungle where she knew it would be eaten by jackals.

She returned to her hut and sat shivering in front of the fire. Having to abandon Tunzing's body—he who had been so bright with love and faith—filled her with anguish. She gazed down at her cracked and calloused hands, the once beautiful hands of Laura Weatherall, 610 Park Avenue, New York City. Although it wasn't cold she felt chilled to the bone and knew she ought to get more wood. But there was enough for the night, to hell with it. In the morning she would get more.

She never got around to it.

The next morning the fever hit her. It was worse than the Sirocco, the burning Sahara wind that scorches everything in its path. It knocked her over. Her thirst was monstrous. She placed a bucket under the eaves of her hut, just outside the door, to collect rainwater. She knew she would soon be too weak to do anything. Somehow she managed to get to Tunzing's hut and pull the wood she had piled there into her own place. There was always a chance someone might come or that she might ride out the sickness. Perhaps Harpal would get her letter and come to rescue her. In it she had given the name and directions to the village down the river. The letter! She had no memory of mailing it. She fumbled in her bag. Her hand felt the crumpled envelope. She had forgotten to renew her cholera shot and now she had forgotten to mail the letter. Something was working to make her forget.

Feeling very alone she began to ask herself final questions, summing up her life. She recalled all the good times—had they been so good?—all her satisfied desires. They made her uneasy. She knew now in her heart that Desire was endless, an endless urge for action and fulfillment. What seemed to stand out were the times she had really extended herself, beyond her own desire into acts of human kindness.

She closed her eyes and began repeating the syllables Indra had given her. During the night, through the steady rain and thunder, she heard the whoops and screams of the jackals as they devoured Tunzing's body. The next day she began vomiting and had diarrhea at the same time. Soon she was too weak to move and could only lie by the fire feeding wood into it.

She would doze off into strange dreams like bad acid trips accompanied by the quick time *thump thump thump* of hard rock music. Finally she lost all track of time and seemed to be drifting in an awful purgatory of boredom and terror.

[346]

One night she thought she heard Indra's voice; she lay half asleep listening to it as though it were in the room with her. "Are you all right?" it repeated solemnly, quietly, over and over. She closed her eyes tightly. Tears poured down her cheeks, mingling with the cold sweat that poured out of her.

"You said you would be with me again," she whispered. "Where are you? I'm lost."

"I am here in the corner on your left."

She raised herself on one elbow, thinking he was there in the room with her.

"Do not look directly," the voice said. "Look into your fire."

She wiped her eyes and stared into the coals.

"Now, can you see me out of the corner of your eye?" the voice said. "Come—without looking directly—you must try. Try!"

Staring at the fire she could just make out on the periphery of her vision the glowing silhouette she knew so well, the unmistakable look of him that had first attracted her in Delhi.

"Yes, I can see you now."

"You must try to sit up then," his voice said. She came totally awake. His voice was in the room. It was not in her head, it was really in the room. Or was it?

She gathered all her remaining strength and sat up.

"Now your strength is coming back. Get wood. You must build up the fire. After you get it blazing well remove all your clothing. Go outside in the rain, let the rain wash you off, cut the rope and let the cow go. Then burn all your soiled things in the fire."

She managed to crawl around the hut and throw the wood from Tunzing's hut into the fire. Then she put her clothes in the flames and crawled out the door. Her body shook with cold. Shuddering she contrived somehow to stand up in the rain which never stopped. Her thighs and buttocks hung in wrinkles like an old woman's flesh. How long had she been lying there, she wondered.

After she had cleaned herself, she staggered through the door. "Good," his voice said as she entered. "Can you sit up now? Sit up in front of the fire, let it dry you off. You can—go ahead."

She tried but fell backwards.

"Try," his voice said harshly. "Do some breathing and try again."

She breathed deeply in the special way he had taught her and after a while was able to sit up.

"Now you must offer all the food you have into the fire—all of it!"

The new wood was catching and the fire began to blaze. She

[347]

crawled to where the supplies were kept and began throwing handfuls of rice, wheat, and lentils into the flames. She watched as the fire began to hiss and crackle and go higher.

"Do not delay," he said urgently. "Throw the whole lot in. Have you any ghee?"

She nodded.

"After you have finished offering the food take the ghee and rub your body with it."

She turned toward his voice wanting to ask why.

"Do not look toward me, it is not time yet. You must only follow directions."

She rubbed the ghee over herself. Her skin felt like greased leather but she felt better, as if the fever might be leaving her. "Am I . . . are you?" she stammered, "is the fever leaving, am I . . . ?"

"The fever is not leaving," he said firmly. "You are going to leave the fever. Have you got scissors somewhere, if not a cooking knife will do."

She reached for her bag. As she looked for the scissors, her travelers checks fell out with the letter to Harpal. She counted them and found seven thousand five hundred dollars. She laughed to herself. Now she understood Stan's frustration at having so much bread and getting cancer.

She could hear Indra laughing. "Throw that trash into the fire, throw it all! And toss the scissors to me."

She threw the checks, the letter, and the bag into the fire. Then she threw the scissors in the direction of his voice.

"Good," he said. "Now I am coming behind you and I am going to cut off your hair."

She felt warmth behind her and his hands gathering up her hair. In three snips it was done. She saw the hair go into the fire and burn.

"Terrible smell," he whispered into her ear.

"Now I want you to close your eyes. There are certain things that must be done. Close your eyes and repeat the syllables you learned before. Keep repeating until you see them with your inner eye. Do not open your eyes until I give the word."

She could hear more wood going onto the fire. The heat was intense.

"Did the old man make it?" she asked. "Is he with you?"

"Yes and no," Indra replied. "He got further but he didn't use the proper key although I told him. He didn't believe me. He is fixed, while I am movable."

There was a pause during which she heard him wrestling the large bamboo poles into the fire. She began to see the syllables

[348]

gleaming against the endless blue field, as she had seen them at the cremation ground.

"But you have the guts," he laughed, "and I am the key."

Up to that moment she thought he had come to heal her, to rescue her. Now she realized it was going to be different, very different. For the first time she realized it was going to be the end. She was surprised to note how cool she felt about it.

"Where are you, really?" she whispered.

"Don't ask silly questions," his voice rang out. "Keep your eyes closed. There is not much time left. Are you seeing the syllables?"

"Yes."

"Good. Now you must repeat all three mantras I have given you simultaneously. Have you been practicing that?"

"Yes."

"Then begin now. Repeat them all together on three levels. Can you do it?"

"Yes."

"Good. Then we will begin. Remember: do not under any circumstances open your eyes until I tell you."

The sound of the rain and the fire began blending in her ears. She had a vision of a fountain of liquid fire, like a volcano erupting and obliterating everything. She had no trouble repeating the first, then the second, and finally the third set of syllables. They seemed to be working in tandem. She felt high and exhilarated. It was like tuning in three channels at once. She was so filled with their sounds that her exterior senses seemed to have stopped functioning.

Then, as if from far away, from some golden sundrenched island deep in her heart, she heard his voice calling her.

"Open now, open your eyes."

She opened her eyes.

The fire was blazing before her, an inferno that would soon burn down the hut, but she felt no heat. It was like watching a movie of fire and slowly even the sound of it faded. She was getting out. She kept repeating the three mantras and after a few moments Indra's naked form appeared across from her, on the other side of the flames. His body became palpable before her eyes as he extended his arms toward her through the fire.

"Do not be afraid. I am truly with you," he said.

"I'm not afraid any more," she answered calmly.

"Before I was in the room with you," he said smiling. He looked younger than she ever remembered seeing him. She wanted to go with him, to be with him. She burned with desire for him.

"Before I was in your old space, that world's space," he said.

[349]

"Now I am on the other side. That is why the voice you are hearing sounds far away. Can you hear me?"

"Yes," she answered and stopped short. She could no longer hear herself speaking.

"You can hear me but you cannot hear your own voice—is that correct?"

She nodded.

"Or the fire or anything?"

She nodded again.

"Good, that is good." He grinned. "Then it is time. Now look at the point on my body where I have taught you to look, yes?"

"Right."

He reached toward her through the flames. "Concentrate on that place and follow directions. Feel yourself do as I say. Do not take your eyes from the point. Ready?"

"Ready."

"Are you all right?" he said.

She nodded, feeling deliriously happy, as if at last she were about to recover something long lost. Homeward-bound, she thought.

"You look wonderful," he said, his eyes sparkling. "Now squat in front of the fire. . . . Correct. Right. Very good.

"Ah ha!" he cried out. With a roar of laughter that filled her whole being, he leaped into the flames and crouched there, his arms held out. "I am going to catch you. Ready?"

"Yes!"

"Now—JUMP! JUMP!"

His body flashed white before her.